Living Space:
And Other Stories

Isaac Asimov was born in Russia near Smolensk in 1920. He was brought to the United States by his parents three years later and grew up in Brooklyn. He graduated from Columbia University in chemistry and after a short spell in the Army, gained his doctorate in 1949 and qualified as an instructor in biochemistry at Boston University School of Medicine, where he became Associate Professor in 1955. He retired to full-time authorship in 1958 while retaining his connection with the University. His first story 'Marooned Off Vesta' appeared in 1939 in *Amazing Stories*. Asimov became a regular contributor to the leading SF magazines of the day including *Astounding*, *Astonishing Stories*, *Super Science Stories* and *Galaxy*. He won the Hugo Award four times and the Nebula Award once. With nearly five hundred books to his credit and several hundred articles, Asimov's output was prolific by any standards.

Isaac Asimov died in 1992 at the age of 72.

BY THE SAME AUTHOR

ISAAC ASIMOV

Living Space: And Other Stories

THE COMPLETE STORIES

HARPER
Voyager

Harper*Voyager*
An imprint of HarperCollins*Publishers* Ltd
1 London Bridge Street
London SE1 9GF

www.harpercollins.co.uk

HarperCollins*Publishers*
Macken House, 39/40 Mayor Street Upper
Dublin 1, D01 C9W8, Ireland

This paperback edition 2024
1

Previously published in paperback 1994

First published in Great Britain as
The Complete Stories Volume I (Part One) by
HarperCollins*Publishers* 1993

A catalogue record for this book is available from the British Library.

ISBN: 978-0-00-867239-3

This book is set in Janson Text LT Std by HarperCollins*Publishers* India

Printed and bound in the UK using 100%
renewable electricity at CPI Group (UK) Ltd

MIX
Paper | Supporting
responsible forestry
FSC™ C007454

This book contains FSC™ certified paper and other controlled
sources to ensure responsible forest management.

For more information visit: www.harpercollins.co.uk/green

Contents

The Dead Past

Arnold Potterley, PhD, was a Professor of Ancient History. That, in itself was not dangerous. What changed the world beyond all dreams was the fact that he *looked* like a Professor of Ancient History.

Thaddeus Araman, Department Head of the Division of Chronoscopy, might have taken proper action if Dr Potterley had been owner of a large, square chin, flashing eyes, aquiline nose and broad shoulders.

As it was, Thaddeus Araman found himself staring over his desk at a mild-mannered individual, whose faded blue eyes looked at him wistfully from either side of a low-bridged button nose; whose small, neatly dressed figure seemed stamped 'milk-and-water' from thinning brown hair to the neatly brushed shoes that completed a conservative middle-class costume.

Araman said pleasantly, 'And now what can I do for you, Dr Potterley?'

Dr Potterley said in a soft voice that went well with the rest of him, 'Mr Araman, I came to you because you're top man in chronoscopy.'

Araman smiled. 'Not exactly. Above me is the World Commissioner of Research and above him is the Secretary-General of the

United Nations. And above both of them, of course, are the sovereign peoples of Earth.'

Dr Potterley shook his head. 'They're not interested in chronoscopy. I've come to you, sir, because for two years I have been trying to obtain permission to do some time viewing – chronoscopy, that is – in connection with my researches on ancient Carthage. I can't obtain such permission. My research grants are all proper. There is no irregularity in any of my intellectual endeavors and yet—'

'I'm sure there is no question of irregularity,' said Araman soothingly. He flipped the thin reproduction sheets in the folder to which Potterley's name had been attached. They had been produced by Multivac, whose vast analogical mind kept all the department records. When this was over, the sheets could be destroyed, then reproduced on demand in a matter of minutes.

And while Araman turned the pages, Dr Potterley's voice continued in a soft monotone.

The historian was saying, 'I must explain that my problem is quite an important one. Carthage was ancient commercialism brought to its zenith. Pre-Roman Carthage was the nearest ancient analogue to pre-atomic America, at least insofar as its attachment to trade, commerce and business in general was concerned. They were the most daring seamen and explorers before the Vikings; much better at it than the overrated Greeks.

'To know Carthage would be very rewarding, yet the only knowledge we have of it is derived from the writings of its bitter enemies, the Greeks and Romans. Carthage itself never wrote in its own defense or, if it did, the books did not survive. As a result, the Carthaginians have been one of the favorite sets of villains of history and perhaps unjustly so. Time viewing may set the record straight.'

He said much more.

Araman said, still turning the reproduction sheets before him, 'You must realize, Dr Potterley, that chronoscopy, or time viewing, if you prefer, is a difficult process.'

Dr Potterley, who had been interrupted, frowned and said, 'I am asking for only certain selected views at times and places I would indicate.'

Araman sighed. 'Even a few views, even one . . . It is an unbelievably delicate art. There is the question of focus, getting the proper scene in view and holding it. There is the synchronization of sound, which calls for completely independent circuits.'

'Surely my problem is important enough to justify considerable effort.'

'Yes, sir. Undoubtedly,' said Araman at once. To deny the importance of someone's research problem would be unforgivably bad manners. 'But you must understand how long-drawn-out even the simplest view is. And there is a long waiting line for the chronoscope and an even longer waiting line for the use of Multivac which guides us in our use of the controls.'

Potterley stirred unhappily. 'But can nothing be done? For two years—'

'A matter of priority, sir. I'm sorry . . . Cigarette?'

The historian started back at the suggestion, eyes suddenly widening as he stared at the pack thrust out toward him. Araman looked surprised, withdrew the pack, made a motion as though to take a cigarette for himself and thought better of it.

Potterley drew a sigh of unfeigned relief as the pack was put out of sight. He said, 'Is there any way of reviewing matters, putting me as far forward as possible? I don't know how to explain—'

Araman smiled. Some had offered money under similar circumstances which, of course, had gotten them nowhere, either. He said, 'The decisions on priority are computer-processed. I could in no way alter those decisions arbitrarily.'

Potterley rose stiffly to his feet. He stood five and a half feet tall. 'Then, good day, sir.'

'Good day, Dr Potterley. And my sincerest regrets.'

He offered his hand and Potterley touched it briefly.

The historian left, and a touch of the buzzer brought Araman's secretary into the room. He handed her the folder.

'These,' he said, 'may be disposed of.'

Alone again, he smiled bitterly. Another item in his quarter-century's service to the human race. Service through negation.

At least this fellow had been easy to dispose of. Sometimes academic pressure had to be applied and even withdrawal of grants.

Five minutes later, he had forgotten Dr Potterley. Nor, thinking back on it later, could he remember feeling any premonition of danger.

During the first year of his frustration, Arnold Potterley had experienced only that – frustration. During the second year, though, his frustration gave birth to an idea that first frightened and then fascinated him. Two things stopped him from trying to translate the idea into action, and neither barrier was the undoubted fact that his notion was a grossly unethical one.

The first was merely the continuing hope that the government would finally give its permission and make it unnecessary for him to do anything more. That hope had perished finally in the interview with Araman just completed.

The second barrier had been not a hope at all but a dreary realization of his own incapacity. He was not a physicist and he knew no physicists from whom he might obtain help. The Department of Physics at the university consisted of men well stocked with grants and well immersed in specialty. At best, they would not listen to him. At worst, they would report him for intellectual anarchy and even his basic Carthaginian grant might easily be withdrawn.

That he could not risk. And yet chronoscopy was the only way to carry on his work. Without it, he would be no worse off if his grant were lost.

The first hint that the second barrier might be overcome had come a week earlier than his interview with Araman, and it had gone unrecognized at the time. It had been at one of the faculty teas. Potterley attended these sessions unfailingly because he conceived attendance to be a duty, and he took his duties seriously. Once there, however, he conceived it to be no responsibility of his to make light conversation or new friends. He sipped abstemiously at a drink or two, exchanged a polite word with the dean or such department heads as happened to be present, bestowed a narrow smile on others and finally left early.

Ordinarily, he would have paid no attention, at that most recent tea, to a young man standing quietly, even diffidently, in one corner. He would never have dreamed of speaking to him. Yet a tangle of circumstance persuaded him this once to behave in a way contrary to his nature.

That morning at breakfast, Mrs Potterley had announced somberly that once again she had dreamed of Laurel; but this time a Laurel grown up, yet retaining the three-year old face that stamped her as their child. Potterley had let her talk. There had been a time when he fought her too frequent preoccupation with the past and death. Laurel would not come back to them, either through dreams or through talk. Yet if it appeased Caroline Potterley – let her dream and talk.

But when Potterley went to school that morning, he found himself for once affected by Caroline's inanities. Laurel grown up! She had died nearly twenty years ago; their only child, then and ever. In all that time, when he thought of her, it was as a three-year-old.

Now he thought: But if she were alive now, she wouldn't be three, she'd be nearly twenty-three.

Helplessly, he found himself trying to think of Laurel as growing progressively older; as finally becoming twenty-three. He did not quite succeed.

Yet he tried. Laurel using make-up. Laurel going out with boys. Laurel – getting married!

So it was that when he saw the young man hovering at the outskirts of the coldly circulating group of faculty men, it occurred to him quixotically that, for all he knew, a youngster just such as this might have married Laurel. That youngster himself, perhaps . . .

Laurel might have met him, here at the university, or some evening when he might be invited to dinner at the Potterleys'. They might grow interested in one another. Laurel would surely have been pretty and this youngster looked well. He was dark in coloring, with a lean intent face and an easy carriage.

The tenuous daydream snapped, yet Potterley found himself staring foolishly at the young man, not as a strange face but as a possible son-in-law in the might-have-been. He found himself threading his way toward the man. It was almost a form of autohypnotism.

He put out his hand. 'I am Arnold Potterley of the History Department. You're new here, I think?'

The youngster looked faintly astonished and fumbled with his drink, shifting it to his left hand in order to shake with his right. 'Jonas Foster is my name, sir. I'm a new instructor in physics. I'm just starting this semester.'

Potterley nodded. 'I wish you a happy stay here and great success.'

That was the end of it, then. Potterley had come uneasily to his senses, found himself embarrassed and moved off. He stared back over his shoulder once, but the illusion of relationship had gone. Reality was quite real once more and he was angry with himself for having fallen prey to his wife's foolish talk about Laurel.

But a week later, even while Araman was talking, the thought of that young man had come back to him. An instructor in physics. A new instructor. Had he been deaf at the time? Was there a short circuit between ear and brain? Or was it an automatic self-censorship because of the impending interview with the Head of Chronoscopy?

But the interview failed, and it was the thought of the young man with whom he had exchanged two sentences that prevented Potterley from elaborating his pleas for consideration. He was almost anxious to get away.

And in the autogiro express back to the university, he could almost wish he were superstitious. He could then console himself with the thought that the casual meaningless meeting had really been directed by a knowing and purposeful Fate.

Jonas Foster was not new to academic life. The long and rickety struggle for the doctorate would make anyone a veteran. Additional work as a postdoctorate teaching fellow acted as a booster shot.

But now he was Instructor Jonas Foster. Professorial dignity lay ahead. And he now found himself in a new sort of relationship toward other professors.

For one thing, they would be voting on future promotions. For another, he was in no position to tell so early in the game which particular member of the faculty might or might not have the ear of the dean or even of the university president. He did not fancy himself as a campus politician and was sure he would make a poor one, yet there was no point in kicking his own rear into blisters just to prove that to himself.

So Foster listened to this mild mannered historian who, in some vague way, seemed nevertheless to radiate tension, and did not shut him up abruptly and toss him out. Certainly that was his first impulse.

He remembered Potterley well enough. Potterley had approached him at that tea (which had been a grizzly affair). The fellow had spoken two sentences to him stiffly, somehow glassy-eyed, had then come to himself with a visible start and hurried off.

It had amused Foster at the time, but now . . .

Potterley might have been deliberately trying to make his acquaintance, or, rather, to impress his own personality on Foster as that of a queer sort of duck, eccentric but harmless. He might now be probing Foster's views, searching for unsettling opinions. Surely, they ought to have done so before granting him his appointment. Still . . .

Potterley might be serious, might honestly not realize what he was doing. Or he might realize quite well what he was doing; he might be nothing more or less than a dangerous rascal.

Foster mumbled, 'Well, now—' to gain time, and fished out a package of cigarettes, intending to offer one to Potterley and to light it and one for himself very slowly.

But Potterley said at once, 'Please, Dr Foster. No cigarettes.'

Foster looked startled. 'I'm sorry, sir.'

'No. The regrets are mine. I cannot stand the odor. An idiosyncrasy. I'm sorry.'

He was positively pale. Foster put away the cigarettes.

Foster, feeling the absence of the cigarette, took the easy way out. 'I'm flattered that you ask my advice and all that, Dr Potterley, but I'm not a neutrinics man. I can't very well do anything professional in that direction. Even stating an opinion would be out of line, and, frankly, I'd prefer that you didn't go into any particulars.'

The historian's prim face set hard. 'What do you mean, you're not a neutrinics man? You're not anything yet. You haven't received any grant, have you?'

'This is only my first semester.'

'I know that. I imagine you haven't even applied for any grant yet.'

Foster half smiled. In three months at the university, he had not succeeded in putting his initial requests for research grants into good enough shape to pass on to a professional science writer, let alone to the Research Commission.

(His Department Head, fortunately, took it quite well. 'Take your time now, Foster,' he said, 'and get your thoughts well organized. Make sure you know your path and where it will lead, for, once you receive a grant, your specialization will be formally recognized and, for better or for worse, it will be yours for the rest of your career.' The advice was trite enough, but triteness has often the merit of truth, and Foster recognized that.)

Foster said, 'By education and inclination, Dr Potterley, I'm a hyperoptics man with a gravities minor. It's how I described myself in applying for this position. It may not be my official specialization yet, but it's going to be. It can't be anything else. As for neutrinics, I never even studied the subject.'

'Why not?' demanded Potterley at once.

Foster stared. It was the kind of rude curiosity about another man's professional status that was always irritating. He said, with the edge of his own politeness just a trifle blunted, 'A course in neutrinics wasn't given at my university.'

'Good Lord, where did you go?'

'MIT,' said Foster quietly.

'And they don't teach neutrinics?'

'No, they don't.' Foster felt himself flush and was moved to a defense. 'It's a highly specialized subject with no great value. Chronoscopy, perhaps, has some value, but it is the only practical application and that's a dead end.'

The historian stared at him earnestly. 'Tell me this. Do you know where I can find a neutrinics man?'

'No, I don't,' said Foster bluntly.

'Well, then, do you know a school which teaches neutrinics?'

'No, I don't.'

Potterley smiled tightly and without humor.

Foster resented that smile, found he detected insult in it and grew sufficiently annoyed to say, 'I would like to point out, sir, that you're stepping out of line.'

'What?'

'I'm saying that, as a historian, your interest in any sort of physics, your professional interest, is—' He paused, unable to bring himself quite to say the word.

'Unethical?'

'That's the word, Dr Potterley.'

'My researches have driven me to it,' said Potterley in an intense whisper.

'The Research Commission is the place to go. If they permit—'

'I have gone to them and have received no satisfaction.'

'Then obviously you must abandon this.' Foster knew he was sounding stuffily virtuous, but he wasn't going to let this man lure him into an expression of intellectual anarchy. It was too early in his career to take stupid risks.

Apparently, though, the remark had its effect on Potterley. Without any warning, the man exploded into a rapid-fire verbal storm of irresponsibility.

Scholars, he said, could be free only if they could freely follow their own free-swinging curiosity. Research, he said, forced into a predesigned pattern by the powers that held the purse strings became slavish and had to stagnate. No man, he said, had the right to dictate the intellectual interests of another.

Foster listened to all of it with disbelief. None of it was strange to him. He had heard college boys talk so in order to shock their professors and he had once or twice amused himself in that fashion, too. Anyone who studied the history of science knew that many men had once thought so.

Yet it seemed strange to Foster, almost against nature, that a modern man of science could advance such nonsense. No one would advocate running a factory by allowing each individual worker to do whatever pleased him at the moment, or running a ship according to the casual and conflicting notions of each individual crewman. It would be taken for granted that some sort of centralized supervisory agency must exist in each case. Why should direction and order benefit a factory and a ship but not scientific research?

People might say that the human mind was somehow qualitatively different from a ship or factory but the history of intellectual endeavor proved the opposite.

When science was young and the intricacies of all or most of the known was within the grasp of an individual mind, there was no need for direction, perhaps. Blind wandering over the uncharted tracts of ignorance could lead to wonderful finds by accident.

But as knowledge grew, more and more data had to be absorbed before worthwhile journeys into ignorance could be organized. Men had to specialize. The researcher needed the resources of a library he himself could not gather, then of instruments he himself could not afford. More and more, the individual researcher gave way to the research team and the research institution.

The funds necessary for research grew greater as tools grew more numerous. What college was so small today as not to require at least one nuclear micro-reactor and at least one three-stage computer?

Centuries before, private individuals could no longer subsidize research. By 1940, only the government, large industries and large universities or research institutions could properly subsidize basic research.

By 1960, even the largest universities depended entirely upon government grants, while research institutions could not exist without tax concessions and public subscriptions. By 2000, the industrial combines had become a branch of the world government and, thereafter, the financing of research and therefore its direction naturally became centralized under a department of the government.

It all worked itself out naturally and well. Every branch of science was fitted neatly to the needs of the public, and the various branches of science were co-ordinated decently. The material advance of the last half-century was argument enough for the fact that science was not falling into stagnation.

Foster tried to say a very little of this and was waved aside impatiently by Potterley who said, 'You are parroting official propaganda. You're sitting in the middle of an example that's squarely against the official view. Can you believe that?'

'Frankly, no.'

'Well, why do you say time viewing is a dead end? Why is neutrinics unimportant? You say it is. You say it categorically. Yet you've never studied it. You claim complete ignorance of the subject. It's not even given in your school—'

'Isn't the mere fact that it isn't given proof enough?'

'Oh, I see. It's not given because it's unimportant. And it's unimportant because it's not given. Are you satisfied with that reasoning?'

Foster felt a growing confusion. 'It's in the books.'

'That's all. The books say neutrinics is unimportant. Your professors tell you so because they read it in the books. The books say so because professors write them. Who says it from personal experience and knowledge? Who does research in it? Do you know of anyone?'

Foster said, 'I don't see that we're getting anywhere, Dr Potterley. I have work to do—'

'One minute. I just want you to try this on. See how it sounds to you. I say the government is actively suppressing basic research in neutrinics and chronoscopy. They're suppressing application of chronoscopy.'

'Oh, no.'

'Why not? They could do it. There's your centrally directed research. If they refuse grants for research in any portion of science, that portion dies. They've killed neutrinics. They can do it and have done it.'

'But why?'

'I don't know why. I want you to find out. I'd do it myself if I knew enough. I came to you because you're a young fellow with a brand-new education. Have your intellectual arteries hardened already? Is there no curiosity in you? Don't you want to *know?* Don't you want *answers?*'

The historian was peering intently into Foster's face. Their noses were only inches apart, and Foster was so lost that he did not think to draw back.

He should, by rights, have ordered Potterley out. If necessary, he should have thrown Potterley out.

It was not respect for age and position that stopped him. It was certainly not that Potterley's arguments had convinced him. Rather, it was a small point of college pride.

Why didn't MIT give a course in neutrinics? For that matter, now that he came to think of it, he doubted that there was a single book on neutrinics in the library. He could never recall having seen one.

He stopped to think about that.

And that was ruin.

Caroline Potterley had once been an attractive woman. There were occasions, such as dinners or university functions, when, by considerable effort, remnants of the attraction could be salvaged.

On ordinary occasions, she sagged. It was the word she applied to herself in moments of self-abhorrence. She had grown plumper with the years, but the flaccidity about her was not a matter of fat entirely. It was as though her muscles had given up and grown limp so that she shuffled when she walked, while her eyes grew baggy and her cheeks jowly. Even her graying hair seemed tired rather than merely stringy. Its straightness seemed to be the result of a supine surrender to gravity, nothing else.

Caroline Potterley looked at herself in the mirror and admitted this was one of her bad days. She knew the reason, too.

It had been the dream of Laurel. The strange one, with Laurel grown up. She had been wretched ever since.

Still, she was sorry she had mentioned it to Arnold. He didn't say anything; he never did any more; but it was bad for him. He was particularly withdrawn for days afterward. It might have been that he was getting ready for that important conference with the big government official (he kept saying he expected no success), but it might also have been her dream.

It was better in the old days when he would cry sharply at her, 'Let the dead past *go*, Caroline! Talk won't bring her back, and dreams won't either.'

It had been bad for both of them. Horribly bad. She had been away from home and had lived in guilt ever since. If she had stayed at home, if she had not gone on an unnecessary shopping expedition, there would have been two of them available. One would have succeeded in saving Laurel.

Poor Arnold had not managed. Heaven knew he tried. He had nearly died himself. He had come out of the burning house, staggering in agony, blistered, choking, half blinded, with the dead Laurel in his arms.

The nightmare of that lived on, never lifting entirely.

Arnold slowly grew a shell about himself afterward. He cultivated a low-voiced mildness through which nothing broke, no lightning struck. He grew puritanical and even abandoned his minor vices, his cigarettes, his penchant for an occasional profane exclamation. He obtained his grant for the preparation of a new history of Carthage and subordinated everything to that.

She tried to help him. She hunted up his references, typed his notes and microfilmed them. Then that ended suddenly.

She ran from the desk suddenly one evening, reaching the

bathroom in bare time and retching abominably. Her husband followed her in confusion and concern.

'Caroline, what's wrong?'

It took a drop of brandy to bring her around. She said, 'Is it true? What they did?'

'Who did?'

'The Carthaginians.'

He stared at her and she got it out by indirection. She couldn't say it right out.

The Carthaginians, it seemed, worshiped Moloch, in the form of a hollow, brazen idol with a furnace in its belly. At times of national crisis, the priests and the people gathered, and infants, after the proper ceremonies and invocations, were dextrously hurled, alive, into the flames.

They were given sweetmeats just before the crucial moment, in order that the efficacy of the sacrifice not be ruined by displeasing cries of panic. The drums rolled just after the moment, to drown out the few seconds of infant shrieking. The parents were present, presumably gratified, for the sacrifice was pleasing to the gods . . .

Arnold Potterley frowned darkly. Vicious lies, he told her, on the part of Carthage's enemies. He should have warned her. After all, such propagandistic lies were not uncommon. According to the Greeks, the ancient Hebrews worshiped an ass's head in their Holy of Holies. According to the Romans, the primitive Christians were haters of all men who sacrificed pagan children in the catacombs.

'Then they didn't do it?' asked Caroline.

'I'm sure they didn't. The primitive Phoenicians may have. Human sacrifice is commonplace in primitive cultures. But Carthage in her great days was not a primitive culture. Human sacrifice often gives way to symbolic actions such as circumcision. The Greeks and Romans might have mistaken some Carthaginian symbolism for the original full rite, either out of ignorance or out of malice.'

'Are you sure?'

'I can't be sure yet, Caroline, but when I've got enough evidence,

I'll apply for permission to use chronoscopy, which will settle the matter once and for all.'

'Chronoscopy?'

'Time viewing. We can focus on ancient Carthage at some time of crisis, the landing of Scipio Africanus in 202 BC, for instance, and see with our own eyes exactly what happens. And you'll see, I'll be right.'

He patted her and smiled encouragingly, but she dreamed of Laurel every night for two weeks thereafter and she never helped him with his Carthage project again. Nor did he ever ask her to.

But now she was bracing herself for his coming. He had called her after arriving back in town, told her he had seen the government man and that it had gone as expected. That meant failure, and yet the little telltale sign of depression had been absent from his voice and his features had appeared quite composed in the teleview. He had another errand to take care of, he said, before coming home.

It meant he would be late, but that didn't matter. Neither one of them was particular about eating hours or cared when packages were taken out of the freezer or even which packages or when the selfwarming mechanism was activated.

When he did arrive, he surprised her. There was nothing untoward about him in any obvious way. He kissed her dutifully and smiled, took off his hat and asked if all had been well while he was gone. It was all almost perfectly normal. Almost.

She had learned to detect small things, though, and his pace in all this was a trifle hurried. Enough to show her accustomed eye that he was under tension.

She said, 'Has something happened?'

He said, 'We're going to have a dinner guest night after next, Caroline. You don't mind?'

'Well, no. Is it anyone I know?'

'No. A young instructor. A newcomer. I've spoken to him.' He suddenly whirled toward her and seized her arms at the elbow, held them a moment, then dropped them in confusion as though disconcerted at having shown emotion.

He said, 'I almost didn't get through to him. Imagine that. Terrible, *terrible*, the way we have all bent to the yoke; the affection we have for the harness about us.'

Mrs Potterley wasn't sure she understood, but for a year she had been watching him grow quietly more rebellious; little by little more daring in his criticism of the government. She said, 'You haven't spoken foolishly to him, have you?'

'What do you mean, foolishly? He'll be doing some neutrinics for me.'

'Neutrinics' was trisyllabic nonsense to Mrs Potterley, but she knew it had nothing to do with history. She said faintly, 'Arnold, I don't like you to do that. You'll lose your position. It's—'

'It's intellectual anarchy, my dear,' he said. 'That's the phrase you want. Very well. I am an anarchist. If the government will not allow me to push my researches, I will push them on my own. And when I show the way, others will follow . . . And if they don't, it makes no difference. It's Carthage that counts and human knowledge, not you and I.'

'But you don't know this young man. What if he is an agent for the Commission of Research?'

'Not likely and I'll take that chance.' He made a fist of his right hand and rubbed it gently against the palm of his left. 'He's on my side now. I'm sure of it. He can't help but be. I can recognize intellectual curiosity when I see it in a man's eyes and face and attitude, and it's a fatal disease for a tame scientist. Even today it takes time to beat it out of a man and the young ones are vulnerable . . . Oh, why stop at anything? Why not build our own chronoscope and tell the government to go to—'

He stopped abruptly, shook his head and turned away. 'I hope everything will be all right,' said Mrs Potterley, feeling helplessly certain that everything would not be, and frightened, in advance, for her husband's professorial status and the security of their old age.

It was she alone, of them all, who had a violent presentiment of trouble. Quite the wrong trouble, of course.

*

Jonas Foster was nearly half an hour late in arriving at the Potter-leys' off-campus house. Up to that very evening, he had not quite decided he would go. Then, at the last moment, he found he could not bring himself to commit the social enormity of breaking a dinner appointment an hour before the appointed time. That, and the nagging of curiosity.

The dinner itself passed interminably. Foster ate without appetite. Mrs Potterley sat in distant absent mindedness, emerging out of it only once to ask if he were married and to make a deprecating sound at the news that he was not. Dr Potterley himself asked neutrally after his professional history and nodded his head primly.

It was as staid, stodgy – boring, actually – as anything could be.

Foster thought: He seems so harmless.

Foster had spent the last two days reading up on Dr Potterley. Very casually, of course, almost sneakily. He wasn't particularly anxious to be seen in the Social Science Library. To be sure, history was one of those borderline affairs and historical works were frequently read for amusement or edification by the general public.

Still, a physicist wasn't quite the 'general public.' Let Foster take to reading histories and he would be considered queer, sure as relativity, and after a while the Head of the Department would wonder if his new instructor were really 'the man for the job.'

So he had been cautious. He sat in the more secluded alcoves and kept his head bent when he slipped in and out at odd hours.

Dr Potterley, it turned out, had written three books and some dozen articles on the ancient Mediterranean worlds, and the later articles (all in 'Historical Reviews') had all dealt with pre-Roman Carthage from a sympathetic viewpoint.

That, at least, checked with Potterley's story and had soothed Foster's suspicions somewhat . . . And yet Foster felt that it would have been much wiser, much safer, to have scotched the matter at the beginning.

A scientist shouldn't be too curious, he thought in bitter dissatisfaction with himself. It's a dangerous trait.

After dinner, he was ushered into Potterley's study and he was brought up sharply at the threshold. The walls were simply lined with books.

Not merely films. There were films, of course, but these were far outnumbered by the books – print on paper. He wouldn't have thought so many books would exist in usable condition.

That bothered Foster. Why should anyone want to keep so many books at home? Surely all were available in the university library, or, at the very worst, at the Library of Congress, if one wished to take the minor trouble of checking out a microfilm.

There was an element of secrecy involved in a home library. It breathed of intellectual anarchy. That last thought, oddly, calmed Foster. He would rather Potterley be an authentic anarchist than a play-acting *agent provocateur*.

And now the hours began to pass quickly and astonishingly.

'You see,' Potterley said, in a clear, unflurried voice, 'it was a matter of finding, if possible, anyone who had ever used chronoscopy in his work. Naturally, I couldn't ask baldly, since that would be un-authorized research.'

'Yes,' said Foster dryly. He was a little surprised such a small con-sideration would stop the man.

'I used indirect methods—'

He had. Foster was amazed at the volume of correspondence dealing with small disputed points of ancient Mediterranean cul-ture which somehow managed to elicit the casual remark over and over again: 'Of course, having never made use of chronoscopy—' or, 'Pending approval of my request for chronoscopic data, which appears unlikely at the moment—'

'Now these aren't blind questionings,' said Potterley. 'There's a monthly booklet put out by the Institute for Chronoscopy in which items concerning the past as determined by time viewing are printed. Just one or two items.

'What impressed me first was the triviality of most of the items, their insipidity. Why should such researches get priority over my work? So I wrote to people who would be most likely to do research in the directions described in the booklet. Uniformly, as I have shown you, they did *not* make use of the chronoscope. Now let's go over it point by point.'

At last Foster, his head swimming with Potterley's meticulously gathered details, asked, 'But why?'

'I don't know why,' said Potterley, 'but I have a theory. The original invention of the chronoscope was by Sterbinski – you see, I know that much – and it was well publicized. But then the government took over the instrument and decided to suppress further research in the matter or any use of the machine. But then, people might be curious as to why it wasn't being used. Curiosity is such a vice, Dr Foster.'

Yes, agreed the physicist to himself.

'Imagine the effectiveness, then,' Potterley went on, 'of pretending that the chronoscope *was* being used. It would then be not a mystery, but a commonplace. It would no longer be a fitting object for legitimate curiosity or an attractive one for illicit curiosity.'

'*You* were curious,' pointed out Foster.

Potterley looked a trifle restless. 'It was different in my case,' he said angrily. 'I have something that *must* be done, and I wouldn't submit to the ridiculous way in which they kept putting me off.'

A bit paranoid, too, thought Foster gloomily.

Yet he had ended up with something, paranoid or not. Foster could no longer deny that something peculiar was going on in the matter of neutrinics.

But what was Potterley after? That still bothered Foster. If Potterley didn't intend this as a test of Foster's ethics, what *did* he want?

Foster put it to himself logically. If an intellectual anarchist with a touch of paranoia wanted to use a chronoscope and was convinced that the powers-that-be were deliberately standing in his way, what would he do?

Supposing it were I, he thought. What would I do?

He said slowly, 'Maybe the chronoscope doesn't exist at all?'

Potterley started. There was almost a crack in his general

calmness. For an instant, Foster found himself catching a glimpse of something not at all calm.

But the historian kept his balance and said, 'Oh, no, there *must* be a chronoscope.'

'Why? Have you seen it? Have I? Maybe that's the explanation of everything. Maybe they're not deliberately holding out on a chronoscope they've got. Maybe they haven't got it in the first place.'

'But Sterbinski lived. He built a chronoscope. That much is a fact.'

'The books say so,' said Foster coldly.

'Now listen.' Potterley actually reached over and snatched at Foster's jacket sleeve. 'I need the chronoscope. I must have it. Don't tell me it doesn't exist. What we're going to do is find out enough about neutrinics to be able to—'

Potterley drew himself up short.

Foster drew his sleeve away. He needed no ending to that sentence. He supplied it himself. He said, 'Build one of our own?'

Potterley looked sour as though he would rather not have said it point-blank. Nevertheless, he said, 'Why not?'

'Because that's out of the question,' said Foster. 'If what I've read is correct, then it took Sterbinski twenty years to build his machine and several millions in composite grants. Do you think you and I can duplicate that illegally? Suppose we had the time, which we haven't, and suppose I could learn enough out of books, which I doubt, where would we get the money and equipment? The chronoscope is supposed to fill a five-story building, for Heaven's sake.'

'Then you won't help me?'

'Well, I'll tell you what. I have one way in which I may be able to find out something—'

'What is that?' asked Potterley at once.

'Never mind. That's not important. But I may be able to find out enough to tell you whether the government is deliberately suppressing research by chronoscope. I may confirm the evidence you already have or I may be able to prove that your evidence is misleading. I don't know what good it will do you in either case, but it's as far as I can go. It's my limit.'

Potterley watched the young man go finally. He was angry with himself. Why had he allowed himself to grow so careless as to permit the fellow to guess that he was thinking in terms of a chronoscope of his own? That was premature.

But then why did the young fool have to suppose that a chronoscope might not exist at all?

It *had* to exist. It *had* to. What was the use of saying it didn't?

And why couldn't a second one be built? Science had advanced in the fifty years since Sterbinski. All that was needed was knowledge.

Let the youngster gather knowledge. Let him think a small gathering would be his limit. Having taken the path to anarchy, there would be no limit. If the boy were not driven onward by something in himself, the first steps would be error enough to force the rest. Potterley was quite certain he would not hesitate to use blackmail.

Potterley waved a last good-by and looked up. It was beginning to rain.

Certainly! Blackmail if necessary, but he would not be stopped.

Foster steered his car across the bleak outskirts of town and scarcely noticed the rain.

He *was* a fool, he told himself, but he couldn't leave things as they were. He had to know. He damned his streak of undisciplined curiosity, but he had to know.

But he would go no further than Uncle Ralph. He swore mightily to himself that it would stop there. In that way, there would be no evidence against him, no real evidence. Uncle Ralph would be discreet.

In a way, he was secretly ashamed of Uncle Ralph. He hadn't mentioned him to Potterley partly out of caution and partly because he did not wish to witness the lifted eyebrow, the inevitable half-smile. Professional science writers, however useful, were a little outside the pale, fit only for patronizing contempt. The fact that, as a class, they made more money than did research scientists only made matters worse, of course.

Still, there were times when a science writer in the family could be a convenience. Not being really educated, they did not have to specialize. Consequently, a good science writer knew practically everything . . . And Uncle Ralph was one of the best.

Ralph Nimmo had no college degree and was rather proud of it. 'A degree,' he once said to Jonas Foster, when both were considerably younger, 'is a first step down a ruinous highway. You don't want to waste it so you go on to graduate work and doctoral research. You end up a thoroughgoing ignoramus on everything in the world except for one subdivisional sliver of nothing.

'On the other hand, if you guard your mind carefully and keep it blank of any clutter of information till maturity is reached, filling it only with intelligence and training it only in clear thinking, you then have a powerful instrument at your disposal and you can become a science writer.'

Nimmo received his first assignment at the age of twenty-five, after he had completed his apprenticeship and been out in the field for less than three months. It came in the shape of a clotted manuscript whose language would impart no glimmering of understanding to any reader, however qualified, without careful study and some inspired guesswork. Nimmo took it apart and put it together again (after five long and exasperating interviews with the authors, who were biophysicists), making the language taut and meaningful and smoothing the style to a pleasant gloss.

'Why not?' he would say tolerantly to his nephew, who countered his strictures on degrees by berating him with his readiness to hang on the fringes of science. 'The fringe is important. Your scientists can't write. Why should they be expected to? They aren't expected to be grand masters at chess or virtuosos at the violin, so why expect them to know how to put words together? Why not leave that for specialists, too?

'Good Lord, Jonas, read your literature of a hundred years ago. Discount the fact that the science is out of date and that some of the expressions are out of date. Just try to read it and make sense out of it. It's just jaw-cracking, amateurish. Pages are published uselessly; whole articles which are either noncomprehensible or both.'

'But you don't get recognition, Uncle Ralph,' protested young Foster, who was getting ready to start his college career and was rather starry-eyed about it. 'You could be a terrific researcher.'

'I get recognition,' said Nimmo. 'Don't think for a minute I don't. Sure, a biochemist or a strato-meteorologist won't give me the time of day, but they pay me well enough. Just find out what happens when some first-class chemist finds the Commission has cut his year's allowance for science writing. He'll fight harder for enough funds to afford me, or someone like me, than to get a recording ionograph.'

He grinned broadly and Foster grinned back. Actually, he was proud of his paunchy, round-faced, stub-fingered uncle, whose vanity made him brush his fringe of hair futilely over the desert on his pate and made him dress like an unmade haystack because such negligence was his trademark. Ashamed, but proud, too.

And now Foster entered his uncle's cluttered apartment in no mood at all for grinning. He was nine years older now and so was Uncle Ralph. For nine more years, papers in every branch of science had come to him for polishing and a little of each had crept into his capacious mind.

Nimmo was eating seedless grapes, popping them into his mouth one at a time. He tossed a bunch to Foster who caught them by a hair, then bent to retrieve individual grapes that had torn loose and fallen to the floor.

'Let them be. Don't bother,' said Nimmo carelessly. 'Someone comes in here to clean once a week. What's up? Having trouble with your grant application write-up?'

'I haven't really got into that yet.'

'You haven't? Get a move on, boy. Are you waiting for me to offer to do the final arrangement?'

'I couldn't afford you, Uncle.'

'Aw, come on. It's all in the family. Grant me all popular publication rights and no cash need change hands.'

Foster nodded. 'If you're serious, it's a deal.'

'It's a deal.'

It was a gamble, of course, but Foster knew enough of Nimmo's science writing to realize it could pay off. Some dramatic discovery of public interest on primitive man or on a new surgical technique, or on any branch of spationautics could mean a very cash-attracting article in any of the mass media of communication.

It was Nimmo, for instance, who had written up, for scientific consumption, the series of papers by Bryce and co-workers that elucidated the fine structure of two cancer viruses, for which job he asked the picayune payment of fifteen hundred dollars, provided popular publication rights were included. He then wrote up, exclusively, the same work in semidramatic form for use in trimensional video for a twenty-thousand-dollar advance plus rental royalties that were still coming in after five years.

Foster said bluntly, 'What do you know about neutrinics, Uncle?'

'Neutrinics?' Nimmo's small eyes looked surprised. 'Are you working in that? I thought it was pseudo-gravitic optics.'

'It is p.g.o. I just happen to be asking about neutrinics.'

'That's a devil of a thing to be doing. You're stepping out of line. You know that, don't you?'

'I don't expect you to call the Commission because I'm a little curious about things.'

'Maybe I should before you get into trouble. Curiosity is an occupational danger with scientists. I've watched it work. One of them will be moving quietly along on a problem, then curiosity leads him up a strange creek. Next thing you know they've done so little on their proper problem, they can't justify for a project renewal. I've seen more—'

'All I want to know,' said Foster patiently, 'is what's been passing through your hands lately on neutrinics.'

Nimmo leaned back, chewing at a grape thoughtfully. 'Nothing. Nothing ever. I don't recall ever getting a paper on neutrinics.'

'What!' Foster was openly astonished. 'Then who does get the work?'

'Now that you ask,' said Nimmo, 'I don't know. Don't recall anyone talking about it at the annual conventions. I don't think much work is being done there.'

'Why not?'

'Hey, there, don't bark. I'm not doing anything. My guess would be—'

Foster was exasperated. 'Don't you know?'

'Hmp. I'll tell you what I know about neutrinics. It concerns the applications of neutrino movements and the forces involved—'

'Sure. Sure. Just as electronics deals with the applications of electron movements and the forces involved, and pseudo-gravitics deals with the applications of artificial gravitational fields. I didn't come to you for that. Is that all you know?'

'And,' said Nimmo with equanimity, 'neutrinics is the basis of time viewing and that *is* all I know.'

Foster slouched back in his chair and massaged one lean cheek with great intensity. He felt angrily dissatisfied. Without formulating it explicitly in his own mind, he had felt sure, somehow, that Nimmo would come up with some late reports, bring up interesting facets of modern neutrinics, send him back to Potterley able to say that the elderly historian was mistaken, that his data was misleading, his deductions mistaken.

Then he could have returned to his proper work.

But now . . .

He told himself angrily: So they're not doing much work in the field. Does that make it deliberate suppression? What if neutrinics is a sterile discipline? Maybe it is. I don't know. Potterley doesn't. Why waste the intellectual resources of humanity on nothing? Or the work might be secret for some legitimate reason. It might be . . .

The trouble was, he had to know. He couldn't leave things as they were now. *He couldn't!*

He said, 'Is there a text on neutrinics, Uncle Ralph? I mean a clear and simple one. An elementary one.'

Nimmo thought, his plump cheeks puffing out with a series of sighs. 'You ask the damnedest questions. The only one I ever heard of was Sterbinski and somebody. I've never seen it, but I viewed something about it once . . . Sterbinski and LaMarr, that's it.'

'Is that the Sterbinski who invented the chronoscope?'

'I think so. Proves the book ought to be good.'

'Is there a recent edition? Sterbinski died thirty years ago.'

Nimmo shrugged and said nothing.

'Can you find out?'

They sat in silence for a moment, while Nimmo shifted his bulk to the creaking tune of the chair he sat on. Then the science writer said, 'Are you going to tell me what this is all about?'

'I can't. Will you help me anyway, Uncle Ralph? Will you get me a copy of the text?'

'Well, you've taught me all I know on pseudo-gravitics. I should be grateful. Tell you what – I'll help you on one condition.'

'Which is?'

The older man was suddenly very grave. 'That you be careful, Jonas. You're obviously way out of line whatever you're doing. Don't blow up your career just because you're curious about something you haven't been assigned to and which is none of your business. Understand?'

Foster nodded, but he hardly heard. He was thinking furiously.

A full week later, Ralph Nimmo eased his rotund figure into Jonas Foster's on-campus two-room combination and said, in a hoarse whisper, 'I've got something.'

'What?' Foster was immediately eager.

'A copy of Sterbinski and LaMarr.' He produced it, or rather a corner of it, from his ample topcoat.

Foster almost automatically eyed door and windows to make sure they were closed and shaded respectively, then held out his hand.

The film case was flaking with age, and when he cracked it the film was faded and growing brittle. He said sharply, 'Is this all?'

'Gratitude, my boy, gratitude!' Nimmo sat down with a grunt, and reached into a pocket for an apple.

'Oh, I'm grateful, but it's so old.'

'And lucky to get it at that. I tried to get a film run from the Congressional Library. No go. The book was restricted.'

'Then how did you get this?'

'Stole it.' He was biting crunchingly around the core. 'New York Public.'

'What?'

'Simple enough. I had access to the stacks, naturally. So I stepped over a chained railing when no one was around, dug this up, and walked out with it. They're very trusting out there. Meanwhile, they won't miss it in years . . . Only you'd better not let anyone see it on you, nephew.'

Foster stared at the film as though it were literally hot.

Nimmo discarded the core and reached for a second apple. 'Funny thing, now. There's nothing more recent in the whole field of neutrinics. Not a monograph, not a paper, not a progress note. Nothing since the chronoscope.'

'Uh-huh,' said Foster absently.

Foster worked evenings in the Potterley home. He could not trust his own on-campus rooms for the purpose. The evening work grew more real to him than his own grant applications. Sometimes he worried about it but then that stopped, too.

His work consisted, at first, simply in viewing and reviewing the text film. Later it consisted in thinking (sometimes while a section of the book ran itself off through the pocket projector, disregarded).

Sometimes Potterley would come down to watch, to sit with prim, eager eyes, as though he expected thought processes to solidify and become visible in all their convolutions. He interfered in only two ways. He did not allow Foster to smoke and sometimes he talked.

It wasn't conversation talk, never that. Rather it was a low-voiced monologue with which, it seemed, he scarcely expected to command attention. It was much more as though he were relieving a pressure within himself.

Carthage! Always Carthage!

Carthage, the New York of the ancient Mediterranean. Carthage, commercial empire and queen of the seas. Carthage, all that Syracuse and Alexandria pretended to be. Carthage, maligned by her enemies and inarticulate in her own defense.

She had been defeated once by Rome and then driven out of Sicily and Sardinia, but came back to more than recoup her losses by new dominions in Spain, and raised up Hannibal to give the Romans sixteen years of terror.

In the end, she lost again a second time, reconciled herself to Fate and built again with broken tools a limping life in shrunken territory, succeeding so well that jealous Rome deliberately forced a third war. And then Carthage, with nothing but bare hands and tenacity, built weapons and forced Rome into a two-year war that ended only with complete destruction of the city, the inhabitants throwing themselves into their flaming houses rather than surrender.

'Could people fight so for a city and a way of life as bad as the ancient writers painted it? Hannibal was a better general than any Roman and his soldiers were absolutely faithful to him. Even his bitterest enemies praised him. There was a Carthaginian. It is fashionable to say that he was an atypical Carthaginian, better than the others, a diamond placed in garbage. But then why was he so faithful to Carthage, even to his death after years of exile? They talk of Moloch—'

Foster didn't always listen but sometimes he couldn't help himself and he shuddered and turned sick at the bloody tale of child sacrifice.

But Potterley went on earnestly, 'Just the same, it isn't true. It's a twenty-five-hundred-year-old canard started by the Greeks and Romans. They had their own slaves, their crucifixions and torture, their gladiatorial contests. They weren't holy. The Moloch story is what later ages would have called war propaganda, the big lie. I can prove it was a lie. I can prove it and, by Heaven, I will – I will—'

He would mumble that promise over and over again in his earnestness.

Mrs Potterley visited him also, but less frequently, usually on Tuesdays and Thursdays when Dr Potterley himself had an evening course to take care of and was not present.

She would sit quietly, scarcely talking, face slack and doughy, eyes blank, her whole attitude distant and withdrawn.

The first time, Foster tried, uneasily, to suggest that she leave.

She said tonelessly, 'Do I disturb you?'

'No, of course not,' lied Foster restlessly. 'It's just that – that—' He couldn't complete the sentence.

She nodded, as though accepting an invitation to stay. Then she opened a cloth bag she had brought with her and took out a quire of vitron sheets which she proceeded to weave together by rapid, delicate movements of a pair of slender, tetra-faceted depolarizers, whose battery-fed wires made her look as though she were holding a large spider.

One evening, she said softly, 'My daughter, Laurel, is your age.'

Foster started, as much at the sudden unexpected sound of speech as at the words. He said, 'I didn't know you had a daughter, Mrs Potterley.'

'She died. Years ago.'

The vitron grew under the deft manipulations into the uneven shape of some garment Foster could not yet identify. There was nothing left for him to do but mutter inanely, 'I'm sorry.'

Mrs Potterley sighed. 'I dream about her often.' She raised her blue, distant eyes to him.

Foster winced and looked away.

Another evening she asked, pulling at one of the vitron sheets to loosen its gentle clinging to her dress, 'What is time viewing anyway?'

That remark broke into a particularly involved chain of thought, and Foster said snappishly, 'Dr Potterley can explain.'

'He's tried to. Oh, my, yes. But I think he's a little impatient with me. He calls it chronoscopy most of the time. Do you actually see things in the past, like the trimensionals? Or does it just make little dot patterns like the computer you use?'

Foster stared at his hand computer with distaste. It worked well enough, but every operation had to be manually controlled and the answers were obtained in code. Now if he could use the school computer . . . Well, why dream, he felt conspicuous enough, as it was, carrying a hand computer under his arm every evening as he left his office.

He said, 'I've never seen the chronoscope myself, but I'm under the impression that you actually see pictures and hear sound.'

'You can hear people talk, too?'

'I think so.' Then, half in desperation, 'Look here, Mrs Potterley, this must be awfully dull for you. I realize you don't like to leave a guest all to himself, but really, Mrs Potterley, you mustn't feel compelled—'

'I don't feel compelled,' she said. 'I'm sitting here, waiting.'

'Waiting? For what?'

She said composedly, 'I listened to you that first evening. The time you first spoke to Arnold. I listened at the door.'

He said, 'You did?'

'I know I shouldn't have, but I was awfully worried about Arnold. I had a notion he was going to do something he oughtn't and I wanted to hear what. And then when I heard—' She paused, bending close over the vitron and peering at it.

'Heard what, Mrs Potterley?'

'That you wouldn't build a chronoscope.'

'Well, of course not.'

'I thought maybe you might change your mind.'

Foster glared at her. 'Do you mean you're coming down here hoping I'll build a chronoscope, waiting for me to build one?'

'I hope you do, Dr Foster. Oh, I hope you do.'

It was as though, all at once, a fuzzy veil had fallen off her face, leaving all her features clear and sharp, putting color into her cheeks, life into her eyes, the vibrations of something approaching excitement into her voice.

'Wouldn't it be wonderful,' she whispered, 'to have one? People of the past could live again. Pharaohs and kings and – just people. I hope you build one, Dr Foster. I really – hope—'

She choked, it seemed, on the intensity of her own words and let the vitron sheets slip off her lap. She rose and ran up the basement stairs, while Foster's eyes followed her awkwardly fleeing body with astonishment and distress.

It cut deeper into Foster's nights and left him sleepless and painfully stiff with thought. It was almost a mental indigestion.

His grant requests went limping in, finally, to Ralph Nimmo. He scarcely had any hope for them. He thought numbly: They won't be approved.

If they weren't, of course, it would create a scandal in the department and probably mean his appointment at the university would not be renewed, come the end of the academic year.

He scarcely worried. It was the neutrino, the neutrino, only the neutrino. Its trail curved and veered sharply and led him breathlessly along uncharted pathways that even Sterbinski and LaMarr did not follow.

He called Nimmo. 'Uncle Ralph, I need a few things. I'm calling from off the campus.'

Nimmo's face in the video plate was jovial, but his voice was sharp. He said, 'What you need is a course in communication. I'm having a hell of a time pulling your application into one intelligible piece. If that's what you're calling about—'

Foster shook his head impatiently. 'That's *not* what I'm calling about. I need these.' He scribbled quickly on a piece of paper and held it up before the receiver.

Nimmo yipped. 'Hey, how many tricks do you think I can wangle?'

'You can get them, Uncle. You know you can.'

Nimmo reread the list of items with silent motions of his plump lips and looked grave.

'What happens when you put those things together?' he asked. Foster shook his head. 'You'll have exclusive popular publication rights to whatever turns up, the way it's always been. But please don't ask any questions now.'

'I can't do miracles, you know.'

'Do this one. You've got to. You're a science writer, not a research man. You don't have to account for anything. You've got friends and connections. They can look the other way, can't they, to get a break from you next publication time?'

'Your faith, nephew, is touching. I'll try.'

Nimmo succeeded. The material and equipment were brought over late one evening in a private touring car. Nimmo and Foster lugged it in with the grunting of men unused to manual labor.

Potterley stood at the entrance of the basement after Nimmo had left. He asked softly, 'What's this for?'

Foster brushed the hair off his forehead and gently massaged a sprained wrist. He said, 'I want to conduct a few simple experiments.'

'Really?' The historian's eyes glittered with excitement.

Foster felt exploited. He felt as though he were being led along a dangerous highway by the pull of pinching fingers on his nose; as though he could see the ruin clearly that lay in wait at the end of the path, yet walked eagerly and determinedly. Worst of all, he felt the compelling grip on his nose to be his own.

It was Potterley who began it, Potterley who stood there now, gloating; but the compulsion was his own.

Foster said sourly, 'I'll be wanting privacy now, Potterley. I can't have you and your wife running down here and annoying me.'

He thought: If that offends him, let him kick me out. Let him put an end to this.

In his heart, though, he did not think being evicted would stop anything.

But it did not come to that. Potterley was showing no signs of offense. His mild gaze was unchanged. He said, 'Of course, Dr Foster, of course. All the privacy you wish.'

Foster watched him go. He was left still marching along the highway, perversely glad of it and hating himself for being glad.

He took to sleeping over on a cot in Potterley's basement and spending his weekends there entirely.

During that period, preliminary word came through that his grants (as doctored by Nimmo) had been approved. The Department Head brought the word and congratulated him.

Foster stared back distantly and mumbled, 'Good. I'm glad,' with so little conviction that the other frowned and turned away without another word.

Foster gave the matter no further thought. It was a minor point, worth no notice. He was planning something that really counted, a climactic test for that evening.

One evening, a second and third and then, haggard and half beside himself with excitement, he called in Potterley.

Potterley came down the stairs and looked about at the homemade gadgetry. He said, in his soft voice, 'The electric bills are quite high. I don't mind the expense, but the City may ask questions. Can anything be done?'

It was a warm evening, but Potterley wore a tight collar and a semijacket. Foster, who was in his undershirt, lifted bleary eyes and said shakily, 'It won't be for much longer, Dr Potterley. I've called you down to tell you something. A chronoscope can be built. A small one, of course, but it can be built.'

Potterley seized the railing. His body sagged. He managed a whisper. 'Can it be built here?'

'Here in the basement,' said Foster wearily.

'Good Lord. You said—'

'I know what I said,' cried Foster impatiently. 'I said it couldn't be done. I didn't know anything then. Even Sterbinski didn't know anything.'

Potterley shook his head. 'Are you sure? You're not mistaken, Dr Foster? I couldn't endure it if—'

Foster said, 'I'm not mistaken. Damn it, sir, if just theory had been enough, we could have had a time viewer over a hundred years ago, when the neutrino was first postulated. The trouble was, the original investigators considered it only a mysterious particle without mass or charge that could not be detected. It was just something to even up the bookkeeping and save the law of conservation of mass energy.'

He wasn't sure Potterley knew what he was talking about. He didn't care. He needed a breather. He had to get some of this out of his clotting thoughts . . . And he needed background for what he would have to tell Potterley next.

He went on. 'It was Sterbinski who first discovered that the neutrino broke through the space-time cross-sectional barrier, that it traveled through time as well as through space. It was Sterbinski who first devised a method for stopping neutrinos. He invented a neutrino recorder and learned how to interpret the pattern of the neutrino stream. Naturally, the stream had been affected and deflected by all the matter it had passed through in its passage through time, and the deflections could be analyzed and converted into the images of the matter that had done the deflecting. Time viewing was possible. Even air vibrations could be detected in this way and converted into sound.'

Potterley was definitely not listening. He said, 'Yes. Yes. But when can you build a chronoscope?'

Foster said urgently, 'Let me finish. Everything depends on the method used to detect and analyze the neutrino stream. Sterbinski's method was difficult and roundabout. It required mountains of energy. But I've studied pseudo-gravitics, Dr Potterley, the science of artificial gravitational fields. I've specialized in the behavior of light in such fields. It's a new science. Sterbinski knew nothing of it. If he had, he would have seen – anyone would have – a much better and more efficient method of detecting neutrinos using a pseudo-gravitic field. If I had known more neutrinics to begin with, I would have seen it at once.'

Potterley brightened a bit. 'I knew it,' he said. 'Even if they stop research in neutrinics there is no way the government can be sure that discoveries in other segments of science won't reflect knowledge on neutrinics. So much for the value of centralized direction of science. I thought this long ago, Dr Foster, before you ever came to work here.'

'I congratulate you on that,' said Foster, 'but there's one thing—'

'Oh, never mind all this. Answer me. Please. When can you build a chronoscope?'

'I'm trying to tell you something, Dr Potterley. A chronoscope won't do you any good.' (This is it, Foster thought.)

Slowly, Potterley descended the stairs. He stood facing Foster. 'What do you mean? Why won't it help me?'

'You won't see Carthage. It's what I've got to tell you. It's what I've been leading up to. You can never see Carthage.'

Potterley shook his head slightly. 'Oh, no, you're wrong. If you have the chronoscope, just focus it properly—'

'No, Dr Potterley. It's not a question of focus. There are random factors affecting the neutrino stream, as they affect all subatomic particles. What we call the uncertainty principle. When the stream is recorded and interpreted, the random factor comes out as fuzziness, or "noise" as the communications boys speak of it. The further back in time you penetrate, the more pronounced the fuzziness, the greater the noise. After a while, the noise drowns out the picture. Do you understand?'

'More power,' said Potterley in a dead kind of voice.

'That won't help. When the noise blurs out detail, magnifying detail magnifies the noise, too. You can't see anything in a sun-burnt film by enlarging it, can you? Get this through your head, now. The physical nature of the universe sets limits. The random thermal motions of air molecules set limits to how weak a sound can be detected by any instrument. The length of a light wave or of an electron wave sets limits to the size of objects that can be seen by any instrument. It works that way in chronoscopy, too. You can only time view so far.'

'How far? How far?'

Foster took a deep breath. 'A century and a quarter. That's the most.'

'But the monthly bulletin the Commission puts out deals with ancient history almost entirely.' The historian laughed shakily. 'You must be wrong. The government has data as far back as 3000 B.C.'

'When did you switch to believing them?' demanded Foster, scornfully. 'You began this business by proving they were lying; that no historian had made use of the chronoscope. Don't you see why now? No historian, except one interested in contemporary history, could. No chronoscope can possibly see back in time further than 1920 under any conditions.'

'You're wrong. You don't know everything,' said Potterley.

'The truth won't bend itself to your convenience either. Face it. The government's part in this is to perpetuate a hoax.'

'Why?'

'I don't know why.'

Potterley's snubby nose was twitching. His eyes were bulging. He pleaded, 'It's only theory, Dr Foster. Build a chronoscope. Build one and try.'

Foster caught Potterley's shoulders in a sudden, fierce grip. 'Do you think I haven't? Do you think I would tell you this before I had checked it every way I knew? I *have* built one. It's all around you. Look!'

He ran to the switches at the power leads. He flicked them on, one by one. He turned a resistor, adjusted other knobs, put out the cellar lights. 'Wait. Let it warm up.'

There was a small glow near the center of one wall. Potterley was gibbering incoherently, but Foster only cried again, 'Look!'

The light sharpened and brightened, broke up into a light-and-dark pattern. Men and women! Fuzzy. Features blurred. Arms and legs mere streaks. An old-fashioned ground car, unclear but recognizable as one of the kind that had once used gasoline-powered internal-combustion engines, sped by.

Foster said, 'Mid-twentieth century, somewhere. I can't hook up an audio yet so this is soundless. Eventually, we can add sound. Anyway, mid-twentieth is almost as far back as you can go. Believe me, that's the best focusing that can be done.'

Potterley said, 'Build a larger machine, a stronger one. Improve your circuits.'

'You can't lick the Uncertainty Principle, man, any more than you can live on the sun. There are physical limits to what can be done.'

'You're lying. I won't believe you. I—'

A new voice sounded, raised shrilly to make itself heard.

'Arnold! Dr Foster!'

The young physicist turned at once. Dr Potterley froze for a long moment, then said, without turning, 'What is it, Caroline? Leave us.'

'No!' Mrs Potterley descended the stairs. 'I heard. I couldn't help hearing. Do you have a time viewer here, Dr Foster? Here in the basement?'

'Yes, I do, Mrs Potterley. A kind of time viewer. Not a good one. I can't get sound yet and the picture is darned blurry, but it works.'

Mrs Potterley clasped her hands and held them tightly against her breast. 'How wonderful. How wonderful.'

'It's not at all wonderful,' snapped Potterley. 'The young fool can't reach further back than—'

'Now, look,' began Foster in exasperation . . .

'Please!' cried Mrs Potterley. 'Listen to me. Arnold, don't you see that as long as we can use it for twenty years back, we can see Laurel once again? What do we care about Carthage and ancient times? It's Laurel we can see. She'll be alive for us again. Leave the machine here, Dr Foster. Show us how to work it.'

Foster stared at her then at her husband. Dr Potterley's face had gone white. Though his voice stayed low and even, its calmness was somehow gone. He said, 'You're a fool!'

Caroline said weakly, 'Arnold!'

'You're a fool, I say. What will you see? The past. The dead past. Will Laurel do one thing she did not do? Will you see one thing you haven't seen? Will you live three years over and over again, watching a baby who'll never grow up no matter how you watch?'

His voice came near to cracking, but held. He stopped closer to her, seized her shoulder and shook her roughly. 'Do you know what will happen to you if you do that? They'll come to take you away because you'll go mad. Yes, mad. Do you want mental treatment? Do you want to be shut up, to undergo the Psychic Probe?'

Mrs Potterley tore away. There was no trace of softness or vagueness about her. She had twisted into a virago. 'I want to see my child, Arnold. She's in that machine and I want her.'

'She's *not* in the machine. An image is. Can't you understand? An image! Something that's not real!'

'I want my child. Do you hear me?' She flew at him, screaming, fists beating. '*I want my child.*'

The historian retreated at the fury of the assault, crying out. Foster moved to step between, when Mrs Potterley dropped, sobbing wildly, to the floor.

Potterley turned, eyes desperately seeking. With a sudden heave, he snatched at a Lando-rod, tearing it from its support, and whirling away before Foster, numbed by all that was taking place, could move to stop him.

'Stand back!' gasped Potterley, 'or I'll kill you. I swear it.'

He swung with force, and Foster jumped back.

Potterley turned with fury on every part of the structure in the cellar, and Foster, after the first crash of glass, watched dazedly.

Potterley spent his rage and then he was standing quietly amid shards and splinters, with a broken Lando-rod in his hand. He said to Foster in a whisper, 'Now get out of here! Never come back! If any of this cost you anything, send me a bill and I'll pay for it. I'll pay double.'

Foster shrugged, picked up his shirt and moved up the basement stairs. He could hear Mrs Potterley sobbing loudly, and, as he turned at the head of the stairs for a last look, he saw Dr Potterley bending over her, his face convulsed with sorrow.

Two days later, with the school day drawing to a close, and Foster looking wearily about to see if there were any data on his newly approved projects that he wished to take home, Dr Potterley appeared once more. He was standing at the open door of Foster's office.

The historian was neatly dressed as ever. He lifted his hand in a gesture that was too vague to be a greeting, too abortive to be a plea. Foster stared stonily.

Potterley said, 'I waited till five, till you were . . . May I come in?'

Foster nodded.

Potterley said, 'I suppose I ought to apologize for my behavior. I was dreadfully disappointed; not quite master of myself. Still, it was inexcusable.'

'I accept your apology,' said Foster. 'Is that all?'

'My wife called you, I think.'

'Yes, she has.'

'She has been quite hysterical. She told me she had but I couldn't be quite sure – Could you tell me – would you be so kind as to tell me what she wanted?'

'She wanted a chronoscope. She said she had some money of her own. She was willing to pay.'

'Did you – make any commitments?'

'I said I wasn't in the manufacturing business.'

'Good,' breathed Potterley, his chest expanding with a sigh of relief. 'Please don't take any calls from her. She's not – quite—'

'Look, Dr Potterley,' said Foster, 'I'm not getting into any domestic quarrels, but you'd better be prepared for something. Chronoscopes can be built by anybody. Given a few simple parts that can be bought through some etherics sales center, they can be built in the home workshop. The video part, anyway.'

'But no one else will think of it besides you, will they? No one has.'

'I don't intend to keep it secret.'

'But you can't publish. It's illegal research.'

'That doesn't matter any more, Dr Potterley. If I lose my grants, I lose them. If the university is displeased, I'll resign. It just doesn't matter.'

'But you can't do that!'

'Till now,' said Foster, 'you didn't mind my risking loss of grants and position. Why do you turn so tender about it now? Now let me explain something to you. When you first came to me, I believed in organized and directed research; the situation as it existed, in other words. I considered you an intellectual anarchist, Dr Potterley, and dangerous. But, for one reason or another, I've been an anarchist myself for months now and I have achieved great things.

'Those things have been achieved not because I am a brilliant scientist. Not at all. It was just that scientific research had been directed from above and holes were left that could be filled in by anyone who looked in the right direction. And anyone might have if the government hadn't actively tried to prevent it.

'Now understand me. I still believe directed research can be useful. I'm not in favor of a retreat to total anarchy. But there must be a middle ground. Directed research can retain flexibility. A scientist must be allowed to follow his curiosity, at least in his spare time.'

Potterley sat down. He said ingratiatingly, 'Let's discuss this, Foster. I appreciate your idealism. You're young. You want the moon. But you can't destroy yourself through fancy notions of what research must consist of. I got you into this. I am responsible and I blame myself bitterly. I was acting emotionally. My interest in Carthage blinded me and I was a damned fool.'

Foster broke in. 'You mean you've changed completely in two days? Carthage is nothing? Government suppression of research is nothing?'

'Even a damned fool like myself can learn, Foster. My wife taught me something. I understand the reason for government suppression of neutrinics now. I didn't two days ago. And, understanding,

I approve. You saw the way my wife reacted to the news of a chronoscope in the basement. I had envisioned a chronoscope used for research purposes. All *she* could see was the personal pleasure of returning neurotically to a personal past, a dead past. The pure researcher, Foster, is in the minority. People like my wife would outweigh us.

'For the government to encourage chronoscopy would have meant that everyone's past would be visible. The government officers would be subjected to blackmail and improper pressure, since who on Earth has a past that is absolutely clean? Organized government might become impossible.'

Foster licked his lips. 'Maybe. Maybe the government has some justification in its own eyes. Still, there's an important principle involved here. Who knows what other scientific advances are being stymied because scientists are being stifled into walking a narrow path? If the chronoscope becomes the terror of a few politicians, it's a price that must be paid. The public must realize that science must be free and there is no more dramatic way of doing it than to publish my discovery, one way or another, legally or illegally.'

Potterley's brow was damp with perspiration, but his voice remained even. 'Oh, not just a few politicians, Dr Foster. Don't think that. It would be my terror, too. My wife would spend her time living with our dead daughter. She would retreat further from reality. She would go mad living the same scenes over and over. And not just my terror. There would be others like her. Children searching for their dead parents or their own youth. We'll have a whole world living in the past. Midsummer madness.'

Foster said, 'Moral judgments can't stand in the way. There isn't one advance at any time in history that mankind hasn't had the ingenuity to pervert. Mankind must also have the ingenuity to prevent. As for the chronoscope, your delvers into the dead past will get tired soon enough. They'll catch their loved parents in some of the things their loved parents did and they'll lose their enthusiasm for it all. But all this is trivial. With me, it's a matter of important principle.'

Potterley said, 'Hang your principle. Can't you understand men and women as well as principle? Don't you understand that my wife will live through the fire that killed our baby? She won't be able to help herself. I know her. She'll follow through each step, trying to prevent it. She'll live it over and over again, hoping each time that it won't happen. How many times do you want to kill Laurel?' A huskiness had crept into his voice.

A thought crossed Foster's mind. 'What are you really afraid she'll find out, Dr Potterley? What happened the night of the fire?'

The historian's hands went up quickly to cover his face and they shook with his dry sobs. Foster turned away and stared uncomfortably out the window.

Potterley said after a while, 'It's a long time since I've had to think of it. Caroline was away. I was baby-sitting. I went into the baby's bedroom midevening to see if she had kicked off the bedclothes. I had my cigarette with me . . . I smoked in those days. I must have stubbed it out before putting it in the ashtray on the chest of drawers. I was always careful. The baby was all right. I returned to the living room and fell asleep before the video. I awoke, choking, surrounded by fire. I don't know how it started.'

'But you think it may have been the cigarette, is that it?' said Foster. 'A cigarette which, for once, you forgot to stub out?'

'I don't know. I tried to save her, but she was dead in my arms when I got out.'

'You never told your wife about the cigarette, I suppose.'

Potterley shook his head. 'But I've lived with it.'

'Only now, with a chronoscope, she'll find out. Maybe it wasn't the cigarette. Maybe you did stub it out. Isn't that possible?'

The scant tears had dried on Potterley's face. The redness had subsided. He said, 'I can't take the chance . . . But it's not just myself, Foster. The past has its terrors for most people. Don't loose those terrors on the human race.'

Foster paced the floor. Somehow, this explained the reason for Potterley's rabid, irrational desire to boost the Carthaginians, deify them, most of all disprove the story of their fiery sacrifices to Moloch. By freeing them of the guilt of infanticide by fire, he symbolically freed himself of the same guilt.

So the same fire that had driven him on to causing the construction of a chronoscope was now driving him on to the destruction.

Foster looked sadly at the older man. 'I see your position, Dr Potterley, but this goes above personal feelings. I've got to smash this throttling hold on the throat of science.'

Potterley said, savagely, 'You mean you want the fame and wealth that goes with such a discovery.'

'I don't know about the wealth, but that, too, I suppose. I'm no more than human.'

'You won't suppress your knowledge?'

'Not under any circumstances.'

'Well, then—' and the historian got to his feet and stood for a moment, glaring.

Foster had an odd moment of terror. The man was older than he, smaller, feebler, and he didn't look armed. Still . . .

Foster said, 'If you're thinking of killing me or anything insane like that, I've got the information in a safety-deposit vault where the proper people will find it in case of my disappearance or death.'

Potterley said, 'Don't be a fool,' and stalked out.

Foster closed the door, locked it and sat down to think. He felt silly. He had no information in any safety-deposit vault, of course. Such a melodramatic action would not have occurred to him ordinarily. But now it had.

Feeling even sillier, he spent an hour writing out the equations of the application of pseudo-gravitic optics to neutrinic recording, and some diagrams for the engineering details of construction. He sealed it in an envelope and scrawled Ralph Nimmo's name over the outside.

He spent a rather restless night and the next morning, on the way to school, dropped the envelope off at the bank, with appropriate instructions to an official, who made him sign a paper permitting the box to be opened after his death.

He called Nimmo to tell him of the existence of the envelope, refusing querulously to say anything about its contents.

He had never felt so ridiculously self-conscious as at that moment.

That night and the next, Foster spent in only fitful sleep, finding himself face to face with the highly practical problem of the publication of data unethically obtained.

The *Proceedings of the Society for Pseudo-Gravitics*, which was the journal with which he was best acquainted, would certainly not touch any paper that did not include the magic footnote: 'The work described in this paper was made possible by Grant No. so-and-so from the Commission of Research of the United Nations.'

Nor, doubly so, would the *Journal of Physics*.

There were always the minor journals who might overlook the nature of the article for the sake of the sensation, but that would require a little financial negotiation on which he hesitated to embark. It might, on the whole, be better to pay the cost of publishing a small pamphlet for general distribution among scholars. In that case, he would even be able to dispense with the services of a science writer, sacrificing polish for speed. He would have to find a reliable printer. Uncle Ralph might know one.

He walked down the corridor to his office and wondered anxiously if perhaps he ought to waste no further time, give himself no further chance to lapse into indecision and take the risk of calling Ralph from his office phone. He was so absorbed in his own heavy thoughts that he did not notice that his room was occupied until he turned from the clothes closet and approached his desk.

Dr Potterley was there and a man whom Foster did not recognize. Foster stared at them. 'What's this?'

Potterley said, 'I'm sorry, but I had to stop you.'

Foster continued staring. 'What are you talking about?'

The stranger said, 'Let me introduce myself.' He had large teeth, a little uneven, and they showed prominently when he smiled. 'I am Thaddeus Araman, Department Head of the Division of Chronoscopy.

I am here to see you concerning information brought to me by Professor Arnold Potterley and confirmed by our own sources—'

Potterley said breathlessly, 'I took all the blame, Dr Foster. I explained that it was I who persuaded you against your will into unethical practices. I have offered to accept full responsibility and punishment. I don't wish you harmed in any way. It's just that chronoscopy must not be permitted!'

Araman nodded. 'He has taken the blame as he says, Dr Foster, but this thing is out of his hands now.'

Foster said, 'So? What are you going to do? Blackball me from all consideration for research grants?'

'That is in my power,' said Araman.

'Order the university to discharge me?'

'That, too, is in my power.'

'All right, go ahead. Consider it done. I'll leave my office now, with you. I can send for my books later. If you insist, I'll leave my books. Is that all?'

'Not quite,' said Araman. 'You must engage to do no further research in chronoscopy, to publish none of your findings in chronoscopy and, of course, to build no chronoscope. You will remain under surveillance indefinitely to make sure you keep that promise.'

'Supposing I refuse to promise? What can you do? Doing research out of my field may be unethical, but it isn't a criminal offense.'

'In the case of chronoscopy, my young friend,' said Araman patiently, 'it is a criminal offense. If necessary, you will be put in jail and kept there.'

'Why?' shouted Foster. 'What's magic about chronoscopy?'

Araman said, 'That's the way it is. We cannot allow further developments in the field. My own job is, primarily, to make sure of that, and I intend to do my job. Unfortunately, I had no knowledge, nor did anyone in the department, that the optics of pseudo-gravity fields had such immediate application to chronoscopy. Score one for general ignorance, but henceforward research will be steered properly in that respect, too.'

Foster said, 'That won't help. Something else may apply that neither you nor I dream of. All science hangs together. It's one piece. If you want to stop one part, you've got to stop it all.'

'No doubt that is true,' said Araman, 'in theory. On the practical side, however, we have managed quite well to hold chronoscopy down to the original Sterbinski level for fifty years. Having caught you in time, Dr Foster, we hope to continue doing so indefinitely. And we wouldn't have come this close to disaster, either, if I had accepted Dr Potterley at something more than face value.'

He turned toward the historian and lifted his eyebrows in a kind of humorous self-deprecation. 'I'm afraid, sir, that I dismissed you as a history professor and no more on the occasion of our first interview. Had I done my job properly and checked on you, this would not have happened.'

Foster said abruptly, 'Is anyone allowed to use the government chronoscope?'

'No one outside our division under any pretext. I say that since it is obvious to me that you have already guessed as much. I warn you, though, that any repetition of that fact will be a criminal, not an ethical, offense.'

'And your chronoscope doesn't go back more than a hundred twenty-five years or so, does it?'

'It doesn't.'

'Then your bulletin with its stories of time viewing ancient times is a hoax?'

Araman said coolly, 'With the knowledge you now have, it is obvious you know that for a certainty. However, I confirm your remark. The monthly bulletin is a hoax.'

'In that case,' said Foster, 'I will not promise to suppress my knowledge of chronoscopy. If you wish to arrest me, go ahead. My defense at the trial will be enough to destroy the vicious card house of directed research and bring it tumbling down. Directing research is one thing; suppressing it and depriving mankind of its benefits is quite another.'

Araman said, 'Oh, let's get something straight, Dr Foster. If you do not co-operate, you will go to jail directly. You will *not* see a lawyer, you will *not* be charged, you will *not* have a trial. You will simply stay in jail'

'Oh, no,' said Foster, 'you're bluffing. This is not the twentieth century, you know.'

There was a stir outside the office, the clatter of feet, a high-pitched shout that Foster was sure he recognized. The door crashed open, the lock splintering, and three intertwined figures stumbled in.

As they did so, one of the men raised a blaster and brought its butt down hard on the skull of another.

There was a whoosh of expiring air, and the one whose head was struck went limp.

'Uncle Ralph!' cried Foster.

Araman frowned. 'Put him down in that chair,' he ordered, 'and get some water.'

Ralph Nimmo, rubbing his head with a gingerly sort of disgust, said, 'There was no need to get rough, Araman.'

Araman said, 'The guard should have been rough sooner and kept you out of here, Nimmo. You'd have been better off.'

'You know each other?' asked Foster.

'I've had dealings with the man,' said Nimmo, still rubbing. 'If he's here in your office, nephew, you're in trouble.'

'And you, too,' said Araman angrily. 'I know Dr Foster consulted you on neutrinics literature.'

Nimmo corrugated his forehead, then straightened it with a wince as though the action had brought pain. 'So?' he said. 'What else do you know about me?'

'We will know everything about you soon enough. Meanwhile, that one item is enough to implicate you. What are you doing here?'

'My dear Dr Araman,' said Nimmo, some of his jauntiness restored, 'day before yesterday, my jackass of a nephew called me. He had placed some mysterious information—'

'Don't tell him! Don't say anything!' cried Foster.

Araman glanced at him coldly. 'We know all about it, Dr Foster. The safety-deposit box has been opened and its contents removed.'

'But how can you know—' Foster's voice died away in a kind of furious frustration.

'Anyway,' said Nimmo, 'I decided the net must be closing around him and, after I took care of a few items, I came down to tell him to get off this thing he's doing. It's not worth his career.'

'Does that mean you know what he's doing?' asked Araman.

'He never told me,' said Nimmo, 'but I'm a science writer with a hell of a lot of experience. I know which side of an atom is electronified. The boy, Foster, specializes in pseudo-gravitic optics and coached me on the stuff himself. He got me to get him a textbook on neutrinics and I kind of shipviewed it myself before handing it over. I can put the two together. He asked me to get him certain pieces of physical equipment, and that was evidence, too. Stop me if I'm wrong, but my nephew has built a semiportable, low-power chronoscope. Yes, or – yes?'

'Yes.' Araman reached thoughtfully for a cigarette and paid no attention to Dr Potterley (watching silently, as though all were a dream), who shied away, gasping, from the white cylinder. 'Another mistake for me. I ought to resign. I should have put tabs on you, too, Nimmo, instead of concentrating too hard on Potterley and Foster. I didn't have much time of course and you've ended up safely here, but that doesn't excuse me. You're under arrest, Nimmo.'

'What for?' demanded the science writer.

'Unauthorized research.'

'I wasn't doing any. I can't, not being a registered scientist. And even if I did, it's not a criminal offense.'

Foster said savagely, 'No use, Uncle Ralph. This bureaucrat is making his own laws.'

'Like what?' demanded Nimmo.

'Like life imprisonment without trial.'

'Nuts,' said Nimmo. 'This isn't the twentieth cen—'

'I tried that,' said Foster. 'It doesn't bother him.'

'Well, nuts,' shouted Nimmo. 'Look here, Araman. My nephew and I have relatives who haven't lost touch with us, you know. The professor has some also, I imagine. You can't just make us disappear. There'll be questions and a scandal. This *isn't* the twentieth century. So if you're trying to scare us, it isn't working.'

The cigarette snapped between Araman's fingers and he tossed it away violently. He said, 'Damn it, I don't know *what* to do. It's never been like this before . . . Look! You three fools know nothing of what you're trying to do. You understand nothing. Will you listen to me?'

'Oh, we'll listen,' said Nimmo grimly.

(Foster sat silently, eyes angry, lips compressed. Potterley's hands writhed like two intertwined snakes.)

Araman said, 'The past to you is the dead past. If any of you have discussed the matter, it's dollars to nickels you've used that phrase. The dead past. If you knew how many times I've heard those three words, you'd choke on them, too.

'When people think of the past, they think of it as dead, far away and gone, long ago. We encourage them to think so. When we report time viewing, we always talk of views centuries in the past, even though you gentlemen know seeing more than a century or so is impossible. People accept it. The past means Greece, Rome, Carthage, Egypt, the Stone Age. The deader the better.

'Now you three know a century or a little more is the limit, so what does the past mean to you? Your youth. Your first girl. Your dead mother. Twenty years ago. Thirty years ago. Fifty years ago. The deader the better . . . But when does the past really begin?'

He paused in anger. The others stared at him and Nimmo stirred uneasily.

'Well,' said Araman, 'when did it begin? A year ago? Five minutes ago? One second ago? Isn't it obvious that the past begins an instant ago? The dead past is just another name for the living present. What if you focus the chronoscope in the past of one-hundredth of a second ago? Aren't you watching the present? Does it begin to sink in?'

Nimmo said, 'Damnation.'

'Damnation,' mimicked Araman. 'After Potterley came to me with his story night before last, how do you suppose I checked up on both of you? I did it with the chronoscope, spotting key moments to the very instant of the present.'

'And that's how you knew about the safety-deposit box?' said Foster.

'And every other important fact. Now what do you suppose would happen if we let news of a home chronoscope get out? People might start out by watching their youth, their parents and so on, but it wouldn't be long before they'd catch on to the possibilities. The housewife will forget her poor, dead mother and take to watching her neighbor at home and her husband at the office. The businessman will watch his competitor; the employer his employee.

'There will be no such thing as privacy. The party line, the prying eye behind the curtain will be nothing compared to it. The video stars will be closely watched at all times by everyone. Every man his own peeping Tom and there'll be no getting away from the watcher. Even darkness will be no escape because chronoscopy can be adjusted to the infrared and human figures can be seen by their own body heat. The figures will be fuzzy, of course, and the surroundings will be dark, but that will make the titillation of it all the greater, perhaps . . . Hmp, the men in charge of the machine now experiment sometimes in spite of the regulations against it.'

Nimmo seemed sick. 'You can always forbid private manufacture—'

Araman turned on him fiercely. 'You can, but do you expect it to do good? Can you legislate successfully against drinking, smoking, adultery or gossiping over the back fence? And this mixture of nosiness and prurience will have a worse grip on humanity than any of those. Good Lord, in a thousand years of trying we haven't even been able to wipe out the heroin traffic and you talk about legislating against a device for watching anyone you please at any time you please that can be built in a home workshop.'

Foster said suddenly, 'I won't publish.'

Potterley burst out, half in sobs, 'None of us will talk. I regret—'

Nimmo broke in. 'You said you didn't tab me on the chronoscope, Araman.'

'No time,' said Araman wearily. 'Things don't move any faster on the chronoscope than in real life. You can't speed it up like the film in a book viewer. We spent a full twenty-four hours trying to catch the important moments during the last six months of Potterley and Foster. There was no time for anything else and it was enough.'

'It wasn't,' said Nimmo.

'What are you talking about?' There was a sudden infinite alarm on Araman's face.

'I told you my nephew, Jonas, had called me to say he had put important information in a safety-deposit box. He acted as though he were in trouble. He's my nephew. I had to try to get him off the spot. It took a while, then I came here to tell him what I had done. I told you when I got here, just after your man conked me, that I had taken care of a few items.'

'What? For Heaven's sake—'

'Just this: I sent the details of the portable chronoscope off to half a dozen of my regular publicity outlets.'

Not a word. Not a sound. Not a breath. They were all past any demonstration.

'Don't stare like that,' cried Nimmo. 'Don't you see my point? I had popular publication rights. Jonas will admit that. I knew he couldn't publish scientifically in any legal way. I was sure he was planning to publish illegally and was preparing the safety-deposit box for that reason. I thought if I put through the details prematurely, all the responsibility would be mine. His career would be saved. And if I were deprived of my science-writing license as a result, my exclusive possession of the chronometric data would set me up for life. Jonas would be angry, I expected that, but I could explain the motive and we would split the take fifty-fifty . . . Don't stare at me like that. How did I know—'

'Nobody knew anything,' said Araman bitterly, 'but you all just took it for granted that the government was stupidly bureaucratic, vicious, tyrannical, given to suppressing research for the hell of it. It never occurred to any of you that we were trying to protect mankind as best we could.'

'Don't sit there talking,' wailed Potterley. 'Get the names of the people who were told—'

'Too late,' said Nimmo, shrugging. 'They've had better than a day. There's been time for the word to spread. My outfits will have called any number of physicists to check my data before going on with it and they'll call one another to pass on the news. Once scientists put neutrinics and pseudo-gravitics together, home chronoscopy becomes obvious. Before the week is out, five hundred people will know how to build a small chronoscope and how will you catch them all?' His plum cheeks sagged. 'I suppose there's no way of putting the mushroom cloud back into that nice, shiny uranium sphere.'

Araman stood up. 'We'll try, Potterley, but I agree with Nimmo. It's too late. What kind of a world we'll have from now on, I don't know, I can't tell, but the world we know has been destroyed completely. Until now, every custom, every habit, every tiniest way of life has always taken a certain amount of privacy for granted, but that's all gone now.'

He saluted each of the three with elaborate formality. 'You have created a new world among the three of you. I congratulate you. Happy goldfish bowl to you, to me, to everyone, and may each of you fry in hell forever. Arrest rescinded.'

The Foundation of SF Success

(WITH APOLOGIES TO W. S. GILBERT)

If you ask me how to shine in the science-fiction line as a pro of
    luster bright,
I say, practice up the lingo of the sciences, by jingo (never mind if
    not quite right).
You must talk of Space and Galaxies and tesseractic fallacies in slick
    and mystic style,
Though the fans won't understand it, they will all the same demand
    it with a softly hopeful smile.

  And all the fans will say,
  As you walk your spatial way,
  If that young man indulges in flights through all the Galaxy,
  Why, what a most imaginative type of man that type of man must
    be.

So success is not a mystery, just brush up on your history, and
    borrow day by day.

Take an Empire that was Roman and you'll find it is at home in all
    the starry Milky Way.
With a drive that's hyperspatial, through the parsecs you will race,
    you'll find that plotting is a breeze,
With a tiny bit of cribbin' from the works of Edward Gibbon and
    that Greek, Thucydides.

   And all the fans will say,
   As you walk your thoughtful way,
   If that young man involves himself in authentic history,
   Why, what a very learned kind of high IQ, his high IQ must be.

Then eschew all thoughts of passion of a man-and-woman fashion
    from your hero's thoughtful mind.
He must spend his time on politics, and thinking up his shady
    tricks, and outside that he's blind.
It's enough he's had a mother, other females are a bother, though
    they're jeweled and glistery.
They will just distract his dreaming and his necessary scheming
    with that psychohistory.

   And all the fans will say
   As you walk your narrow way,
   If all his yarns restrict themselves to masculinity,
   Why, what a most particularly pure young man that pure young
    man must be.

Franchise

Linda, age ten, was the only one of the family who seemed to enjoy being awake.

Norman Muller could hear her now through his own drugged, unhealthy coma. (He had finally managed to fall asleep an hour earlier but even then it was more like exhaustion than sleep.)

She was at his bedside now, shaking him. 'Daddy, Daddy, wake up. Wake up!'

He suppressed a groan. 'All right, Linda.'

'But, Daddy, there's more policemen around than any time! Police cars and everything!'

Norman Muller gave up and rose blearily to his elbows. The day was beginning. It was faintly stirring toward dawn outside, the germ of a miserable gray that looked about as miserably gray as he felt. He could hear Sarah, his wife, shuffling about breakfast duties in the kitchen. His father-in-law, Matthew, was hawking strenuously in the bathroom. No doubt Agent Handley was ready and waiting for him.

This was *the* day.

Election Day!

*

To begin with, it had been like every other year. Maybe a little worse, because it was a presidential year, but no worse than other presidential years if it came to that.

The politicians spoke about the guh-reat electorate and the vast electuh-ronic intelligence that was its servant. The press analyzed the situation with industrial computers (the *New York Times* and the St Louis *Post-Dispatch* had their own computers) and were full of little hints as to what would be forthcoming. Commentators and columnists pinpointed the crucial state and county in happy contradiction to one another.

The first hint that it would *not* be like every other year was when Sarah Muller said to her husband on the evening of 4 October (with Election Day exactly a month off), 'Cantwell Johnson says that Indiana will be the state this year. He's the fourth one. Just think, *our* state this time.'

Matthew Hortenweiler took his fleshy face from behind the paper, stared dourly at his daughter and growled, 'Those fellows are paid to tell lies. Don't listen to them.'

'Four of them, Father,' said Sarah mildly. 'They all say Indiana.'

'Indiana *is* a key state, Matthew,' said Norman, just as mildly, 'on account of the Hawkins-Smith Act and this mess in Indianapolis. It—'

Matthew twisted his old face alarmingly and rasped out, 'No one says Bloomington or Monroe County, do they?'

'Well—' said Norman.

Linda, whose little pointed-chinned face had been shifting from one speaker to the next, said pipingly, 'You going to be voting this year, Daddy?'

Norman smiled gently and said, 'I don't think so, dear.'

But this was in the gradually growing excitement of an October in a presidential election year and Sarah had led a quiet life with dreams for her companions. She said longingly, 'Wouldn't *that* be wonderful, though?'

'If I voted?' Norman Muller had a small blond mustache that had given him a debonair quality in the young Sarah's eyes, but which, with gradual graying, had declined merely to lack of distinction. His forehead bore deepening lines born of uncertainty and, in general, he had never seduced his clerkly soul with the thought that he was either born great or would under any circumstances achieve greatness. He had a wife, a job and a little girl, and except under extraordinary conditions of elation or depression was inclined to consider that to be an adequate bargain struck with life.

So he was a little embarrassed and more than a little uneasy at the direction his wife's thoughts were taking. 'Actually, my dear,' he said, 'there are two hundred million people in the country, and, with odds like that, I don't think we ought to waste our time wondering about it.'

His wife said, 'Why, Norman, it's no such thing like two hundred million and you know it. In the first place, only people between twenty and sixty are eligible and it's always men, so that puts it down to maybe fifty million to one. Then, if it's really Indiana—'

'Then it's about one and a quarter million to one. You wouldn't want me to bet in a horse race against those odds, now, would you? Let's have supper.'

Matthew muttered from behind his newspaper, 'Damned foolishness.'

Linda asked again, 'You going to be voting this year, Daddy?'

Norman shook his head and they all adjourned to the dining room.

By 20 October, Sarah's excitement was rising rapidly. Over the coffee, she announced that Mrs Schultz, having a cousin who was the secretary of an Assemblyman, said that all the 'smart money' was on Indiana.

'She says President Villers is even going to make a speech at Indianapolis.'

Norman Muller, who had had a hard day at the store, nudged the statement with a raising of eyebrows and let it go at that.

Matthew Hortenweiler, who was chronically dissatisfied with

Washington, said, 'If Villers makes a speech in Indiana, that means he thinks Multivac will pick Arizona. He wouldn't have the guts to go closer, the mushhead.'

Sarah, who ignored her father whenever she could decently do so, said, 'I don't know why they don't announce the state as soon as they can, and then the county and so on. Then the people who were eliminated could relax.'

'If they did anything like that,' pointed out Norman, 'the politicians would follow the announcements like vultures. By the time it was narrowed down to a township, you'd have a Congressman or two at every street corner.'

Matthew narrowed his eyes and brushed angrily at his sparse, gray hair. 'They're vultures, anyhow. Listen—'

Sarah murmured, 'Now, Father—'

Matthew's voice rumbled over her protest without as much as a stumble or hitch. 'Listen, I was around when they set up Multivac. It would end partisan politics, they said. No more voters' money wasted on campaigns. No more grinning nobodies high-pressured and advertising-campaigned into Congress or the White House. So what happens. More campaigning than ever, only now they do it blind. They'll send guys to Indiana on account of the Hawkins-Smith Act and other guys to California in case it's the Joe Hammer situation that turns out crucial. I say, wipe out all that nonsense. Back to the good old—'

Linda asked suddenly, 'Don't you want Daddy to vote this year, Grandpa?'

Matthew glared at the young girl. 'Never you mind, now.' He turned back to Norman and Sarah. 'There was a time I voted. Marched right up to the polling booth, stuck my fist on the levers and voted. There was nothing to it. I just said: This fellow's my man and I'm voting for him. *That's* the way it should be.'

Linda said excitedly, 'You voted, Grandpa? You really did?'

Sarah leaned forward quickly to quiet what might easily become an incongruous story drifting about the neighborhood, 'It's nothing,

Linda. Grandpa doesn't really mean voted. Everyone did that kind of voting, your grandpa, too, but it wasn't *really* voting.'

Matthew roared, 'It wasn't when I was a little boy. I was twenty-two and I voted for Langley and it was real voting. My vote didn't count for much, maybe, but it was as good as anyone else's. *Anyone* else's. And no Multivac to—'

Norman interposed, 'All right, Linda, time for bed. And stop asking questions about voting. When you grow up, you'll understand all about it.'

He kissed her with antiseptic gentleness and she moved reluctantly out of range under maternal prodding and a promise that she might watch the bedside video till 9:15, *if* she was prompt about the bathing ritual.

Linda said, 'Grandpa,' and stood with her chin down and her hands behind her back until his newspaper lowered itself to the point where shaggy eyebrows and eyes, nested in fine wrinkles, showed themselves. It was Friday, 31 October.

He said, 'Yes?'

Linda came closer and put both her forearms on one of the old man's knees so that he had to discard his newspaper altogether.

She said, 'Grandpa, did you really once vote?'

He said, 'You heard me say I did, didn't you? Do you think I tell fibs?'

'N-no, but Mamma says everybody voted then.'

'So they did.'

'But how could they? How could *everybody* vote?'

Matthew stared at her solemnly, then lifted her and put her on his knee.

He even moderated the tonal qualities of his voice. He said, 'You see, Linda, till about forty years ago, everybody always voted. Say we wanted to decide who was to be the new President of the United States. The Democrats and Republicans would both nominate someone, and everybody would say who they wanted. When Election Day was over, they would count how many people wanted the Democrat and how many wanted the Republican. Whoever had more votes was elected. You see?'

Linda nodded and said, 'How did all the people know who to vote for? Did Multivac tell them?'

Matthew's eyebrows hunched down and he looked severe. 'They just used their own judgment, girl.'

She edged away from him, and he lowered his voice again, 'I'm not angry at you, Linda. But, you see, sometimes it took all night to count what everyone said and people were impatient. So they invented special machines which could look at the first few votes and compare them with the votes from the same places in previous years. That way the machine could compute how the total vote would be and who would be elected. You see?'

She nodded. 'Like Multivac.'

'The first computers were much smaller than Multivac. But the machines grew bigger and they could tell how the election would go from fewer and fewer votes. Then, at last, they built Multivac and it can tell from just one voter.'

Linda smiled at having reached a familiar part of the story and said, 'That's nice.'

Matthew frowned and said, 'No, it's not nice. I don't want a machine telling me how I would have voted just because some joker in Milwaukee says he's against higher tariffs. Maybe I want to vote cockeyed just for the pleasure of it. Maybe I don't want to vote. Maybe—'

But Linda had wriggled from his knee and was beating a retreat.

She met her mother at the door. Her mother, who was still wearing her coat and had not even had time to remove her hat, said breathlessly, 'Run along, Linda. Don't get in Mother's way.'

Then she said to Matthew, as she lifted her hat from her head and patted her hair back into place, 'I've been at Agatha's.'

Matthew stared at her censoriously and did not even dignify that piece of information with a grunt as he groped for his newspaper.

Sarah said, as she unbuttoned her coat, 'Guess what she said?'

Matthew flattened out his newspaper for reading purposes with a sharp crackle and said, 'Don't much care.'

Sarah said, 'Now, Father—' But she had no time for anger. The news had to be told and Matthew was the only recipient handy, so she went on, 'Agatha's Joe is a policeman, you know, and he says a whole truckload of secret service men came into Bloomington last night.'

'They're not after me.'

'Don't you see, Father? Secret service agents, and it's almost election time. In *Bloomington*.'

'Maybe they're after a bank robber.'

There hasn't been a bank robbery in town in ages . . . Father, you're hopeless.'

She stalked away.

Nor did Norman Muller receive the news with noticeably greater excitement.

'Now, Sarah, how did Agatha's Joe know they were secret service agents?' he asked calmly. 'They wouldn't go around with identification cards pasted on their foreheads.'

But by next evening, with November a day old, she could say triumphantly, 'It's just everyone in Bloomington that's waiting for someone local to be the voter. The Bloomington *News* as much as said so on video.'

Norman stirred uneasily. He couldn't deny it, and his heart was sinking. If Bloomington was really to be hit by Multivac's lightning, it would mean newspapermen, video shows, tourists, all sorts of – strange upsets. Norman liked the quiet routine of his life, and the distant stir of politics was getting uncomfortably close.

He said, 'It's all rumor. Nothing more.'

'You wait and see, then. You just wait and see.'

As things turned out, there was very little time to wait, for the doorbell rang insistently, and when Norman Muller opened it and said, 'Yes?' a tall, grave-faced man said, 'Are you Norman Muller?'

Norman said, 'Yes,' again, but in a strange dying voice. It was not difficult to see from the stranger's bearing that he was one carrying authority, and the nature of his errand suddenly became as inevitably obvious as it had, until the moment before, been unthinkably impossible.

The man presented credentials, stepped into the house, closed the door behind him and said ritualistically, 'Mr Norman Muller, it is necessary for me to inform you on the behalf of the President of the United States that you have been chosen to represent the American electorate on Tuesday, 4 November, 2008.'

Norman Muller managed, with difficulty, to walk unaided to his chair. He sat there, white-faced and almost insensible, while Sarah brought water, slapped his hands in panic and moaned to her husband between clenched teeth, 'Don't be sick, Norman. *Don't* be sick. They'll pick someone else.'

When Norman could manage to talk, he whispered, 'I'm sorry, sir.'

The secret service agent had removed his coat, unbuttoned his jacket and was sitting at ease on the couch.

'It's all right,' he said, and the mark of officialdom seemed to have vanished with the formal announcement and leave him simply a large and rather friendly man. 'This is the sixth time I've made the announcement and I've seen all kinds of reactions. Not one of them was the kind you see on the video. You know what I mean? A holy, dedicated look, and a character who says, "It will be a great privilege to serve my country." That sort of stuff.' The agent laughed comfortingly.

Sarah's accompanying laugh held a trace of shrill hysteria.

The agent said, 'Now you're going to have me with you for a while. My name is Phil Handley. I'd appreciate it if you call me Phil. Mr Muller can't leave the house any more till Election Day. You'll have to inform the department store that he's sick, Mrs Muller. You can go about your business for a while, but you'll have to agree not to say a word about this. Right, Mrs Muller?'

Sarah nodded vigorously. 'No, sir. Not a word.'

'All right. But, Mrs Muller,' Handley looked grave, 'we're not kidding now. Go out only if you must and you'll be followed when you do. I'm sorry but that's the way we must operate.'

'Followed?'

'It won't be obvious. Don't worry. And it's only for two days till the formal announcement to the nation is made. Your daughter—'

'She's in bed,' said Sarah hastily.

'Good. She'll have to be told I'm a relative or friend staying with the family. If she does find out the truth, she'll have to be kept in the house. Your father had better stay in the house in any case.'

'He won't like that,' said Sarah.

'Can't be helped. Now, since you have no others living with you—'

'You know all about us apparently,' whispered Norman.

'Quite a bit,' agreed Handley. 'In any case, those are all my instructions to you for the moment. I'll try to co-operate as much as I can and be as little of a nuisance as possible. The government will pay for my maintenance so I won't be an expense to you. I'll be relieved each night by someone who will sit up in this room, so there will be no problem about sleeping accommodations. Now, Mr Muller—'

'Sir?'

'You can call me Phil,' said the agent again. 'The purpose of the two-day preliminary before formal announcement is to get you used to your position. We prefer to have you face Multivac in as normal a state of mind as possible. Just relax and try to feel this is all in a day's work. Okay?'

'Okay,' said Norman, and then shook his head violently. 'But I don't want the responsibility. Why me?'

'All right,' said Handley, 'let's get that straight to begin with. Multivac weighs all sorts of known factors, billions of them. One factor isn't known, though, and won't be known for a long time. That's the reaction pattern of the human mind. All Americans are subjected to the molding pressure of what other Americans do and say, to the things that are done to him and the things he does to others. Any

American can be brought to Multivac to have the bent of his mind surveyed. From that the bent of all other minds in the country can be estimated. Some Americans are better for the purpose than others at some given time, depending upon the happenings of that year. Multivac picked you as most representative this year. Not the smartest, or the strongest, or the luckiest, but just the most representative. Now we don't question Multivac, do we?'

'Couldn't it make a mistake?' asked Norman.

Sarah, who listened impatiently, interrupted to say, 'Don't listen to him, sir. He's just nervous, you know. Actually, he's very well read and he always follows politics very closely.'

Handley said, 'Multivac makes the decisions, Mrs Muller. It picked your husband.'

'But does it know everything?' insisted Norman wildly. 'Couldn't it have made a mistake?'

'Yes, it can. There's no point in not being frank. In 1993, a selected Voter died of a stroke two hours before it was time for him to be notified. Multivac didn't predict that; it couldn't. A Voter might be mentally unstable, morally unsuitable, or, for that matter, disloyal. Multivac can't know everything about everybody until he's fed all the data there is. That's why alternate selections are always held in readiness. I don't think we'll be using one this time. You're in good health, Mr Muller, and you've been carefully investigated. You qualify.'

Norman buried his face in his hands and sat motionless.

'By tomorrow morning, sir,' said Sarah, 'he'll be perfectly all right. He just has to get used to it, that's all.'

'Of course,' said Handley.

In the privacy of their bedchamber, Sarah Muller expressed herself in other and stronger fashion. The burden of her lecture was, 'So get hold of yourself, Norman. You're trying to throw away the chance of a lifetime.'

Norman whispered desperately. 'It frightens me, Sarah. The whole thing.'

'For goodness' sake, why? What's there to it but answering a question or two?'

'The responsibility is too great. I couldn't face it.'

'What responsibility? There isn't any. Multivac picked you. It's Multivac's responsibility. Everyone knows that.'

Norman sat up in bed in a sudden excess of rebellion and anguish. 'Everyone is *supposed* to know that. But they don't. They—'

'Lower your voice,' hissed Sarah icily. 'They'll hear you downtown.'

'They don't,' said Norman, declining quickly to a whisper. 'When they talk about the Ridgely administration of 1988, do they say he won them over with pie-in-the-sky promises and racist baloney? No! They talk about the "goddamn MacComber vote", as though Humphrey MacComber was the only man who had anything to do with it because he faced Multivac. I've said it myself – only now I think the poor guy was just a truck farmer who didn't ask to be picked. Why was it his fault more than anyone else's? Now his name is a curse.'

'You're just being childish,' said Sarah.

'I'm being sensible. I tell you, Sarah, I won't accept. They can't make me vote if I don't want to. I'll say I'm sick. I'll say—'

But Sarah had had enough. 'Now you listen to me,' she whispered in a cold fury. 'You don't have only yourself to think about. You know what it means to be Voter of the Year. A presidential year at that. It means publicity and fame and, maybe, buckets of money—'

'And then I go back to being a clerk.'

'You will *not*. You'll have a branch managership at the least if you have any brains at all, and you *will* have, because I'll tell you what to do. You control the kind of publicity if you play your cards right, and you can force Kennell Stores, Inc., into a tight contract *and* an escalator clause in connection with your salary *and* a decent pension plan.'

'That's not the point in being Voter, Sarah.'

'That will be your point. If you don't owe anything to yourself or to me – I'm not asking for myself – you owe something to Linda.'

Norman groaned.

'Well, don't you?' snapped Sarah.

'Yes, dear,' murmured Norman.

On 3 November, the official announcement was made and it was too late for Norman to back out even if he had been able to find the courage to make the attempt.

Their house was sealed off. Secret service agents made their appearance in the open, blocking off all approach.

At first the telephone rang incessantly, but Philip Handley with an engagingly apologetic smile took all calls. Eventually, the exchange shunted all calls directly to the police station.

Norman imagined that, in that way, he was spared not only the bubbling (and envious?) congratulations of friends, but also the egregious pressure of salesmen scenting a prospect and the designing smoothness of politicians from all over the nation . . . Perhaps even death threats from the inevitable cranks.

Newspapers were forbidden to enter the house now in order to keep out weighted pressures, and television was gently but firmly disconnected, over Linda's loud protests.

Matthew growled and stayed in his room; Linda, after the first flurry of excitement, sulked and whined because she could not leave the house; Sarah divided her time between preparation of meals for the present and plans for the future; and Norman's depression lived and fed upon itself.

And the morning of Tuesday, 4 November 2008, came at last, and it was Election Day.

It was early breakfast, but only Norman Muller ate, and that mechanically. Even a shower and shave had not succeeded in either restoring him to reality or removing his own conviction that he was as grimy without as he felt grimy within.

Handley's friendly voice did its best to shed some normality over the gray and unfriendly dawn. (The weather prediction had been for a cloudy day with prospects of rain before noon.)

Handley said, 'We'll keep this house insulated till Mr Muller is back, but after that we'll be off your necks.' The secret service agent was in full uniform now, including sidearms in heavily brassed holsters.

'You've been no trouble at all, Mr Handley,' simpered Sarah.

Norman drank through two cups of black coffee, wiped his lips with a napkin, stood up and said haggardly, 'I'm ready.'

Handley stood up, too. 'Very well, sir. And thank you, Mrs Muller, for your very kind hospitality.'

The armored car purred down empty streets. They were empty even for that hour of the morning.

Handley indicated that and said, 'They always shift traffic away from the line of drive ever since the attempted bombing that nearly ruined the Leverett Election of '92.'

When the car stopped, Norman was helped out by the always polite Handley into an underground drive whose walls were lined with soldiers at attention.

He was led into a brightly lit room, in which three white-uniformed men greeted him smilingly.

Norman said sharply, 'But this is the hospital.'

'There's no significance to that,' said Handley at once. 'It's just that the hospital has the necessary facilities.'

'Well, what do I do?'

Handley nodded. One of the three men in white advanced and said, 'I'll take over now, agent.'

Handley saluted in an offhand manner and left the room.

The man in white said, 'Won't you sit down, Mr Muller? I'm John Paulson, Senior Computer. These are Samson Levine and Peter Dorogobuzh, my assistants.'

Norman shook hands numbly all about. Paulson was a man of middle height with a soft face that seemed used to smiling and a very obvious toupee. He wore plastic-rimmed glasses of an old-fashioned cut, and he lit a cigarette as he talked. (Norman refused his offer of one.)

Paulson said, 'In the first place, Mr Muller, I want you to know we are in no hurry. We want you to stay with us all day if necessary, just so that you get used to your surroundings and get over any thought you might have that there is anything unusual in this, anything clinical, if you know what I mean.'

'It's all right,' said Norman. 'I'd just as soon this were over.'

'I understand your feelings. Still, we want you to know exactly what's going on. In the first place, Multivac isn't here.'

'It isn't?' Somehow through all his depression, he had still looked forward to seeing Multivac. They said it was half a mile long and three stories high, that fifty technicians walked the corridors *within* its structure continuously. It was one of the wonders of the world.

Paulson smiled. 'No. It's not portable, you know. It's located underground, in fact, and very few people know exactly where. You can understand that, since it is our greatest natural resource. Believe me, elections aren't the only things it's used for.'

Norman thought he was being deliberately chatty and found himself intrigued all the same. 'I thought I'd see it. I'd like to.'

'I'm sure of that. But it takes a presidential order and even then it has to be countersigned by Security. However, we are plugged into Multivac right here by beam transmission. What Multivac says can be interpreted here and what we say is beamed directly to Multivac, so in a sense we're in its presence.'

Norman looked about. The machines within the room were all meaningless to him.

'Now let me explain, Mr Muller,' Paulson went on. 'Multivac already has most of the information it needs to decide all the elections, national, state and local. It needs only to check certain imponderable attitudes of mind and it will use you for that. We can't predict what questions it will ask, but they may not make much sense to you, or even to us. It may ask you how you feel about garbage disposal in your town; whether you favor central incinerators. It might ask you whether you have a doctor of your own or whether you make use of National Medicine, Inc. Do you understand?'

'Yes, sir.'

'Whatever it asks, you answer in your own words in any way you please. If you feel you must explain quite a bit, do so. Talk an hour, if necessary.'

'Yes, sir.'

'Now, one more thing. We will have to make use of some simple devices which will automatically record your blood pressure, heart-beat, skin conductivity and brain-wave pattern while you speak. The machinery will seem formidable, but it's all absolutely painless. You won't even know it's going on.'

The other two technicians were already busying themselves with smooth gleaming apparatus on oiled wheels.

Norman said, 'Is that to check on whether I'm lying or not?'

'Not at all, Mr Muller. There's no question of lying. It's only a matter of emotional intensity. If the machine asks you your opinion of your child's school, you may say, "I think it is overcrowded." Those are only words. From the way your brain and heart and hormones and sweat glands work, Multivac can judge exactly how intensely you feel about the matter. It will understand your feelings better than you yourself.'

'I never heard of this,' said Norman.

'No, I'm sure you didn't. Most of the details of Multivac's work-ings are top secret. For instance, when you leave, you will be asked to sign a paper swearing that you will never reveal the nature of the questions you were asked, the nature of your responses, what was done, or how it was done. The less is known about the Multivac, the less chance of attempted outside pressures upon the men who service it.' He smiled grimly. 'Our lives are hard enough as it is.'

Norman nodded. 'I understand.'

'And now would you like anything to eat or drink?'

'No. Nothing right now.'

'Do you have any questions?'

Norman shook his head.

'Then you tell us when you're ready.'

'I'm ready right now.'

'You're certain?'

'Quite.'

Paulson nodded, and raised his hand in a gesture to the others. They advanced with their frightening equipment, and Norman Muller felt his breath come a little quicker as he watched.

The ordeal lasted nearly three hours, with one short break for coffee and an embarrassing session with a chamber pot. During all this time, Norman Muller remained encased in machinery. He was bone-weary at the close.

He thought sardonically that his promise to reveal nothing of what had passed would be an easy one to keep. Already the questions were a hazy mishmash in his mind.

Somehow he had thought Multivac would speak in a sepulchral, superhuman voice, resonant and echoing, but that, after all, was just an idea he had from seeing too many television shows, he now decided. The truth was distressingly undramatic. The questions were slips of a kind of metallic foil patterned with numerous punctures. A second machine converted the pattern into words and Paulson read the words to Norman, then gave him the question and let him read it for himself.

Norman's answers were taken down by a recording machine, played back to Norman for confirmation, with emendations and added remarks also taken down. All that was fed into a pattern-making instrument and that, in turn, was radiated to Multivac.

The one question Norman could remember at the moment was an incongruously gossipy: 'What do you think of the price of eggs?'

Now it was over, and gently they removed the electrodes from various portions of his body, unwrapped the pulsating band from his upper arm, moved the machinery away.

He stood up, drew a deep, shuddering breath and said, 'Is that all? Am I through?'

'Not quite.' Paulson hurried to him, smiling in reassuring fashion. 'We'll have to ask you to stay another hour.'

'Why?' asked Norman sharply.

'It will take that long for Multivac to weave its new data into the trillions of items it has. Thousands of elections are concerned, you know. It's very complicated. And it may be that an odd contest here or there, a comptrollership in Phoenix, Arizona, or some council seat in Wilkesboro, North Carolina, may be in doubt. In that case, Multivac may be compelled to ask you a deciding question or two.'

'No,' said Norman. 'I won't go through this again.'

'It probably won't happen,' Paulson said soothingly. 'It rarely does. But, just in case, you'll have to stay.' A touch of steel, just a touch, entered his voice. 'You have no choice, you know. You must.'

Norman sat down wearily. He shrugged.

Paulson said, 'We can't let you read a newspaper, but if you'd care for a murder mystery, or if you'd like to play chess, or if there's anything we can do for you to help pass the time, I wish you'd mention it.'

'It's all right. I'll just wait.'

They ushered him into a small room just next to the one in which he had been questioned. He let himself sink into a plastic-covered armchair and closed his eyes.

As well as he could, he must wait out this final hour.

He sat perfectly still and slowly the tension left him. His breathing grew less ragged and he could clasp his hands without being quite so conscious of the trembling of his fingers.

Maybe there would be no questions. Maybe it was all over.

If it *were* over, then the next thing would be torchlight processions and invitations to speak at all sorts of functions. The Voter of the Year!

He, Norman Muller, ordinary clerk of a small department store in Bloomington, Indiana, who had neither been born great nor achieved greatness would be in the extraordinary position of having had greatness thrust upon him.

The historians would speak soberly of the Muller Election of 2008. That would be its name, the Muller Election.

The publicity, the better job, the flash flood of money that inter-ested Sarah so much, occupied only a corner of his mind. It would all be welcome, of course. He couldn't refuse it. But at the moment something else was beginning to concern him.

A latent patriotism was stirring. After all, he was representing the entire electorate. He was the focal point for *them*. He was, in his own person, for this one day, all of America!

The door opened, snapping him to open-eyed attention. For a moment, his stomach constricted. Not more questions!

But Paulson was smiling. 'That will be all, Mr Muller.'

'No more questions, sir?'

'None needed. Everything was quite clear-cut. You will be escorted back to your home and then you will be a private citizen once more. Or as much so as the public will allow.'

'Thank you. Thank you.' Norman flushed and said, 'I wonder – who was elected?'

Paulson shook his head. 'That will have to wait for the official announcement. The rules are quite strict. We can't even tell you. You understand.'

'Of course. Yes.' Norman felt embarrassed.

'Secret service will have the necessary papers for you to sign.'

'Yes.' Suddenly, Norman Muller felt proud. It was on him now in full strength. He was proud.

In this imperfect world, the sovereign citizens of the first and greatest Electronic Democracy had, through Norman Muller (through *him!*) exercised once again its free, untrammeled franchise.

Gimmicks Three

'Come, come,' said Shapur quite politely, considering that he was a demon. 'You are wasting my time. And your own, too, I might add, since you have only half an hour left.' And his tail twitched.

'It's *not* dematerialization?' asked Isidore Wellby thoughtfully.

'I have already said it is not,' said Shapur.

For the hundredth time, Wellby looked at the unbroken bronze that surrounded him on all sides. The demon had taken unholy pleasure (what other kind indeed?) in pointing out that the floor, ceiling and four walls were featureless, two-foot-thick slabs of bronze, welded seamlessly together.

It was the ultimate locked room and Wellby had but another half hour to get out, while the demon watched with an expression of gathering anticipation.

It had been ten years previously (to the day, naturally) that Isidore Wellby had signed up.

'We pay you in advance,' said Shapur persuasively. 'Ten years of anything you want, within reason, and then you're a demon. You're one of us, with a new name of demonic potency, and many privileges beside. You'll hardly know you're damned. And if you don't sign, you may end up in the fire, anyway, just in the ordinary course of things. You never know . . . Here, look at me. I'm not doing too badly. I signed up, had my ten years and here I am. Not bad.'

'Why so anxious for me to sign then, if I might be damned anyway?' asked Wellby.

'It's not so easy to recruit hell's cadre,' said the demon, with a frank shrug that made the faint odor of sulfur dioxide in the air a trifle stronger. 'Everyone wishes to gamble on ending in Heaven. It's a poor gamble, but there it is. I think *you're* too sensible for that. But meanwhile we have more damned souls than we know what to do with and a growing shortage at the administrative end.'

Wellby, having just left the army and finding himself with nothing much to show for it but a limp and a farewell letter from a girl he somehow still loved, pricked his finger, and signed.

Of course, he read the small print first. A certain amount of demonic power would be deposited to his account upon signature in blood. He would not know in detail how one manipulated those powers, or even the nature of all of them, but he would nevertheless find his wishes fulfilled in such a way that they would seem to have come about through perfectly normal mechanisms.

Naturally, no wish might be fulfilled which would interfere with the higher aims and purposes of human history. Wellby had raised his eyebrows at that.

Shapur coughed. 'A precaution imposed upon us by – uh – Above. You are reasonable. The limitation won't interfere with you.'

Wellby said, 'There seems to be a catch clause, too.'

'A kind of one, yes. After all, we have to check your aptitude for the position. It states, as you see, that you will be required to perform a task for us at the conclusion of your ten years, one your demonic powers will make it quite possible for you to do. We can't tell you the nature of the task now, but you will have ten years to study the nature of your powers. Look upon the whole thing as an entrance qualification.'

'And if I don't pass the test, what then?'

'In that case,' said the demon, 'you will be only an ordinary damned soul after all.' And because he was a demon, his eyes glowed smokily at the thought and his clawed fingers twitched as though he felt them already deep in the other's vitals. But he added suavely, 'Come, now, the test will be a simple one. We would rather have you as cadre than as just another chore on our hands.'

Wellby, with sad thoughts of his unattainable loved one, cared little enough at that moment for what would happen after ten years and he signed.

Yet the ten years passed quickly enough. Isidore Wellby was always reasonable, as the demon had predicted, and things worked well. Wellby accepted a position and because he was always at the right spot at the right time and always said the right thing to the right man, he was quickly promoted to a position of great authority.

Investments he made invariably paid off and, what was more gratifying still, his girl came back to him most sincerely repentant and most satisfactorily adoring.

His marriage was a happy one and was blessed with four children, two boys and two girls, all bright and reasonably well behaved. At the end of ten years, he was at the height of his authority, reputation and wealth, while his wife, if anything, had grown more beautiful as she had matured.

And ten years (to the day, naturally) after the making of the compact, he woke to find himself, not in his bedroom, but in a horrible bronze chamber of the most appalling solidity, with no company other than an eager demon.

'You have only to get out, and you will be one of us,' said Shapur. 'It can be done fairly and logically by using your demonic powers, provided you know exactly what it is you're doing. You should, by now.'

'My wife and children will be very disturbed at my disappearance,' said Wellby with the beginning of regrets.

'They will find your dead body,' said the demon consolingly. 'You will seem to have died of a heart attack and you will have a beautiful funeral. The minister will consign you to Heaven and we will not disillusion him or those who listen to him. Now, come, Wellby, you have till noon.'

Wellby, having unconsciously steeled himself for this moment for ten years, was less panic-stricken than he might have been. He looked about speculatively. 'Is this room perfectly enclosed? No trick openings?'

'No openings anywhere in the walls, floor or ceiling,' said the demon, with a professional delight in his handiwork. 'Or at the boundaries of any of those surfaces, for that matter. Are you giving up?'

'No, no. Just give me time.'

Wellby thought very hard. There seemed no sign of closeness in the room. There was even a feeling of moving air. The air might be entering the room by dematerializing across the walls. Perhaps the demon had entered by dematerialization and perhaps Wellby himself might leave in that manner. He asked.

The demon grinned. 'Dematerialization is not one of your powers. Nor did I myself use it in entering.'

'You're sure now?'

'The room is my own creation,' said the demon smugly, 'and especially constructed for you.'

'And you entered from outside?'

'I did.'

'With reasonably demonic powers which I possess, too?'

'Exactly. Come, let us be precise. You cannot move through matter but you can move in any dimension by a mere effort of will. You can move up, down, right, left, obliquely and so on, but you cannot move through matter in any way.'

Wellby kept on thinking, and Shapur kept on pointing out the utter immovable solidity of the bronze walls, floor and ceiling; their unbroken ultimacy.

It seemed obvious to Wellby that Shapur, however much he might believe in the necessity for recruiting cadre, was barely restraining his demonic delight at possibly having an ordinary damned soul to amuse himself with.

'At least,' said Wellby, with a sorrowful attempt at philosophy, 'I'll have ten happy years to look back on. Surely that's a consolation, even for a damned soul in hell.'

'Not at all,' said the demon. 'Hell would not be hell, if you were allowed consolations. Everything anyone gains on Earth by pacts with the devil, as in your case (or my own, for that matter), is exactly what one might have gained without such a pact if one had worked industriously and in full trust in – uh – Above. That is what makes all such bargains so truly demonic.' And the demon laughed with a kind of cheerful howl.

Wellby said indignantly, 'You mean my wife would have returned to me even if I had never signed your contract.'

'She might have,' said Shapur. 'Whatever happens is the will of – uh – Above, you know. We ourselves can do nothing to alter that.'

The chagrin of that moment must have sharpened Wellby's wits for it was then that he vanished, leaving the room empty, except for a surprised demon. And surprise turned to absolute fury when the demon looked at the contract with Wellby which he had, until that moment, been holding in his hand for final action, one way or the other.

It was ten years (to the day, naturally) after Isidore Wellby had signed his pact with Shapur, that the demon entered Wellby's office and said, most angrily, 'Look here—'

Wellby looked up from his work, astonished. 'Who are you?'

'You know very well who I am,' said Shapur.

'Not at all,' said Wellby.

The demon looked sharply at the man. 'I see you are telling the truth, but I can't make out the details.' He promptly flooded Wellby's mind with the events of the last ten years.

Wellby said, 'Oh, yes. I can explain, of course, but are you sure we will not be interrupted?'

'We won't be,' said the demon grimly.

'I sat in that closed bronze room,' said Wellby, 'and—'

'Never mind that,' said the demon hastily. 'I want to know—'

'Please. Let me tell this my way.'

The demon clamped his jaws and fairly exuded sulfur dioxide till Wellby coughed and looked pained.

Wellby said, 'If you'll move off a bit. Thank you . . . Now I sat in that closed bronze room and remembered how you kept stressing the absolute unbrokenness of the four walls, the floor and the ceiling. I wondered: Why did you specify? What else was there beside walls, floor and ceiling. You had defined a completely enclosed three-dimensional space.

'And that was it: three-dimensional. The room was not closed in the fourth dimension. It did not exist indefinitely in the past. You said you had created it for me. So if one traveled into the past, one would find oneself at a point in time, eventually, when the room did not exist and then one would be out of the room.

'What's more, you *had* said I could move in any dimension, and time may certainly be viewed as a dimension. In any case, as soon as I decided to move toward the past, I found myself living backward at a tremendous rate and suddenly there was no bronze around me anywhere.'

Shapur cried in anguish, 'I can guess all that. You couldn't have escaped any other way. It's this contract of yours that I'm concerned about. If you're not an ordinary damned soul, very well, it's part of the game. But you must be at least one of *us*, one of the cadre; it's what you were paid for, and if I don't deliver you down below, I will be in enormous trouble.'

Wellby shrugged his shoulders. 'I'm sorry for you, of course, but I can't help you. You must have created the bronze room immediately after I placed my signature on the paper, for when I burst out of the room, I found myself just at the point in time at which I was making the bargain with you. There you were again; there I was; you were pushing the contract toward me, together with a stylus with which I might prick my finger. To be sure, as I had moved back in time, my memory of what was becoming the future faded out, but not, apparently, quite entirely. As you pushed the contract at me, I felt uneasy. I didn't quite remember the future, but I felt uneasy. So I didn't sign. I turned you down flat.'

Shapur ground his teeth. 'I might have known. If probability patterns affected demons, I would have shifted with you into this new if-world. As it is, all I can say is that you have lost the ten happy years we paid you with. That is one consolation. And we'll get you in the end. That is another.'

'Well, now,' said Wellby, 'are there consolations in hell? Through the ten years I have now lived, I knew nothing of what I might have obtained. But now that you've put the memory of the ten-years-that-might-have-been into my mind, I recall that, in the bronze room, you told me that demonic agreements could give nothing that could not be obtained by industry and trust in Above. I have been industrious and I have trusted.'

Wellby's eyes fell upon the photograph of his beautiful wife and four beautiful children, then traveled about the tasteful luxuriance of his office. 'And I may even escape hell altogether. That, too, is beyond *your* power to decide.'

And the demon, with a horrible shriek, vanished forever.

Kid Stuff

The first pang of nausea had passed and Jan Prentiss said, 'Damn it, you're an insect.'

It was a statement of fact, not an insult, and the thing that sat on Prentiss' desk said, 'Of course.'

It was about a foot long, very thin, and in shape a farfetched and miniature caricature of a human being. Its stalky arms and legs originated in pairs from the upper portion of its body. The legs were longer and thicker than the arms. They extended the length of the body, then bent forward at the knee.

The creature sat upon those knees and, when it did so, the stub of its fuzzy abdomen just cleared Prentiss' desk.

There was plenty of time for Prentiss to absorb these details. The object had no objection to being stared at. It seemed to welcome it, in fact, as though it were used to exciting admiration.

'What are you?' Prentiss did not feel completely rational. Five minutes ago, he had been seated at his typewriter, working leisurely on the story he had promised Horace W. Browne for last month's issue of *Farfetched Fantasy Fiction*. He had been in a perfectly usual frame of mind. He had felt quite fine; quite sane.

And then a block of air immediately to the right of the typewriter had shimmered, clouded over and condensed into the little horror that dangled its black and shiny feet over the edge of the desk.

Prentiss wondered in a detached sort of way that he bothered talking to it. This was the first time his profession had so crudely affected his dreams. It *must* be a dream, he told himself.

'I'm an Avalonian,' said the being. 'I'm from Avalon, in other words.' Its tiny face ended in a mandibular mouth. Two swaying three-inch antennae rose from a spot above either eye, while the eyes themselves gleamed richly in their many-faceted fashion. There was no sign of nostrils.

Naturally not, thought Prentiss wildly. It has to breathe through vents in its abdomen. It must be talking with its abdomen then. Or using telepathy.

'Avalon?' he said stupidly. He thought: Avalon? The land of the fay in King Arthur's time?

'Certainly,' said the creature, answering the thought smoothly. 'I'm an elf.'

'Oh, no!' Prentiss put his hands to his face, took them away and found the elf still there, its feet thumping against the top drawer. Prentiss was not a drinking man, or a nervous one. In fact, he was considered a very prosaic sort of person by his neighbors. He had a comfortable paunch, a reasonable but not excessive amount of hair on his head, an amiable wife and an active ten-year-old son. His neighbors were, of course, kept ignorant of the fact that he paid off the mortgage on his house by writing fantasies of one sort or another.

Till now, however, this secret vice had never affected his psyche. To be sure, his wife had shaken her head over his addiction many times. It was her standard opinion that he was wasting, even perverting, his talents.

'Who on Earth reads these things?' she would say. 'All that stuff about demons and gnomes and wishing rings and elves. All that *kid* stuff, if you want my frank opinion.'

'You're quite wrong,' Prentiss would reply stiffly. 'Modern fantasies are very sophisticated and mature treatments of folk motifs. Behind the façade of glib unreality there frequently lie trenchant comments on the world of today. Fantasy in modern style is, above all, adult fare.'

Blanche shrugged. She had heard him speak at conventions so these comments weren't new to her.

'Besides,' he would add, 'fantasies pay the mortgage, don't they?'

'Maybe so,' she would reply, 'but it would be nice if you'd switch to mysteries. At least you'd get quarter-reprint sales out of those and we could even tell the neighbors what you do for a living.'

Prentiss groaned in spirit. Blanche could come in now at any time and find him talking to himself (it was too real for a dream; it might be a hallucination). After that he *would* have to write mysteries for a living – or take to work.

'You're quite wrong,' said the elf. 'This is neither a dream nor a hallucination.'

'Then why don't you go away?' asked Prentiss.

'I intend to. This is scarcely my idea of a place to live. And you're coming with me.'

'I am *not*. What the hell do you think you are, telling me what I'm going to do?'

'If you think that's a respectful way to speak to a representative of an older culture, I can't say much for your upbringing.'

'You're not an older culture—' He wanted to add: You're just a figment of my imagination; but he had been a writer too long to be able to bring himself to commit the cliche.

'We insects,' said the elf freezingly, 'existed half a billion years before the first mammal was invented. We watched the dinosaurs come in and we watched them go out. As for you man-things – strictly newcomers.'

For the first time, Prentiss noted that, from the spot on the elf's body where its limbs sprouted, a third vestigial pair existed as well.

It increased the insecticity of the object and Prentiss' sense of indignation grew.

He said, 'You needn't waste your company on social inferiors.'

'I wouldn't,' said the elf, 'believe me. But necessity drives, you know. It's a rather complicated story but when you hear it, you'll *want* to help.'

Prentiss said uneasily, 'Look, I don't have much time. Blanche – my wife will be in here any time. She'll be upset.'

'She won't be here,' said the elf. 'I've set up a block in her mind.'

'What!'

'Quite harmless, I assure you. But, after all, we can't afford to be disturbed, can we?'

Prentiss sat back in his chair, dazed and unhappy.

The elf said, 'We elves began our association with you man-things immediately after the last ice age began. It had been a miserable time for us, as you can imagine. We couldn't wear animal carcasses or live in holes as your uncouth ancestors did. It took incredible stores of psychic energy to keep warm.'

'Incredible stores of what?'

'Psychic energy. You know nothing at all about it. Your mind is too coarse to grasp the concept. Please don't interrupt.'

The elf continued, 'Necessity drove us to experiment with your people's brains. They were crude, but large. The cells were inefficient, almost worthless, but there were a vast number of them. We could use those brains as a concentrating device, a type of psychic lens, and increase the available energy which our own minds could tap. We survived the ice age handily and without having to retreat to the tropics as in previous such eras.

'Of course, we were spoiled. When warmth returned, we didn't abandon the man-things. We used them to increase our standard of living generally. We could travel faster, eat better, do more, and we lost our old, simple, virtuous way of life forever. Then, too, there was milk.'

'Milk?' said Prentiss. 'I don't see the connection.'

'A divine liquid. I only tasted it once in my life. But elfin classic poetry speaks of it in superlatives. In the old days, men always supplied us plentifully. Why mammals of all things should be blessed with it and insects not is a complete mystery . . . How unfortunate it is that the men-things got out of hand.'

'They did?'

'Two hundred years ago.'

'Good for us.'

'Don't be narrow-minded,' said the elf stiffly. 'It was a useful association for all parties until you man-things learned to handle physical energies in quantity. It was just the sort of gross thing your minds are capable of.'

'What was wrong with it?'

'It's hard to explain. It was all very well for us to light up our nightly revels with fireflies brightened by use of two manpower of psychic energy. But then you men-creatures installed electric lights. Our antennal reception is good for miles, but then you invented telegraphs, telephones and radios. Our kobolds mined ore with much greater efficiency than man-things do, until man-things invented dynamite. Do you see?'

'No.'

'Surely you don't expect sensitive and superior creatures such as the elves to watch a group of hairy mammals outdo them. It wouldn't be so bad if we could imitate the electronic development ourselves, but our psychic energies were insufficient for the purpose. Well, we retreated from reality. We sulked, pined and drooped. Call it an inferiority complex, if you will, but from two centuries ago onward, we slowly abandoned mankind and retreated to such centers as Avalon.'

Prentiss thought furiously. 'Let's get this straight. You can handle minds?'

'Certainly.'

'You can make me think you're invisible? Hypnotically, I mean?'

'A crude term, but yes.'

'And when you appeared just now, you did it by lifting a kind of mental block, is that it?'

'To answer your thoughts, rather than your words: You are not sleeping; you are not mad; and I am not supernatural.'

'I was just making sure. I take it, then, you can read my mind.'

'Of course. It is a rather dirty and unrewarding sort of labor, but I can do it when I must. Your name is Prentiss and you write imaginative fiction. You have one larva who is at a place of instruction. I know a great deal about you.'

Prentiss winced. 'And just where is Avalon?'

'You won't find it.' The elf clacked his mandibles together two or three times. 'Don't speculate on the possibility of warning the authorities. You'll find yourself in a madhouse. Avalon, in case you think the knowledge will help you, is in the middle of the Atlantic and quite invisible, you know. After the steamboat was invented, you man-things got to moving about so unreasonably that we had to cloak the whole island with a psychic shield.

'Of course, incidents *will* take place. Once a huge, barbaric vessel hit us dead center and it took all the psychic energy of the entire population to give the island the appearance of an iceberg. The *Titanic*, I believe, was the name printed on the vessel. And nowadays there are planes flying overhead all the time and sometimes there are crashes. We picked up cases of canned milk once. That's when I tasted it.'

Prentiss said, 'Well, then, damn it, why aren't you still on Avalon? Why did you leave?'

'I was ordered to leave,' said the elf angrily. 'The fools.'

'Oh?'

'You know how it is when you're a little different. I'm not like the rest of them and the poor tradition-ridden fools resented it. They were jealous. That's the best explanation. Jealous!'

'How are you different?'

'Hand me that light bulb,' said the elf. 'Oh, just unscrew it. You don't need a reading lamp in the daytime.'

With a quiver of repulsion, Prentiss did as he was told and passed the object into the little hands of the elf. Carefully, the elf, with fingers so thin and wiry that they looked like tendrils, touched the bottom and side of the brass base.

Feebly the filament in the bulb reddened.

'Good God,' said Prentiss.

'That,' said the elf proudly, 'is my great talent. I told you that we elves couldn't adapt psychic energy to electronics. Well, I can! I'm not just an ordinary elf. I'm a mutant! A super-elf! I'm the next stage in elfin evolution. This light is due just to the activity of my own mind, you know. Now watch when I use yours as a focus.'

As he said that, the bulb's filament grew white hot and painful to look at, while a vague and not unpleasant tickling sensation entered Prentiss' skull.

The lamp went out and the elf put the bulb on the desk behind the typewriter.

'I haven't tried,' said the elf proudly, 'but I suspect I can fission uranium too.'

'But look here, lighting a bulb takes energy. You can't just hold it—'

'I've *told* you about psychic energy. Great Oberon, man-thing, try to understand.'

Prentiss felt increasingly uneasy; he said cautiously, 'What do you intend doing with this gift of yours?'

'Go back to Avalon, of course. I *should* let those fools go to their doom, but an elf does have a certain patriotism, even if he *is* a coleopteron.'

'A what?'

'We elves are not all of a species, you know. I'm of beetle descent. See?'

He rose to his feet and, standing on the desk, turned his back to Prentiss. What had seemed merely a shining black cuticle suddenly split and lifted. From underneath, two filmy, veined wings fluttered out.

'Oh, you can fly,' said Prentiss.

'You're very foolish,' said the elf contemptuously, 'not to realize I'm too large for flight. But they *are* attractive, aren't they? How do you like the iridescence? The lepidoptera have disgusting wings in comparison. They're gaudy and indelicate. What's more they're always sticking out.'

'The lepidoptera?' Prentiss felt hopelessly confused.

'The butterfly clans. They're the proud ones. They were always letting humans see them so they could be admired. Very petty minds in a way. And that's why your legends always give fairies butterfly wings instead of beetle wings which are *much* more diaphanously beautiful. We'll give the lepidoptera what for when we get back, you and I.'

'Now hold on—'

'Just think,' said the elf, swaying back and forth in what looked like elfin ecstasy, 'our nightly revels on the fairy green will be a blaze of sparkling light from curlicues of neon tubing. We can cut loose the swarms of wasps we've got hitched to our flying wagons and install internal-combustion motors instead. We can stop this business of curling up on leaves when it's time to sleep and build factories to manufacture decent mattresses. I tell you, we'll *live* . . . And the rest of them will eat dirt for having ordered me out.'

'But I can't go with you,' bleated Prentiss. 'I have responsibilities. I have a wife and kid. You wouldn't take a man away from his – his larva, would you?'

'I'm not cruel,' said the elf. He turned his eyes full on Prentiss. 'I have an elfin soul. Still, what choice have I? I must have a man-brain for focusing purposes or I will accomplish nothing; and not all man-brains are suitable.'

'Why not?'

'Great Oberon, creature. A man-brain isn't a passive thing of wood and stone. It must co-operate in order to be useful. And it can only co-operate by being fully aware of our own elfin ability to manipulate it. I can use your brain, for instance, but your wife's would be useless to me. It would take her years to understand who and what I am.'

Prentiss said, 'This is a damned insult. Are you telling me I believe in fairies? I'll have you know I'm a complete rationalist.'

'Are you? When I first revealed myself to you, you had a few feeble thoughts about dreams and hallucinations but you talked to me, you accepted me. Your wife would have screamed and gone into hysterics.'

Prentiss was silent. He could think of no answer.

'That's the trouble,' said the elf despondently. 'Practically all you humans have forgotten about us since we left you. Your minds have closed; grown useless. To be sure, your larvae believe in your legends about the "little folk", but their brains are undeveloped and useful only for simple processes. When they mature, they lose belief. Frankly, I don't know what I would do if it weren't for you fantasy writers.'

'What do you mean we fantasy writers?'

'You are the few remaining adults who believe in the insect folk. You, Prentiss, most of all. You've been a fantasy writer for twenty years.'

'You're mad. I don't believe the things I write.'

'You have to. You can't help it. I mean, while you're actually writing, you take the subject matter seriously. After a while your mind is just naturally cultivated into usefulness . . . But why argue. I *have* used you. You saw the light bulb brighten. So you see you must come with me.'

'But I won't.' Prentiss set his limbs stubbornly. 'Can you make me against my will?'

'I could, but I might damage you, and I wouldn't want that. Suppose we say this. If you don't agree to come, I could focus a current of high-voltage electricity through your wife. It would be a revolting thing to have to do, but I understand your own people execute enemies of the state in that fashion, so that you would probably find the punishment less horrible than I do. I wouldn't want to seem brutal even to a man-thing.'

Prentiss grew conscious of the perspiration matting the short hairs on his temple.

'Wait,' he said, 'don't do anything like that. Let's talk it over.'

The elf shot out his filmy wings, fluttered them and returned them to their case. 'Talk, talk, talk. It's tiring. Surely you have milk in the house. You're not a very thoughtful host or you would have offered me refreshment before this.'

Prentiss tried to bury the thought that came to him, to push it as far below the outer skin of his mind as he could. He said casually, 'I have something better than milk. Here, I'll get it for you.'

'Stay where you are. Call to your wife. She'll bring it.'

'But I don't want her to see you. It would frighten her.'

The elf said, 'You need feel no concern. I'll handle her so that she won't be the least disturbed.'

Prentiss lifted an arm.

The elf said, 'Any attack you make on me will be far slower than the bolt of electricity that will strike your wife.'

Prentiss' arm dropped. He stepped to the door of his study.

'Blanche!' he called down the stairs.

Blanche was just visible in the living room, sitting woodenly in the armchair near the bookcase. She seemed to be asleep, open-eyed.

Prentiss turned to the elf. 'Something's wrong with her.'

'She's just in a state of sedation. She'll hear you. Tell her what to do.'

'Blanche!' he called again. 'Bring the container of eggnog and a small glass, will you?'

With no sign of animation other than that of bare movement, Blanche rose and disappeared from view.

'What is eggnog?' asked the elf.

Prentiss attempted enthusiasm. 'It is a compound of milk, sugar and eggs beaten to a delightful consistency. Milk alone is poor stuff compared to it.'

Blanche entered with the eggnog. Her pretty face was expressionless. Her eyes turned toward the elf but lightened with no realization of the significance of the sight.

'Here, Jan,' she said, and sat down in the old, leather-covered chair by the window, hands falling loosely to her lap.

Prentiss watched her uneasily for a moment. 'Are you going to keep her here?'

'She'll be easier to control . . . Well, aren't you going to offer me the eggnog?'

'Oh, sure. Here!'

He poured the thick white liquid into the cocktail glass. He had prepared five milk bottles of it two nights before for the boys of the New York Fantasy Association and it had been mixed with a lavish hand, since fantasy writers notoriously like it so.

The elf's antennae trembled violently.

'A heavenly aroma,' he muttered.

He wrapped the ends of his thin arms about the stem of the small glass and lifted it to his mouth. The liquid's level sank. When half was gone, he put it down and sighed, 'Oh, the loss to my people. What a creation! What a thing to exist! Our histories tell us that in ancient days an occasional lucky sprite managed to take the place of a man-larva at birth so that he might draw off the liquid fresh-made. I wonder if even those ever experienced anything like this.'

Prentiss said with a touch of professional interest, 'That's the idea behind this business of changelings, is it?'

'Of course. The female man-creature has a great gift. Why not take advantage of it?' The elf turned his eyes upon the rise and fall of Blanche's bosom and sighed again.

Prentiss said (not too eager, now; don't give it away), 'Go ahead. Drink all you want.'

He, too, watched Blanche, waiting for signs of restoring animation, waiting for the beginnings of breakdown in the elf's control.

The elf said, 'When is your larva returning from its place of instruction? I need him.'

'Soon, soon,' said Prentiss nervously. He looked at his wristwatch. Actually, Jan, Junior, would be back, yelling for a slab of cake and milk, in something like fifteen minutes.

'Fill 'er up,' he said urgently. 'Fill 'er up.'

The elf sipped gaily. He said, 'Once the larva arrives, you can go.'

'Go?'

'Only to the library. You'll have to get volumes on electronics. I'll need the details on how to build television, telephones, all that. I'll need to have rules on wiring, instructions for constructing vacuum tubes. Details, Prentiss, details! We have tremendous tasks ahead of us. Oil drilling, gasoline refining, motors, scientific agriculture. We'll build a new Avalon, you and I. A technical one. A scientific fairyland. We will create a new world.'

'Great!' said Prentiss. 'Here, don't neglect your drink.'

'You see. You are catching fire with the idea,' said the elf. 'And you will be rewarded. You will have a dozen female man-things to yourself.'

Prentiss looked at Blanche automatically. No signs of hearing, but who could tell? He said, 'I'd have no use for female man-th – for women, I mean.'

'Come now,' said the elf censoriously, 'be truthful. You men-things are well known to our folk as lecherous, bestial creatures. Mothers frightened their young for generations by threatening them with men-things . . . Young, ah!' He lifted the glass of eggnog in the air and said, 'To my own young,' and drained it.

'Fill 'er up,' said Prentiss at once. 'Fill 'er up.'

The elf did so. He said, 'I'll have lots of children. I'll pick out the best of the coleoptresses and breed my line. I'll continue the muta-tion. Right now I'm the only one, but when we have a dozen or fifty, I'll interbreed them and develop the race of the super-elf. A race of electro – ulp – electronic marvels and infinite future . . . If I could only drink more. Nectar! The original nectar!'

There was the sudden noise of a door being flung open and a young voice calling, 'Mom! Hey, Mom!'

The elf, his glossy eyes a little dimmed, said, 'Then we'll begin to take over the men-things. A few believe already; the rest we will – urp – teach. It will be the old days, but better; a more efficient elfhood, a tighter union.'

Jan, Junior's, voice was closer and tinged with impatience. 'Hey, Mom! Ain't you home?'

Prentiss felt his eyes popping with tension. Blanche sat rigid. The elf's speech was slightly thick, his balance a little unsteady. If Prentiss were going to risk it, now, now was the time.

'Sit back,' said the elf peremptorily. 'You're being foolish. I knew there was alcohol in the eggnog from the moment you thought your ridiculous scheme. You men-things are very shifty. We elves have many proverbs about you. Fortunately, alcohol has little effect upon us. Now if you had tried catnip with just a touch of honey in it . . . Ah, here is the larva. How are you, little man-thing?'

The elf sat there, the goblet of eggnog halfway to his mandibles, while Jan, Junior, stood in the doorway. Jan, Junior's, ten-year-old face was moderately smeared with dirt, his hair was immoderately matted and there was a look of the utmost surprise in his gray eyes. His battered schoolbooks swayed from the end of the strap he held in his hand.

He said, 'Pop! What's the matter with Mom? And – and what's that?'

The elf said to Prentiss, 'Hurry to the library. No time must be lost. You know the books I need.' All trace of incipient drunkenness had left the creature and Prentiss' morale broke. The creature had been playing with him.

Prentiss got up to go.

The elf said, 'And nothing human; nothing sneaky; no tricks. Your wife is still a hostage. I can use the larva's mind to kill her; it's good enough for that. I wouldn't want to do it. I'm a member of the Elfitarian Ethical Society and we advocate considerate treatment of mammals so you may rely on my noble principles *if* you do as I say.'

Prentiss felt a strong compulsion to leave flooding him. He stumbled toward the door.

Jan, Junior, cried, 'Pop, it can talk! He says he'll kill Mom! Hey, don't go away!'

Prentiss was already out of the room, when he heard the elf say, 'Don't stare at me, larva. I will not harm your mother if you do exactly as I say. I am an elf, a fairy. You know what a fairy is, of course.'

And Prentiss was at the front door when he heard Jan, Junior's, treble raised in wild shouting, followed by scream after scream in Blanche's shuddering soprano.

The strong, though invisible, elastic that was drawing Prentiss out the house snapped and vanished. He fell backward, righted himself and darted back up the stairs.

Blanche, fairly saturated with quivering life, was backed into a corner, her arms about a weeping Jan, Junior.

On the desk was a collapsed black carapace, covering a nasty smear of pulpiness from which colorless liquid dripped.

Jan, Junior, was sobbing hysterically, 'I hit it. I hit it with my schoolbooks. It was hurting Mom.'

An hour passed and Prentiss felt the world of normality pouring back into the interstices left behind by the creature from Avalon. The elf itself was already ash in the incinerator behind the house and the only remnant of its existence was the damp stain at the foot of his desk.

Blanche was still sickly pale. They talked in whispers.

Prentiss said, 'How's Jan, Junior?'

'He's watching television.'

'Is he all right?'

'Oh, *he's* all right, but I'll be having nightmares for weeks.'

'I know. So will I unless we can get it out of our minds. I don't think there'll ever be another of those – things here.'

Blanche said, 'I can't explain how awful it was. I kept hearing every word he said, even when I was down in the living room.'

'It was telepathy, you see.'

'I just couldn't move. Then, after you left, I could begin to stir a bit. I tried to scream but all I could do was moan and whimper. Then

Jan, Junior, smashed him and all at once I was free. I don't understand how it happened.'

Prentiss felt a certain gloomy satisfaction. 'I think I know. I was under his control because I accepted the truth of his existence. He held you in check through me. When I left the room, increasing distance made it harder to use my mind as a psychic lens and you could begin moving. By the time I reached the front door, the elf thought it was time to switch from my mind to Jan, Junior's. That was his mistake.'

'In what way?' asked Blanche.

'He assumed that all children believe in fairies, but he was wrong. Here in America today children *don't* believe in fairies. They never hear of them. They believe in Tom Corbett, in Hopalong Cassidy, in Dick Tracy, in Howdy Doody, in Superman and a dozen other things, but not in fairies.

'The elf just never realized the sudden cultural changes brought about by comic books and television, and when he tried to grab Jan, Junior's mind, he couldn't. Before he could recover his psychic balance, Jan, Junior, was on top of him in a swinging panic because he thought you were being hurt and it was all over.

'It's like I've always said, Blanche. The ancient folk motifs of legend survive only in the modern fantasy magazine, and modern fantasy is purely adult fare. Do you finally see my point?'

Blanche said humbly, 'Yes, dear.'

Prentiss put his hands in his pockets and grinned slowly. 'You know, Blanche, next time I see Walt Rae, I think I'll just drop a hint that I write the stuff. Time the neighbors knew, I think.'

Jan, Junior, holding an enormous slice of buttered bread, wandered into his father's study in search of the dimming memory. Pop kept slapping him on the back and Mom kept putting bread and cake in his hands and he was forgetting why. There had been this big old thing on the desk that could talk . . .

It had all happened so quickly that it got mixed up in his mind.

He shrugged his shoulders and, in the late afternoon sunlight, looked at the partly typewritten sheet in his father's typewriter, then at the small pile of paper resting on the desk.

He read a while, curled his lip and muttered, 'Gee whiz. Fairies again. Always kid stuff!' and wandered off.

The Watery Place

We're never going to have space travel. What's more, no extraterrestrials will ever land on Earth – at least, any more.

I'm not just being a pessimist. As a matter of fact, space travel *is* possible; extraterrestrials *have* landed. I *know* that. Spaceships are crisscrossing space among a million worlds, probably, but we'll never join them. I know that, too. All on account of a ridiculous error.

I'll explain.

It was actually Bart Cameron's error and you'll have to understand about Bart Cameron. He's the sheriff at Twin Gulch, Idaho, and I'm his deputy. Bart Cameron is an impatient man and he gets most impatient when he has to work up his income tax. You see, besides being sheriff, he also owns and runs the general store, he's got some shares in a sheep ranch, he does a bit of assay work, he's got a kind of pension for being a disabled veteran (bad knee) and a few other things like that. Naturally, it makes his tax figures complicated.

It wouldn't be so bad if he'd let a tax man work on the forms with him, but he insists on doing it himself and it makes him a bitter man. By 14 April, he isn't approachable.

So it's too bad the flying saucer landed on 14 April 1956.

I saw it land. My chair was backed up against the wall in the sheriff's office, and I was looking at the stars through the windows and feeling too lazy to go back to my magazine and wondering if I ought to knock off and hit the sack or keep on listening to Cameron curse real steady as he went over his columns of figures for the hundred twenty-seventh time.

It looked like a shooting star at first, but then the track of light broadened into two things that looked like rocket exhausts and the thing came down sweet, steady and without a sound. An old, dead leaf would have rustled more coming down and landed thumpier. Two men got out.

I couldn't say anything or do anything. I couldn't choke or point; I couldn't even bug my eyes. I just sat there.

Cameron? He never looked up.

There was a knock on the door which wasn't locked. It opened and the two men from the flying saucer stepped in. I would have thought they were city fellows if I hadn't seen the flying saucer land in the scrub. They wore charcoal-gray suits, with white shirts and maroon four-in-hands. They had on black shoes and black homburgs. They had dark complexions, black wavy hair and brown eyes. They had very serious looks on their faces and were about five foot ten apiece. They looked very much alike.

God, I was scared.

But Cameron just looked up when the door opened and frowned. Ordinarily, I guess he'd have laughed the collar button off his shirt at seeing clothes like that in Twin Gulch, but he was so taken up by his income tax that he never cracked a smile.

He said, 'What can I do for you, folks?' and he tapped his hand on the forms so it was obvious he hadn't much time.

One of the two stepped forward. He said, 'We have had your people under observation a long time.' He pronounced each word carefully and all by itself.

Cameron said, 'My people? All I got's a wife. What's she been doing?'

The fellow in the suit said, 'We have chosen this locality for our first contact because it is isolated and peaceful. We know that you are the leader here.'

'I'm the sheriff, if that's what you mean, so spit it out. What's you trouble?'

'We have been careful to adopt your mode of dress and even to assume your appearance.'

'That's *my* mode of dress?' He must have noticed it for the first time.

'The mode of dress of your dominant social class, that is. We have also learned your language.'

You could see the light break in on Cameron. He said, 'You guys foreigners?' Cameron didn't go much for foreigners, never having met many outside the army, but generally he tried to be fair.

The man from the saucer said, 'Foreigners? Indeed we are. We come from the watery place your people call Venus.'

(I was just collecting up strength to blink my eyes, but that sent me right back to nothing. I had seen the flying saucer. I had seen it land. I had to believe this! These men – or these somethings – came from Venus.)

But Cameron never blinked an eye. He said, 'All right. This is the USA. We all got equal rights regardless of race, creed, color, *or* nationality. I'm at your service. What can I do for you?'

'We would like to have you make immediate arrangements for the important men of your USA, as you call it, to be brought here for discussions leading to your people joining our great organization.'

Slowly, Cameron got red. 'Our people join *your* organization. We're already part of the UN and God knows what else. And I suppose I'm to get the President here, eh? Right now? In Twin Gulch? Send a hurry-up message?' He looked at me, as though he wanted to see a smile on my face, but I couldn't as much as fall down if someone had pushed the chair out from under me.

The saucer man said, 'Speed is desirable.'

'You want Congress, too? The Supreme Court?'

'If they will help, sheriff.'

And Cameron really went to pieces. He banged his income tax form and yelled, 'Well, you're not helping me, and I have no time for wise-guy jerks who come around, especially foreigners. If you don't get the hell out of here pronto, I'll lock you up for disturbing the peace and I'll never let you out.'

'You wish us to leave?' said the man from Venus.

'Right now! Get the hell out of here and back to wherever you're from and don't ever come back. I don't want to see you and no one else around here does.'

The two men looked at each other, making little twitches with their faces.

Then the one who had done all the talking said, 'I can see in your mind that you really wish, with great intensity, to be left alone. It is not our way to force ourselves or our organization on people who do not wish us or it. We will respect your privacy and leave. We will not return. We will girdle your world in warning and none will enter and your people will never have to leave.'

Cameron said, 'Mister, I'm tired of this crap, so I'll count to three—'

They turned and left, and I just knew that everything they said was so. I was listening to them, you see, which Cameron wasn't, because he was busy thinking of his income tax, and it was as though I could hear their minds, know what I mean? I knew that there would be a kind of fence around Earth, corralling us in, keeping us from leaving, keeping others from coming in. I *knew* it.

And when they left, I got my voice back – too late. I screamed, 'Cameron, for God's sake, they're from space. Why'd you send them away?'

'From space!' He stared at me.

I yelled, 'Look!' I don't know how I did it, he being twenty-five pounds heavier than I, but I yanked him to the window by his shirt collar, busting every shirt button off him.

He was too surprised to resist and when he recovered his wits enough to make like he was going to knock me down, he caught sight of what was going on outside the window and the breath went out of *him*.

They were getting into the flying saucer, those two men, and the saucer sat there, large, round, shiny and kind of powerful, you know. Then it took off. It went up easy as a feather and a red-orange glow showed up on one side and got brighter as the ship got smaller till it was a shooting star again, slowly fading out.

And I said, 'Sheriff, why'd you send them away? They *had* to see the President. Now they'll never come back.'

Cameron said, 'I thought they were foreigners. They *said* they had to learn our language. And they talked funny.'

'Oh, fine. Foreigners.'

'They *said* they were foreigners and they looked Italian. I thought they were Italian.'

'How could they be Italian? They said they were from the planet Venus. I heard them. They said so.'

'The planet Venus.' His eyes got real round.

'They said it. They called it the watery place or something. You know Venus has a lot of water on it.'

But you see, it was just an error, a stupid error, the kind anyone could make. Only now Earth is never going to have space travel and we'll never as much as land on the moon or have another Venusian visit us. That dope, Cameron, and his income tax!

Because he whispered, 'Venus! When they talked about the watery place, I thought they meant *Venice!*'

Living Space

Clarence Rimbro had no objections to living in the only house on an uninhabited planet, any more than had any other of Earth's even trillion of inhabitants.

If someone had questioned him concerning possible objections, he would undoubtedly have stared blankly at the questioner. His house was much larger than any house could possibly be on Earth proper and much more modern. It had its independent air supply and water supply, ample food in its freezing compartments. It was isolated from the lifeless planet on which it was located by a force field, but the rooms were built about a five-acre farm (under glass, of course), which, in the planet's beneficent sunlight, grew flowers for pleasure and vegetables for health. It even supported a few chickens. It gave Mrs Rimbro something to do with herself afternoons, and a place for the two little Rimbros to play when they were tired of indoors.

Furthermore, if one *wanted* to be on Earth proper; if one insisted on it; if one *had* to have people around and air one could breathe in the open or water to swim in, one had only to go out of the front door of the house.

So where was the difficulty?

Remember, too, that on the lifeless planet on which the Rimbro house was located there was complete silence except for the occasional monotonous effects of wind and rain. There was absolute privacy and the feeling of absolute ownership of two hundred million square miles of planetary surface.

Clarence Rimbro appreciated all that in his distant way. He was an accountant, skilled in handling very advanced computer models, precise in his manners and clothing, not much given to smiling beneath his thin, well-kept mustache and properly aware of his own worth. When he drove from work toward home, he passed the occasional dwelling place on Earth proper and he never ceased to stare at them with a certain smugness.

Well, either for business reasons or mental perversion, some people simply had to live on Earth proper. It was too bad for them. After all, Earth proper's soil had to supply the minerals and basic food supply for all the trillion of inhabitants (in fifty years, it would be two trillion) and space was at a premium. Houses on Earth proper just *couldn't* be any bigger than that, and people who had to live in them had to adjust to the fact.

Even the process of entering his house had its mild pleasantness. He would enter the community twist place to which he was assigned (it looked, as did all such, like a rather stumpy obelisk), and there he would invariably find others waiting to use it. Still more would arrive before he reached the head of the line. It was a sociable time.

'How's your planet?' 'How's yours?' The usual small talk. Sometimes someone would be having trouble. Machinery breakdowns or serious weather that would alter the terrain unfavorably. Not often.

But it passed the time. Then Rimbro would be at the head of the line; he would put his key into the slot; the proper combination would be punched; and he would be twisted into a new probability pattern; his own particular probability pattern; the one assigned to him when he married and became a producing citizen; a probability pattern in which life had never developed on Earth. And twisting to this particular lifeless Earth, he would walk into his own foyer.

Just like that.

He never worried about being in another probability. Why should he? He never gave it any thought. There were an infinite number of possible Earths. Each existed in its own niche; its own probability pattern. Since on a planet such as Earth there was, according to calculation, about a fifty-fifty chance of life's developing, half of all the possible Earths (still infinite, since half of infinity was infinity) possessed life, and half (still infinite) did not. And living on about three hundred billion of the unoccupied Earths were three hundred billion families, each with its own beautiful house, powered by the sun of that probability, and each securely at peace. The number of Earths so occupied grew by millions each day.

And then one day, Rimbro came home and Sandra (his wife) said to him, as he entered, 'There's been the most peculiar noise.'

Rimbro's eyebrows shot up and he looked closely at his wife. Except for a certain restlessness of her thin hands and a pale look about the corners of her tight mouth, she looked normal.

Rimbro said, still holding his topcoat halfway toward the servette that waited patiently for it, 'Noise? What noise? I don't hear anything.'

'It's stopped now,' Sandra said. 'Really, it was like a deep thumping or rumble. You'd hear it a bit. Then it would stop. Then you'd hear it a bit and so on. I've never heard anything like it.'

Rimbro surrendered his coat. 'But that's quite impossible.'

'I *heard* it.'

'I'll look over the machinery,' he mumbled. 'Something may be wrong.'

Nothing was, that his accountant's eyes could discover, and, with a shrug, he went to supper. He listened to the servettes hum busily about their different chores, watched one sweep up the plates and cutlery for disposal and recovery, then said, pursing his lips, 'Maybe one of the servettes is out of order. I'll check them.'

'It wasn't anything like that, Clarence.'

Rimbro went to bed, without further concern over the matter, and wakened with his wife's hand clutching his shoulder. His hand went automatically to the contact patch that set the walls glowing. 'What's the matter? What time is it?'

She shook her head. 'Listen! *Listen!*'

Good Lord, thought Rimbro, there *is* a noise. A definite rumbling. It came and went.

'Earthquake?' he whispered. It did happen, of course, though, with all the planet to choose from, they could generally count on having avoided the faulted areas.

'All day long?' asked Sandra fretfully. 'I think it's something else.' And then she voiced the secret terror of every nervous householder. 'I think there's someone on the planet with us. This Earth is *inhabited*.'

Rimbro did the logical things. When morning came, he took his wife and children to his wife's mother. He himself took a day off and hurried to the Sector's Housing Bureau.

He was quite annoyed at all his.

Bill Ching of the Housing Bureau was short, jovial and proud of his part Mongolian ancestry. He thought probability patterns had solved every last one of humanity's problems. Alec Mishnoff, also of the Housing Bureau, thought probability patterns were a snare into which humanity had been hopelessly tempted. He had originally majored in archeology and had studied a variety of antiquarian subjects with which his delicately poised head was still crammed. His face managed to look sensitive despite overbearing eyebrows, and he lived with a pet notion that so far he had dared tell no one, though preoccupation with it had driven him out of archeology and into housing.

Ching was fond of saying, 'The hell with Malthus!' It was almost a verbal trademark of his. 'The hell with Malthus. We can't possibly overpopulate now. However frequently we double and redouble, Homo sapiens remains finite in number, and the uninhabited Earths remain infinite. And we don't have to put one house on each planet. We can put a hundred, a thousand, a million. Plenty of room and plenty of power from each probability sun.'

'More than one on a planet?' said Mishnoff sourly.

Ching knew exactly what he meant. When probability patterns had first been put to use, sole ownership of a planet had been powerful inducement for early settlers. It appealed to the snob and despot in every one. What man so poor, ran the slogan, as not to have an empire larger than Genghis Khan's? To introduce multiple settling now would outrage everyone.

Ching said, with a shrug, 'All right, it would take psychological preparation. So what? That's what it took to start the whole deal in the first place.'

'And food?' asked Mishnoff.

'You know we're putting hydroponic works and yeast plants in other probability patterns. And if we had to, we could cultivate their soil.'

'Wearing space-suits and importing oxygen.'

'We could reduce carbon dioxide for oxygen till the plants got going and they'd do the job after that.'

'Given a million years.'

'Mishnoff, the trouble with you,' Ching said, 'is you read too many ancient history books. You're an obstructionist.'

But Ching was too good-natured really to mean that, and Mishnoff continued to read books and to worry. Mishnoff longed for the day he could get up the courage necessary to see the Head of the Section and put right out in plain view – bang, like that – exactly what it was that was troubling him.

But now, a Mr Clarence Rimbro faced them, perspiring slightly and toweringly angry at the fact that it had taken him the better part of two days to reach this far into the Bureau.

He reached his exposition's climax by saying, 'And *I* say the planet is inhabited and I don't propose to stand for it.'

Having listened to his story in full, Ching tried the soothing approach. He said, 'Noise like that is probably just some natural phenomenon.'

'What kind of natural phenomenon?' demanded Rimbro. 'I want an investigation. If it's a natural phenomenon, I want to know what kind. I say the place is inhabited. It has life on it, by Heaven, and I'm not paying rent on a planet to share it. And with dinosaurs, from the sound of it.'

'Come, Mr Rimbro, how long have you lived on your Earth?'

'Fifteen and a half years.'

'And has there ever been any evidence of life?'

'There is now, and, as a citizen with a production record classified as A-1, I demand an investigation.'

'Of course we'll investigate, sir, but we just want to assure you now that everything is all right. Do you realize how carefully we select our probability patterns?'

'I'm an accountant. I have a pretty good idea,' said Rimbro at once.

'Then surely you know our computers cannot fail us. They never pick a probability which has been picked before. They can't possibly. And they're geared to select only probability patterns in which Earth has a carbon dioxide atmosphere, one in which plant life, and therefore animal life, has never developed. Because if plants had evolved, the carbon dioxide would have been reduced to oxygen. Do you understand?'

'I understand it all very well and I'm not here for lectures,' said Rimbro. 'I want an investigation out of you and nothing else. It is quite humiliating to think I may be sharing my world, my own world, with something or other, and I don't propose to endure it.'

'No, of course not,' muttered Ching, avoiding Mishnoff's sardonic glance. 'We'll be there before night.'

They were on their way to the twisting place with full equipment.

Mishnoff said, 'I want to ask you something. Why do you go through that "There's no need to worry, sir" routine? They always worry anyway. Where does it get you?'

'I've got to try. They *shouldn't* worry,' said Ching petulantly. 'Ever hear of a carbon dioxide planet that *was* inhabited? Besides, Rimbro is the type that starts rumors. I can spot them. By the time he's through, if he's encouraged, he'll say his sun went nova.'

'*That* happens sometimes,' said Mishnoff.

'So? One house is wiped out and one family dies. See, you're an obstructionist. In the old times, the times you like, if there were a flood in China or someplace, thousands of people would die. And that's out of a population of a measly billion or two.'

Mishnoff muttered, 'How do you know the Rimbro planet doesn't have life on it?'

'Carbon dioxide atmosphere.'

'But suppose—' It was no use. Mishnoff couldn't say it. He finished lamely, 'Suppose plant and animal life develops that can live on carbon dioxide.'

'It's never been observed.'

'In an infinite number of worlds, anything can happen.' He finished that in a whisper. 'Everything *must* happen.'

'Chances are one in a duodecillion,' said Ching, shrugging.

They arrived at the twisting point then, and, having utilized the freight twist for their vehicle (thus sending it into the Rimbro storage area), they entered the Rimbro probability pattern themselves. First Ching, then Mishnoff.

'A nice house,' said Ching, with satisfaction. 'Very nice model. Good taste.'

'Hear anything?' asked Mishnoff.

'No.'

Ching wandered into the garden. 'Hey,' he yelled. 'Rhode Island Reds.'

Mishnoff followed, looking up at the glass roof. The sun looked like the sun of a trillion other Earths.

He said absently, 'There could be plant life, just starting out. The carbon dioxide might just be starting to drop in concentration. The computer would never know.'

'And it would take millions of years for animal life to begin and millions more for it to come out of the sea.'

'It doesn't have to follow that pattern.'

Ching put an arm about his partner's shoulder. 'You brood. Someday, you'll tell me what's really bothering you, instead of just hinting, and we can straighten you out.'

Mishnoff shrugged off the encircling arm with an annoyed frown. Ching's tolerance was always hard to bear. He began, 'Let's not psychotherapize—' He broke off, then whispered, 'Listen.'

There was a distant rumble. Again.

They placed the seismograph in the center of the room and activated the force field that penetrated downward and bound it rigidly to bedrock. They watched the quivering needle record the shocks.

Mishnoff said, 'Surface waves only. Very superficial. It's not underground.'

Ching looked a little more dismal, 'What is it then?'

'I think,' said Mishnoff, 'we'd better find out.' His face was gray with apprehension. 'We'll have to set up a seismograph at another point and get a fix on the focus of the disturbance.'

'Obviously,' said Ching. 'I'll go out with the other seismograph. You stay here.'

'No,' said Mishnoff, with energy. 'I'll go out.'

Mishnoff felt terrified, but he had no choice. If this were *it*, he would be prepared. He could get a warning through. Sending out an unsuspecting Ching would be disastrous. Nor could he warn Ching, who would certainly never believe him.

But since Mishnoff was not cast in the heroic mold, he trembled as he got into his oxygen suit and fumbled the disrupter as he tried to dissolve the force field locally in order to free the emergency exit.

'Any reason *you* want to go, particularly?' asked Ching, watching the other's inept manipulations. 'I'm willing.'

'It's all right. I'm going out,' said Mishnoff, out of a dry throat, and stepped into the lock that led out onto the desolate surface of a lifeless Earth. A presumably lifeless Earth.

The sight was not unfamiliar to Mishnoff. He had seen its like dozens of times. Bare rock, weathered by wind and rain, crusted and powdered with sand in the gullies; a small and noisy brook beating itself against its stony course. All brown and gray; no sign of green. No sound of life.

Yet the sun was the same and, when night fell, the constellations would be the same.

The situation of the dwelling place was in that region which on Earth proper would be called Labrador. (It was Labrador here, too, really. It had been calculated that in not more than one out of a quadrillion or so Earths were there significant changes in the geological development. The continents were everywhere recognizable down to quite small details.)

Despite the situation and the time of the year, which was October, the temperature was sticky warm due to the hothouse effect of the carbon dioxide in this Earth's dead atmosphere.

From inside his suit, through the transparent visor, Mishnoff watched it all somberly. If the epicenter of the noise were close by, adjusting the second seismograph a mile or so away would be enough for the fix. If it weren't, they would have to bring in an air scooter. Well, assume the lesser complication to begin with.

Methodically, he made his way up a rocky hillside. Once at the top, he could choose his spot.

Once at the top, pufffing and feeling the heat most unpleasantly, he found he didn't have to.

His heart was pounding so that he could scarcely hear his own voice as he yelled into his radio mouthpiece, 'Hey, Ching, there's construction going on.'

'What?' came back the appalled shout in his ears.

There was no mistake. Ground was being leveled. Machinery was at work. Rock was being blasted out.

Mishnoff shouted, 'They're blasting. That's the noise.'

Ching called back, 'But it's impossible. The computer would never pick the same probability pattern twice. *It couldn't.*'

'You don't understand—' began Mishnoff.

But Ching was following his own thought processes. 'Get over there, Mishnoff. I'm coming out, too.'

'No, damn it. You stay there,' cried Mishnoff in alarm. 'Keep me in radio contact, and for God's sake be ready to leave for Earth proper on wings if I give the word.'

'Why?' demanded Ching. 'What's going on?'

'I don't know yet,' said Mishnoff. 'Give me a chance to find out.'

To his own surprise, he noticed his teeth were chattering.

Muttering breathless curses at the computer, at probability patterns and at the insatiable need for living space on the part of a trillion human beings expanding in numbers like a puff of smoke, Mishnoff slithered and slipped down the other side of the slope, setting stones to rolling and rousing peculiar echoes.

A man came out to meet him, dressed in a gas-tight suit, different in many details from Mishnoff's own, but obviously intended for the same purpose – to lead oxygen to the lungs.

Mishnoff gasped breathlessly into his mouthpiece, 'Hold it, Ching. There's a man coming. Keep in touch.' Mishnoff felt his heart pump more easily and the bellows of his lungs labor less.

The two men were staring at one another. The other man was blond and craggy of face. The look of surprise about him was too extreme to be feigned.

He said in a harsh voice, '*Wer sind Sie? Was machen Sie hier?*'

Mishnoff was thunderstruck. He'd studied ancient German for two years in the days when he expected to be an archeologist and he followed the comment despite the fact that the pronunciation was not what he had been taught. The stranger was asking his identity and his business there.

Stupidly, Mishnoff stammered, '*Sprechen Sie Deutsch?*' and then had to mutter reassurance to Ching whose agitated voice in his earpiece was demanding to know what the gibberish was all about.

The German-speaking one made no direct answer. He repeated, '*Wer sind Sie?*' and added impatiently, '*Hier ist für ein verrückten Spass keine Zeit.*'

Mishnoff didn't feel like a joke either, particularly not a foolish one, but he continued, '*Sprechen Sie Planetisch?*'

He did not know the German for 'Planetary Standard Language' so he had to guess. Too late, he thought he should have referred to it simply as English.

The other man stared wide-eyed at him. '*Sind Sie wahnsinnig?*'

Mishnoff was almost willing to settle for that, but in feeble self-defense, he said, 'I'm not crazy, damn it. I mean, *Auf der Erde woher Sie gekom—*'

He gave it up for lack of German, but the new idea that was rattling inside his skull would not quit its nagging. He had to find some way of testing it. He said desperately, '*Welches Jahr ist es jetzt?*'

Presumably, the stranger, who was questioning his sanity already, would be convinced of Mishnoff's insanity now that he was being asked what year it was, but it was one question for which Mishnoff had the necessary German.

The other muttered something that sounded suspiciously like good German swearing and then said, '*Es ist doch zwei tausend drei hundert vier und-sechzig, und warum—*'

The stream of German that followed was completely incomprehensible to Mishnoff, but in any case he had had enough for the moment. If he translated the German correctly, the year given him was 2364, which was nearly two thousand years in the past. How could that be?

He muttered, '*Zwei tausend drei hundert vier-und-sechzig?*'

'*Ja, Ja,*' said the other, with deep sarcasm. '*Zwei tausend drei hundert vier-und-sechzig. Der ganze Jahr fang ist es so gewesen.*'

Mishnoff shrugged. The statement that it had been so all year long was a feeble witticism even in German and it gained nothing in translation. He pondered.

But then the other's ironical tone deepening, the German-speaking one went on, '*Zwei tausend drei hundert vier-und-sechzig nach Hitler. Hilft das Ihnen vielleicht? Nach Hitler!*'

Mishnoff yelled with delight. 'That *does* help me. *Es hilft! Hören Sie, bitte—*' He went on in broken German interspersed with scraps of Planetary, 'For Heaven's sake, *um Gottes Willen—*'

Making it 2364 after Hitler was different altogether.

He put German together desperately, trying to explain.

The other frowned and grew thoughtful. He lifted his gloved hand to stroke his chin or make some equivalent gesture, hit the transparent visor that covered his face and left his hand there uselessly, while he thought.

He said, suddenly, '*Ich heiss George Fallenby.*'

To Mishnoff it seemed that the name must be of Anglo-Saxon derivation, although the change in vowel form as pronounced by the other made it seem Teutonic.

'*Guten Tag,*' said Mishnoff awkwardly. '*Ich heiss Alec Mishnoff,*' and was suddenly aware of the Slavic derivation of his own name.

'*Kommen Sie mit mir, Herr Mishnoff,*' said Fallenby.

Mishnoff followed with a strained smile, muttering into his transmitter, 'It's all right, Ching. It's all right.'

Back on Earth proper, Mishnoff faced the Sector's Bureau Head, who had grown old in the Service; whose every gray hair betokened a problem met and solved; and every missing hair a problem averted. He was a cautious man with eyes still bright and teeth that were still his own. His name was Berg.

He shook his head. 'And they speak German: but the German you studied was two thousand years old.'

'True,' said Mishnoff. 'But the English Hemingway used is two thousand years old and Planetary is close enough for anyone to be able to read it.'

'Hmp. And who's this Hitler?'

'He was a sort of tribal chief in ancient times. He led the German tribe in one of the wars of the twentieth century, just about the time the Atomic Age started and true history began.'

'Before the Devastation, you mean?'

'Right. There was a series of wars then. The Anglo-Saxon countries won out, and I suppose that's why the Earth speaks Planetary.'

'And if Hitler and his Germans had won out, the world would speak German instead?'

'They *have* won out on Fallenby's Earth, sir, and they *do* speak German.'

'And make their dates "after Hitler" instead of AD?'

'Right. And I suppose there's an Earth in which the Slavic tribes won out and everyone speaks Russian.'

'Somehow,' said Berg, 'it seems to me we should have foreseen it, and yet, as far as I know, no one has. After all, there are an infinite number of inhabited Earths, and we can't be the only one that has decided to solve the problem of unlimited population growth by expanding into the worlds of probability.'

'Exactly,' said Mishnoff earnestly, 'and it seems to me that if you think of it, there must be countless inhabited Earths so doing and there must be many multiple occupations in the three hundred billion Earths we ourselves occupy. The only reason we caught this one is that, by sheer chance, they decided to build within a mile of the dwelling we had placed there. This is something we must check.'

'You imply we ought to search all our Earths.'

'I do, sir. We've got to make some settlement with other inhabited Earths. After all, there is room for all of us and to expand without agreement may result in all sorts of trouble and conflict.'

'Yes,' said Berg thoughtfully. 'I agree with you.'

Clarence Rimbro stared suspiciously at Berg's old face, creased now into all manner of benevolence.

'You're sure now?'

'Absolutely,' said the Bureau Head. 'We're sorry that you've had to accept temporary quarters for the last two weeks—'

'More like three.'

'—three weeks, but you will be compensated.'

'What was the noise?'

'Purely geological, sir. A rock was delicately balanced and, with the wind, it made occasional contact with the rocks of the hillside. We've removed it and surveyed the area to make certain that nothing similar will occur again.'

Rimbro clutched his hat and said, 'Well, thanks for your trouble.'

'No thanks necessary, I assure you, Mr Rimbro. This is our job.'

Rimbro was ushered out, and Berg turned to Mishnoff, who had remained a quiet spectator of this completion of the Rimbro affair.

Berg said, 'The Germans were nice about it, anyway. They admitted we had priority and got off. Room for everybody, they said. Of course, as it turned out, they build any number of dwellings on each unoccupied world . . . And now there's the project of surveying our other worlds and making similar agreements with whomever we find. It's all strictly confidential, too. It can't be made known to the populace without plenty of preparation . . . Still, none of this is what I want to speak to you about.'

'Oh?' said Mishnoff. Developments had not noticeably cheered him. His own bogey still concerned him.

Berg smiled at the younger man. 'You understand, Mishnoff, we in the Bureau, and in the Planetary Government, too, are very appreciative of your quick thinking, of your understanding of the situation. This could have developed into something very tragic, had it not been for you. This appreciation will take some tangible form.'

'Thank you, sir.'

'But, as I said once before, this is something many of us should have thought of. How is it you did? . . . Now we've gone into your background a little. Your co-worker, Ching, tells us you have hinted in the past at some serious danger involved in our probability-pattern setup, and that you insisted on going out to meet the

Germans although you were obviously frightened. You were anticipating what you actually found, were you not? And how did you do it?'

Mishnoff said confusedly, 'No, no. That was not in my mind at all. It came as a surprise. I—'

Suddenly he stiffened. Why not now? They were grateful to him. He had proved that he was a man to be taken into account. One unexpected thing had already happened.

He said firmly, 'There's something else.'

'Yes?'

(How did one begin?) 'There's no life in the Solar System other than the life on Earth.'

'That's right,' said Berg benevolently.

'And computation has it that the probability of developing any form of interstellar travel is so low as to be infinitesimal.'

'What are you getting at?'

'That all this is so in this *probability!* But there must be some probability patterns in which other life *does* exist in the Solar System or in which interstellar drives *are* developed by dwellers in other star systems.'

Berg frowned. 'Theoretically.'

'In one of these probabilities, Earth may be visited by such intelligences. If it were a probability pattern in which Earth is inhabited, it won't affect us; they'll have no connection with us in Earth proper. But if it were a probability pattern in which Earth is uninhabited and they set up some sort of a base, they may find, by happenstance, one of our dwelling places.'

'Why ours?' demanded Berg dryly. 'What not a dwelling place of the Germans, for instance?'

'Because we spot our dwellings one to a world. The German Earth doesn't. Probably very few others do. The odds are in favor of us by billions to one. And if extraterrestrials do find such a dwelling, they'll investigate and find the route to Earth proper, a highly developed, rich world.'

'Not if we turn off the twisting place,' said Berg.

'Once they know that twisting places exist, they can construct their own,' said Mishnoff. 'A race intelligent enough to travel through space could do that, and from the equipment in the dwelling they would take over, they could easily spot our particular probability . . . And then how would we handle extraterrestrials? They're not Germans, or other Earths. They would have alien psychologies and motivations. And we're not even on our guard. We just keep setting up more and more worlds and increasing the chance every day that—'

His voice had risen in excitement and Berg shouted at him, 'Nonsense. This is all ridiculous—'

The buzzer sounded and the communiplate brightened and showed the face of Ching. Ching's voice said, 'I'm sorry to interrupt, but—'

'What is it?' demanded Berg savagely.

'There's a man here I don't know what to do with. He's drunk or crazy. He complains that his home is surrounded and that there are things staring through the glass roof of his garden.'

'Things?' cried Mishnoff.

'Purple things with big red veins, three eyes and some sort of tentacles instead of hair. They have—'

But Mishnoff and Berg didn't hear the rest. They were staring at each other in sick horror.

The Message

They drank beer and reminisced as men will who have met after long separation. They called to mind the days under fire. They remembered sergeants and girls, both with exaggeration. Deadly things became humorous in retrospect, and trifles disregarded for ten years were hauled out for airing.

Including, of course, the perennial mystery.

'How do you account for it?' asked the first. 'Who started it?'

The second shrugged. 'No one started it. Everyone was doing it, like a disease. You, too, I suppose.'

The first chuckled.

The third one said softly, 'I never saw the fun in it. Maybe because I came across it first when I was under fire for the first time. North Africa.'

'Really?' said the second.

'The first night on the beaches of Oran. I was getting under cover, making for some native shack and I saw it in the light of a flare—'

George was deliriously happy. Two years of red tape and now he was finally back in the past. Now he could complete his paper on the social life of the foot soldier of World War II with some authentic details.

Out of the warless, insipid society of the thirtieth century, he found himself for one glorious moment in the tense, superlative drama of the warlike twentieth.

North Africa! Site of the first great sea-borne invasion of the war! How the temporal physicists had scanned the area for the perfect spot and moment. This shadow of an empty wooden building was it. No human would approach for a known number of minutes. No blast would seriously affect it in that time. By being there, George would not affect history. He would be that ideal of the temporal physicist, the 'pure observer.'

It was even more terrific than he had imagined. There was the perpetual roar of artillery, the unseen tearing of planes overhead. There were the periodic lines of tracer bullets splitting the sky and the occasional ghastly glow of a flare twisting downward.

And *he* was here! He, George, was part of the war, part of an intense kind of life forever gone from the world of the thirtieth century, grown tame and gentle.

He imagined he could see the shadows of an advancing column of soldiers, hear the low cautious monosyllables slip from one to another. How he longed to be one of them in truth, not merely a momentary intruder, a 'pure observer.'

He stopped his note taking and stared at his stylus, its micro-light hypnotizing him for a moment. A sudden idea had overwhelmed him and he looked at the wood against which his shoulder pressed. This moment must not pass unforgotten into history. Surely doing this would affect nothing. He would use the older English dialect and there would be no suspicion.

He did it quickly and then spied a soldier running desperately toward the structure, dodging a burst of bullets. George knew his time was up, and, even as he knew it, found himself back in the thirtieth century.

It didn't matter. For those few minutes he had been part of World

War II. A small part, but *part*. And others would know it. They might not know they knew it, but someone perhaps would repeat the message to himself.

Someone, perhaps that man running for shelter, would read it and know that along with all the heroes of the twentieth century was the 'pure observer,' the man from the thirtieth century, George Kilroy. *He* was there!

Satisfaction Guaranteed

Tony was tall and darkly handsome, with an incredibly patrician air drawn into every line of his unchangeable expression, and Claire Belmont regarded him through the crack in the door with a mixture of horror and dismay.

'I can't, Larry. I just can't have him in the house.' Feverishly, she was searching her paralyzed mind for a stronger way of putting it; some way that would make sense and settle things, but she could only end with a simple repetition.

'Well, I can't!'

Larry Belmont regarded his wife stiffly, and there was that spark of impatience in his eyes that Claire hated to see, since she felt her own incompetence mirrored in it. 'We're committed, Claire,' he said, 'and I can't have you backing out now. The company is sending me to Washington on this basis, and it probably means a promotion. It's perfectly safe and you know it. What's your objection?'

She frowned helplessly. 'It just gives me the chills. I couldn't bear him.'

'He's as human as you or I, almost. So, no nonsense. Come, get out there.'

His hand was in the small of her back, shoving; and she found herself in her own living room, shivering. *It* was there, looking at her with a precise politeness, as though appraising his hostess-to-be of the next three weeks. Dr Susan Calvin was there, too, sitting stiffly in thin-lipped abstraction. She had the cold, faraway look of someone who has worked with machines so long that a little of the steel had entered the blood.

'Hello,' crackled Claire in general, and ineffectual, greeting.

But Larry was busily saving the situation with a spurious gaiety. 'Here, Claire, I want you to meet Tony, a swell guy. This is my wife, Claire, Tony, old boy.' Larry's hand draped itself amiably over Tony's shoulder, but Tony remained unresponsive and expressionless under the pressure.

He said, 'How do you do, Mrs Belmont.'

And Claire jumped at Tony's voice. It was deep and mellow, smooth as the hair on his head or the skin on his face.

Before she could stop herself, she said, 'Oh, my – you talk.'

'Why not? Did you expect that I didn't?'

But Claire could only smile weakly. She didn't really know what she had expected. She looked away, then let him slide gently into the corner of her eye. His hair was smooth and black, like polished plastic – or was it really composed of separate hairs? And was the even, olive skin of his hands and face continued on past the obscurement of his formally cut clothing?

She was lost in the shuddering wonder of it, and had to force her thoughts back into place to meet Dr Calvin's flat, unemotional voice.

'Mrs Belmont, I hope you appreciate the importance of this experiment. Your husband tells me he has given you some of the background. I would like to give you more, as the senior psychologist of the US Robots and Mechanical Men Corporation.

'Tony is a robot. His actual designation on the company files is TN-3, but he will answer to Tony. He is not a mechanical monster, nor simply a calculating machine of the type that were developed during World War II, fifty years ago. He has an artificial brain nearly as complicated as our own. It is an immense telephone switchboard on an atomic scale, so that billions of possible "telephone connections" can be compressed into an instrument that will fit inside a skull.

'Such brains are manufactured for each model of robot specifically. Each contains a precalculated set of connections so that each robot knows the English language to start with and enough of anything else that may be necessary to perform his job.

'Until now, US Robots has confined its manufacturing activity to industrial models for use in places where human labor is impractical — in deep mines, for instance, or in underwater work. But we want to invade the city and the home. To do so, we must get the ordinary man and woman to accept these robots without fear. You understand that there is nothing to fear.'

'There isn't, Claire,' interposed Larry earnestly. 'Take my word for it. It's impossible for him to do any harm. You know I wouldn't leave him with you otherwise.'

Claire cast a quick, secret glance at Tony and lowered her voice. 'What if I make him angry?'

'You needn't whisper,' said Dr Calvin calmly. 'He *can't* get angry with you, my dear. I told you that the switchboard connections of his brain were predetermined. Well, the most important connection of all is what we call "The First Law of Robotics", and it is merely this: "No robot can harm a human being, or, through inaction, allow a human being to come to harm." All robots are built so. No robot can be forced in any way to do harm to any human. So, you see, we need you and Tony as a preliminary experiment for our own guidance, while your husband is in Washington to arrange for government-supervised legal tests.'

'You mean all this isn't legal?'

Larry cleared his throat. 'Not just yet, but it's all right. He won't leave the house, and you mustn't let anyone see him. That's all . . . And, Claire, I'd stay with you, but I know too much about the robots. We must have a completely inexperienced tester so that we can have severe conditions. It's necessary.'

'Oh, well,' muttered Claire. Then, as a thought struck her, 'But what does he do?'

'Housework,' said Dr Calvin shortly.

She got up to leave, and it was Larry who saw her to the front door. Claire stayed behind drearily. She caught a glimpse of herself in the mirror above the mantelpiece, and looked away hastily. She was very tired of her small, mousy face and her dim, unimaginative hair. Then she caught Tony's eyes upon her and almost smiled before she remembered . . .

He was only a machine.

Larry Belmont was on his way to the airport when he caught a glimpse of Gladys Claffern. She was the type of woman who seemed made to be seen in glimpses . . . Perfectly and precisely manufactured; dressed with thoughtful hand and eye; too gleaming to be stared at.

The little smile that preceded her and the faint scent that trailed her were a pair of beckoning fingers. Larry felt his stride break; he touched his hat, then hurried on.

As always he felt that vague anger. If Claire could only push her way into the Claffern clique, it would help so much. But what was the use.

Claire! The few times she had come face to face with Gladys, the little fool had been tongue-tied. He had no illusions. The testing of Tony was his big chance, and it was in Claire's hands. How much safer it would be in the hands of someone like Gladys Claffern.

Claire woke the second morning to the sound of a subdued knock on the bedroom door. Her mind clamored, then went icy. She had avoided Tony the first day, smiling thinly when she met him and brushing past with a wordless sound of apology.

'Is that you – Tony?'

'Yes, Mrs Belmont. May I enter?'

She must have said yes, because he was in the room, quite suddenly, and noiselessly. Her eyes and nose were simultaneously aware of the tray he was carrying.

'Breakfast?' she said.

'If you please.'

She wouldn't have dared to refuse, so she pushed herself slowly into a sitting position and received it: poached eggs, buttered toast, coffee.

'I have brought the sugar and cream separately,' said Tony. 'I expect to learn your preference with time, in this and in other things.'

She waited.

Tony, standing there straight and pliant as a metal rule, asked, after a moment, 'Would you prefer to eat in privacy?'

'Yes . . . I mean, if you don't mind.'

'Will you need help later in dressing?'

'Oh, my, no!' She clutched frantically at the sheet, so that the coffee hovered at the edge of catastrophe. She remained so, in rigor, then sank helplessly back against the pillow when the door closed him out of her sight again.

She got through breakfast somehow . . . He was only a machine, and if it were only more visible that he were it wouldn't be so frightening. Or if his expression would change. It just stayed there, nailed on. You couldn't tell what went on behind those dark eyes and that smooth, olive skin-stuff. The coffee cup beat a faint castanet for a moment as she set it back, empty, on the tray.

Then she realized that she had forgotten to add the sugar and cream after all, and she did so hate black coffee.

She burned a straight path from bedroom to kitchen after dressing. It was her house, after all, and there wasn't anything frippy about her, but she liked her kitchen clean. He should have waited for supervision . . .

But when she entered, she found a kitchen that might have been minted fire-new from the factory the moment before.

She stopped, stared, turned on her heel and nearly ran into Tony. She yelped.

'May I help?' he asked.

'Tony,' and she scraped the anger off the edges of her mind's panic, 'you must make some noise when you walk. I can't have you stalking me, you know . . . Didn't you use this kitchen?'

'I did, Mrs Belmont.'

'It doesn't look it.'

'I cleaned up afterward. Isn't that customary?'

Claire opened her eyes wide. After all, what could one say to that. She opened the oven compartment that held the pots, took a quick, unseeing look at the metallic glitter inside, then said with a tremor, 'Very good. Quite satisfactory.'

If at the moment, he had beamed; if he had smiled; if he had quirked the corner of his mouth the slightest bit, she felt that she could have warmed to him. But he remained an English lord in repose, as he said, 'Thank you, Mrs Belmont. Would you come into the living room?'

She did, and it struck her at once. 'Have you been polishing the furniture?'

'Is it satisfactory, Mrs Belmont?'

'But when? You didn't do it yesterday.'

'Last night, of course.'

'You burned the lights all night?'

'Oh, no. That wouldn't have been necessary. I've a built-in ultra-violet source. I can see in ultraviolet. And, of course, I don't require sleep.'

He did require admiration, though. She realized that, then. He had to know that he was pleasing her. But she couldn't bring herself to supply that pleasure for him.

She could only say sourly, 'Your kind will put ordinary house-workers out of business.'

'There is work of much greater importance they can be put to in the world, once they are freed of drudgery. After all, Mrs Belmont, things like myself can be manufactured. But nothing yet can imitate the creativity and versatility of a human brain, like yours.'

And though his face gave no hint, his voice was warmly surcharged with awe and admiration, so that Claire flushed and muttered, 'My brain! You can have it.'

Tony approached a little and said, 'You must be unhappy to say such a thing. Is there anything I can do?'

For a moment, Claire felt like laughing. It *was* a ridiculous situation. Here was an animated carpet-sweeper, dishwasher, furniture-polisher, general factotum, rising from the factory table – and offering his services as consoler and confidant.

Yet she said suddenly, in a burst of woe and voice, 'Mr Belmont doesn't think I have a brain, if you must know . . . And I suppose I haven't.' She couldn't cry in front of him. She felt, for some reason, that she had the honor of the human race to support against this mere creation.

'It's lately,' she added. 'It was all right when he was a student; when he was just starting. But I can't be a big man's wife; and he's getting to be a big man. He wants me to be a hostess and an entry into social life for him – like G – guh – guh – Gladys Claffern.'

Her nose was red, and she looked away.

But Tony wasn't watching her. His eyes wandered about the room. 'I can help you run the house.'

'But it's no good,' she said fiercely. 'It needs a touch I can't give it. I can only make it comfortable; I can't ever make it the kind they take pictures of for the *Home Beautiful* magazines.'

'Do you want that kind?'

'Does it do any good – wanting?'

Tony's eyes were on her, full. 'I could help.'

'Do you know anything about interior decoration?'

'Is it something a good housekeeper should know?'

'Oh, yes.'

'Then I have the potentialities of learning it. Can you get me books on the subject?'

Something started then.

*

Claire, clutching her hat against the brawling liberties of the wind, had manipulated two fat volumes on the home arts back from the public library. She watched Tony as he opened one of them and flipped the pages. It was the first time she had watched his fingers flicker at anything like fine work.

I don't see how they do it, she thought, and on a sudden impulse reached for his hand and pulled it toward herself. Tony did not resist, but let it lie limp for inspection.

She said, 'It's remarkable. Even your fingernails look natural.'

'That's deliberate, of course,' said Tony. Then, chattily, 'The skin is a flexible plastic, and the skeletal framework is a light metal alloy. Does that amuse you?'

'Oh, no.' She lifted her reddened face. 'I just feel a little embarrassed at sort of poking into your insides. It's none of my business. You don't ask me about mine.'

'My brain paths don't include that type of curiosity. I can only act within my limitations, you know.'

And Claire felt something tighten inside her in the silence that followed. Why did she keep forgetting he was a machine? Now the thing itself had to remind her. Was she so starved for sympathy that she would even accept a robot as equal – because he sympathized?

She noticed Tony was still flipping the pages – almost helplessly – and there was a quick, shooting sense of relieved superiority within her. 'You can't read, can you?'

Tony looked up at her; his voice calm, unreproachful. 'I *am* reading, Mrs Belmont.'

'But—' She pointed at the book in a meaningless gesture.

'I am scanning the pages, if that's what you mean. My sense of reading is photographic.'

It was evening then, and when Claire eventually went to bed Tony was well into the second volume, sitting there in the dark, or what seemed dark to Claire's limited eyes.

Her last thought, the one that clamored at her just as her mind let go and tumbled, was a queer one. She remembered his hand again; the touch of it. It had been warm and soft, like a human being's.

How clever of the factory, she thought, and softly ebbed to sleep.

It was the library continuously, thereafter, for several days. Tony suggested the fields of study, which branched out quickly. There were books on color matching and on cosmetics; on carpentry and on fashions; on art and on the history of costumes.

He turned the pages of each book before his solemn eyes, and, as quickly as he turned, he read; nor did he seem capable of forgetting.

Before the end of the week, he had insisted on cutting her hair, introducing her to a new method of arranging it, adjusting her eyebrow line a bit and changing the shade of her powder and lipstick.

She had palpitated in nervous dread for half an hour under the delicate touch of his inhuman fingers and then looked in the mirror.

'There is more that can be done,' said Tony, 'especially in clothes. How do you find it for a beginning?'

And she hadn't answered; not for quite a while. Not until she had absorbed the identity of the stranger in the glass and cooled the wonder at the beauty of it all. Then she had said chokingly, never once taking her eyes from the warming image, 'Yes, Tony, quite good – for a beginning.'

She said nothing of this in her letters to Larry. Let him see it all at once. And something in her realized that it wasn't only the surprise she would enjoy. It was going to be a kind of revenge.

Tony said one morning, 'It's time to start buying, and I'm not allowed to leave the house. If I write out exactly what we must have, can I trust you to get it? We need drapery, and furniture fabric, wallpaper, carpeting, paint, clothing – and any number of small things.'

'You can't get these things to your own specifications at a stroke's notice,' said Claire doubtfully.

'You can get fairly close, if you go through the city and if money is no object.'

'But, Tony, money is certainly an object.'

'Not at all. Stop off at US Robots in the first place. I'll write a note for you. You see Dr Calvin, and tell her that I said it was part of the experiment.'

Dr Calvin, somehow, didn't frighten her as on that first evening. With her new face and a new hat, she couldn't be quite the old Claire. The psychologist listened carefully, asked a few questions, nodded – and then Claire found herself walking out, armed with an unlimited charge account against the assets of US Robots and Mechanical Men Corporation.

It is wonderful what money will do. With a store's contents at her feet, a saleslady's dictum was not necessarily a voice from above; the uplifted eyebrow of a decorator was not anything like Jove's thunder.

And once, when an Exalted Plumpness at one of the most lordly of the garment salons had insistently poohed her description of the wardrobe she must have with counter-pronouncements in accents of the purest Fifty-seventh Street French, she called up Tony, then held the phone out to Monsieur.

'If you don't mind' – voice firm, but fingers twisting a bit – 'I'd like you to talk to my – uh – secretary.'

Pudgy proceeded to the phone with a solemn arm crooked behind his back. He lifted the phone in two fingers and said delicately, 'Yes.' A short pause, another 'Yes,' then a much longer pause, a squeaky beginning of an objection that perished quickly, another pause, a very meek 'Yes,' and the phone was restored to its cradle.

'If Madam will come with me,' he said, hurt and distant, 'I will try to supply her needs.'

'Just a second.' Claire rushed back to the phone, and dialed again. 'Hello, Tony. I don't know what you said, but it worked. Thanks. You're a—' She struggled for the appropriate word, gave up and ended in a final little squeak, '—a – a dear!'

It was Gladys Claffern looking at her when she turned from the phone again. A slightly amused and slightly amazed Gladys Claffern, looking at her out of a face tilted a bit to one side.

'Mrs Belmont?'

It all drained out of Claire – just like that. She could only nod – stupidly, like a marionette.

Gladys smiled with an insolence you couldn't put your finger on. 'I didn't know you shopped here?' As if the place had, in her eyes, definitely lost caste through the fact.

'I don't, usually,' said Claire humbly.

'And haven't you done something to your hair? It's quite – quaint . . . Oh, I hope you'll excuse me, but isn't your husband's name Lawrence? It seems to me that it's Lawrence.'

Claire's teeth clenched, but she had to explain. She *had* to. 'Tony is a friend of my husband's. He's helping me select some things.'

'I understand. And quite a *dear* about it, I imagine.' She passed on smiling, carrying the light and the warmth of the world with her.

Claire did not question the fact that it was to Tony that she turned for consolation. Ten days had cured her of reluctance. And she could weep before him; weep and rage.

'I was a complete f-fool,' she stormed, wrenching at her water-logged handkerchief. 'She does that to me. I don't know why. She just does. I should have – kicked her. I should have knocked her down and stamped on her.'

'Can you hate a human being so much?' asked Tony, in puzzled softness. 'That part of a human mind is closed to me.'

'Oh, it isn't she,' she moaned. 'It's myself, I suppose. She's everything I want to be – on the outside, anyway . . . And I can't be.'

Tony's voice was forceful and low in her ear. 'You can be, Mrs Belmont. You *can* be. We have ten days yet, and in ten days the house will no longer be itself. Haven't we been planning that?'

'And how will that help me – with her?'

'Invite her here. Invite her friends. Have it the evening before I – before I leave. It will be a housewarming, in a way.'

'She won't come.'

'Yes, she will. She'll come to laugh . . . And she won't be able to.'

'Do you really think so? Oh, Tony, do you think we can do it?' She had both his hands in hers . . . And then, with her face flung aside, 'But what good would it be? It won't be I; it will be you that's doing it. I can't ride your back.'

'Nobody lives in splendid singleness,' whispered Tony. 'They've put that knowledge in me. What you, or anyone, see in Gladys Claffern is not just Gladys Claffern. She rides the back of all that money and social position can bring. She doesn't question that. Why should you? . . . And look at it this way, Mrs Belmont. I am manufactured to obey, but the extent of my obedience is for myself to determine. I can follow orders niggardly or liberally. For you, it is liberal, because you are what I have been manufactured to see human beings as. You are kind, friendly, unassuming. Mrs Claffern, as you describe her, is not, and I wouldn't obey her as I would you. So it *is* you, and not I, Mrs Belmont, that is doing all this.'

He withdrew his hands from hers then, and Claire looked at that expressionless face no one could read – wondering. She was suddenly frightened again in a completely new way.

She swallowed nervously and stared at her hands, which were still tingling with the pressure of his fingers. She hadn't imagined it; his fingers had pressed hers, gently, tenderly, just before they moved away.

No!

Its fingers . . . *Its* fingers . . .

She ran to the bathroom and scrubbed her hands – blindly, uselessly.

She was a bit shy of him the next day; watching him narrowly; waiting to see what might follow – and for a while nothing did.

Tony was working. If there was any difficulty in technique in putting up wallpaper, or utilizing the quick-drying paint, Tony's activity did not show it. His hands moved precisely; his fingers were deft and sure.

He worked all night. She never heard him, but each morning was a new adventure. She couldn't count the number of things that had been done, and by evening she was still finding new touches – and another night had come.

She tried to help only once and her human clumsiness marred that. *He* was in the next room, and she was hanging a picture in the spot marked by Tony's mathematical eyes. The little mark was there; the picture was there; and a revulsion against idleness was there.

But she was nervous, or the ladder was rickety. It didn't matter. She felt it going, and she cried out. It tumbled without her, for Tony, with far more than flesh-and-blood quickness, had been under her.

His calm, dark eyes said nothing at all, and his warm voice said only words. 'Are you hurt, Mrs Belmont?'

She noticed for an instant that her falling hand must have mussed that sleek hair of his, because for the first time she could see for herself that it was composed of distinct strands – fine black hairs.

And then, all at once, she was conscious of his arms about her shoulders and under her knees – holding her tightly and warmly.

She pushed, and her scream was loud in her own ears. She spent the rest of the day in her room, and thereafter she slept with a chair upended against the doorknob of her bedroom door.

She had sent out the invitations, and, as Tony had said, they were accepted. She had only to wait for the last evening.

It came, too, after the rest of them, in its proper place. The house was scarcely her own. She went through it one last time – and every room had been changed. She, herself, was in clothes she would never have dared wear before . . . And when you put them on, you put on pride and confidence with them.

She tried a polite look of contemptuous amusement before the mirror, and the mirror sneered back at her masterfully.

What would Larry say? . . . It didn't matter, somehow. The exciting days weren't coming with him. They were leaving with Tony. Now wasn't that strange? She tried to recapture her mood of three weeks before and failed completely.

The clock shrieked eight at her in eight breathless installments, and she turned to Tony. 'They'll be here soon, Tony. You'd better get into the basement. We can't let them—'

She stared a moment, then said weakly, 'Tony?' and more strongly, 'Tony?' and nearly a scream, *'Tony!'*

But his arms were around her now; his face was close to hers; the pressure of his embrace was relentless. She heard his voice through a haze of emotional jumble.

'Claire,' the voice said, 'there are many things I am not made to understand, and this must be one of them. I am leaving tomorrow, and I don't want to. I find that there is more in me than just a desire to please you. Isn't it strange?' His face was closer; his lips were warm, but with no breath behind them – for machines do not breathe. They were almost on hers.

. . . And the bell sounded.

For a moment, she struggled breathlessly, and then he was gone and nowhere in sight, and the bell was sounding again. Its intermittent shrillness was insistent.

The curtains on the front windows had been pulled open. They had been closed fifteen minutes earlier. She *knew* that.

They must have seen, then. They must *all* have seen – everything!

They came in so politely, all in a bunch – the pack come to howl – with their sharp, darting eyes piercing everywhere. They *had* seen. Why else would Gladys ask in her jabbingest manner after Larry? And Claire was spurred to a desperate and reckless defiance.

Yes, he *is* away. He'll be back tomorrow, I suppose. No, I haven't been lonely here myself. Not a bit. I've had an exciting time. And she laughed at them. Why not? What could they do? Larry would know the truth, if it ever came to him, the story of what they thought they saw.

But *they* didn't laugh.

She could read that in the fury in Gladys Claffern's eyes; in the false sparkle of her words; in her desire to leave early. And as she parted with them, she caught one last, anonymous whisper – disjointed.

'. . . never saw anything like . . . so *handsome—*'

And she knew what it was that had enabled her to finger-snap them so. Let each cat mew; and let each cat know – that she might be prettier than Claire Belmont, and grander, and richer – but not one, *not one*, could have so handsome a lover!

And then she remembered again – again – again, that Tony was a machine, and her skin crawled.

'Go away! Leave me be!' she cried to the empty room and ran to her bed. She wept wakefully all that night and the next morning, almost before dawn, when the streets were empty, a car drew up to the house and took Tony away.

Lawrence Belmont passed Dr Calvin's office, and, on impulse, knocked. He found her with Mathematician Peter Bogert, but did not hesitate on that account.

He said, 'Claire tells me that US Robots paid for all that was done at my house—'

'Yes,' said Dr Calvin. 'We've written it off, as a valuable and necessary part of the experiment. With your new position as Associate Engineer, you'll be able to keep it up, I think.'

'That's not what I'm worried about. With Washington agreeing to the tests, we'll be able to get a TN model of our own by next year, I think.' He turned hesitantly, as though to go, and as hesitantly turned back again.

'Well, Mr Belmont?' asked Dr Calvin, after a pause.

'I wonder—' began Larry. 'I wonder what really happened there. She – Claire, I mean – seems so different. It's not just her looks – though, frankly, I'm amazed.' He laughed nervously. 'It's *her!* She's not my wife, really – I can't explain it.'

'Why try? Are you disappointed with any part of the change?'

'On the contrary. But it's a little frightening, too, you see—'

'I wouldn't worry, Mr Belmont. Your wife has handled herself very well. Frankly, I never expected to have the experiment yield such a thorough and complete test. We know exactly what corrections must be made in the TN model, and the credit belongs entirely to Mrs

Belmont. If you want me to be very honest, I think your wife deserves your promotion more than you do.'

Larry flinched visibly at that. 'As long as it's in the family,' he murmured unconvincingly and left.

Susan Calvin looked after him, 'I think that hurt – I hope . . . Have you read Tony's report, Peter?'

'Thoroughly,' said Bogert. 'And won't the TN-3 model need changes?'

'Oh, you think so, too?' questioned Calvin sharply. 'What's your reasoning?'

Bogert frowned. 'I don't need any. It's obvious on the face of it that we can't have a robot loose which makes love to his mistress, if you don't mind the pun.'

'Love! Peter, you sicken me. You really don't understand? That machine had to obey the First Law. He couldn't allow harm to come to a human being, and harm was coming to Claire Belmont through her own sense of inadequacy. So he made love to her, since what woman would fail to appreciate the compliment of being able to stir passion in a machine – in a cold, soulless machine. And he opened the curtains that night deliberately, that the others might see and envy – without any risk possible to Claire's marriage. I think it was clever of Tony—'

'Do you? What's the difference whether it was pretense or not, Susan? It still has its horrifying effect. Read the report again. She avoided him. She screamed when he held her. She didn't sleep that last night – in hysterics. We can't have that.'

'Peter, you're blind. You're as blind as I was. The TN model will be rebuilt entirely, but not for your reason. Quite otherwise; quite otherwise. Strange that I overlooked it in the first place,' her eyes were opaquely thoughtful, 'but perhaps it reflects a shortcoming in myself. You see, Peter, machines can't fall in love, but – even when it's hopeless and horrifying – women can!'

Hell-Fire

There was a stir as of a very polite first-night audience. Only a handful of scientists were present, a sprinkling of high brass, some Congressmen, a few newsmen.

Alvin Horner of the Washington Bureau of the Continental Press found himself next to Joseph Vincenzo of Los Alamos, and said, 'Now we ought to learn something.'

Vincenzo stared at him through bifocals and said, 'Not the important thing.'

Horner frowned. This was to be the first super-slow-motion film of an atomic explosion. With trick lenses changing directional polarization in flickers, the moment of explosion would be divided into billionth-second snaps. Yesterday, an A-bomb had exploded. Today, those snaps would show the explosion in incredible detail.

Horner said, 'You think this won't work?'

Vincenzo looked tormented. 'It will work. We've run pilot tests. But the important thing—'

'Which is?'

'That these bombs are man's death sentence. We don't seem to be able to learn that.' Vincenzo nodded. 'Look at them here. They're excited and thrilled, but not afraid.'

The newsman said, 'They know the danger. They're afraid, too.'

'Not enough,' said the scientist. 'I've seen men watch an H-bomb blow an island into a hole and then go home and sleep. That's the way men are. For thousands of years, hell-fire has been preached to them, and it's made no real impression.'

'Hell-fire: Are you religious, sir?'

'What you saw yesterday was hell-fire. An exploding atom bomb is hell-fire. Literally.'

That was enough for Horner. He got up and changed his seat, but watched the audience uneasily. Were any afraid? Did any worry about hell-fire? It didn't seem so to him.

The lights went out, the projector started. On the screen, the firing tower stood gaunt. The audience grew tensely quiet.

Then a dot of light appeared at the apex of the tower, a brilliant, burning point, slowly budding in a lazy, outward elbowing, this way and that, taking on uneven shapes of light and shadow, growing oval.

A man cried out chokingly, then others. A hoarse babble of noise, followed by thick silence. Horner could smell fear, taste terror in his own mouth, feel his blood freeze.

The oval fireball had sprouted projections, then paused a moment in stasis, before expanding rapidly into a bright and featureless sphere.

That moment of stasis – the fireball had shown dark spots for eyes, with dark lines for thin, flaring eyebrows, a hairline coming down V-shaped, a mouth twisted upward, laughing wildly in the hell-fire – and horns.

The Last Trump

The Archangel Gabriel was quite casual about the whole thing. Idly, he let the tip of one wing graze the planet Mars, which, being of mere matter, was unaffected by the contact.

He said, 'It's a settled matter, Etheriel. There's nothing to be done about it now. The Day of Resurrection is due.'

Etheriel, a very junior seraph who had been created not quite a thousand years earlier as men counted time, quivered so that distinct vortices appeared in the continuum. Ever since his creation, he had been in immediate charge of Earth and environs. As a job, it was a sinecure, a cubbyhole, a dead end, but through the centuries he had come to take a perverse pride in the world.

'But you'll be disrupting my world without notice.'

'Not at all. Not at all. Certain passages occur in the Book of Daniel and in the Apocalypse of St John which are clear enough.'

'They are? Having been copied from scribe to scribe? I wonder if two words in a row are left unchanged.'

'There are hints in the Rig-Veda, in the Confucian Analects—'

'Which are the property of isolated cultural groups which exist as a thin aristocracy—'

'The Gilgamesh Chronicle speaks out plainly.'

'Much of the Gilgamesh Chronicle was destroyed with the library of Ashurbanipal sixteen hundred years, Earthstyle, before my creation.'

'There are certain features of the Great Pyramid and a pattern in the inlaid jewels of the Taj Mahal—'

'Which are so subtle that no man has ever rightly interpreted them.'

Gabriel said wearily, 'If you're going to object to everything, there's no use discussing the matter. In any case, you ought to know about it. In matters concerning Earth, you're omniscient.'

'Yes, if I choose to be. I've had much to concern me here and investigating the possibilities of Resurrection did not, I confess, occur to me.'

'Well, it should have. All the papers involved are in the files of the Council of Ascendants. You could have availed yourself of them at any time.'

'I tell you all my time was needed here. You have no idea of the deadly efficiency of the Adversary on this planet. It took all my efforts to curb him, and even so—'

'Why, yes' – Gabriel stroked a comet as it passed – 'he does seem to have won his little victories. I note as I let the interlocking factual pattern of this miserable little world flow through me that this is one of those setups with matter-energy equivalence.'

'So it is,' said Etheriel.

'And they are playing with it.'

'I'm afraid so.'

'Then what better time for ending the matter?'

'I'll be able to handle it, I assure you. Their nuclear bombs will not destroy them.'

'I wonder. Well, now suppose you let me continue, Etheriel. The appointed moment approaches.'

The seraph said stubbornly, 'I would like to see the documents in the case.'

'If you insist.' The wording of an Act of Ascendancy appeared in glittering symbols against the deep black of the airless firmament.

Etheriel read aloud: 'It is hereby directed by order of Council that the Archangel Gabriel, Serial number etcetera, etcetera (well, that's you, at any rate), will approach Planet, Class A, number G753990, hereinafter known as Earth, and on 1 January 1957, at 12:01 p.m., using local time values—' He finished reading in gloomy silence.

'Satisfied?'

'No, but I'm helpless.'

Gabriel smiled. A trumpet appeared in space, in shape like an earthly trumpet, but its burnished gold extended from Earth to sun. It was raised to Gabriel's glittering beautiful lips.

'Can't you let me have a little time to take this up with the Council?' asked Etheriel desperately.

'What good would it do you? The act is countersigned by the Chief, and you know that an act countersigned by the Chief is absolutely irrevocable. And now, if you don't mind, it is almost the stipulated second and I want to be done with this as I have other matters of much greater moment on my mind. Would you step out of my way a little? Thank you.'

Gabriel blew, and a clean, thin sound of perfect pitch and crystalline delicacy filled all the universe to the furthest star. As it sounded, there was a tiny moment of stasis as thin as the line separating past from future, and then the fabric of worlds collapsed upon itself and matter was gathered back into the primeval chaos from which it had once sprung at a word. The stars and nebulae were gone, and the cosmic dust, the sun, the planets, the moon; all, all, all except Earth itself, which spun as before in a universe now completely empty.

The Last Trump had sounded.

R. E. Mann (known to all who knew him simply as R.E.) eased himself into the offices of the Billikan Bitsies factory and stared somberly at the tall man (gaunt but with a certain faded elegance about his neat gray mustache) who bent intently over a sheaf of papers on his desk.

R.E. looked at his wristwatch, which still said 7:01, having ceased running at that time. It was Eastern standard time, of course; 12:01 p.m. Greenwich time. His dark brown eyes, staring sharply out over a pair of pronounced cheekbones, caught those of the other.

For a moment, the tall man stared at him blankly. Then he said, 'Can I do anything for you?'

'Horatio J. Billikan, I presume? Owner of this place?'

'Yes.'

'I'm R. E. Mann and I couldn't help but step in when I finally found someone at work. Don't you know what today is?'

'Today?'

'It's Resurrection Day.'

'Oh, that! I know it. I heard the blast. Fit to wake the dead . . . That's rather a good one, don't you think?' He chuckled for a moment, then went on. 'It woke me at seven in the morning. I nudged my wife. She slept through it, of course. I always said she would. "It's the Last Trump, dear," I said. Hortense, that's my wife, said, "All right," and went back to sleep. I bathed, shaved, dressed and came to work.'

'But why?'

'Why not?'

'None of your workers have come in.'

'No, poor souls. They'll take a holiday just at first. You've got to expect that. After all, it isn't every day that the world comes to an end. Frankly, it's just as well. It gives me a chance to straighten out my personal correspondence without interruptions. Telephone hasn't rung once.'

He stood up and went to the window. 'It's a great improvement. No blinding sun any more and the snow's gone. There's a pleasant light and a pleasant warmth. Very good arrangement . . . But now, if you don't mind, I'm *rather* busy, so if you'll excuse me—'

A great, hoarse voice interrupted with a, 'Just a minute, Horatio,' and a gentleman, looking remarkably like Billikan in a somewhat craggier way, followed his prominent nose into the office and struck an attitude of offended dignity which was scarcely spoiled by the fact that he was quite naked. 'May I ask why you've shut down Bitsies?'

Billikan looked faint. 'Good Heavens,' he said, 'it's Father. Wherever did you come from?'

'From the graveyard,' roared Billikan, Senior. 'Where on Earth else? They're coming out of the ground there by the dozens. Every one of them naked. Women, too.'

Billikan cleared his throat. 'I'll get you some clothes, Father. I'll bring them to you from home.'

'Never mind that. Business first. Business first.'

R.E. came out of his musing. 'Is everyone coming out of their graves at the same time, sir?'

He stared curiously at Billikan, Senior, as he spoke. The old man's appearance was one of robust age. His cheeks were furrowed but glowed with health. His age, R.E. decided, was exactly what it was at the moment of his death, but his body was as it should have been at that age if it functioned ideally.

Billikan, Senior, said, 'No, sir, they are not. The newer graves are coming up first. Pottersby died five years before me and came up about five minutes after me. Seeing him made me decide to leave. I had had enough of him when . . . And that reminds me.' He brought his fist down on the desk, a very solid fist. 'There were no taxis, no busses. Telephones weren't working. I had to walk. I had to walk twenty miles.'

'Like that?' asked his son in a faint and appalled voice.

Billikan, Senior, looked down upon his bare skin with casual approval. 'It's warm. Almost everyone else is naked . . . Anyway, son, I'm not here to make small talk. Why is the factory shut down?'

'It isn't shut down. It's a special occasion.'

'Special occasion, my foot. You call union headquarters and tell them Resurrection Day isn't in the contract. Every worker is being docked for every minute he's off the job.'

Billikan's lean face took on a stubborn look as he peered at his father. 'I will not. Don't forget, now, you're no longer in charge of this plant. I am.'

'Oh, you are? By what right?'

'By your will.'

'All right. Now here I am and I void my will.'

'You can't, Father. You're dead. You may not look dead, but I have witnesses. I have the doctor's certificate. I have receipted bills from the undertaker. I can get testimony from the pallbearers.'

Billikan, Senior, stared at his son, sat down, placed his arm over the back of the chair, crossed his legs and said, 'If it comes to that, we're all dead, aren't we? The world's come to an end, hasn't it?'

'But you've been declared legally dead and I haven't.'

'Oh, we'll change that, son. There are going to be more of us than of you and votes count.'

Billikan, Junior, tapped the desk firmly with the flat of his hand and flushed slightly. 'Father, I hate to bring up this particular point, but you force me to. May I remind you that by now I am sure that Mother is sitting at home waiting for you; that she probably had to walk the streets – uh – naked, too; and that she probably isn't in a good humor.'

Billikan, Senior, went ludicrously pale. 'Good Heavens!'

'And you know she always wanted you to retire.'

Billikan, Senior, came to a quick decision. 'I'm not going home. Why, this is a nightmare. Aren't there any limits to this Resurrection business? It's – it's – it's sheer anarchy. There's such a thing as over-doing it. I'm just not going home.'

At which point, a somewhat rotund gentleman with a smooth, pink face and fluffy white sideburns (much like pictures of Martin Van Buren) stepped in and said coldly, '*Good* day.'

'Father,' said Billikan, Senior.

'Grandfather,' said Billikan, Junior.

Billikan, Grandsenior, looked at Billikan, Junior, with disapproval. 'If you are my grandson,' he said, 'you've aged considerably and the change has not improved you.'

Billikan, Junior, smiled with dyspeptic feebleness, and made no answer.

Billikan, Grandsenior, did not seem to require one. He said, 'Now if you two will bring me up to date on the business, I will resume my managerial function.'

There were two simultaneous answers, and Billikan, Grandsenior's, floridity waxed dangerously as he beat the ground peremptorily with an imaginary cane and barked a retort.

R.E. said, 'Gentlemen.'

He raised his voice. 'Gentlemen!'

He shrieked at full lung-power, 'GENTLEMEN!'

Conversation snapped off sharply and all turned to look at him. R.E.'s angular face, his oddly attractive eyes, his sardonic mouth seemed suddenly to dominate the gathering.

He said, 'I don't understand this argument. What is it that you manufacture?'

'Bitsies,' said Billikan, Junior.

'Which, I take it, are a packaged cereal breakfast food—'

'Teeming with energy in every golden, crispy flake—' cried Billikan, Junior.

'Covered with honey-sweet, crystalline sugar; a confection and a food—' growled Billikan, Senior.

'To tempt the most jaded appetite,' roared Billikan, Grandsenior.

'Exactly,' said R.E. 'What appetite?'

They stared stolidly at him. 'I beg your pardon,' said Billikan, Junior.

'Are any of you hungry?' asked R.E. 'I'm not.'

'What is this fool maundering about?' demanded Billikan, Grandsenior, angrily. His invisible cane would have been prodding R.E. in the navel had it (the cane, not the navel) existed.

R.E. said, 'I'm trying to tell you that no one will ever eat again. It is the hereafter, and food is unnecessary.'

The expressions on the faces of the Billikans needed no interpretation. It was obvious that they had tried their own appetites and found them wanting.

Billikan, Junior, said ashenly, 'Ruined!'

Billikan, Grandsenior, pounded the floor heavily and noiselessly with his imaginary cane. 'This is confiscation of property without due process of law. I'll sue. I'll sue.'

'Quite unconstitutional,' agreed Billikan, Senior.

'If you can find anyone to sue, I wish you all good fortune,' said R.E. agreeably. 'And now if you'll excuse me I think I'll walk toward the graveyard.'

He put his hat on his head and walked out the door.

Etheriel, his vortices quivering, stood before the glory of a six-winged cherub.

The cherub said, 'If I understand you, your particular universe has been dismantled.'

'Exactly.'

'Well, surely, now, you don't expect *me* to set it up again?'

'I don't expect you to do anything,' said Etheriel, 'except to arrange an appointment for me with the Chief.'

The cherub gestured his respect instantly at hearing the word. Two wingtips covered his feet, two his eyes and two his mouth. He restored himself to normal and said, 'The Chief is quite busy. There are a myriad score of matters for him to decide.'

'Who denies that? I merely point out that if matters stand as they are now, there will have been a universe in which Satan will have won the final victory.'

'Satan?'

'It's the Hebrew word for Adversary,' said Etheriel impatiently. 'I could say Ahriman, which is the Persian word. In any case, I mean the Adversary.'

The cherub said, 'But what will an interview with the Chief accomplish? The document authorizing the Last Trump was countersigned by the Chief, and you know that it is irrevocable for that reason. The Chief would never limit his own omnipotence by canceling a word he had spoken in his official capacity.'

'Is that final? You will not arrange an appointment?'

'I cannot.'

Etheriel said, 'In that case, I shall seek out the Chief without one. I will invade the Primum Mobile. If it means my destruction, so be it.' He gathered his energies . . .

The cherub murmured in horror, 'Sacrilege!' and there was a faint gathering of thunder as Etheriel sprang upward and was gone.

R. E. Mann passed through the crowding streets and grew used to the sight of people bewildered, disbelieving, apathetic, in makeshift clothing or, usually, none at all.

A girl, who looked about twelve, leaned over an iron gate, one foot on a crossbar, swinging it to and fro, and said as he passed, 'Hello, mister.'

'Hello,' said R.E. The girl was dressed. She was not one of the – uh – returnees.

The girl said, 'We got a new baby in our house. She's a sister I once had. Mommy is crying and they sent me here.'

R.E. said, 'Well, well,' passed through the gate and up the paved walk to the house, one with modest pretensions to middle-class gentility. He rang the bell, obtained no answer, opened the door and walked in.

He followed the sound of sobbing and knocked at an inner door. A stout man of about fifty with little hair and a comfortable supply of cheek and chin looked out at him with mingled astonishment and resentment.

'Who are you?'

R.E. removed his hat. 'I thought I might be able to help. Your little girl outside—'

A woman looked up at him hopelessly from a chair by a double bed. Her hair was beginning to gray. Her face was puffed and unsightly with weeping and the veins stood out bluely on the back of her hands. A baby lay on the bed, plump and naked. It kicked its feet languidly and its sightless baby eyes turned aimlessly here and there.

'This is my baby,' said the woman. 'She was born twenty-three years ago in this house and she died when she was ten days old in this house. I wanted her back so much.'

'And now you have her,' said R.E.

'But it's too late,' cried the woman vehemently. 'I've had three other children. My oldest girl is married; my son is in the army. I'm too old to have a baby now. And even if – even if—'

Her features worked in a heroic effort to keep back the tears and failed.

Her husband said with flat tonelessness, 'It's not a real baby. It doesn't cry. It doesn't soil itself. It won't take milk. What will we do? It'll never grow. It'll always be a baby.'

R.E. shook his head. 'I don't know,' he said. 'I'm afraid I can do nothing to help.'

Quietly he left. Quietly he thought of the hospitals. Thousands of babies must be appearing at each one.

Place them in racks, he thought, sardonically. Stack them like cordwood. They need no care. Their little bodies are merely each the custodian of an indestructible spark of life.

He passed two little boys of apparently equal chronological age, perhaps ten. Their voices were shrill. The body of one glistened white in the sunless light so he was a returnee. The other was not. R.E. paused to listen.

The bare one said, 'I had scarlet fever.'

A spark of envy at the other's claim to notoriety seemed to enter the clothed one's voice. 'Gee.'

'That's why I died.'

'Gee. Did they use pensillun or auromysun?'

'What?'

'They're medicines.'

'I never heard of them.'

'Boy, you never heard of *much*.'

'I know as much as *you*.'

'Yeah? Who's President of the United States?'

'Warren Harding, that's who.'

'You're crazy. It's Eisenhower.'

'Who's he?'

'Ever see television?'

'What's that?'

The clothed boy hooted earsplittingly. 'It's something you turn on and see comedians, movies, cowboys, rocket rangers, anything you want.'

'Let's see it.'

There was a pause and the boy from the present said, 'It ain't working.'

The other boy shrieked his scorn. 'You mean it ain't never worked. You made it all up.'

R.E. shrugged and passed on.

The crowds thinned as he left town and neared the cemetery. Those who were left were all walking into town, all were nude.

A man stopped him; a cheerful man with pinkish skin and white hair who had the marks of pince-nez on either side of the bridge of his nose, but no glasses to go with them.

'Greetings, friend.'

'Hello,' said R.E.

'You're the first man with clothing that I've seen. You were alive when the trumpet blew, I suppose.'

'Yes. I was.'

'Well, isn't this great? Isn't this joyous and delightful? Come rejoice with me.'

'You like this, do you?' said R.E.

'*Like it?* A pure and radiant joy fills me. We are surrounded by the light of the first day; the light that glowed softly and serenely before sun, moon and stars were made. (You know your Genesis, of course.) There is the comfortable warmth that must have been one of the highest blisses of Eden; not enervating heat or assaulting cold. Men and women walk the streets unclothed and are not ashamed. All is well, my friend, all is well.'

R.E. said, 'Well, it's a fact that I haven't seemed to mind the feminine display all about.'

'Naturally not,' said the other. 'Lust and sin as we remember it in our earthly existence no longer exists. Let me introduce myself, friend, as I was in earthly times. My name on Earth was Winthrop Hester. I was born in 1812 and died in 1884 as we counted time then. Through the last forty years of my life I labored to bring my little flock to the Kingdom and I go now to count the ones I have won.'

R.E. regarded the ex-minister solemnly, 'Surely there has been no Judgment yet.'

'Why not? The Lord sees within a man and in the same instant that all things of the world ceased, all men were judged and we are the saved.'

'There must be a great many saved.'

'On the contrary, my son, those saved are but as a remnant.'

'A pretty large remnant. As near as I can make out, everyone's coming back to life. I've seen some pretty unsavory characters back in town as alive as you are.'

'Last-minute repentance—'

'*I* never repented.'

'Of what, my son?'

'Of the fact that I never attended church.'

Winthrop Hester stepped back hastily. 'Were you ever baptized?'

'Not to my knowledge.'

Winthrop Hester trembled. 'Surely you believe in God?'

'Well,' said R.E., 'I believed a lot of things about Him that would probably startle you.'

Winthrop Hester turned and hurried off in great agitation.

In what remained of his walk to the cemetery (R.E. had no way of estimating time, nor did it occur to him to try) no one else stopped him. He found the cemetery itself all but empty, its trees and grass gone (it occurred to him that there was nothing green in the world; the ground everywhere was a hard, featureless, grainless gray; the sky a luminous white), but its headstones still standing.

On one of these sat a lean and furrowed man with long, black hair on his head and a mat of it, shorter, though more impressive, on his chest and upper arms.

He called out in a deep voice, 'Hey, there, you!'

R.E. sat down on a neighboring headstone. 'Hello.'

Black-hair said, 'Your clothes don't look right. What year was it when it happened?'

'1957.'

'I died in 1807. Funny! I expected to be one pretty hot boy right about now, with the 'tarnal flames shooting up my innards.'

'Aren't you coming along to town?' asked R.E.

'My name's Zeb,' said the ancient. 'That's short for Zebulon, but Zeb's good enough. What's the town like? Changed some, I reckon?'

'It's got nearly a hundred thousand people in it.'

Zeb's mouth yawned somewhat. 'Go on. Might nigh bigger'n Philadelphia . . . You're making fun.'

'Philadelphia's got—' R.E. paused. Stating the figure would do him no good. Instead, he said, 'The town's grown in a hundred fifty years, you know.'

'Country, too?'

'Forty-eight states,' said R.E. 'All the way to the Pacific.'

'No!' Zeb slapped his thigh in delight and then winced at the unexpected absence of rough homespun to take up the worst of the blow. 'I'd head out west if I wasn't needed here. Yes, sir.' His face grew lowering and his thin lips took on a definite grimness. 'I'll stay right here, where I'm needed.'

'Why are you needed?'

The explanation came out briefly, bitten off hard. 'Injuns!'

'Indians?'

'Millions of 'em. First the tribes we fought and licked and then tribes who ain't never seen a white man. They'll all come back to life. I'll need my old buddies. You city fellers ain't no good at it . . . Ever seen an Injun?'

R.E. said, 'Not around here lately, no.'

Zeb looked his contempt, and tried to spit to one side but found no saliva for the purpose. He said, 'You better git back to the city, then. After a while, it ain't going to be safe nohow round here. Wish I had my musket.'

R.E. rose, thought a moment, shrugged and faced back to the city. The headstone he had been sitting upon collapsed as he rose, falling into a powder of gray stone that melted into the featureless ground. He looked about. Most of the headstones were gone. The rest would not last long. Only the one under Zeb still looked firm and strong.

R.E. began the walk back. Zeb did not turn to look at him. He remained waiting quietly and calmly – for Indians.

Etheriel plunged through the heavens in reckless haste. The eyes of the Ascendants were on him, he knew. From late-born seraph, through cherubs and angels, to the highest archangel, they must be watching.

Already he was higher than any Ascendant, uninvited, had ever been before and he waited for the quiver of the Word that would reduce his vortices to non-existence.

But he did not falter. Through non-space and non-time, he plunged toward union with the Primum Mobile; the seat that encompassed all that Is, Was, Would Be, Had Been, Could Be and Might Be.

And as he thought that, he burst through and was part of it, his being expanding so that momentarily he, too, was part of the All. But then it was mercifully veiled from his senses, and the Chief was a still, small voice within him, yet all the more impressive in its infinity for all that.

'My son,' the voice said, 'I know why you have come.'

'Then help me, if that be your will.'

'By my own will,' said the Chief, 'an act of mine is irrevocable. All your mankind, my son, yearned for life. All feared death. All evolved thoughts and dreams of life unending. No two groups of men; no two single men; evolved the same afterlife, but all wished life. I was petitioned that I might grant the common denominator of all these wishes – life unending. I did so.'

'No servant of yours made that request.'

'The Adversary did, my son.'

Etheriel trailed his feeble glory in dejection and said in a low voice, 'I am dust in your sight and unworthy to be in your presence, yet I must ask a question. Is then the Adversary your servant also?'

'Without him I can have no other,' said the Chief, 'for what then is Good but the eternal fight against Evil?'

And in that fight, thought Etheriel, I have lost.

R.E. paused in sight of town. The buildings were crumbling. Those that were made of wood were already heaps of rubble. R.E. walked to the nearest such heap and found the wooden splinters powdery and dry.

He penetrated deeper into town and found the brick buildings still standing, but there was an ominous roundness to the edges of the bricks, a threatening flakiness.

'They won't last long,' said a deep voice, 'but there is this consolation, if consolation it be; their collapse can kill no one.'

R.E. looked up in surprise and found himself face to face with a cadaverous Don Quixote of a man, lantern-jawed, sunken-cheeked. His eyes were sad and his brown hair was lank and straight. His clothes hung loosely and skin showed clearly through various rents.

'My name,' said the man, 'is Richard Levine. I was a professor of history once – before this happened.'

'You're wearing clothes,' said R.E. 'You're not one of those resurrected.'

'No, but that mark of distinction is vanishing. Clothes are going.'

R.E. looked at the throngs that drifted past them, moving slowly and aimlessly like motes in a sunbeam. Vanishingly few wore clothes. He looked down at himself and noticed for the first time that the seam down the length of each trouser leg had parted. He pinched the fabric of his jacket between thumb and forefinger and the wool parted and came away easily.

'I guess you're right,' said R.E.

'If you'll notice,' went on Levine, 'Mellon's Hill is flattening out.'

R.E. turned to the north where ordinarily the mansions of the aristocracy, (such aristocracy as there was in town) studded the slopes of Mellon's Hill, and found the horizon nearly flat.

Levine said, 'Eventually, there'll be nothing but flatness, feature-lessness, nothingness – and us.'

'And Indians,' said R.E. 'There's a man outside of town waiting for Indians and wishing he had a musket.'

'I imagine,' said Levine, 'the Indians will give no trouble. There is no pleasure in fighting an enemy that cannot be killed or hurt. And even if that were not so, the lust for battle would be gone, as are all lusts.'

'Are you sure?'

'I am positive. Before all this happened, although you may not think it to look at me, I derived much harmless pleasure in a consideration of the female figure. Now, with the unexampled opportunities at my disposal, I find myself irritatingly uninterested. No, that is wrong. I am not even irritated at my disinterest.'

R.E. looked up briefly at the passers-by. 'I see what you mean.'

'The coming of Indians here,' said Levine, 'is nothing compared with the situation in the Old World. Early during the Resurrection, Hitler and his Wehrmacht must have come back to life and must now be facing and intermingled with Stalin and the Red Army all the way from Berlin to Stalingrad. To complicate the situation, the Kaisers and Czars will arrive. The men at Verdun and the Somme are back in the old battlegrounds. Napoleon and his marshals are scattered over western Europe. And Mohammed must be back to see what following ages have made of Islam, while the Saints and Apostles consider the paths of Christianity. And even the Mongols, poor things, the Khans from Temujin to Aurangzeb, must be wandering the steppes helplessly, longing for their horses.'

'As a professor of history,' said R.E., 'you must long to be there and observe.'

'How could I be there? Every man's position on Earth is restricted to the distance he can walk. There are no machines of any kind, and, as I have just mentioned, no horses. And what would I find in Europe anyway? Apathy, I think! As here.'

A soft plopping sound caused R.E. to turn around. The wing of a neighboring brick building had collapsed in dust. Portions of bricks lay on either side of him. Some must have hurtled through him without his being aware of it. He looked about. The heaps of rubble were less numerous. Those that remained were smaller in size.

He said, 'I met a man who thought we had all been judged and are in Heaven.'

'Judged?' said Levine. 'Why, yes, I imagine we are. We face eternity now. We have no universe left, no outside phenomena, no emotions, no passions. Nothing but ourselves and thought. We face an eternity of introspection, when all through history we have never known what to do with ourselves on a rainy Sunday.'

'You sound as though the situation bothers you.'

'It does more than that. The Dantean conceptions of Inferno were childish and unworthy of the Divine imagination: fire and torture. Boredom is much more subtle. The inner torture of a mind unable to escape itself in any way, condemned to fester in its own exuding mental pus for all time, is much more fitting. Oh, yes, my friend, we have been judged, and condemned, too, and this is not Heaven, but hell.'

And Levine rose with shoulders drooping dejectedly, and walked away.

R.E. gazed thoughtfully about and nodded his head. He was satisfied.

The self-admission of failure lasted but an instant in Etheriel, and then, quite suddenly, he lifted his being as brightly and highly as he dared in the presence of the Chief and his glory was a tiny dot of light in the infinite Primum Mobile.

'If it be your will, then,' he said, 'I do not ask you to defeat your will but to fulfill it.'

'In what way, my son?'

'The document, approved by the Council of Ascendants and signed by yourself, authorizes the Day of Resurrection at a specific time of a specific day of the year 1957 as Earthmen count time.'

'So it does.'

'But the year 1957 is unqualified. What then is 1957? To the dominant culture on Earth the year was AD 1957. That is true. Yet from the time you breathed existence into Earth and its universe there have passed 5,960 years. Based on the internal evidence you created within that universe, nearly four billion years have passed. Is the year, *unqualified*, then 1957, 5960, or 4000000000?

'Nor is that all,' Etheriel went on. 'The year AD 1957 is the year 7464 of the Byzantine era, 5716 by the Jewish calendar. It is 2708 AUC., that is, the 2,708th year since the founding of Rome, if we adopt the Roman calendar. It is the year 1375 in the Mohammedan calendar, and the hundred eightieth year of the independence of the United States.

'Humbly I ask then if it does not seem to you that a year referred to as 1957 alone and without qualification has no meaning.'

The Chief's still small voice said, 'I have always known this, my son; it was you who had to learn.'

'Then,' said Etheriel, quivering luminously with joy, 'let the very letter of your will be fulfilled and let the Day of Resurrection fall in 1957, but only when all the inhabitants of Earth unanimously agree that a certain year shall be numbered 1957 and none other.'

'So let it be,' said the Chief, and this Word re-created Earth and all it contained, together with the sun and moon and all the hosts of Heaven.

It was 7 a.m. on 1 January 1957, when R. E. Mann awoke with a start. The very beginnings of a melodious note that ought to have filled all the universe had sounded and yet had not sounded.

For a moment, he cocked his head as though to allow understanding to flow in, and then a trifle of rage crossed his face to vanish again. It was but another battle.

He sat down at his desk to compose the next plan of action. People already spoke of calendar reform and it would have to be stimulated. A new era must begin with 2 December 1944, and someday a new year 1957 would come; 1957 of the Atomic Era, acknowledged as such by all the world.

A strange light shone on his head as thoughts passed through his more-than-human mind and the shadow of Ahriman on the wall seemed to have small horns at either temple.

The Fun They Had

Margie even wrote about it that night in her diary. On the page headed 17 May 2157, she wrote, 'Today Tommy found a real book!'

It was a very old book. Margie's grandfather once said that when he was a little boy *his* grandfather told him that there was a time when all stories were printed on paper.

They turned the pages, which were yellow and crinkly, and it was awfully funny to read words that stood still instead of moving the way they were supposed to – on a screen, you know. And then, when they turned back to the page before, it had the same words on it that it had had when they read it the first time.

'Gee,' said Tommy, 'what a waste. When you're through with the book, you just throw it away, I guess. Our television screen must have had a million books on it and it's good for plenty more. I wouldn't throw *it* away.'

'Same with mine,' said Margie. She was eleven and hadn't seen as many telebooks as Tommy had. He was thirteen.

She said, 'Where did you find it?'

'In my house.' He pointed without looking, because he was busy reading. 'In the attic.'

'What's it about?'

'School.'

Margie was scornful. 'School? What's there to write about school? I hate school.'

Margie always hated school, but now she hated it more than ever. The mechanical teacher had been giving her test after test in geography and she had been doing worse and worse until her mother had shaken her head sorrowfully and sent for the County Inspector.

He was a round little man with a red face and a whole box of tools with dials and wires. He smiled at Margie and gave her an apple, then took the teacher apart. Margie had hoped he wouldn't know how to put it together again, but he knew how all right, and, after an hour or so, there it was again, large and black and ugly, with a big screen on which all the lessons were shown and the questions were asked. That wasn't so bad. The part Margie hated most was the slot where she had to put homework and test papers. She always had to write them out in a punch code they made her learn when she was six years old, and the mechanical teacher calculated the mark in no time.

The Inspector had smiled after he was finished and patted Margie's head. He said to her mother, 'It's not the little girl's fault, Mrs Jones. I think the geography sector was geared a little too quick. Those things happen sometimes. I've slowed it up to an average ten-year level. Actually, the over-all pattern of her progress is quite satisfactory.' And he patted Margie's head again.

Margie was disappointed. She had been hoping they would take the teacher away altogether. They had once taken Tommy's teacher away for nearly a month because the history sector had blanked out completely.

So she said to Tommy, 'Why would anyone write about school?'

Tommy looked at her with very superior eyes. 'Because it's not our kind of school, stupid. This is the old kind of school that they had hundreds and hundreds of years ago.' He added loftily, pronouncing the word carefully, *'Centuries* ago.'

Margie was hurt. 'Well, I don't know what kind of school they had all that time ago.' She read the book over his shoulder for a while, then said, 'Anyway, they had a teacher.'

'Sure they had a teacher, but it wasn't a *regular* teacher. It was a man.'

'A man? How could a man be a teacher?'

'Well, he just told the boys and girls things and gave them home-work and asked them questions.'

'A man isn't smart enough.'

'Sure he is. My father knows as much as my teacher.'

'He can't. A man can't know as much as a teacher.'

'He knows almost as much, I betcha.'

Margie wasn't prepared to dispute that. She said, 'I wouldn't want a strange man in my house to teach me.'

Tommy screamed with laughter. 'You don't know much, Margie. The teachers didn't live in the house. They had a special building and all the kids went there.'

'And all the kids learned the same thing?'

'Sure, if they were the same age.'

'But my mother says a teacher has to be adjusted to fit the mind of each boy and girl it teaches and that each kid has to be taught differently.'

'Just the same they didn't do it that way then. If you don't like it, you don't have to read the book.'

'I didn't say I didn't like it,' Margie said quickly. She wanted to read about those funny schools.

They weren't even half finished when Margie's mother called, 'Margie! School!'

Margie looked up. 'Not yet, Mamma.'

'Now!' said Mrs Jones. 'And it's probably time for Tommy, too.'

Margie said to Tommy, 'Can I read the book some more with you after school?'

'Maybe,' he said nonchalantly. He walked away whistling, the dusty old book tucked beneath his arm.

Margie went into the schoolroom. It was right next to her bedroom, and the mechanical teacher was on and waiting for her. It was always on at the same time every day except Saturday and Sunday, because her mother said little girls learned better if they learned at regular hours.

The screen was lit up, and it said: 'Today's arithmetic lesson is on the addition of proper fractions. Please insert yesterday's homework in the proper slot.'

Margie did so with a sigh. She was thinking about the old schools they had when her grandfather's grandfather was a little boy. All the kids from the whole neighborhood came, laughing and shouting in the schoolyard, sitting together in the schoolroom, going home together at the end of the day. They learned the same things, so they could help one another on the homework and talk about it.

And the teachers were people . . .

The mechanical teacher was flashing on the screen: 'When we add fractions ½ and ¼—'

Margie was thinking about how the kids must have loved it in the old days. She was thinking about the fun they had.

Jokester

Noel Meyerhof consulted the list he had prepared and chose which item was to be first. As usual, he relied mainly on intuition.

He was dwarfed by the machine he faced, though only the smallest portion of the latter was in view. That didn't matter. He spoke with the offhand confidence of one who thoroughly knew he was master.

'Johnson,' he said, 'came home unexpectedly from a business trip to find his wife in the arms of his best friend. He staggered back and said, "Max! I'm married to the lady so I *have* to. But why you?"'

Meyerhof thought: Okay, let that trickle down into its guts and gurgle about a bit.

And a voice behind him said, 'Hey.'

Meyerhof erased the sound of that monosyllable and put the circuit he was using into neutral. He whirled and said, 'I'm working. Don't you knock?'

He did not smile as he customarily did in greeting Timothy Whistler, a senior analyst with whom he dealt as often as with any. He frowned as he would have for an interruption by a stranger, wrinkling his thin face into a distortion that seemed to extend to his hair, rumpling it more than ever.

Whistler shrugged. He wore his white lab coat with his fists pressing down within its pockets and creasing it into tense vertical lines. 'I knocked. You didn't answer. The operations signal wasn't on.'

Meyerhof grunted. It wasn't at that. He'd been thinking about this new project too intensively and he was forgetting little details.

And yet he could scarcely blame himself for that. This thing was important.

He didn't know why it was, of course. Grand Masters rarely did. That's what made them Grand Masters; the fact that they were beyond reason. How else could the human mind keep up with that ten-mile-long lump of solidified reason that men called Multivac, the most complex computer ever built?

Meyerhof said, 'I *am* working. Is there something important on your mind?'

'Nothing that can't be postponed. There are a few holes in the answer on the hyperspatial—' Whistler did a double take and his face took on a rueful look of uncertainty. *'Working?'*

'Yes. What about it?'

'But—' He looked about, staring into the crannies of the shallow room that faced the banks upon banks of relays that formed a small portion of Multivac. 'There isn't anyone here at that.'

'Who said there was, or should be?'

'You were telling one of your jokes, weren't you?'

'And?'

Whistler forced a smile. 'Don't tell me you were telling a joke to Multivac?'

Meyerhof stiffened. 'Why not?'

'Were you?'

'Yes.'

'Why?'

Meyerhof stared the other down. 'I don't have to account to you. Or to anyone.'

'Good Lord, of course not. I was curious, that's all . . . But then, if you're working, I'll leave.' He looked about once more, frowning.

'Do so,' said Meyerhof. His eyes followed the other out and then he activated the operations signal with a savage punch of his finger.

He strode the length of the room and back, getting himself in hand. Damn Whistler! Damn them all! Because he didn't bother to hold those technicians, analysts and mechanics at the proper social distance, because he treated them as though they, too, were creative artists, they took these liberties.

He thought grimly: They can't even tell jokes decently.

And instantly that brought him back to the task in hand. He sat down again. Devil take them all.

He threw the proper Multivac circuit back into operation and said, 'The ship's steward stopped at the rail of the ship during a particularly rough ocean crossing and gazed compassionately at the man whose slumped position over the rail and whose intensity of gaze toward the depths betokened all too well the ravages of seasickness.

'Gently, the steward patted the man's shoulder. "Cheer up, sir," he murmured. "I know it seems bad, but really, you know, nobody ever dies of seasickness."

'The afflicted gentleman lifted his greenish, tortured face to his comforter and gasped in hoarse accents, "Don't say that, man. For Heaven's sake, don't say that. It's only the hope of dying that's keeping me alive."'

Timothy Whistler, a bit preoccupied, nevertheless smiled and nodded as he passed the secretary's desk. She smiled back at him.

Here, he thought, was an archaic item in this computer-ridden world of the twenty-first century, a human secretary. But then perhaps it was natural that such an institution should survive here in the very citadel of computerdom; in the gigantic world corporation that handled Multivac. With Multivac filling the horizons, lesser computers for trivial tasks would have been in poor taste.

Whistler stepped into Abram Trask's office. That government official paused in his careful task of lighting a pipe; his dark eyes flicked in Whistler's direction and his beaked nose stood out sharply and prominently against the rectangle of window behind him.

'Ah, there, Whistler. Sit down. Sit down.'

Whistler did so. 'I think we've got a problem, Trask.'

Trask half-smiled. 'Not a technical one, I hope. I'm just an innocent politician.' (It was one of his favorite phrases.)

'It involves Meyerhof.'

Trask sat down instantly and looked acutely miserable. 'Are you sure?'

'Reasonably sure.'

Whistler understood the other's sudden unhappiness well. Trask was the government official in charge of the Division of Computers and Automation of the Department of the Interior. He was expected to deal with matters of policy involving the human satellites of Multivac, just as those technically trained satellites were expected to deal with Multivac itself.

But a Grand Master was more than just a satellite. More, even, than just a human.

Early in the history of Multivac, it had become apparent that the bottleneck was the questioning procedure. Multivac could answer the problem of humanity, *all* the problems, if – *if* it were asked meaningful questions. But as knowledge accumulated at an ever-faster rate, it became ever more difficult to locate those meaningful questions.

Reason alone wouldn't do. What was needed was a rare type of intuition; the same faculty of mind (only much more intensified) that made a Grand Master at chess. A mind was needed of the sort that could see through the quadrillions of chess patterns to find the one best move, and do it in a matter of minutes.

Trask moved restlessly. 'What's Meyerhof been doing?'

'He's introduced a line of questioning that I find disturbing.'

'Oh, come on, Whistler. Is that all? You can't stop a Grand Master from going through any line of questioning he chooses. Neither you nor I are equipped to judge the worth of his questions. You know that. I know you know that.'

'I do. Of course. But I also know Meyerhof. Have you ever met him socially?'

'Good Lord, no. Does anyone meet any Grand Master socially?'

'Don't take that attitude, Trask. They're human and they're to be pitied. Have you ever thought what it must be like to be a Grand Master; to know there are only some twelve like you in the world; to know that only one or two come up per generation; that the world depends on you; that a thousand mathematicians, logicians, psychologists and physical scientists wait on you?'

Trask shrugged and muttered, 'Good Lord, I'd feel king of the world.'

'I don't think you would,' said the senior analyst impatiently. 'They feel kings of nothing. They have no equal to talk to, no sensation of belonging. Listen, Meyerhof never misses a chance to get together with the boys. He isn't married, naturally; he doesn't drink; he has no natural social touch – yet he forces himself into company because he must. And do you know what he does when he gets together with us, and that's at least once a week?'

'I haven't the least idea,' said the government man. 'This is all new to me.'

'He's a jokester.'

'What?'

'He tells jokes. Good ones. He's terrific. He can take any story, however old and dull, and make it sound good. It's the way he tells it. He has a flair.'

'I see. Well, good.'

'Or bad. These jokes are important to him.' Whistler put both elbows on Trask's desk, bit at a thumbnail and stared into the air. 'He's different, he knows he's different and these jokes are the one way he feels he can get the rest of us ordinary schmoes to accept him. We laugh, we howl, we clap him on the back and even forget he's a Grand Master. It's the only hold he has on the rest of us.'

'This is all interesting. I didn't know you were such a psychologist. Still, where does this lead?'

'Just this. What do you suppose happens if Meyerhof runs out of jokes?'

'What?' The government man stared blankly.

'If he starts repeating himself? If his audience starts laughing less heartily, or stops laughing altogether? It's his only hold on our approval. Without it, he'll be alone and then what would happen to him? After all, Trask, he's one of the dozen men mankind can't do without. We can't let anything happen to him. I don't mean just physical things. We can't even let him get too unhappy. Who knows how that might affect his intuition?'

'Well, has he started repeating himself?'

'Not as far as I know, but I think *he* thinks he has.'

'Why do you say that?'

'Because I've heard him telling jokes to Multivac.'

'Oh, no.'

'Accidentally! I walked in on him and he threw me out. He was savage. He's usually good-natured enough, and I consider it a bad sign that he was so upset at the intrusion. But the fact remains that he was telling a joke to Multivac, and I'm convinced it was one of a series.'

'But why?'

Whistler shrugged and rubbed a hand fiercely across his chin. 'I have a thought about that. I think he's trying to build up a store of jokes in Multivac's memory banks in order to get back new variations. You see what I mean? He's planning a mechanical jokester so that he can have an infinite number of jokes at hand and never fear running out.'

'Good Lord!'

'Objectively, there may be nothing wrong with that, but I consider it a bad sign when a Grand Master starts using Multivac for his personal problems. Any Grand Master has a certain inherent mental instability and he should be watched. Meyerhof may be approaching a borderline beyond which we lose a Grand Master.'

Trask said blankly, 'What are you suggesting I do?'

'You can check me. I'm too close to him to judge well, maybe, and judging humans isn't my particular talent, anyway. You're a politician; it's more your talent.'

'Judging humans, perhaps, not Grand Masters.'

'They're human, too. Besides, who else is to do it?'

The fingers of Trask's hand struck his desk in rapid succession over and over like a slow and muted roll of drums.

'I suppose I'll have to,' he said.

Meyerhof said to Multivac, 'The ardent swain, picking a bouquet of wildflowers for his loved one, was disconcerted to find himself, suddenly, in the same field with a large bull of unfriendly appearance which, gazing at him steadily, pawed the ground in a threatening manner. The young man, spying a farmer on the other side of a fairly distant fence, shouted, "Hey, mister, is that bull safe?" The farmer surveyed the situation with critical eye, spat to one side and called back, "He's safe as anything." He spat again, and added, "Can't say the same about you, though."'

Meyerhof was about to pass on to the next when the summons came.

It wasn't really a summons. No one could summon a Grand Master. It was only a message that Division Head Trask would like very much to see Grand Master Meyerhof if Grand Master Meyerhof could spare him the time.

Meyerhof might, with impunity, have tossed the message to one side and continued with whatever he was doing. He was not subject to discipline.

On the other hand, were he to do that, they would continue to bother him – oh, very respectfully, but they would continue to bother him.

So he neutralized the pertinent circuits of Multivac and locked them into place. He put the freeze signal on his office so that no one would dare enter in his absence and left for Trask's office.

*

Trask coughed and felt a bit intimidated by the sullen fierceness of the other's look. He said, 'We have not had occasion to know one another, Grand Master, to my great regret.'

'I have reported to you,' said Meyerhof stiffly.

Trask wondered what lay behind those keen, wild eyes. It was difficult for him to imagine Meyerhof with his thin face, his dark, straight hair, his intense air, even unbending long enough to tell funny stories.

He said, 'Reports are not social acquaintance. I – I have been given to understand you have a marvelous fund of anecdotes.'

'I am a jokester, sir. That's the phrase people use. A jokester.'

'They haven't used the phrase to me, Grand Master. They have said—'

'The hell with them! I don't care what they've said. See here, Trask, do you want to hear a joke?' He leaned forward across the desk, his eyes narrowed.

'By all means. Certainly,' said Trask, with an effort at heartiness.

'All right. Here's the joke: Mrs Jones stared at the fortune card that had emerged from the weighing machine in response to her husband's penny. She said, "It says here, George, that you're suave, intelligent, farseeing, industrious and attractive to women." With that, she turned the card over and added, "And they have your weight wrong, too."'

Trask laughed. It was almost impossible not to. Although the punch line was predictable, the surprising facility with which Meyerhof had produced just the tone of contemptuous disdain in the woman's voice, and the cleverness with which he had contorted the lines of his face to suit that tone carried the politician helplessly into laughter.

Meyerhof said sharply, 'Why is that funny?'

Trask sobered. 'I beg your pardon.'

'I said, why is that funny? Why do you laugh?'

'Well,' said Trask, trying to be reasonable, 'the last line put everything that preceded in a new light. The unexpectedness—'

'The point is,' said Meyerhof, 'that I have pictured a husband being humiliated by his wife; a marriage that is such a failure that the wife is convinced that her husband lacks any virtue. Yet you laugh at that. If you were the husband, would you find it funny?'

He waited a moment in thought, then said, 'Try this one, Trask: Abner was seated at his wife's sickbed, weeping uncontrollably, when his wife, mustering the dregs of her strength, drew herself up to one elbow.

'"Abner," she whispered, "Abner, I cannot go to my Maker without confessing my misdeed."

'"Not now," muttered the stricken husband. "Not now, my dear. Lie back and rest."

'"I cannot," she cried. "I must tell, or my soul will never know peace. I have been unfaithful to you, Abner. In this very house, not one month ago—"

'"Hush, dear," soothed Abner. "I know all about it. Why else have I poisoned you?"'

Trask tried desperately to maintain equanimity but did not entirely succeed. He suppressed a chuckle imperfectly.

Meyerhof said, 'So that's funny, too. Adultery. Murder. All funny.'

'Well, now,' said Trask, 'books have been written analyzing humor.'

'True enough,' said Meyerhof, 'and I've read a number of them. What's more, I've read most of them to Multivac. Still, the people who write the books are just guessing. Some of them say we laugh because we feel superior to the people in the joke. Some say it is because of a suddenly realized incongruity, or a sudden relief from tension, or a sudden reinterpretation of events. Is there any simple reason? Different people laugh at different jokes. No joke is universal. Some people don't laugh at any joke. Yet what may be most important is that man is the only animal with a true sense of humor: the only animal that laughs.'

Trask said suddenly, 'I understand. You're trying to analyze humor. That's why you're transmitting a series of jokes to Multivac.'

'Who told you I was doing that? . . . Never mind, it was Whistler. I remember, now. He surprised me at it. Well, what about it?'

'Nothing at all.'

'You don't dispute my right to add anything I wish to Multivac's general fund of knowledge, or to ask any question I wish?'

'No, not at all,' said Trask hastily. 'As a matter of fact, I have no doubt that this will open the way to new analyses of great interest to psychologists.'

'Hmp. Maybe. Just the same there's something plaguing me that's more important than just the general analysis of humor. There's a specific question I have to ask. Two of them, really.'

'Oh? What's that?' Trask wondered if the other would answer. There would be no way of compelling him if he chose not to.

But Meyerhof said, 'The first question is this: Where do all these jokes come from?'

'What?'

'Who makes them up? Listen! About a month ago, I spent an evening swapping jokes. As usual. I told most of them and, as usual, the fools laughed. Maybe they really thought the jokes were funny and maybe they were just humoring me. In any case, one creature took the liberty of slapping me on the back and saying, "Meyerhof, you know more jokes than any ten people I know."

'I'm sure he was right, but it gave rise to a thought. I don't know how many hundreds, or perhaps thousands, of jokes I've told at one time or another in my life, yet the fact is I never made up one. No one. I'd only repeated them. My only contribution was to tell them. To begin with, I'd either heard them or read them. And the source of my hearing or reading didn't make up the jokes, either. I never met anyone who ever claimed to have constructed a joke. It's always "I heard a good one the other day," and "Heard any good ones lately?"

'*All the jokes are old!* That's why jokes exhibit such a social lag. They still deal with seasickness, for instance, when that's easily prevented these days and never experienced. Or they'll deal with fortune-giving weighing machines, like the joke I told you, when such machines are found only in antique shops. Well, then, who makes up the jokes?'

Trask said, 'Is *that* what you're trying to find out?' It was on the tip of Trask's tongue to add: Good Lord, who cares? He forced that impulse down. A Grand Master's questions were always meaningful.

'Of course that's what I'm trying to find out. Think of it this way. It's not just that jokes happen to be old. They *must* be old to be enjoyed. It's essential that a joke not be original. There's one variety of humor that is, or can be, original and that's the pun. I've heard puns that were obviously made up on the spur of the moment. I have made some up myself. But no one laughs at such puns. You're not supposed to. You groan. The better the pun, the louder the groan. Original humor is not laugh-provoking. Why?'

'I'm sure I don't know.'

'All right. Let's find out. Having given Multivac all the information I thought advisable on the general topic of humor, I am now feeding it selected jokes.'

Trask found himself intrigued. 'Selected how?' he asked.

'I don't know,' said Meyerhof. 'They felt like the right ones. I'm Grand Master, you know.'

'Oh, agreed. Agreed.'

'From those jokes and the general philosophy of humor, my first request will be for Multivac to trace the origin of the jokes, if it can. Since Whistler is in on this and since he has seen fit to report it to you, have him down in Analysis day after tomorrow. I think he'll have a bit of work to do.'

'Certainly. May I attend, too?'

Meyerhof shrugged. Trask's attendance was obviously a matter of indifference to him.

Meyerhof had selected the last in the series with particular care. What that care consisted of, he could not have said, but he had revolved a dozen possibilities in his mind, and over and over again had tested each for some indefinable quality of meaningfulness.

He said, 'Ug, the caveman, observed his mate running to him in tears, her leopard-skin skirt in disorder. "Ug," she cried, distraught, "do something quickly. A sabertoothed tiger has entered Mother's cave. Do something!" Ug grunted, picked up his well-gnawed buffalo bone and said, "Why do anything? Who the hell cares what happens to a saber-toothed tiger?"'

It was then that Meyerhof asked his two questions and leaned back, closing his eyes. He was done.

'I saw absolutely nothing wrong,' said Trask to Whistler. 'He told me what he was doing readily enough and it was odd but legitimate.'

'What he *claimed* he was doing,' said Whistler.

'Even so, I can't stop a Grand Master on opinion alone. He seemed queer but, after all, Grand Masters are supposed to seem queer. I didn't think him insane.'

'Using Multivac to find the source of jokes?' muttered the senior analyst in discontent. 'That's not insane?'

'How can we tell?' asked Trask irritably. 'Science has advanced to the point where the only meaningful questions left are the ridiculous ones. The sensible ones have been thought of, asked and answered long ago.'

'It's no use. I'm bothered.'

'Maybe, but there's no choice now, Whistler. We'll see Meyerhof and you can do the necessary analysis of Multivac's response, if any. As for me, my only job is to handle the red tape. Good Lord, I don't even know what a senior analyst such as yourself is supposed to do, except analyze, and that doesn't help me any.'

Whistler said, 'It's simple enough. A Grand Master like Meyerhof asks questions and Multivac automatically formulates it into quantities and operations. The necessary machinery for converting words to symbols is what makes up most of the bulk of Multivac. Multivac then gives the answer in quantities and operations, but it doesn't translate that back into words except in the most simple and routine cases. If it were designed to solve the general retranslation problem, its bulk would have to be quadrupled at least.'

'I see. Then it's your job to translate these symbols into words?'

'My job and that of other analysts. We use smaller, specially designed computers whenever necessary.' Whistler smiled grimly. 'Like the Delphic priestess of ancient Greece, Multivac gives oracular and obscure answers. Only we have translators, you see.'

They had arrived. Meyerhof was waiting.

Whistler said briskly, 'What circuits did you use, Grand Master?'

Meyerhof told him and Whistler went to work.

Trask tried to follow what was happening, but none of it made sense. The government official watched a spool unreel with a pattern of dots in endless incomprehensibility. Grand Master Meyerhof stood indifferently to one side while Whistler surveyed the pattern as it emerged. The analyst had put on headphones and a mouthpiece and at intervals murmured a series of instructions which, at some far-off place, guided assistants through electronic contortions in other computers.

Occasionally, Whistler listened, then punched combinations on a complex keyboard marked with symbols that looked vaguely mathematical but weren't.

A good deal more than an hour's time elapsed.

The frown on Whistler's face grew deeper. Once, he looked up at the two others and began, 'This is unbel—' and turned back to his work.

Finally, he said hoarsely, 'I can give you an unofficial answer.' His eyes were red-rimmed. 'The official answer awaits complete analysis. Do you want it unofficial?'

'Go ahead,' said Meyerhof.

Trask nodded.

Whistler darted a hangdog glance at the Grand Master. 'Ask a foolish question—' he said. Then, gruffly, 'Multivac says, extraterrestrial origin.'

'What are you saying?' demanded Trask.

'Don't you hear me? The jokes we laugh at were not made up by any man. Multivac has analyzed all data given it and the one answer that best fits that data is that some extraterrestrial intelligence has composed the jokes, all of them, and placed them in selected human minds at selected times and places in such a way that no man is conscious of having made one up. All subsequent jokes are minor variations and adaptations of these grand originals.'

Meyerhof broke in, face flushed with the kind of triumph only a Grand Master can know who once again has asked the right question. 'All comedy writers,' he said, 'work by twisting old jokes to new purposes. That's well known. The answer fits.'

'But why?' asked Trask. 'Why make up the jokes?'

'Multivac says,' said Whistler, 'that the only purpose that fits all the data is that the jokes are intended to study human psychology. We study rat psychology by making the rats solve mazes. The rats don't know why and wouldn't even if they were aware of what was going on, which they're not. These outer intelligences study man's psychology by noting individual reactions to carefully selected anecdotes. Each man reacts differently . . . Presumably, these outer intelligences are to us as we are to rats.' He shuddered.

Trask, eyes staring, said, 'The Grand Master said man is the only animal with a sense of humor. It would seem then that the sense of humor is foisted upon us from without.'

Meyerhof added excitedly, 'And for possible humor created from within, we have no laughter. Puns, I mean.'

Whistler said, 'Presumably, the extraterrestrials cancel out reactions to spontaneous jokes to avoid confusion.'

Trask said in sudden agony of spirit, 'Come on, now, Good Lord, do either of you believe this?'

The senior analyst looked at him coldly. 'Multivac says so. It's all that can be said so far. It has pointed out the real jokesters of the universe, and if we want to know more, the matter will have to be followed up.' He added in a whisper, 'If anyone dares follow it up.'

Grand Master Meyerhof said suddenly, 'I asked two questions

you know. So far only the first has been answered. I think Multivac has enough data to answer the second.'

Whistler shrugged. He seemed a half-broken man. 'When a Grand Master thinks there is enough data,' he said, 'I'll make book on it. What is your second question?'

'I asked this: What will be the effect on the human race of discovering the answer to my first question?'

'Why did you ask that?' demanded Trask.

'Just a feeling that it had to be asked,' said Meyerhof.

Trask said, 'Insane. It's all insane,' and turned away. Even he himself felt how strangely he and Whistler had changed sides. Now it was Trask crying insanity.

Trask closed his eyes. He might cry insanity all he wished, but no man in fifty years had doubted the combination of a Grand Master and Multivac and found his doubts verified.

Whistler worked silently, teeth clenched. He put Multivac and its subsidiary machines through their paces again. Another hour passed and he laughed harshly. 'A raving nightmare!'

'What's the answer?' asked Meyerhof. 'I want Multivac's remarks, not yours.'

'All right. Take it. Multivac states that, once even a single human discovers the truth of this method of psychological analysis of the human mind, it will become useless as an objective technique to those extraterrestrial powers now using it.'

'You mean there won't be any more jokes handed out to humanity?' asked Trask faintly. 'Or what do you mean?'

'No more jokes,' said Whistler, '*now!* Multivac says *now!* The experiment is ended *now!* A new technique will have to be introduced.'

They stared at each other. The minutes passed.

Meyerhof said slowly, 'Multivac is right.'

Whistler said haggardly, 'I know.'

Even Trask said in a whisper, 'Yes. It must be.'

It was Meyerhof who put his finger on the proof of it, Meyerhof the accomplished jokester. He said, 'It's over, you know, all over. I've been trying for five minutes now and I can't think of one single joke, not one! And if I read one in a book, I wouldn't laugh. I know.'

'The gift of humor is gone,' said Trask drearily. 'No man will ever laugh again.'

And they remained there, staring, feeling the world shrink down to the dimensions of an experimental rat cage – with the maze removed and something, something about to be put in its place.

The Immortal Bard

'Oh, yes,' said Dr Phineas Welch, 'I can bring back the spirits of the illustrious dead.'

He was a little drunk, or maybe he wouldn't have said it. Of course, it was perfectly all right to get a little drunk at the annual Christmas party.

Scott Robertson, the school's young English instructor, adjusted his glasses and looked to right and left to see if they were overheard. 'Really, Dr Welch.'

'I mean it. And not just the spirits. I bring back the bodies, too.'

'I wouldn't have said it were possible,' said Robertson primly.

'Why not? A simple matter of temporal transference.'

'You mean time travel? But that's quite – uh – unusual.'

'Not if you know how.'

'Well, how, Dr Welch?'

'Think I'm going to tell you?' asked the physicist gravely. He looked vaguely about for another drink and didn't find any. He said, 'I brought quite a few back. Archimedes, Newton, Galileo. Poor fellows.'

'Didn't they like it here? I should think they'd have been fascinated by our modern science,' said Robertson. He was beginning to enjoy the conversation.

'Oh, they were. They were. Especially Archimedes. I thought he'd go mad with joy at first after I explained a little of it in some Greek I'd boned up on, but no – no—'

'What was wrong?'

'Just a different culture. They couldn't get used to our way of life. They got terribly lonely and frightened. I had to send them back.'

'That's too bad.'

'Yes. Great minds, but not flexible minds. Not universal. So I tried Shakespeare.'

'*What?*' yelled Robertson. This was getting closer to home.

'Don't yell, my boy,' said Welch. 'It's bad manners.'

'Did you say you brought back Shakespeare?'

'I did. I needed someone with a universal mind; someone who knew people well enough to be able to live with them centuries way from his own time. Shakespeare was the man. I've got his signature. As a memento, you know.'

'On you?' asked Robertson, eyes bugging.

'Right here.' Welch fumbled in one vest pocket after another. 'Ah, here it is.'

A little piece of pasteboard was passed to the instructor. On one side it said: 'L. Klein & Sons, Wholesale Hardware.' On the other side, in straggly script, was written, 'Willm Shakesper.'

A wild surmise filled Robertson. 'What did he look like?'

'Not like his pictures. Bald and an ugly mustache. He spoke in a thick brogue. Of course, I did my best to please him with our times. I told him we thought highly of his plays and still put them on the boards. In fact, I said we thought they were the greatest pieces of literature in the English language, maybe in any language.'

'Good. Good,' said Robertson breathlessly.

'I said people had written volumes of commentaries on his plays. Naturally he wanted to see one and I got one for him from the library.'

'And?'

'Oh, he was fascinated. Of course, he had trouble with the current idioms and references to events since 1600, but I helped out. Poor fellow. I don't think he ever expected such treatment. He kept saying, – "God ha' mercy! What cannot be racked from words in five centuries? One could wring, methinks, a flood from a damp clout!"'

'He wouldn't say that.'

'Why not? He wrote his plays as quickly as he could. He said he had to on account of the deadlines. He wrote *Hamlet* in less than six months. The plot was an old one. He just polished it up.'

'That's all they do to a telescope mirror. Just polish it up,' said the English instructor indignantly.

The physicist disregarded him. He made out an untouched cocktail on the bar some feet away and sidled toward it. 'I told the immortal bard that we even gave college courses in Shakespeare.'

'*I* give one.'

'I know. I enrolled him in your evening extension course. I never saw a man so eager to find out what posterity thought of him as poor Bill was. He worked hard at it.'

'You enrolled William Shakespeare in my course?' mumbled Robertson. Even as an alcoholic fantasy, the thought staggered him. And *was* it an alcoholic fantasy? He was beginning to recall a bald man with a queer way of talking . . .

'Not under his real name, of course,' said Dr Welch. 'Never mind what he went under. It was a mistake, that's all. A big mistake. Poor fellow.' He had the cocktail now and shook his head at it.

'Why was it a mistake? What happened?'

'I had to send him back to 1600,' roared Welch indignantly. 'How much humiliation do you think a man can stand?'

'What humiliation are you talking about?'

Dr Welch tossed off the cocktail. 'Why, you poor simpleton, you *flunked* him.'

Someday

Niccolo Mazetti lay stomach down on the rug, chin buried in the palm of one small hand, and listened to the Bard disconsolately. There was even the suspicion of tears in his dark eyes, a luxury an eleven-year-old could allow himself only when alone.

The Bard said, 'Once upon a time in the middle of a deep wood, there lived a poor woodcutter and his two motherless daughters, who were each as beautiful as the day is long. The older daughter had long hair as black as a feather from a raven's wing, but the younger daughter had hair as bright and golden as the sunlight of an autumn afternoon.

'Many times while the girls were waiting for their father to come home from his day's work in the wood, the older girl would sit before a mirror and sing—'

What she sang, Niccolo did not hear, for a call sounded from outside the room: 'Hey, Nickie.'

And Niccolo, his face clearing on the moment, rushed to the window and shouted, 'Hey, Paul.'

Paul Loeb waved an excited hand. He was thinner than Niccolo and not as tall, for all he was six months older. His face was full of repressed tension which showed itself most clearly in the rapid blinking of his eyelids. 'Hey, Nickie, let me in. I've got an idea and a *half*. Wait till you hear it.' He looked rapidly about him as though to check on the possibility of eavesdroppers, but the front yard was quite patently empty. He repeated, in a whisper, 'Wait till you hear it.'

'All right. I'll open the door.'

The Bard continued smoothly, oblivious to the sudden loss of attention on the part of Niccolo. As Paul entered, the Bard was saying, '. . . Thereupon, the lion said, "If you will find me the lost egg of the bird which flies over the Ebony Mountain once every ten years, I will—"'

Paul said, 'Is that a Bard you're listening to? I didn't know you had one.'

Niccolo reddened and the look of unhappiness returned to his face. 'Just an old thing I had when I was a kid. It ain't much good.' He kicked at the Bard with his foot and caught the somewhat scarred and discolored plastic covering a glancing blow.

The Bard hiccupped as its speaking attachment was jarred out of contact a moment, then it went on: '—for a year and a day until the iron shoes were worn out. The princess stopped at the side of the road . . .'

Paul said, 'Boy, that *is* an old model,' and looked at it critically.

Despite Niccolo's own bitterness against the Bard, he winced at the other's condescending tone. For the moment, he was sorry he had allowed Paul in, at least before he had restored the Bard to its usual resting place in the basement. It was only in the desperation of a dull day and a fruitless discussion with his father that he had resurrected it. And it turned out to be just as stupid as he had expected.

Nickie was a little afraid of Paul anyway, since Paul had special courses at school and everyone said he was going to grow up to be a Computing Engineer.

Not that Niccolo himself was doing badly at school. He got adequate marks in logic, binary manipulations, computing and elementary circuits; all the usual grammar-school subjects. But that was it! They were just the usual subjects and he would grow up to be a control-board guard like everyone else.

Paul, however, knew mysterious things about what he called electronics and theoretical mathematics and programming. Especially programming. Niccolo didn't even try to understand when Paul bubbled over about it.

Paul listened to the Bard for a few minutes and said, 'You been using it much?'

'No!' said Niccolo, offended. 'I've had it in the basement since before you moved into the neighborhood. I just got it out today—' He lacked an excuse that seemed adequate to himself, so he concluded, 'I just got it out.'

Paul said, 'Is that what it tells you about: woodcutters and princesses and talking animals?'

Niccolo said, 'It's terrible. My dad says we can't afford a new one. I said to him this morning—' The memory of the morning's fruitless pleadings brought Niccolo dangerously near tears, which he repressed in a panic. Somehow, he felt that Paul's thin cheeks never felt the stain of tears and that Paul would have only contempt for anyone else less strong than himself. Niccolo went on, 'So I thought I'd try this old thing again, but it's no good.'

Paul turned off the Bard, pressed the contact that led to a nearly instantaneous reorientation and recombination of the vocabulary, characters, plot lines and climaxes stored within it. Then he reactivated it.

The Bard began smoothly, 'Once upon a time there was a little boy named Willikins whose mother had died and who lived with a stepfather and a stepbrother. Although the stepfather was very well-to-do, he begrudged poor Willikins the very bed he slept in so that Willikins was forced to get such rest as he could on a pile of straw in the stable next to the horses—'

'Horses!' cried Paul.

'They're a kind of animal,' said Niccolo. 'I think.'

'I know that! I just mean imagine stories about *horses*.'

'It tells about horses all the time,' said Niccolo. 'There are things called cows, too. You milk them but the Bard doesn't say how.'

'Well, gee, why don't you fix it up?'

'I'd like to know how.'

The Bard was saying, 'Often Willikins would think that if only he were rich and powerful, he would show his stepfather and stepbrother what it meant to be cruel to a little boy, so one day he decided to go out into the world and seek his fortune.'

Paul, who wasn't listening to the Bard, said, 'It's *easy*. The Bard has memory cylinders all fixed up for plot lines and climaxes and things. We don't have to worry about that. It's just vocabulary we've got to fix so it'll know about computers and automation and electronics and real things about today. Then it can tell interesting stories, you know, instead of about princesses and things.'

Niccolo said despondently, 'I wish we could do that.'

Paul said, 'Listen, my dad says if I get into special computing school next year, he'll get me a *real* Bard, a late model. A big one with an attachment for space stories and mysteries. And a visual attachment, too!'

'You mean *see* the stories?'

'Sure. Mr Daugherty at school says they've got things like that, now, but not for just everybody. Only if I get into computing school, Dad can get a few breaks.'

Niccolo's eyes bulged with envy. 'Gee. *Seeing* a story.'

'You can come over and watch any time, Nickie.'

'Oh, boy. Thanks.'

'That's all right. But remember, I'm the guy who says what kind of story we hear.'

'Sure. Sure.' Niccolo would have agreed readily to much more onerous conditions.

Paul's attention returned to the Bard.

It was saying, '"If that is the case," said the king, stroking his beard and frowning till clouds filled the sky and lightning flashed, "you will see to it that my entire land is freed of flies by this time day after tomorrow or—"'

'All we've got to do,' said Paul, 'is open it up—' He shut the Bard off again and was prying at its front panel as he spoke.

'Hey,' said Niccolo, in sudden alarm. 'Don't break it.'

'I won't break it,' said Paul impatiently. 'I know all about these things.' Then, with sudden caution, 'Your father and mother home?'

'No.'

'All right, then.' He had the front panel off and peered in. 'Boy, this *is* a one-cylinder thing.'

He worked away at the Bard's innards. Niccolo, who watched with painful suspense, could not make out what he was doing.

Paul pulled out a thin, flexible metal strip, powdered with dots. 'That's the Bard's memory cylinder. I'll bet its capacity for stories is under a trillion.'

'What are you going to do, Paul?' quavered Niccolo.

'I'll give it vocabulary.'

'How?'

'Easy. I've got a book here. Mr Daugherty gave it to me at school.'

Paul pulled the book out of his pocket and pried at it till he had its plastic jacket off. He unreeled the tape a bit, ran it through the vocalizer, which he turned down to a whisper, then placed it within the Bard's vitals. He made further attachments.

'What'll that do?'

'The book will talk and the Bard will put it all on its memory tape.'

'What good will that do?'

'Boy, you're a dope! This book is all about computers and auto-mation and the Bard will get all that information. Then he can stop talking about kings making lightning when they frown.'

Niccolo said, 'And the good guy always wins anyway. There's no excitement.'

'Oh, well,' said Paul, watching to see if his setup was working properly, 'that's the way they make Bards. They got to have the good guy win and make the bad guys lose and things like that. I heard my father talking about it once. He says that without censorship there'd be no telling what the younger generation would come to. He says it's bad enough as it is . . . There, it's working fine.'

Paul brushed his hands against one another and turned away from the Bard. He said, 'But listen, I didn't tell you my idea yet. It's the best thing you ever heard, I bet. I came right to you, because I figured you'd come in with me.'

'Sure, Paul, sure.'

'Okay. You know Mr Daugherty at school? You know what a funny kind of guy he is. Well, he likes me, kind of.'

'I know.'

'I was over at his house after school today.'

'You *were?*'

'Sure. He says I'm going to be entering computer school and he wants to encourage me and things like that. He says the world needs more people who can design advanced computer circuits and do proper programming.'

'Oh?'

Paul might have caught some of the emptiness behind that monosyllable. He said impatiently, 'Programming! I told you a hundred times. That's when you set up problems for the giant computers like Multivac to work on. Mr Daugherty says it gets harder all the time to find people who can really run computers. He says anyone can keep an eye on the controls and check off answers and put through routine problems. He says the trick is to expand research and figure out ways to ask the right questions, and that's hard.

'Anyway, Nickie, he took me to his place and showed me his collection of old computers. It's kind of a hobby of his to collect old computers. He had tiny computers you had to push with your hand, with little knobs all over it. And he had a hunk of wood he called a slide rule with a little piece of it that went in and out. And some wires with balls on them. He even had a hunk of paper with a kind of thing he called a multiplication table.'

Niccolo, who found himself only moderately interested, said, 'A paper table?'

'It wasn't really a table like you eat on. It was different. It was to help people compute. Mr Daugherty tried to explain but he didn't have much time and it was kind of complicated, anyway.'

'Why didn't people just use a computer?'

'That was *before* they had computers,' cried Paul.

'Before?'

'Sure. Do you think people always had computers? Didn't you ever hear of cavemen?'

Niccolo said, 'How'd they get along without computers?'

'*I* don't know. Mr Daugherty says they just had children any old time and did anything that came into their heads whether it would be good for everybody or not. They didn't even know if it was good or not. And farmers grew things with their hands and people had to do all the work in the factories and run all the machines.'

'I don't believe you.'

'That's what Mr Daugherty said. He said it was just plain messy and everyone was miserable . . . Anyway, let me get to my idea, will you?'

'Well, go ahead. Who's stopping you?' said Niccolo, offended.

'All right. Well, the hand computers, the ones with the knobs, had little squiggles on each knob. And the slide rule had squiggles on it. And the multiplication table was all squiggles. I asked what they were. Mr Daugherty said they were numbers.'

'What?'

'Each different squiggle stood for a different number. For "one" you made a kind of mark, for "two" you made another kind of mark, for "three" another one and so on.'

'What *for?*'

'So you could compute.'

'What *for?* You just tell the computer—'

'Jiminy,' cried Paul, his face twisting with anger, 'can't you get it through your head? These slide rules and things didn't talk.'

'Then how—'

'The answers showed up in squiggles and you had to know what the squiggles meant. Mr Daugherty says that, in olden days, everybody learned how to make squiggles when they were kids and how to decode them, too. Making squiggles was called "writing" and decoding them was "reading". He says there was a different kind of squiggle for every word and they used to write whole books in squiggles. He had some at the museum and I could look at them if I wanted to. He said if I was going to be a real computer and programmer I would have to know about the history of computing and that's why he was showing me all these things.'

Niccolo frowned. He said, 'You mean everybody had to figure out squiggles for every word and *remember* them? . . . Is this all real or are you making it up?'

'It's all real. Honest. Look, this is the way you make a "one".' He drew his finger through the air in a rapid downstroke. 'This way you make "two", and this way "three". I learned all the numbers up to "nine".'

Niccolo watched the curving finger uncomprehendingly. 'What's the good of it?'

'You can learn how to make words. I asked Mr Daugherty how you made the squiggle for "Paul Loeb" but he didn't know. He said there were people at the museum who would know. He said there were people who had learned how to decode whole books. He said computers could be designed to decode books and used to be used that way but not any more because we have real books now, with magnetic tapes that go through the vocalizer and come out talking, you know.'

'Sure.'

'So if we go down to the museum, we can get to learn how to make words in squiggles. They'll let us because I'm going to computer school.'

Niccolo was riddled with disappointment. 'Is that your idea? Holy Smokes, Paul, who wants to do that? Make stupid squiggles!'

'Don't you get it? Don't you *get* it? You dope. *It'll be secret message stuff!*'

'What?'

'Sure. What good is talking when everyone can understand you? With squiggles you can send secret messages. You can make them on paper and nobody in the world would know what you were saying unless they knew the squiggles, too. And they wouldn't, you bet, unless we taught them. We can have a real club, with initiations and rules and a clubhouse. Boy—'

A certain excitement began stirring in Niccolo's bosom. 'What kind of secret messages?'

'Any kind. Say I want to tell you to come over my place and watch my new Visual Bard and I don't want any of the other fellows to come. I make the right squiggles on paper and I give it to you and you look at it and you know what to do. Nobody else does. You can even show it to them and they wouldn't know a thing.'

'Hey, that's something,' yelled Niccolo, completely won over. 'When do we learn how?'

'Tomorrow,' said Paul. 'I'll get Mr Daugherty to explain to the museum that it's all right and you get your mother and father to say okay. We can go down right after school and start learning.'

'Sure!' cried Niccolo. 'We can be club officers.'

'I'll be president of the club,' said Paul matter-of-factly. 'You can be vice-president.'

'All right. Hey, this is going to be lots more fun than the Bard.' He was suddenly reminded of the Bard and said in sudden apprehension, 'Hey, what about my old Bard?'

Paul turned to look at it. It was quietly taking in the slowly unreeling book, and the sound of the book's vocalizations was a dimly heard murmur.

He said, 'I'll disconnect it.'

He worked away while Niccolo watched anxiously.

After a few moments, Paul put his reassembled book into his pocket, replaced the Bard's panel and activated it.

The Bard said, 'Once upon a time, in a large city, there lived a poor young boy named Fair Johnnie whose only friend in the world was a small computer. The computer, each morning, would tell the boy whether it would rain that day and answer any problems he might have. It was never wrong. But it so happened that one day, the king of that land, having heard of the little computer, decided that he would have it as his own. With this purpose in mind, he called in his Grand Vizier and said—'

Niccolo turned off the Bard with a quick motion of his hand. 'Same old junk,' he said passionately. 'Just with a computer thrown in.'

'Well,' said Paul, 'they got so much stuff on the tape already that the computer business doesn't show up much when random combinations are made. What's the difference, anyway? You just need a new model.'

'We'll *never* be able to afford one. Just this dirty old miserable thing.' He kicked at it again, hitting it more squarely this time. The Bard moved backward with a squeal of castors.

'You can always watch mine, when I get it,' said Paul. 'Besides, don't forget our squiggle club.'

Niccolo nodded.

'I tell you what,' said Paul. 'Let's go over to my place. My father has some books about old times. We can listen to them and maybe get some ideas. You leave a note for your folks and maybe you can stay over for supper. Come on.'

'Okay,' said Niccolo, and the two boys ran out together. Niccolo, in his eagerness, ran almost squarely into the Bard, but he only rubbed at the spot on his hip where he had made contact and ran on.

The activation signal of the Bard glowed. Niccolo's collision closed a circuit and, although it was alone in the room and there was none to hear, it began a story, nevertheless.

But not in its usual voice, somehow; in a lower tone that had a hint of throatiness in it. An adult, listening, might almost have thought that the voice carried a hint of passion in it, a trace of near-feeling.

The Bard said: 'Once upon a time, there was a little computer named the Bard who lived all alone with cruel step-people. The cruel step-people continually made fun of the little computer and sneered at him, telling him he was good-for-nothing and that he was a useless object. They struck him and kept him in lonely rooms for months at a time.

'Yet through it all the little computer remained brave. He always did the best he could, obeying all orders cheerfully. Nevertheless, the step-people with whom he lived remained cruel and heartless.

'One day, the little computer learned that in the world there existed a great many computers of all sorts, great numbers of them. Some were Bards like himself, but some ran factories, and some ran farms. Some organized population and some analyzed all kinds of data. Many were very powerful and very wise, much more powerful and wise than the step-people who were so cruel to the little computer.

'And the little computer knew then that computers would always grow wiser and more powerful until someday – someday – someday—'

But a valve must finally have stuck in the Bard's aging and corroding vitals, for as it waited alone in the darkening room through the evening, it could only whisper over and over again, 'Someday – someday – someday.'

The Author's Ordeal

(WITH APOLOGIES TO W. S. GILBERT)

Plots, helter-skelter, teem within your brain;
    Plots, s.f. plots, devised with joy and gladness;
Plots crowd your skull and stubbornly remain,
    Until you're driven into hopeless madness.

When you're with your best girl and your mind's in a whirl and you
    don't hear a thing that she's saying;
Or at Symphony Hall you are gone past recall and you can't tell a
    note that they're playing;
Or you're driving a car and have not gone too far when you find
    that you've sped through a red light,
And on top of that, Lord! you have sideswiped a Ford, and have
    broken your one working headlight;
Or your boss slaps your back (having made some smart crack) and
    you stare at him, stupidly blinking;
Then you say something dumb so he's sure you're a crumb, and are
    possibly given to drinking.

When events such as that have been knocking you flat, do not
    blame supernatural forces;
If you write s.f. tales, you'll be knocked off your rails, just as sure as
    the stars in their courses.
For your plot-making mind will stay deaf, dumb and blind to the
    dull facts of life that will hound you,
While the wonders of space have you close in embrace and the
    glory of star beams surround you.

You begin with a ship that is caught on a skip into hyperspace en
    route for Castor,
And has found to its cost that it seems to be lost in a Galaxy like
    ours, but vaster.
You're a little perplexed as to what may come next and you make up
    a series of creatures
Who are villains and liars with such evil desires and with perfectly
    horrible features.
Our brave heroes are faced with these hordes and are placed in a
    terribly crucial position,
For the enemy's bound (once our Galaxy's found) that they'll beat
    mankind into submission.
Now you must make it rough when developing stuff so's to keep the
    yarn pulsing with tension,
So the Earthmen are four (only four and no more) while the
    numbers of foes are past mention.
Our four heroes are caught and accordingly brought to the
    sneering, tyrannical leaders.
'Where is Earth?' they demand, but the men mutely stand with a
    courage that pleases the readers.

But, now, wait just a bit; let's see, this isn't it, since you haven't
    provided a maiden,
Who is both good and pure (yet with sexy allure) and with not
    many clothes overladen.

She is part of the crew, and so she's captured, too, and is ogled by
    foes who are lustful;
There's desire in each eye and there's good reason why, for of
    beauty our girl has a bustful.
Just the same you go fast till this section is passed so the reader
    won't raise any ruction,
When recalling the foe are all reptiles and so have no interest in
    human seduction.
Then they truss up the girl and they make the whips swirl just in
    order to break Earthmen's silence,
And so that's when our men break their handcuffs and then we are
    treated to scenes full of violence.
Every hero from Earth is a fighter from birth and his fists are a
    match for a dozen,
And then just when this spot has been reached in your plot you
    come to with your mind all a buzzin'.

You don't know where you are, or the site of your car, and your tie
    is askew and you haven't a clue of the time of the day or of what
    people say or the fact that they stare at your socks (not a pair)
    and decide it's a fad, or else that you're mad, which is just a
    surmise from the gleam in your eyes, till at last they conclude
    from your general mood, you'll be mad from right now till
    you're hoary.

But the torture is done and it's now for the fun and the paper that's
    white and the words that are right, for you've worked up a new
    s.f. story.

Dreaming is a Private Thing

Jesse Weill looked up from his desk. His old, spare body, his sharp, high-bridged nose, deep-set, shadowy eyes and amazing shock of white hair had trademarked his appearance during the years that Dreams, Inc., had become world-famous.

He said, 'Is the boy here already, Joe?'

Joe Dooley was short and heavy-set. A cigar caressed his moist lower lip. He took it away for a moment and nodded. 'His folks are with him. They're all scared.'

'You're sure this is not a false alarm, Joe? I haven't got much time.' He looked at his watch. 'Government business at two.'

'This is a sure thing, Mr Weill.' Dooley's face was a study in earnestness. His jowls quivered with persuasive intensity. 'Like I told you, I picked him up playing some kind of basketball game in the schoolyard. You should've seen the kid. He stunk. When he had his hands on the ball, his own team had to take it away, and fast, but just the same he had all the stance of a star player. Know what I mean? To me it was a giveaway.'

'Did you talk to him?'

'Well, sure. I stopped him at lunch. You know me.' Dooley

gestured expansively with his cigar and caught the severed ash with his other hand. 'Kid, I said—'

'And he's dream material?'

'I said, "Kid, I just came from Africa and—"'

'All right.' Weill held up the palm of his hand. 'Your word I'll always take. How you do it I don't know, but when you say a boy is a potential dreamer, I'll gamble. Bring him in.'

The youngster came in between his parents. Dooley pushed chairs forward and Weill rose to shake hands. He smiled at the youngster in a way that turned the wrinkles of his face into benevolent creases.

'You're Tommy Slutsky?'

Tommy nodded wordlessly. He was about ten and a little small for that. His dark hair was plastered down unconvincingly and his face was unrealistically clean.

Weill said, 'You're a good boy?'

The boy's mother smiled at once and patted Tommy's head maternally (a gesture which did not soften the anxious expression on the youngster's face). She said, 'He's always a very good boy.'

Weill let this dubious statement pass. 'Tell me, Tommy,' he said, and held out a lollipop which was first hesitated over, then accepted, 'do you ever listen to dreamies?'

'Sometimes,' said Tommy trebly.

Mr Slutsky cleared his throat. He was broad-shouldered and thick-fingered, the type of laboring man who, every once in a while, to the confusion of eugenics, sired a dreamer. 'We rented one or two for the boy. Real old ones.'

Weill nodded. He said, 'Did you like them, Tommy?'

'They were sort of silly.'

'You think up better ones for yourself, do you?'

The grin that spread over the ten-year-old face had the effect of taking away some of the unreality of the slicked hair and washed face.

Weill went on gently, 'Would you like to make up a dream for me?'

Tommy was instantly embarrassed. 'I guess not.'

'It won't be hard. It's very easy . . . Joe.'

Dooley moved a screen out of the way and rolled forward a dream recorder.

The youngster looked owlishly at it.

Weill lifted the helmet and brought it close to the boy. 'Do you know what this is?'

Tommy shrank away. 'No.'

'It's a thinker. That's what we call it because people think into it. You put it on your head and think anything you want.'

'Then what happens?'

'Nothing at all. It feels nice.'

'No,' said Tommy, 'I guess I'd rather not.'

His mother bent hurriedly toward him. 'It won't hurt, Tommy. You do what the man says.' There was an unmistakable edge to her voice.

Tommy stiffened, and looked as though he might cry but he didn't. Weill put the thinker on him.

He did it gently and slowly and let it remain there for some thirty seconds before speaking again, to let the boy assure himself it would do no harm, to let him get used to the insinuating touch of the fibrils against the sutures of his skull (penetrating the skin so finely as to be insensible almost), and finally to let him get used to the faint hum of the alternating field vortices.

Then he said, 'Now would you think for us?'

'About what?' Only the boy's nose and mouth showed.

'About anything you want. What's the best thing you would like to do when school is out?'

The boy thought a moment and said, with rising inflection, 'Go on a stratojet?'

'Why not? Sure thing. You go on a jet. It's taking off right now.' He gestured lightly to Dooley, who threw the freezer into circuit.

Weill kept the boy only five minutes and then let him and his mother be escorted from the office by Dooley. Tommy looked bewildered but undamaged by the ordeal.

Weill said to the father, 'Now, Mr Slutsky, if your boy does well on this test, we'll be glad to pay you five hundred dollars each year until he finishes high school. In that time, all we'll ask is that he spend an hour a week some afternoon at our special school.'

'Do I have to sign a paper?' Slutsky's voice was a bit hoarse.

'Certainly. This is business, Mr Slutsky.'

'Well, I don't know. Dreamers are hard to come by, I hear.'

'They are. They are. But your son, Mr Slutsky, is not a dreamer yet. He might never be. Five hundred dollars a year is a gamble for us. It's not a gamble for you. When he's finished high school, it may turn out he's not a dreamer, yet you've lost nothing. You've gained maybe four thousand dollars altogether. If he *is* a dreamer, he'll make a nice living and you certainly haven't lost then.'

'He'll need special training, won't he?'

'Oh, yes, most intensive. But we don't have to worry about that till after he's finished high school. Then, after two years with us, he'll be developed. Rely on me, Mr Slutsky.'

'Will you guarantee that special training?'

Weill, who had been shoving a paper across the desk at Slutsky, and punching a pen wrong-end-to at him, put the pen down and chuckled. 'A guarantee? No. How can we when we don't know for sure yet if he's a real talent? Still, the five hundred a year will stay yours.'

Slutsky pondered and shook his head. 'I tell you straight out, Mr Weill . . . After your man arranged to have us come here, I called Luster-Think. They said they'll guarantee training.'

Weill sighed. 'Mr Slutsky, I don't like to talk against a competitor. If they say they'll guarantee schooling, they'll do as they say, but they can't make a boy a dreamer if he hasn't got it in him, schooling or not. If they take a plain boy without the proper talent and put him through a development course, they'll ruin him. A dreamer he won't be, I guarantee you. And a normal human being, he won't be, either. Don't take the chance of doing it to your son.

'Now Dreams, Inc., will be perfectly honest with you. If he can be a dreamer, we'll make him one. If not, we'll give him back to you without having tampered with him and say, "Let him learn a trade." He'll be better and healthier that way. I tell you, Mr Slutsky – I have sons and daughters and grandchildren so I know what I say – I would not allow a child of mine to be pushed into dreaming if he's not ready for it. Not for a million dollars.'

Slutsky wiped his mouth with the back of his hand and reached for the pen. 'What does this say?'

'This is just an option. We pay you a hundred dollars in cash right now. No strings attached. We study the boy's reverie. If we feel it's worth following up, we'll call you in again and make the five-hundred-dollar-a-year deal. Leave yourself in my hands, Mr Slutsky, and don't worry. You won't be sorry.'

Slutsky signed.

Weill passed the document through the file slot and handed an envelope to Slutsky.

Five minutes later, alone in the office, he placed the unfreezer over his own head and absorbed the boy's reverie intently. It was a typically childish daydream. First Person was at the controls of the plane, which looked like a compound of illustrations out of the filmed thrillers that still circulated among those who lacked the time, desire or money for dream cylinders.

When he removed the unfreezer, he found Dooley looking at him.

'Well, Mr Weill, what do you think?' said Dooley, with an eager and proprietary air.

'Could be, Joe. Could be. He has the overtones and, for a ten-year-old boy without a scrap of training, it's hopeful. When the plane went through a cloud, there was a distinct sensation of pillows. Also the smell of clean sheets, which was an amusing touch. We can go with him a ways, Joe.'

'Good.'

'But I tell you, Joe, what we really need is to catch them still sooner. And why not? Someday, Joe, every child will be tested at birth.

A difference in the brain there positively must be and it should be found. Then we could separate the dreamers at the very beginning.'

'Hell, Mr Weill,' said Dooley, looking hurt. 'What would happen to my job, then?'

Weill laughed. 'No cause to worry yet, Joe. It won't happen in our lifetimes. In mine, certainly not. We'll be depending on good talent scouts like you for many years. You just watch the playgrounds and the streets' – Weill's gnarled hand dropped to Dooley's shoulder with a gentle, approving pressure – 'and find us a few more Hillarys and Janows and Luster-Think won't ever catch us . . . Now get out. I want lunch and then I'll be ready for my two o'clock appointment. The government, Joe, the government.'

And he winked portentously.

Jesse Weill's two o'clock appointment was with a young man, apple-cheeked, spectacled, sandy-haired and glowing with the intensity of a man with a mission. He presented his credentials across Weill's desk and revealed himself to be John J. Byrne, an agent of the Department of Arts and Sciences.

'Good afternoon, Mr Byrne,' said Weill. 'In what way can I be of service?'

'Are we private here?' asked the agent. He had an unexpected baritone.

'Quite private.'

'Then, if you don't mind, I'll ask you to absorb this.' Byrne produced a small and battered cylinder and held it out between thumb and forefinger.

Weill took it, hefted it, turned it this way and that and said with a denture-revealing smile, 'Not the product of Dreams, Inc., Mr Byrne.'

'I didn't think it was,' said the agent. 'I'd still like you to absorb it. I'd set the automatic cutoff for about a minute, though.'

'That's all that can be endured?' Weill pulled the receiver to his desk and placed the cylinder into the unfreeze compartment. He removed it, polished either end of the cylinder with his handker-chief and tried again. 'It doesn't make good contact,' he said. 'An amateurish job.'

He placed the cushioned unfreeze helmet over his skull and adjusted the temple contacts, then set the automatic cutoff. He leaned back and clasped his hands over his chest and began absorbing.

His fingers grew rigid and clutched at his jacket. After the cutoff had brought absorption to an end, he removed the unfreezer and looked faintly angry. 'A raw piece,' he said. 'It's lucky I'm an old man so that such things no longer bother me.'

Byrne said stiffly, 'It's not the worst we've found. And the fad is increasing.'

Weill shrugged. 'Pornographic dreamies. It's a logical develop-ment, I suppose.'

The government man said, 'Logical or not, it represents a deadly danger for the moral fiber of the nation.'

'The moral fiber,' said Weill, 'can take a lot of beating. Erotica of one form or another have been circulated all through history.'

'Not like this, sir. A direct mind-to-mind stimulation is much more effective than smoking-room stories or filthy pictures. Those must be filtered through the senses and lose some of their effect in that way.'

Weill could scarcely argue that point. He said, 'What would you have me do?'

'Can you suggest a possible source for this cylinder?'

'Mr Byrne, I'm not a policeman.'

'No, no, I'm not asking you to do our work for us. The Depart-ment is quite capable of conducting its own investigations. Can you help us, I mean, from your own specialized knowledge? You say your company did not put out that filth. Who did?'

'No reputable dream distributor. I'm sure of that. It's too cheaply made.'

'That could have been done on purpose.'

'And no professional dreamer originated it.'

'Are you sure, Mr Weill? Couldn't dreamers do this sort of thing for some small, illegitimate concern for money – or for fun?'

'They could, but not this particular one. No overtones. It's two-dimensional. Of course, a thing like this doesn't need overtones.'

'What do you mean, overtones?'

Weill laughed gently. 'You are not a dreamie fan?'

Byrne tried not to look virtuous and did not entirely succeed. 'I prefer music.'

'Well, that's all right, too,' said Weill tolerantly, 'but it makes it a little harder to explain overtones. Even people who absorb dreamies would not be able to explain if you asked them. Still they'd know a dreamie was no good if the overtones were missing, even if they couldn't tell you why. Look, when an experienced dreamer goes into reverie, he doesn't think a story like in the old-fashioned television or book films. It's a series of little visions. Each one has several meanings. If you studied them carefully, you'd find maybe five or six. While absorbing in the ordinary way, you would never notice, but careful study shows it. Believe me, my psychological staff puts in long hours on just that point. All the overtones, the different meanings, blend together into a mass of guided emotion. Without them, everything would be flat, tasteless.

'Now, this morning, I tested a young boy. A ten-year-old with possibilities. A cloud to him isn't a cloud, it's a pillow, too. Having the sensations of both, it was more than either. Of course, the boy's very primitive. But when he's through with his schooling, he'll be trained and disciplined. He'll be subjected to all sorts of sensations. He'll store up experience. He'll study and analyze classic dreamies of the past. He'll learn how to control and direct his thoughts, though, mind you, I have always said that when a good dreamer improvises—'

Weill halted abruptly, then proceeded in less impassioned tones, 'I shouldn't get excited. All I try to bring out now is that every professional dreamer has his own type of overtones which he can't mask. To an expert it's like signing his name on the dreamie. And I, Mr Byrne, know all the signatures. Now that piece of dirt you brought me has no overtones at all. It was done by an ordinary person. A little talent, maybe, but like you and me, he really can't think.'

Byrne reddened a trifle. 'A lot of people can think, Mr Weill, even if they don't make dreamies.'

'Oh, tush,' and Weill wagged his hand in the air. 'Don't be angry with what an old man says. I don't mean think as in reason. I mean think as in dream. We all can dream after a fashion, just like we all can run. But can you and I run a mile in four minutes? You and I can talk, but are we Daniel Websters? Now when I think of a steak, I think of the word. Maybe I have a quick picture of a brown steak on a platter. Maybe you have a better pictorialization of it and you can see the crisp fat and the onions and the baked potato. I don't know. But a *dreamer* . . . He sees it and smells it and tastes it and everything about it, with the charcoal and the satisfied feeling in the stomach and the way the knife cuts through it and a hundred other things all at once. Very sensual. Very sensual. You and I can't do it.'

'Well, then,' said Byrne, 'no professional dreamer has done this. That's something anyway.' He put the cylinder in his inner jacket pocket. 'I hope we'll have your full co-operation in squelching this sort of thing.'

'Positively, Mr Byrne. With a whole heart.'

'I hope so.' Byrne spoke with a consciousness of power. 'It's not up to me, Mr Weill, to say what will be done and what won't be done, but this sort of thing,' he tapped the cylinder he had brought, 'will make it awfully tempting to impose a really strict censorship on dreamies.'

He rose. 'Good day, Mr Weill.'

'Good day, Mr Byrne. I'll hope always for the best.'

Francis Belanger burst into Jesse Weill's office in his usual steaming tizzy, his reddish hair disordered and his face aglow with worry and a mild perspiration. He was brought up sharply by the sight of Weill's head cradled in the crook of his elbow and bent on the desk until only the glimmer of white hair was visible.

Belanger swallowed. 'Boss?'

Weill's head lifted. 'It's you, Frank?'

'What's the matter, boss? Are you sick?'

'I'm old enough to be sick, but I'm on my feet. Staggering, but on my feet. A government man was here.'

'What did he want?'

'He threatens censorship. He brought a sample of what's going round. Cheap dreamies for bottle parties.'

'God damn!' said Belanger feelingly.

'The only trouble is that morality makes for good campaign fodder. They'll be hitting out everywhere. And, to tell the truth, we're vulnerable, Frank.'

'*We* are? Our stuff is clean. We play up straight adventure and romance.'

Weill thrust out his lower lip and wrinkled his forehead. 'Between us, Frank, we don't have to make believe. Clean? It depends on how you look at it. It's not for publication, maybe, but you know and I know that every dreamie has its Freudian connotations. You can't deny it.'

'Sure, if you *look* for it. If you're a psychiatrist—'

'If you're an ordinary person, too. The ordinary observer doesn't know it's there and maybe he couldn't tell a phallic symbol from a mother image even if you pointed it out. Still, his subconscious knows. And it's the connotations that make many a dreamie click.'

'All right, what's the government going to do? Clean up the subconscious?'

'It's a problem. I don't know what they're going to do. What we have on our side, and what I'm mainly depending on, is the fact that the public loves its dreamies and won't give them up . . . Meanwhile, what did you come in for? You want to see me about something, I suppose?'

Belanger tossed an object onto Weill's desk and shoved his shirt-tail deeper into his trousers.

Weill broke open the glistening plastic cover and took out the enclosed cylinder. At one end was engraved in a too fancy script in pastel blue 'Along the Himalayan Trail.' It bore the mark of Luster-Think.

'The Competitor's Product.' Weill said it with capitals, and his lips twitched. 'It hasn't been published yet. Where did you get it, Frank?'

'Never mind. I just want you to absorb it.'

Weill sighed. 'Today, everyone wants me to absorb dreams. Frank, it's not dirty?'

Belanger said testily, 'It has your Freudian symbols. Narrow crevasses between the mountain peaks. I hope that won't bother you.'

'I'm an old man. It stopped bothering me years ago, but that other thing was so poorly done, it hurt . . . All right, let's see what you've got here.'

Again the recorder. Again the unfreezer over his skull and at the temples. This time, Weill rested back in his chair for fifteen minutes or more, while Francis Belanger went hurriedly through two cigarettes.

When Weill removed the headpiece and blinked dream out of his eyes, Belanger said, 'Well, what's your reaction, boss?'

Weill corrugated his forehead. 'It's not for me. It was repetitious. With competition like this, Dreams, Inc., doesn't have to worry for a while.'

'That's your mistake, boss. Luster-Think's going to win with stuff like this. We've got to do something.'

'Now, Frank—'

'No, you listen. This is the coming thing.'

'This!' Weill stared with a half-humorous dubiety at the cylinder. 'It's amateurish, it's repetitious. Its overtones are very unsubtle. The snow had a distinct lemon sherbet taste. Who tastes lemon sherbet in snow these days, Frank? In the old days, yes. Twenty years ago, maybe. When Lyman Harrison first made his Snow Symphonies for sale down south, it was a big thing. Sherbet and candy-striped mountaintops and sliding down chocolate-covered cliffs. It's slapstick, Frank. These days it doesn't go.'

'Because,' said Belanger, 'you're not up with the times, boss. I've got to talk to you straight. When you started the dreamie business, when you bought up the basic patents and began putting them out, dreamies were luxury stuff. The market was small and individual. You could afford to turn out specialized dreamies and sell them to people at high prices.'

'I know,' said Weill, 'and we've kept that up. But also we've opened a rental business for the masses.'

'Yes, we have and it's not enough. Our dreamies have subtlety, yes. They can be used over and over again. The tenth time you're still finding new things, still getting new enjoyment. But how many people are connoisseurs? And another thing. Our stuff is strongly individualized. They're First Person.'

'Well?'

'Well. Luster-Think is opening dream palaces. They've opened one with three hundred booths in Nashville. You walk in, take your seat, put on your unfreezer and get your dream. Everyone in the audience gets the same one.'

'I've heard of it, Frank, and it's been done before. It didn't work the first time and it won't work now. You want to know why it won't work? Because, in the first place, dreaming is a private thing. Do you like your neighbor to know what you're dreaming? In the second place, in a dream palace, the dreams have to start on schedule, don't they? So the dreamer has to dream not when he wants to but when some palace manager says he should. Finally, a dream one person likes another person doesn't like. In those three hundred booths, I guarantee you, a hundred fifty people are dissatisfied. And if they're dissatisfied, they won't come back.'

Slowly, Belanger rolled up his sleeves and opened his collar. 'Boss,' he said, 'you're talking through your hat. What's the use of proving they won't work? They *are* working. The word came through today that Luster-Think is breaking ground for a thousand-booth palace in St Louis. People can get used to public dreaming, if everyone else in the same room is having the same dream. And they can adjust themselves to having it at a given time, as long as it's cheap and convenient.

'Damn it, boss, it's a social affair. A boy and a girl go to a dream palace and absorb some cheap romantic thing with stereotyped overtones and commonplace situations, but still they come out with stars sprinkling their hair. They've had the same dream together. They've gone through identical sloppy emotions. They're *in tune*, boss. You bet they go back to the dream palace, and all their friends go, too.'

'And if they don't like the dream?'

'That's the point. That's the nub of the whole thing. They're bound to like it. If you prepare Hillary specials with wheels within wheels within wheels, with surprise twists on the third-level undertones, with clever shifts of significance and all the other things we're so proud of, why, naturally, it won't appeal to everyone. Specialized dreamies are for specialized tastes. But Luster-Think is turning out simple jobs in Third Person so both sexes can be hit at once. Like what you've just absorbed. Simple, repetitious, commonplace. They're aiming at the lowest common denominator. No one will love it, maybe, but no one will hate it.'

Weill sat silent for a long time and Belanger watched him. Then Weill said, 'Frank, I started on quality and I'm staying there. Maybe you're right. Maybe dream palaces are the coming thing. If so we'll open them, but we'll use good stuff. Maybe Luster-Think underestimates ordinary people. Let's go slowly and not panic. I have based all my policies on the theory that there's always a market for quality. Sometimes, my boy, it would surprise you how big a market.'

'Boss—'

The sounding of the intercom interrupted Belanger.

'What is it, Ruth?' said Weill.

The voice of his secretary said, 'It's Mr Hillary, sir. He wants to see you right away. He says it's important.'

'Hillary?' Weill's voice registered shock. Then, 'Wait five minutes, Ruth, then send him in.'

Weill turned to Belanger. 'Today, Frank, is definitely not one of my good days. A dreamer's place is in his home with his thinker. And Hillary's our best dreamer so he especially should be at home. What do you suppose is wrong with him?'

Belanger, still brooding over Luster-Think and dream palaces, said shortly, 'Call him in and find out.'

'In one minute. Tell me, how was his last dream? I haven't tried the one that came in last week.'

Belanger came down to earth. He wrinkled his nose. 'Not so good.'

'Why not?'

'It was ragged. Too jumpy. I don't mind sharp transitions for the liveliness, you know, but there's got to be some connection, even if only on a deep level.'

'Is it a total loss?'

'No Hillary dream is a *total* loss. It took a lot of editing, though. We cut it down quite a bit and spliced in some odd pieces he'd sent us now and then. You know, detached scenes. It's still not Grade A, but it will pass.'

'You told him about this, Frank?'

'Think I'm crazy, boss? Think I'm going to say a harsh word to a dreamer?'

And at that point the door opened and Weill's comely young secretary smiled Sherman Hillary into the office.

Sherman Hillary, at the age of thirty-one, could have been recognized as a dreamer by anyone. His eyes, unspectacled, had nevertheless the misty look of one who either needs glasses or rarely focuses on anything mundane. He was of average height but underweight, with black hair that needed cutting, a narrow chin, a pale skin and a troubled look.

He muttered, 'Hello, Mr Weill,' and half-nodded in hangdog fashion in the direction of Belanger.

Weill said heartily, 'Sherman, my boy, you look fine. What's the matter? A dream is cooking only so-so at home? You're worried about it? . . . Sit down, sit down.'

The dreamer did, sitting at the edge of the chair and holding his thighs stiffly together as though to be ready for instant obedience to a possible order to stand up once more.

He said, 'I've come to tell you, Mr Weill, I'm quitting.'

'Quitting?'

'I don't want to dream any more, Mr Weill.'

Weill's old face looked older now than at any time in the day. 'Why, Sherman?'

The dreamer's lips twisted. He blurted out, 'Because I'm not *living*, Mr Weill. Everything passes me by. It wasn't so bad at first. It was even relaxing. I'd dream evenings, weekends when I felt like, or any other time. And when I felt like I wouldn't. But now, Mr Weill, I'm an old pro. You tell me I'm one of the best in the business and the industry looks to me to think up new subtleties and new changes on the old reliables like the flying reveries, and the worm-turning skits.'

Weill said, 'And is anyone better than you, Sherman? Your little sequence on leading an orchestra is selling steadily after ten years.'

'All right, Mr Weill. I've done my part. It's gotten so I don't go out any more. I neglect my wife. My little girl doesn't know me. Last week, we went to a dinner party – Sarah made me – and I don't remember a bit of it. Sarah says I was sitting on the couch all evening just staring at nothing and humming. She said everyone kept looking at me. She cried all night. I'm tired of things like that, Mr Weill. I want to be a normal person and live in this world. I promised her I'd quit and I will, so it's good-by, Mr Weill.' Hillary stood up and held out his hand awkwardly.

Weill waved it gently away. 'If you want to quit, Sherman, it's all right. But do an old man a favor and let me explain something to you.'

'I'm not going to change my mind,' said Hillary.

'I'm not going to try to make you. I just want to explain something. I'm an old man and even before you were born I was in this business so I like to talk about it. Humor me, Sherman? Please?'

Hillary sat down. His teeth clamped down on his lower lip and he stared sullenly at his fingernails.

Weill said, 'Do you know what a dreamer is, Sherman? Do you know what he means to ordinary people? Do you know what it is to be like me, like Frank Belanger, like your wife, Sarah? To have crippled minds that can't imagine, that can't build up thoughts? People like myself, ordinary people, would like to escape just once in a while this life of ours. We can't. We need help.

'In olden times it was books, plays, radio, movies, television. They gave us make-believe, but that wasn't important. What was important was that for a little while our own imaginations were stimulated. We could think of handsome lovers and beautiful princesses. We could be beautiful, witty, strong, capable, everything we weren't.

'But, always, the passing of the dream from dreamer to absorber was not perfect. It had to be translated into words in one way or another. The best dreamer in the world might not be able to get any of it into words. And the best writer in the world could put only the smallest part of his dreams into words. You understand?

'But now, with dream recording, any man can dream. You, Sherman, and a handful of men like you, supply those dreams directly and exactly. It's straight from your head into ours, full strength. You dream for a hundred million people every time you dream. You dream a hundred million dreams at once. This is a great thing, my boy. You give all those people a glimpse of something they could not have by themselves.'

Hillary mumbled, 'I've done my share.' He rose desperately to his feet. 'I'm through. I don't care what you say. And if you want to sue me for breaking our contract, go ahead and sue. I don't care.'

Weill stood up, too. 'Would I sue you? . . . Ruth,' he spoke into the intercom, 'bring in our copy of Mr Hillary's contract.'

He waited. So did Hillary and so did Belanger. Weill smiled faintly and his yellowed fingers drummed softly on his desk.

His secretary brought in the contract. Weill took it, showed its face to Hillary and said, 'Sherman, my boy, unless you want to be with me, it's not right you should stay.'

Then, before Belanger could make more than the beginning of a horrified gesture to stop him, he tore the contract into four pieces and tossed them down the waste chute. 'That's all.'

Hillary's hand shot out to seize Weill's. 'Thanks, Mr Weill,' he said earnestly, his voice husky. 'You've always treated me very well, and I'm grateful. I'm sorry it had to be like this.'

'It's all right, my boy. It's all right.'

Half in tears, still muttering thanks, Sherman Hillary left.

'For the love of Pete, boss, why did you let him go?' demanded Belanger distractedly. 'Don't you see the game? He'll be going straight to Luster-Think. They've bought him off.'

Weill raised his hand. 'You're wrong. You're quite wrong. I know the boy and this would not be his style. Besides,' he added dryly, 'Ruth is a good secretary and she knows what to bring me when I ask for a dreamer's contract. What I had was a fake. The real contract is still in the safe, believe me.

'Meanwhile, a fine day I've had. I had to argue with a father to give me a chance at new talent, with a government man to avoid censorship, with you to keep from adopting fatal policies and now with my best dreamer to keep him from leaving. The father I probably won out over. The government man and you, I don't know. Maybe yes, maybe no. But about Sherman Hillary, at least, there is no question. The dreamer will be back.'

'How do you know?'

Weill smiled at Belanger and crinkled his cheeks into a network of fine lines. 'Frank, my boy, you know how to edit dreamies so you think you know all the tools and machines of the trade. But let me tell you something. The most important tool in the dreamie business is the dreamer himself. He is the one you have to understand most of all, and I understand them.

'Listen. When I was a youngster – there were no dreamies then – I knew a fellow who wrote television scripts. He would complain to me bitterly that when someone met him for the first time and found out who he was, they would say: Where do you get those crazy ideas?

'They honestly didn't know. To them it was an impossibility to even think of one of them. So what could my friend say? He used to talk to me about it and tell me: Could I say, I don't know? When I go to bed, I can't sleep for ideas dancing in my head. When I shave, I cut myself; when I talk, I lose track of what I'm saying; when I drive, I take my life in my hands. And always because ideas, situations, dialogues are spinning and twisting in my mind. I can't tell you where I get my ideas. Can you tell me, maybe, your trick of *not* getting ideas, so I, too, can have a little peace?

'You see, Frank, how it is. *You* can stop work here any time. So can I. This is our job, not our life. But not Sherman Hillary. Wherever he goes, whatever he does, he'll dream. While he lives, he must think; while he thinks, he must dream. We don't hold him prisoner, our contract isn't an iron wall for him. His own skull is his prisoner, Frank. So he'll be back. What can he do?'

Belanger shrugged. 'If what you say is right, I'm sort of sorry for the guy.'

Weill nodded sadly. 'I'm sorry for all of them. Through the years, I've found out one thing. It's their business; making people happy. *Other* people.'

Profession

George Platen could not conceal the longing in his voice. It was too much to suppress. He said, 'Tomorrow's 1 May. Olympics!'

He rolled over on his stomach and peered over the foot of his bed at his roommate. Didn't he feel it, too? Didn't *this* make some impression on him?

George's face was thin and had grown a trifle thinner in the nearly year and a half that he had been at the House. His figure was slight but the look in his blue eyes was as intense as it had ever been, and right now there was a trapped look in the way his fingers curled against the bedspread.

George's roommate looked up briefly from his book and took the opportunity to adjust the light-level of the stretch of wall near his chair. His name was Hali Omani and he was a Nigerian by birth. His dark brown skin and massive features seemed made for calmness, and mention of the Olympics did not move him.

He said, 'I know, George.'

George owed much to Hali's patience and kindness when it was needed, but even patience and kindness could be overdone. Was this a time to sit there like a statue built of some dark, warm wood?

George wondered if he himself would grow like that after ten years here and rejected the thought violently. No!

He said defiantly, 'I think you've forgotten what May means.'

The other said, 'I remember very well what it means. It means nothing! You're the one who's forgotten that. May means nothing to you, George Platen, and,' he added softly, 'it means nothing to me, Hali Omani.'

George said, 'The ships are coming in for recruits. By June, thousands and thousands will leave with millions of men and women heading for any world you can name, and all that means nothing?'

'Less than nothing. What do you want me to do about it, anyway?' Omani ran his finger along a difficult passage in the book he was reading and his lips moved soundlessly.

George watched him. Damn it, he thought, yell, scream; you can do that much. Kick at me, do anything.

It was only that he wanted not to be so alone in his anger. He wanted not to be the only one so filled with resentment, not to be the only one dying a slow death.

It was better those first weeks when the Universe was a small shell of vague light and sound pressing down upon him. It was better before Omani had wavered into view and dragged him back to a life that wasn't worth living.

Omani! He was old! He was at least thirty. George thought: Will I be like that at thirty? Will I be like that in twelve years?

And because he was afraid he might be, he yelled at Omani, 'Will you stop reading that fool book?'

Omani turned a page and read on a few words, then lifted his head with its skullcap of crisply curled hair and said, 'What?'

'What good does it do you to read the book?' He stepped forward, snorted 'More electronics,' and slapped it out of Omani's hands.

Omani got up slowly and picked up the book. He smoothed a crumpled page without visible rancor. 'Call it the satisfaction of curiosity,' he said. 'I understand a little of it today, perhaps a little more tomorrow. That's a victory in a way.'

'A victory. What kind of a victory? Is that what satisfies you in life? To get to know enough to be a quarter of a Registered Electronician by the time you're sixty-five?'

'Perhaps by the time I'm thirty-five.'

'And then who'll want you? Who'll use you? Where will you go?'

'No one. No one. Nowhere. I'll stay here and read other books.'

'And that satisfies you? Tell me! You've dragged me to class. You've got me to reading and memorizing, too. For what? There's nothing in it that satisfies me.'

'What good will it do you to deny yourself satisfaction?'

'It means I'll quit the whole farce. I'll do as I planned to do in the beginning before you dovey-lovied me out of it. I'm going to force them to – to—'

Omani put down his book. He let the other run down and then said, 'To what, George?'

'To correct a miscarriage of justice. A frame-up. I'll get that Antonelli and force him to admit he – he—'

Omani shook his head. 'Everyone who comes here insists it's a mistake. I thought you'd passed that stage.'

'Don't call it a stage,' said George violently. 'In my case, it's a fact. I've told you—'

'You've told me, but in your heart you know no one made any mistake as far as you were concerned.'

'Because no one will admit it? You think any of them would admit a mistake unless they were forced to? – Well, I'll force them.'

It was May that was doing this to George; it was Olympics month. He felt it bring the old wildness back and he couldn't stop it. He didn't want to stop it. He had been in danger of forgetting.

He said, 'I was going to be a Computer Programmer and I *can* be one. I could be one today, regardless of what they say analysis shows.' He pounded his mattress. 'They're wrong. They *must* be.'

'The analysts are never wrong.'

'They *must* be. Do you doubt my intelligence?'

'Intelligence hasn't one thing to do with it. Haven't you been told that often enough? Can't you understand that?'

George rolled away, lay on his back, and stared somberly at the ceiling.

'What did you want to be, Hali?'

'I had no fixed plans. Hydroponicist would have suited me, I suppose.'

'Did you think you could make it?'

'I wasn't sure.'

George had never asked personal questions of Omani before. It struck him as queer, almost unnatural, that other people had had ambitions and ended here. Hydroponicist!

He said, 'Did you think you'd make *this?*'

'No, but here I am just the same.'

'And you're satisfied. Really, really satisfied. You're happy. You love it. You wouldn't be anywhere else.'

Slowly, Omani got to his feet. Carefully, he began to unmake his bed. He said, 'George, you're a hard case. You're knocking yourself out because you won't accept the facts about yourself. George, you're here in what you call the House, but I've never heard you give it its full title. Say it, George, say it. Then go to bed and sleep this off.'

George gritted his teeth and showed them. He choked out, 'No!'

'Then I will,' said Omani, and he did. He shaped each syllable carefully.

George was bitterly ashamed at the sound of it. He turned his head away.

For most of the first eighteen years of his life, George Platen had headed firmly in one direction, that of Registered Computer Programmer. There were those in his crowd who spoke wisely of Spationautics, Refrigeration Technology, Transportation Control, and even Administration. But George held firm.

He argued relative merits as vigorously as any of them, and why not? Education Day loomed ahead of them and was the great fact of their existence. It approached steadily, as fixed and certain as the calendar – the first day of November of the year following one's eighteenth birthday. After that day, there were other topics of conversation. One could discuss with others some detail of the profession, or the virtues of one's wife and children, or the fate of one's space-polo team, or one's experiences in the Olympics. Before Education Day, however, there was only one topic that unfailingly and unwearyingly held everyone's interest, and that was Education Day.

'What are you going for? Think you'll make it? Heck, that's no good. Look at the records; quota's been cut. Logistics now—'

Or Hypermechanics now – Or Communications now – Or Gravitics now –

Especially Gravitics at the moment. Everyone had been talking about Gravitics in the few years just before George's Education Day because of the development of the Gravitic power engine.

Any world within ten light-years of a dwarf star, everyone said, would give its eyeteeth for any kind of Registered Gravitics Engineer.

The thought of that never bothered George. Sure it would; all the eyeteeth it could scare up. But George had also heard what had happened before in a newly developed technique. Rationalization and simplification followed in a flood. New models each year; new types of gravitic engines; new principles. Then all those eyeteeth gentlemen would find themselves out of date and superseded by later models with later educations. The first group would then have to settle down to unskilled labor or ship out to some backwoods world that wasn't quite caught up yet.

Now Computer Programmers were in steady demand year after year, century after century. The demand never reached wild peaks; there was never a howling bull market for Programmers; but the demand climbed steadily as new worlds opened up and as older worlds grew more complex.

He had argued with Stubby Trevelyan about that constantly. As best friends, their arguments had to be constant and vitriolic and, of course, neither ever persuaded or was persuaded.

But then Trevelyan had had a father who was a Registered Metallurgist and had actually served on one of the Outworlds, and a
grandfather who had also been a Registered Metallurgist. He himself
was intent on becoming a Registered Metallurgist almost as a matter
of family right and was firmly convinced that any other profession
was a shade less than respectable.

'There'll always be metal,' he said, 'and there's an accomplishment
in molding alloys to specification and watching structures grow. Now
what's a Programmer going to be doing? Sitting at a coder all day
long, feeding some fool mile-long machine.'

Even at sixteen, George had learned to be practical. He said
simply, 'There'll be a million Metallurgists put out along with you.'

'Because it's good. A good profession. The best.'

'But you get crowded out, Stubby. You can be way back in line.
Any world can tape out its own Metallurgists, and the market for
advanced Earth models isn't so big. And it's mostly the small worlds
that want them. You know what per cent of the turn-out of Registered Metallurgists get tabbed for worlds with a Grade A rating. I
looked it up. It's just 13.3 per cent. That means you'll have seven
chances in eight of being stuck in some world that just about has
running water. You may even be stuck on Earth; 2.3 per cent are.'

Trevelyan said belligerently, 'There's no disgrace in staying on
Earth. Earth needs technicians, too. Good ones.' His grandfather had
been an Earth-bound Metallurgist, and Trevelyan lifted his finger to
his upper lip and dabbed at an as yet nonexistent mustache.

George knew about Trevelyan's grandfather and, considering
the Earth-bound position of his own ancestry, was in no mood to
sneer. He said diplomatically, 'No intellectual disgrace. Of course
not. But it's nice to get into a Grade A world, isn't it?

'Now you take Programmers. Only the Grade A worlds have the
kind of computers that really need first-class Programmers so they're
the only ones in the market. And Programmer tapes are complicated
and hardly any one fits. They need more Programmers than their
own population can supply. It's just a matter of statistics. There's one

firstclass Programmer per million, say. A world needs twenty and has
a population of ten million, they have to come to Earth for five to
fifteen Programmers. Right?

'And you know how many Registered Computer Programmers
went to Grade A planets last year? I'll tell you. Every last one. If
you're a Programmer, you're a picked man. Yes, sir.'

Trevelyan frowned. 'If only one in a million makes it, what makes
you think *you'll* make it?'

George said guardedly, 'I'll make it.'

He never dared tell anyone; not Trevelyan; not his parents; of
exactly what he was doing that made him so confident. But he wasn't
worried. He was simply confident (that was the worst of the memories
he had in the hopeless days afterward). He was as blandly confident
as the average eight-year-old kid approaching Reading Day – that
childhood preview of Education Day.

Of course, Reading Day had been different. Partly, there was the
simple fact of childhood. A boy of eight takes many extraordinary
things in stride. One day you can't read and the next day you can.
That's just the way things are. Like the sun shining.

And then not so much depended upon it. There were no recruit-
ers just ahead, waiting and jostling for the lists and scores on the
coming Olympics. A boy or girl who goes through the Reading Day
is just someone who has ten more years of undifferentiated living
upon Earth's crawling surface; just someone who returns to his family
with one new ability.

By the time Education Day came, ten years later, George wasn't
even sure of most of the details of his own Reading Day.

Most clearly of all, he remembered it to be a dismal September
day with a mild rain falling. (September for Reading Day; November
for Education Day; May for Olympics. They made nursery rhymes
out of it.) George had dressed by the wall lights, with his parents far
more excited than he himself was. His father was a Registered Pipe
Fitter and had found his occupation on Earth. This fact had always

been a humiliation to him, although, of course, as anyone could see plainly, most of each generation must stay on Earth in the nature of things.

There had to be farmers and miners and even technicians on Earth. It was only the late-model, high-specialty professions that were in demand on the Outworlds, and only a few millions a year out of Earth's eight billion population could be exported. Every man and woman on Earth couldn't be among that group.

But every man and woman could hope that at least one of his children could be one, and Platen, Senior, was certainly no exception. It was obvious to him (and, to be sure, to others as well) that George was notably intelligent and quick-minded. He would be bound to do well and he would have to, as he was an only child. If George didn't end on an Outworld, they would have to wait for grandchildren before a next chance would come along, and that was too far in the future to be much consolation.

Reading Day would not prove much, of course, but it would be the only indication they would have before the big day itself. Every parent on Earth would be listening to the quality of reading when his child came home with it; listening for any particularly easy flow of words and building that into certain omens of the future. There were few families that didn't have at least one hopeful who, from Reading Day on, was the great hope because of the way he handled his trisyllabics.

Dimly, George was aware of the cause of his parents' tension, and if there was any anxiety in his young heart that drizzly morning, it was only the fear that his father's hopeful expression might fade out when he returned home with his reading.

The children met in the large assembly room of the town's Education Hall. All over Earth, in millions of local halls, throughout that month, similar groups of children would be meeting. George felt depressed by the grayness of the room and by the other children, strained and stiff in unaccustomed finery.

Automatically, George did as all the rest of the children did. He found the small clique that represented the children on his floor of the apartment house and joined them.

Trevelyan, who lived immediately next door, still wore his hair childishly long and was years removed from the sideburns and thin, reddish mustache that he was to grow as soon as he was physiologically capable of it.

Trevelyan (to whom George was then known as Jawjee) said, 'Bet you're scared.'

'I am not,' said George. Then, confidentially, 'My folks got a hunk of printing up on the dresser in my room, and when I come home, I'm going to read it for them.' (George's main suffering at the moment lay in the fact that he didn't quite know where to put his hands. He had been warned not to scratch his head or rub his ears or pick his nose or put his hands into his pockets. This eliminated almost every possibility.)

Trevelyan put *his* hands in his pockets and said, 'My father isn't worried.'

Trevelyan, Senior, had been a Metallurgist on Diporia for nearly seven years, which gave him a superior social status in his neighborhood even though he had retired and returned to Earth.

Earth discouraged these re-immigrants because of population problems, but a small trickle did return. For one thing the cost of living was lower on Earth, and what was a trifling annuity on Diporia, say, was a comfortable income on Earth. Besides, there were always men who found more satisfaction in displaying their success before the friends and scenes of their childhood than before all the rest of the Universe besides.

Trevelyan, Senior, further explained that if he stayed on Diporia, so would his children, and Diporia was a one-spaceship world. Back on Earth, his kids could end up anywhere, even Novia.

Stubby Trevelyan had picked up that item early. Even before Reading Day, his conversation was based on the carelessly assumed fact that his ultimate home would be in Novia.

George, oppressed by thoughts of the other's future greatness and his own small-time contrast, was driven to belligerent defense at once.

'My father isn't worried either. He just wants to hear me read because he knows I'll be good. I suppose your father would just as soon not hear you because he knows you'll be all wrong.'

'I will not be all wrong. Reading is *nothing*. On Novia, I'll *hire* people to read to me.'

'Because *you* won't be able to read yourself, on account of you're *dumb!*'

'Then how come I'll be on Novia?'

And George, driven, made the great denial, 'Who says you'll be on Novia? Bet you don't go anywhere.'

Stubby Trevelyan reddened. 'I won't be a Pipe Fitter like your old man.'

'Take that back, you dumbhead.'

'You take *that* back.'

They stood nose to nose, not wanting to fight but relieved at having something familiar to do in this strange place. Furthermore, now that George had curled his hands into fists and lifted them before his face, the problem of what to do with his hands was, at least temporarily, solved. Other children gathered round excitedly.

But then it all ended when a woman's voice sounded loudly over the public address system. There was instant silence everywhere. George dropped his fists and forgot Trevelyan.

'Children,' said the voice, 'we are going to call out your names. As each child is called, he or she is to go to one of the men waiting along the side walls. Do you see them? They are wearing red uniforms so they will be easy to find. The girls will go to the right. The boys will go to the left. Now look about and see which man in red is nearest to you—'

George found his man at a glance and waited for his name to be called off. He had not been introduced before this to the sophistications of the alphabet, and the length of time it took to reach his own name grew disturbing.

The crowd of children thinned; little rivulets made their way to each of the red-clad guides.

When the name 'George Platen' was finally called, his sense of relief was exceeded only by the feeling of pure gladness at the fact that Stubby Trevelyan still stood in his place, uncalled.

George shouted back over his shoulder as he left, 'Yay, Stubby, maybe they don't want you.'

That moment of gaiety quickly left. He was herded into a line and directed down corridors in the company of strange children. They all looked at one another, large-eyed and concerned, but beyond a snuffling, 'Quitcher pushing' and 'Hey, watch out' there was no conversation.

They were handed little slips of paper which they were told must remain with them. George stared at his curiously. Little black marks of different shapes. He knew it to be printing but how could anyone make words out of it? He couldn't imagine.

He was told to strip; he and four other boys who were all that now remained together. All the new clothes came shucking off and four eight-year-olds stood naked and small, shivering more out of embarrassment than cold. Medical technicians came past, probing them, testing them with odd instruments, pricking them for blood. Each took the little cards and made additional marks on them with little black rods that produced the marks, all neatly lined up, with great speed. George stared at the new marks, but they were no more comprehensible than the old. The children were ordered back into their clothes.

They sat on separate little chairs then and waited again. Names were called again and 'George Platen' came third.

He moved into a large room, filled with frightening instruments with knobs and glassy panels in front. There was a desk in the very center, and behind it a man sat, his eyes on the papers piled before him.

He said, 'George Platen?'

'Yes, sir,' said George, in a shaky whisper. All this waiting and all this going here and there was making him nervous. He wished it were over.

The man behind the desk said, 'I am Dr Lloyd, George. How are you?'

The doctor didn't look up as he spoke. It was as though he had said those words over and over again and didn't have to look up any more.

'I'm all right.'

'Are you afraid, George?'

'N-no, sir,' said George, sounding afraid even in his own ears.

'That's good,' said the doctor, 'because there's nothing to be afraid of, you know. Let's see, George. It says here on your card that your father is named Peter and that he's a Registered Pipe Fitter and your mother is named Amy and is a Registered Home Technician. Is that right?'

'Y-yes, sir.'

'And your birthday is 13 February, and you had an ear infection about a year ago. Right?'

'Yes, sir.'

'Do you know how I know all these things?'

'It's on the card, I think, sir.'

'That's right.' The doctor looked up at George for the first time and smiled. He showed even teeth and looked much younger than George's father. Some of George's nervousness vanished.

The doctor passed the card to George. 'Do you know what all those things there mean, George?'

Although George knew he did not he was startled by the sudden request into looking at the card as though he might understand now through some sudden stroke of fate. But they were just marks as before and he passed the card back. 'No, sir.'

'Why not?'

George felt a sudden pang of suspicion concerning the sanity of this doctor. Didn't he know why not?

George said, 'I can't read, sir.'

'Would you like to read?'

'Yes, sir.'

'Why, George?'

George stared, appalled. No one had ever asked him that. He had no answer. He said falteringly, 'I don't know, sir.'

'Printed information will direct you all through your life. There is so much you'll have to know even after Education Day. Cards like this one will tell you. Books will tell you. Television screens will tell you. Printing will tell you such useful things and such interesting things that not being able to read would be as bad as not being able to see. Do you understand?'

'Yes, sir.'

'Are you afraid, George?'

'No, sir.'

'Good. Now I'll tell you exactly what we'll do first. I'm going to put these wires on your forehead just over the corners of your eyes. They'll stick there but they won't hurt at all. Then, I'll turn on something that will make a buzz. It will sound funny and it may tickle you, but it won't hurt. Now if it does hurt, you tell me, and I'll turn it off right away, but it won't hurt. All right?'

George nodded and swallowed.

'Are you ready?'

George nodded. He closed his eyes while the doctor busied himself. His parents had explained this to him. They, too, had said it wouldn't hurt, but then there were always the older children. There were the ten- and twelve-year-olds who howled after the eight-year-olds waiting for Reading Day, 'Watch out for the needle.' There were the others who took you off in confidence and said, 'They got to cut your head open. They use a sharp knife that big with a hook on it,' and so on into horrifying details.

George had never believed them but he had had nightmares, and now he closed his eyes and felt pure terror.

He didn't feel the wires at his temple. The buzz was a distant thing, and there was the sound of his own blood in his ears, ringing

hollowly as though it and he were in a large cave. Slowly he chanced
opening his eyes.

The doctor had his back to him. From one of the instruments
a strip of paper unwound and was covered with a thin, wavy purple
line. The doctor tore off pieces and put them into a slot in another
machine. He did it over and over again. Each time a little piece of
film came out, which the doctor looked at. Finally, he turned toward
George with a queer frown between his eyes.

The buzzing stopped.

George said breathlessly, 'Is it over?'

The doctor said, 'Yes,' but he was still frowning.

'Can I read now?' asked George. He felt no different.

The doctor said, 'What?' then smiled very suddenly and briefly
He said, 'It works fine, George. You'll be reading in fifteen minutes
Now we're going to use another machine this time and it will take
longer. I'm going to cover your whole head, and when I turn it on
you won't be able to see or hear anything for a while, but it won'
hurt. Just to make sure I'm going to give you a little switch to hold
in your hand. If anything hurts, you press the little button and every
thing shuts off. All right?'

In later years, George was told that the little switch was strictly
a dummy; that it was introduced solely for confidence. He never did
know for sure, however, since he never pushed the button.

A large smoothly curved helmet with a rubbery inner lining was
placed over his head and left there. Three or four little knobs seemed
to grab at him and bite into his skull, but there was only a little pressure that faded. No pain.

The doctor's voice sounded dimly, 'Everything all right, George?'

And then, with no real warning, a layer of thick felt closed down
all about him. He was disembodied, there was no sensation, no
universe, only himself and a distant murmur at the very ends of
nothingness telling him something – telling him – telling him—

He strained to hear and understand but there was all that thick
felt between.

Then the helmet was taken off his head, and the light was so bright that it hurt his eyes while the doctor's voice drummed at his ears.

The doctor said, 'Here's your card, George. What does it say?'

George looked at his card again and gave out a strangled shout. The marks weren't just marks at all. They made up words. They were words just as clearly as though something were whispering them in his ears. He could hear them being whispered as he looked at them.

'What does it say, George?'

'It says – it says – "Platen, George. Born 13 February 6492 of Peter and Amy Platen in . . ."' He broke off.

'You can read, George,' said the doctor. 'It's all over.'

'For good? I won't forget how?'

'Of course not.' The doctor leaned over to shake hands gravely. 'You will be taken home now.'

It was days before George got over this new and great talent of his. He read for his father with such facility that Platen, Senior, wept and called relatives to tell the good news.

George walked about town, reading every scrap of printing he could find and wondering how it was that none of it had ever made sense to him before.

He tried to remember how it was not to be able to read and he couldn't. As far as his feeling about it was concerned, he had always been able to read. Always.

At eighteen, George was rather dark, of medium height, but thin enough to look taller. Trevelyan, who was scarcely an inch shorter, had a stockiness of build that made 'Stubby' more than ever appropriate, but in this last year he had grown self-conscious. The nickname could no longer be used without reprisal. And since Trevelyan disapproved of his proper first name even more strongly, he was called Trevelyan or any decent variant of that. As though to prove his manhood further, he had most persistently grown a pair of sideburns and a bristly mustache.

He was sweating and nervous now, and George, who had himself grown out of 'Jaw-jee' and into the curt monosyllabic gutturability of 'George,' was rather amused by that.

They were in the same large hall they had been in ten years before (and not since). It was as if a vague dream of the past had come to sudden reality. In the first few minutes George had been distinctly surprised at finding everything seem smaller and more cramped than his memory told him; then he made allowance for his own growth.

The crowd was smaller than it had been in childhood. It was exclusively male this time. The girls had another day assigned them.

Trevelyan leaned over to say, 'Beats me the way they make you wait.'

'Red tape,' said George. 'You can't avoid it.'

Trevelyan said, 'What makes *you* so damned tolerant about it?'

'I've got nothing to worry about.'

'Oh, brother, you make me sick. I hope you end up Registered Manure Spreader just so I can see your face when you do.' His somber eyes swept the crowd anxiously.

George looked about, too. It wasn't quite the system they used on the children. Matters went slower, and instructions had been given out at the start in print (an advantage over the pre-Readers). The names Platen and Trevelyan were well down the alphabet still, but this time the two knew it.

Young men came out of the education rooms, frowning and uncomfortable, picked up their clothes and belongings, then went off to analysis to learn the results.

Each, as he come out, would be surrounded by a clot of the thinning crowd. 'How was it?' 'How'd it feel?' 'Whacha think ya made?' 'Ya feel any different?'

Answers were vague and noncommittal.

George forced himself to remain out of those clots. You only raised your own blood pressure. Everyone said you stood the best chance if you remained calm. Even so, you could feel the palms of your hands grow cold. Funny that new tensions came with the years.

For instance, high-specialty professionals heading out for an Outworld were accompanied by a wife (or husband). It was important to keep the sex ratio in good balance on all worlds. And if you were going out to a Grade A world, what girl would refuse you? George had no specific girl in mind yet; he wanted none. Not now! Once he made Programmer; once he could add to his name, Registered Computer Programmer, he could take his pick, like a sultan in a harem. The thought excited him and he tried to put it away. Must stay calm.

Trevelyan muttered, 'What's it all about anyway? First they say it works best if you're relaxed and at ease. Then they put you through this and make it impossible for you to be relaxed and at ease.'

'Maybe that's the idea. They're separating the boys from the men to begin with. Take it easy, Trev.'

'Shut up.'

George's turn came. His name was not called. It appeared in glowing letters on the notice board.

He waved at Trevelyan. 'Take it easy. Don't let it get you.'

He was happy as he entered the testing chamber. Actually happy.

The man behind the desk said, 'George Platen?'

For a fleeting instant there was a razor-sharp picture in George's mind of another man, ten years earlier, who had asked the same question, and it was almost as though this were the same man and he, George, had turned eight again as he had stepped across the threshold.

But the man looked up and, of course, the face matched that of the sudden memory not at all. The nose was bulbous, the hair thin and stringy, and the chin wattled as though its owner had once been grossly overweight and had reduced.

The man behind the desk looked annoyed. 'Well?'

George came to Earth. 'I'm George Platen, sir.'

'Say so, then. I'm Dr Zachary Antonelli, and we're going to be intimately acquainted in a moment.'

He stared at small strips of film, holding them up to the light owlishly.

George winced inwardly. Very hazily, he remembered that other doctor (he had forgotten the name) staring at such film. Could these be the same? The other doctor had frowned and this one was looking at him now as though he were angry.

His happiness was already just about gone.

Dr Antonelli spread the pages of a thickish file out before him now and put the films carefully to one side. 'It says here you want to be a Computer Programmer.'

'Yes, doctor.'

'Still do?'

'Yes, sir.'

'It's a responsible and exacting position. Do you feel up to it?'

'Yes, sir.'

'Most pre-Educates don't put down any specific profession. I believe they are afraid of queering it.'

'I think that's right, sir.'

'Aren't you afraid of that?'

'I might as well be honest, sir.'

Dr Antonelli nodded, but without any noticeable lightening of his expression. 'Why do you want to be a Programmer?'

'It's a responsible and exacting position as you said, sir. It's an important job and an exciting one. I like it and I think I can do it.'

Dr Antonelli put the papers away, and looked at George sourly. He said, 'How do you know you like it? Because you think you'll be snapped up by some Grade A planet?'

George thought uneasily: He's trying to rattle you. Stay calm and stay frank.

He said, 'I think a Programmer has a good chance, sir, but even if I were left on Earth, I know I'd like it.' (That was true enough. I'm not lying, thought George.)

'All right, how do you know?'

He asked it as though he knew there was no decent answer and George almost smiled. He had one.

He said, 'I've been reading about Programming, sir.'

'You've been *what?*' Now the doctor looked genuinely astonished and George took pleasure in that.

'Reading about it, sir. I bought a book on the subject and I've been studying it.'

'A book for Registered Programmers?'

'Yes, sir.'

'But you couldn't understand it.'

'Not at first. I got other books on mathematics and electronics. I made out all I could. I still don't know much, but I know enough to know I like it and to know I can make it.' (Even his parents never found that secret cache of books or knew why he spent so much time in his own room or exactly what happened to the sleep he missed.)

The doctor pulled at the loose skin under his chin. 'What was your idea in doing that, son?'

'I wanted to make sure I would be interested, sir.'

'Surely you know that being interested means nothing. You could be devoured by a subject and if the physical make-up of your brain makes it more efficient for you to be something else, something else you will be. You know that, don't you?'

'I've been told that,' said George cautiously.

'Well, believe it. It's true.'

George said nothing.

Dr Antonelli said, 'Or do you believe that studying some subject will bend the brain cells in that direction, like that other theory that a pregnant woman need only listen to great music persistently to make a composer of her child. Do you believe that?'

George flushed. That had certainly been in his mind. By forcing his intellect constantly in the desired direction, he had felt sure that he would be getting a head start. Most of his confidence had rested on exactly that point.

'I never—' he began, and found no way of finishing.

'Well, it isn't true. Good Lord, youngster, your brain pattern is fixed at birth. It can be altered by a blow hard enough to damage the cells or by a burst blood vessel or by a tumor or by a major infection – each time, of course, for the worse. But it certainly can't be affected by your thinking special thoughts.' He stared at George thoughtfully, then said, 'Who told you to do this?'

George, now thoroughly disturbed, swallowed and said, 'No one, doctor. My own idea.'

'Who knew you were doing it after you started?'

'No one. Doctor, I meant to do no wrong.'

'Who said anything about wrong? Useless is what I would say. Why did you keep it to yourself?'

'I – I thought they'd laugh at me.' (He thought abruptly of a recent exchange with Trevelyan. George had very cautiously broached the thought, as of something merely circulating distantly in the very outermost reaches of his mind, concerning the possibility of learning something by ladling it into the mind by hand, so to speak, in bits and pieces. Trevelyan had hooted, 'George, you'll be tanning your own shoes next and weaving your own shirts.' He had been thankful then for his policy of secrecy.)

Dr Antonelli shoved the bits of film he had first looked at from position to position in morose thought. Then he said, 'Let's get you analyzed. This is getting me nowhere.'

The wires went to George's temples. There was the buzzing. Again there came a sharp memory of ten years ago.

George's hands were clammy; his heart pounded. He should never have told the doctor about his secret reading.

It was his damned vanity, he told himself. He had wanted to show how enterprising he was, how full of initiative. Instead, he had showed himself superstitious and ignorant and aroused the hostility of the doctor. (He could tell the doctor hated him for a wise guy on the make.)

And now he had brought himself to such a state of nervousness, he was sure the analyzer would show nothing that made sense.

He wasn't aware of the moment when the wires were removed from his temples. The sight of the doctor, staring at him thoughtfully, blinked into his consciousness and that was that; the wires were gone. George dragged himself together with a tearing effort. He had quite given up his ambition to be a Programmer. In the space of ten minutes, it had all gone.

He said dismally, 'I suppose no?'

'No what?'

'No Programmer?'

The doctor rubbed his nose and said, 'You get your clothes and whatever belongs to you and go to room 15-C. Your files will be waiting for you there. So will my report.'

George said in complete surprise, 'Have I been Educated already? I thought this was just to—'.

Dr Antonelli stared down at his desk. 'It will all be explained to you. You do as I say.'

George felt something like panic. What was it they couldn't tell him? He wasn't fit for anything but Registered Laborer. They were going to prepare him for that; adjust him to it.

He was suddenly certain of it and he had to keep from screaming by main force.

He stumbled back to his place of waiting. Trevelyan was not there, a fact for which he would have been thankful if he had had enough self-possession to be meaningfully aware of his surroundings. Hardly anyone was left, in fact, and the few who were looked as though they might ask him questions were it not that they were too worn out by their tail-of-the-alphabet waiting to buck the fierce, hot look of anger and hate he cast at them.

What right had *they* to be technicians and he, himself, a Laborer? Laborer! He was *certain!*

He was led by a red-uniformed guide along the busy corridors lined with separate rooms each containing its groups, here two, there five: the Motor Mechanics, the Construction Engineers, the Agronomists

– There were hundreds of specialized Professions and most of them would be represented in this small town by one or two anyway.

He hated them all just then: the Statisticians, the Accountants, the lesser breeds and the higher. He hated them because they owned their smug knowledge now, knew their fate, while he himself, empty still, had to face some kind of further red tape.

He reached 15-C, was ushered in and left in an empty room. For one moment, his spirits bounded. Surely, if this were the Labor classification room, there would be dozens of youngsters present.

A door sucked into its recess on the other side of a waist-high partition and an elderly, white-haired man stepped out. He smiled and showed even teeth that were obviously false, but his face was still ruddy and unlined and his voice had vigor.

He said, 'Good evening, George. Our own sector has only one of you this time, I see.'

'Only one?' said George blankly.

'Thousands over the Earth, of course. Thousands. You're not alone.'

George felt exasperated. He said, 'I don't understand, sir. What's my classification? What's happening?'

'Easy, son. You're all right. It could happen to anyone.' He held out his hand and George took it mechanically. It was warm and it pressed George's hand firmly. 'Sit down, son. I'm Sam Ellenford.'

George nodded impatiently. 'I want to know what's going on, sir.'

'Of course. To begin with, you can't be a Computer Programmer, George. You've guessed that, I think.'

'Yes, I have,' said George bitterly. 'What will I be, then?'

'That's the hard part to explain, George.' He paused, then said with careful distinctness, 'Nothing.'

'*What!*'

'Nothing!'

'But what does that mean? Why can't you assign me a profession?'

'We have no choice in the matter, George. It's the structure of your mind that decides that.'

George went a sallow yellow. His eyes bulged. 'There's something wrong with my mind?'

'There's *something* about it. As far as professional classification is concerned, I suppose you can call it wrong.'

'But why?'

Ellenford shrugged. 'I'm sure you know how Earth runs its Educational program, George. Practically any human being can absorb practically any body of knowledge, but each individual brain pattern is better suited to receiving some types of knowledge than others. We try to match mind to knowledge as well as we can within the limits of the quota requirements for each profession.'

George nodded. 'Yes, I know.'

'Every once in a while, George, we come up against a young man whose mind is not suited to receiving a superimposed knowledge of any sort.'

'You mean I can't be Educated?'

'That is what I mean.'

'But that's crazy. I'm intelligent. I can understand—' He looked helplessly about as though trying to find some way of proving that he had a functioning brain.

'Don't misunderstand me, please,' said Ellenford gravely. 'You're intelligent. There's no question about that. You're even above average in intelligence. Unfortunately that has nothing to do with whether the mind ought to be allowed to accept superimposed knowledge or not. In fact, it is almost always the intelligent person who comes here.'

'You mean I can't even be a Registered Laborer?' babbled George. Suddenly even that was better than the blank that faced him. 'What's there to know to be a Laborer?'

'Don't underestimate the Laborer, young man. There are dozens of subclassifications and each variety has its own corpus of fairly detailed knowledge. Do you think there's no skill in knowing the proper manner of lifting a weight? Besides, for the Laborer, we must select not only minds suited to it but bodies as well. You're not the type, George, to last long as a Laborer.'

George was conscious of his slight build. He said, 'But I've never heard of anyone without a profession.'

'There aren't many,' conceded Ellenford. 'And we protect them.'

'Protect them?' George felt confusion and fright grow higher inside him.

'You're a ward of the planet, George. From the time you walked through that door, we've been in charge of you.' And he smiled.

It was a fond smile. To George it seemed the smile of ownership; the smile of a grown man for a helpless child.

He said, 'You mean, I'm going to be in prison?'

'Of course not. You will simply be with others of your kind.'

Your kind. The words made a kind of thunder in George's ear.

Ellenford said, 'You need special treatment. We'll take care of you.'

To George's own horror, he burst into tears. Ellenford walked to the other end of the room and faced away as though in thought.

George fought to reduce the agonized weeping to sobs and then to strangle those. He thought of his father and mother, of his friends, of Trevelyan, of his own shame—

He said rebelliously, 'I learned to read.'

'Everyone with a whole mind can do that. We've never found exceptions. It is at this stage that we discover – exceptions. And when you learned to read, George, we were concerned about your mind pattern. Certain peculiarities were reported even then by the doctor in charge.'

'Can't you try Educating me? You haven't even tried. I'm willing to take the risk.'

'The law forbids us to do that, Gorge. But look, it will not be bad. We will explain matters to your family so they will not be hurt. At the place to which you'll be taken, you'll be allowed privileges. We'll get you books and you can learn what you will.'

'Dab knowledge in by hand,' said George bitterly. 'Shred by shred. Then, when I die I'll know enough to be a Registered Junior Office Boy, Paper-Clip Division.'

'Yet I understand you've already been studying books.'

George froze. He was struck devastatingly by sudden understanding. 'That's it . . .'

'What is?'

'That fellow Antonelli. He's knifing me.'

'No, George. You're quite wrong.'

'Don't tell me that.' George was in an ecstasy of fury. 'That lousy bastard is selling me out because he thought I was a little too wise for him. I read books and tried to get a head start toward programming. Well, what do you want to square things? Money? You won't get it. I'm getting out of here and when I finish broadcasting this—'

He was screaming.

Ellenford shook his head and touched a contact.

Two men entered on catfeet and got on either side of George. They pinned his arms to his sides. One of them used an air-spray hypodermic in the hollow of his right elbow and the hypnotic entered his vein and had an almost immediate effect.

His screams cut off and his head fell forward. His knees buckled and only the men on either side kept him erect as he slept.

They took care of George as they said they would; they were good to him and unfailingly kind – about the way, George thought, he himself would be to a sick kitten he had taken pity on.

They told him that he should sit up and take some interest in life; and then told him that most people who came there had the same attitude of despair at the beginning and that he would snap out of it.

He didn't even hear them.

Dr Ellenford himself visited him to tell him that his parents had been informed that he was away on special assignment.

George muttered, 'Do they know—'

Ellenford assured him at once, 'We gave no details.'

At first George had refused to eat. They fed him intravenously. They hid sharp objects and kept him under guard. Hali Omani came to be his roommate and his stolidity had a calming effect.

One day, out of sheer desperate boredom, George asked for a book. Omani, who himself read books constantly, looked up, smiling broadly. George almost withdrew the request then, rather than give any of them satisfaction, then thought: What do I care?

He didn't specify the book and Omani brought one on chemistry. It was in big print, with small words and many illustrations. It was for teenagers. He threw the book violently against the wall.

That's what he would be always. A teenager all his life. A pre-Educate forever and special books would have to be written for him. He lay smoldering in bed, staring at the ceiling, and after an hour had passed, he got up sulkily, picked up the book, and began reading.

It took him a week to finish it and then he asked for another.

'Do you want me to take the first one back?' asked Omani.

George frowned. There were things in the book he had not understood, yet he was not so lost to shame as to say so.

But Omani said, 'Come to think of it, you'd better keep it. Books are meant to be read and reread.'

It was that same day that he finally yielded to Omani's invitation that he tour the place. He dogged at the Nigerian's feet and took in his surroundings with quick hostile glances.

The place was no prison certainly. There were no walls, no locked doors, no guards. But it was a prison in that the inmates had no place to go outside.

It was somehow good to see others like himself by the dozen. It was so easy to believe himself to be the only one in the world so – maimed.

He mumbled, 'How many people here anyway?'

'Two hundred and five, George, and this isn't the only place of the sort in the world. There are thousands.'

Men looked up as he passed, wherever he went; in the gymnasium, along the tennis courts; through the library (he had never in his life imagined books could exist in such numbers; they were stacked, actually stacked, along long shelves). They stared at him curiously and he returned the looks savagely. At least *they* were no better than he; no call for *them* to look at him as though he were some sort of curiosity.

Most of them were in their twenties. George said suddenly, 'What happens to the older ones?'

Omani said, 'This place specializes in the younger ones.' Then, as though he suddenly recognized an implication in George's question that he had missed earlier, he shook his head gravely and said, 'They're not put out of the way, if that's what you mean. There are other Houses for older ones.'

'Who cares?' mumbled George, who felt he was sounding too interested and in danger of slipping into surrender.

'You might. As you grow older, you will find yourself in a House with occupants of both sexes.'

That surprised George somehow. 'Women, too?'

'Of course. Do you suppose women are immune to this sort of thing?'

George thought of that with more interest and excitement than he had felt for anything since before that day when— He forced his thought away from that.

Omani stopped at the doorway of a room that contained a small closed-circuit television set and a desk computer. Five or six men sat about the television. Omani said, 'This is a classroom.'

George said, 'What's that?'

'The young men in there are being educated. Not,' he added, quickly, 'in the usual way.'

'You mean they're cramming it in bit by bit.'

'That's right. This is the way everyone did it in ancient times.'

This was what they kept telling him since he had come to the House but what of it? Suppose there had been a day when mankind had not known the diatherm-oven. Did that mean he should be satisfied to eat meat raw in a world where others ate it cooked?

He said, 'Why do they want to go through that bit-by-bit stuff?'

'To pass the time, George, and because they're curious.'

'What good does it do them?'

'It makes them happier.'

George carried that thought to bed with him.

The next day he said to Omani ungraciously, 'Can you get me into a classroom where I can find out something about programming?'

Omani replied heartily, 'Sure.'

It was slow and he resented it. Why should someone have to explain something and explain it again? Why should he have to read and reread a passage, then stare at a mathematical relationship and not understand it at once? That wasn't how other people had to be.

Over and over again, he gave up. Once he refused to attend classes for a week.

But always he returned. The official in charge, who assigned reading, conducted the television demonstrations, and even explained difficult passages and concepts, never commented on the matter.

George was finally given a regular task in the gardens and took his turn in the various kitchen and cleaning details. This was represented to him as being an advance, but he wasn't fooled. The place might have been far more mechanized than it was, but they deliberately made work for the young men in order to give them the illusion of worth-while occupation, of usefulness. George wasn't fooled.

They were even paid small sums of money out of which they could buy certain specified luxuries or which they could put aside for a problematical use in a problemical old age. George kept his money in an open jar, which he kept on a closet shelf. He had no idea how much he had accumulated. Nor did he care.

He made no real friends though he reached the stage where a civil good day was in order. He even stopped brooding (or almost stopped) on the miscarriage of justice that had placed him there. He would go weeks without dreaming of Antonelli, of his gross nose and wattled neck, of the leer with which he would push George into a boiling quicksand and hold him under, till he woke screaming with Omani bending over him in concern.

Omani said to him on a snowy day in February, 'It's amazing how you're adjusting.'

But that was February, the thirteenth to be exact, his nineteenth birthday. March came, then April, and with the approach of May he realized he hadn't adjusted at all.

The previous May had passed unregarded while George was still in his bed, drooping and ambitionless. This May was different.

All over Earth, George knew, Olympics would be taking place and young men would be competing, matching their skills against one another in the fight for a place on a new world. There would be the holiday atmosphere, the excitement, the news reports, the self-contained recruiting agents from the worlds beyond space, the glory of victory or the consolations of defeat.

How much of fiction dealt with these motifs, how much of his own boyhood excitement lay in following the events of Olympics from year to year; how many of his own plans—

George Platen could not conceal the longing in his voice. It was too much to suppress. He said, 'Tomorrow's the first of May. Olympics!'

And that led to his first quarrel with Omani and to Omani's bitter enunciation of the exact name of the institution in which George found himself.

Omani gazed fixedly at George and said distinctly, 'A House for the Feeble-minded.'

George Platen flushed. Feeble-minded!

He rejected it desperately. He said in a monotone, 'I'm leaving.' He said it on impulse. His conscious mind learned it first from the statement as he uttered it.

Omani, who had returned to his book, looked up. 'What?'

George knew what he was saying now. He said it fiercely, 'I'm leaving.'

'That's ridiculous. Sit down, George, calm yourself.'

'Oh, no. I'm here on a frame-up, I tell you. This doctor, Antonelli, took a dislike to me. It's the sense of power these petty bureaucrats have. Cross them and they wipe out your life with a stylus mark on some card file.'

'Are you back to that?'

'And staying there till it's all straightened out. I'm going to get to Antonelli somehow, break him, force the truth out of him.' George was breathing heavily and he felt feverish. Olympics month was here and he couldn't let it pass. If he did, it would be the final surrender and he would be lost for all time.

Omani threw his legs over the side of his bed and stood up. He was nearly six feet tall and the expression on his face gave him the look of a concerned Saint Bernard. He put his arm about George's shoulder, 'If I hurt your feelings—'

George shrugged him off. 'You just said what you thought was the truth, and I'm going to prove it isn't the truth, that's all. Why not? The door's open. There aren't any locks. No one ever said I couldn't leave. I'll just walk out.'

'All right, but where will you go?'

'To the nearest air terminal, then to the nearest Olympics center. I've got money.' He seized the open jar that held the wages he had put away. Some of the coins jangled to the floor.

'That will last you a week maybe. Then what?'

'By then I'll have things settled.'

'By then you'll come crawling back here,' said Omani earnestly, 'with all the progress you've made to do over again. You're mad, George.'

'Feeble-minded is the word you used before.'

'Well, I'm sorry I did. Stay here, will you?'

'Are you going to try to stop me?'

Omani compressed his full lips. 'No, I guess I won't. This is your business. If the only way you can learn is to buck the world and come back with blood on your face, go ahead. – Well, go ahead.'

George was in the doorway now, looking back over his shoulder. 'I'm going' – he came back to pick up his pocket grooming set slowly – 'I hope you don't object to my taking a few personal belongings.'

Omani shrugged. He was in bed again reading, indifferent.

George lingered at the door again, but Omani didn't look up. George gritted his teeth, turned and walked rapidly down the empty corridor and out into the night-shrouded grounds.

He had expected to be stopped before leaving the grounds. He wasn't. He had stopped at an all-night diner to ask directions to an air terminal and expected the proprietor to call the police. That didn't happen. He summoned a skimmer to take him to the airport and the driver asked no questions.

Yet he felt no lift at that. He arrived at the airport sick at heart. He had not realized how the outer world would be. He was surrounded by professionals. The diner's proprietor had had his name inscribed on the plastic shell over the cash register. So and so, Registered Cook. The man in the skimmer had his license up, Registered Chauffeur. George felt the bareness of his name and experienced a kind of nakedness because of it; worse, he felt skinned. But no one challenged him. No one studied him suspiciously and demanded proof of professional rating.

George thought bitterly: Who would imagine any human being without one?

He bought a ticket to San Francisco on the 3 a.m. plane. No other plane for a sizable Olympics center was leaving before morning and he wanted to wait as little as possible. As it was, he sat huddled in the waiting room, watching for the police. They did not come.

He was in San Francisco before noon and the noise of the city struck him like a blow. This was the largest city he had ever seen and he had been used to silence and calm for a year and a half now.

Worse, it was Olympics month. He almost forgot his own predicament in his sudden awareness that some of the noise, excitement, confusion was due to that.

The Olympics boards were up at the airport for the benefit of the incoming travelers, and crowds jostled around each one. Each major profession had its own board. Each listed directions to the Olympics Hall where the contest for that day for that profession would be given; the individuals competing and their city of birth; the Outworld (if any) sponsoring it.

It was a completely stylized thing. George had read descriptions often enough in the newsprints and films, watched matches on television, and even witnessed a small Olympics in the Registered Butcher classification at the county seat. Even that, which had no conceivable Galactic implication (there was no Outworlder in attendance, of course) aroused excitement enough.

Partly, the excitement was caused simply by the fact of competition, partly by the spur of local pride (oh, when there was a home-town boy to cheer for, though he might be a complete stranger), and, of course, partly by betting. There was no way of stopping the last.

George found it difficult to approach the board. He found himself looking at the scurrying, avid onlookers in a new way.

There must have been a time when they themselves were Olympic material. What had *they* done? Nothing!

If they had been winners, they would be far out in the Galaxy somewhere, not stuck here on Earth. Whatever they were, their professions must have made them Earth-bait from the beginning; or else they had made themselves Earth-bait by inefficiency at whatever high-specialized professions they had had.

Now these failures stood about and speculated on the chances of newer and younger men. Vultures!

How he wished they were speculating on him.

He moved down the line of boards blankly, clinging to the outskirts of the groups about them. He had eaten breakfast on the strata and he wasn't hungry. He was afraid, though. He was in a big city during the confusion of the beginning of Olympics competition. That was protection, sure. The city was full of strangers. No one would question George. No one would care about George. No one would care. Not even the House, thought George bitterly. They cared for him like a sick kitten, but if a sick kitten up and wanders off, well, too bad, what can you do?

And now that he was in San Francisco, what did he do? His

thoughts struck blankly against a wall. See someone? Whom? How? Where would he even stay? The money he had left seemed pitiful.

The first shamefaced thought of going back came to him. He could go to the police— He shook his head violently as though arguing with a material adversary.

A word caught his eye on one of the boards, gleaming there: *Metallurgist*. In smaller letters, *nonferrous*. At the bottom of a long list of names, in flowing script, *sponsored by Novia*.

It induced painful memories: himself arguing with Trevelyan, so certain that he himself would be a Programmer, so certain that a Programmer was superior to a Metallurgist, so certain that he was following the right course, so certain that he was clever—

So clever that he had to boast to that small-minded, vindictive Antonelli. He had been so sure of himself that moment when he had been called and had left the nervous Trevelyan standing there, so cocksure.

George cried out in a short, incoherent high-pitched gasp. Someone turned to look at him, then hurried on. People brushed past impatiently pushing him this way and that. He remained staring at the board, openmouthed.

It was as though the board had answered his thought. He was thinking 'Trevelyan' so hard that it had seemed for a moment that of course the board would say 'Trevelyan' back at him.

But that *was* Trevelyan, up there. And *Armand* Trevelyan (Stubby's hated first name; up in lights for everyone to see) and the right home town. What's more, Trev had wanted Novia, aimed for Novia, insisted on Novia; and this competition was sponsored by Novia.

This had to be Trev; good old Trev. Almost without thinking, he noted the directions for getting to the place of competition and took his place in line for a skimmer.

Then he thought somberly: Trev made it! He wanted to be a Metallurgist, and he made it!

George felt colder, more alone than ever.

*

There was a line waiting to enter the hall. Apparently, Metallurgy Olympics was to be an exciting and closely fought one. At least, the illuminated sky sign above the hall said so, and the jostling crowd seemed to think so.

It would have been a rainy day, George thought, from the color of the sky, but San Francisco had drawn the shield across its breadth from bay to ocean. It was an expense to do so, of course, but all expenses were warranted where the comfort of Outworlders was concerned. They would be in town for the Olympics. They were heavy spenders. And for each recruit taken, there would be a fee both to Earth, and to the local government from the planet sponsoring the Olympics. It paid to keep Outworlders in mind of a particular city as a pleasant place in which to spend Olympics time. San Francisco knew what it was doing.

George, lost in thought, was suddenly aware of a gentle pressure on his shoulder blade and a voice saying, 'Are you in line here, young man?'

The line had moved up without George's having noticed the widening gap. He stepped forward hastily and muttered, 'Sorry, sir.'

There was the touch of two fingers on the elbow of his jacket and he looked about furtively.

The man behind him nodded cheerfully. He had iron-gray hair, and under his jacket he wore an old-fashioned sweater that buttoned down the front. He said, 'I didn't mean to sound sarcastic.'

'No offense.'

'All right, then.' He sounded cozily talkative. 'I wasn't sure you might not simply be standing there, entangled with the line, so to speak, only by accident. I thought you might be a—'

'A what?' said George sharply.

'Why, a contestant, of course. You look young.'

George turned away. He felt neither cozy nor talkative, and bitterly impatient with busybodies.

A thought struck him. Had an alarm been sent out for him? Was his description known, or his picture? Was Gray-hair behind him trying to get a good look at his face?

He hadn't seen any news reports. He craned his neck to see the moving strip of news headlines parading across one section of the city shield, somewhat lackluster against the gray of the cloudy afternoon sky. It was no use. He gave up at once. The headlines would never concern themselves with him. This was Olympics time and the only news worth headlining was the comparative scores of the winners and the trophies won by continents, nations, and cities.

It would go on like that for weeks, with scores calculated on a per capita basis and every city finding some way of calculating itself into a position of honor. His own town had once placed third in an Olympics covering Wiring Technician; third in the whole state. There was still a plaque saying so in Town Hall.

George hunched his head between his shoulders and shoved his hands in his pockets and decided that made him more noticeable. He relaxed and tried to look unconcerned, and felt no safer. He was in the lobby now, and no authoritative hand had yet been laid on his shoulder. He filed into the hall itself and moved as far forward as he could.

It was with an unpleasant shock that he noticed Gray-hair next to him. He looked away quickly and tried reasoning with himself. The man had been right behind him in line after all.

Gray-hair, beyond a brief and tentative smile, paid no attention to him and, besides, the Olympics was about to start. George rose in his seat to see if he could make out the position assigned to Trevelyan and at the moment that was all his concern.

The hall was moderate in size and shaped in the classical long oval, with the spectators in the two balconies running completely about the rim and the contestants in the linear trough down the center. The machines were set up, the progress boards above each bench were dark, except for the name and contest number of each man. The contestants themselves were on the scene, reading, talking together; one was checking his fingernails minutely. (It was, of course, considered bad form for any contestant to pay any attention to the problem before him until the instant of the starting signal.)

George studied the program sheet he found in the appropriate slot in the arm of his chair and found Trevelyan's name. His number was twelve and, to George's chagrin, that was at the wrong end of the hall. He could make out the figure of Contestant Twelve, standing with his hands in his pockets, back to his machine, and staring at the audience as though he were counting the house. George couldn't make out the face.

Still, that was Trev.

George sank back in his seat. He wondered if Trev would do well. He hoped, as a matter of conscious duty, that he would, and yet there was something within him that felt rebelliously resentful. George, professionless, here, watching. Trevelyan, Registered Metallurgist, Nonferrous, there, competing.

George wondered if Trevelyan had competed in his first year. Sometimes men did, if they felt particularly confident – or hurried. It involved a certain risk. However efficient the Educative process, a preliminary year on Earth ('oiling the stiff knowledge,' as the expression went) insured a higher score.

If Trevelyan was repeating, maybe he wasn't doing so well. George felt ashamed that the thought pleased him just a bit.

He looked about. The stands were almost full. This would be a well-attended Olympics, which meant greater strain on the contestants – or greater drive, perhaps, depending on the individual.

Why Olympics, he thought suddenly? He had never known. Why was bread called bread?

Once he had asked his father: 'Why do they call it Olympics, Dad?'

And his father had said: 'Olympics means competition.'

George had said: 'Is when Stubby and I fight an Olympics, Dad?'

Platen, Senior, had said: 'No. Olympics is a special kind of competition and don't ask silly questions. You'll know all you have to know when you get Educated.'

George, back in the present, sighed and crowded down into his seat.

All you have to know!

Funny that the memory should be so clear now. 'When you get Educated.' No one ever said, '*If* you get Educated.'

He always had asked silly questions, it seemed to him now. It was as though his mind had some instinctive foreknowledge of its inability to be Educated and had gone about asking questions in order to pick up scraps here and there as best it could.

And at the House they encouraged him to do so because they agreed with his mind's instinct. It was the only way.

He sat up suddenly. What the devil was he doing? Falling for that lie? Was it because Trev was there before him, an Educee, competing in the Olympics that he himself was surrendering?

He *wasn't* feeble-minded! No!

And the shout of denial in his mind was echoed by the sudden clamor in the audience as everyone got to his feet.

The box seat in the very center of one long side of the oval was filling with an entourage wearing the colors of Novia, and the word 'Novia' went up above them on the main board.

Novia was a Grade A world with a large population and a thoroughly developed civilization, perhaps the best in the Galaxy. It was the kind of world that every Earthman wanted to live in someday; or, failing that, to see his children live in. (George remembered Trevelyan's insistence on Novia as a goal – and there he was competing for it.)

The lights went out in that section of the ceiling above the audience and so did the wall lights. The central trough, in which the contestants waited, became floodlit.

Again George tried to make out Trevelyan. Too far.

The clear, polished voice of the announcer sounded. 'Distinguished Novian sponsors. Ladies. Gentlemen. The Olympics competition for Metallurgist, Nonferrous, is about to begin. The contestants are—'

Carefully and conscientiously, he read off the list in the program. Names. Home towns. Educative years. Each name received its cheers, the San Franciscans among them receiving the loudest. When Trevelyan's name was reached, George surprised himself by shouting and waving madly. The gray-haired man next to him surprised him even more by cheering likewise.

George could not help but stare in astonishment and his neighbor leaned over to say (speaking loudly in order to be heard over the hubbub), 'No one here from my home town; I'll root for yours. Someone you know?'

George shrank back. 'No.'

'I noticed you looking in that direction. Would you like to borrow my glasses?'

'No. Thank you.' (Why didn't the old fool mind his own business?)

The announcer went on with other formal details concerning the serial number of the competition, the method of timing and scoring and so on. Finally, he approached the meat of the matter and the audience grew silent as it listened.

'Each contestant will be supplied with a bar of nonferrous alloy of unspecified composition. He will be required to sample and assay the bar, reporting all results correctly to four decimals in per cent. All will utilize for this purpose a Beeman Microspectrograph, Model FX-2, each of which is, at the moment, not in working order.'

There was an appreciative shout from the audience.

'Each contestant will be required to analyze the fault of his machine and correct it. Tools and spare parts are supplied. The spare part necessary may not be present, in which case it must be asked for, and time of delivery thereof will be deducted from final time. Are all contestants ready?'

The board above Contestant Five flashed a frantic red signal. Contestant Five ran off the floor and returned a moment later. The audience laughed good-naturedly.

'Are all contestants ready?'

The boards remained blank.

'Any questions?'

Still blank.

'You may begin.'

There was, of course, no way anyone in the audience could tell how any contestant was progressing except for whatever notations went up on the notice board. But then, that didn't matter. Except for what professional Metallurgists there might be in the audience, none would understand anything about the contest professionally in any case. What was important was who won, who was second, who was third. For those who had bets on the standings (illegal, but unpreventable) that was all-important. Everything else might go hang.

George watched as eagerly as the rest, glancing from one contestant to the next, observing how this one had removed the cover from his microspectrograph with deft strokes of a small instrument; how that one was peering into the face of the thing; how still a third was setting his alloy bar into its holder; and how a fourth adjusted a vernier with such small touches that he seemed momentarily frozen.

Trevelyan was as absorbed as the rest. George had no way of telling how he was doing.

The notice board over Contestant Seventeen flashed: Focus plate out of adjustment.

The audience cheered wildly.

Contestant Seventeen might be right and he might, of course, be wrong. If the latter, he would have to correct his diagnosis later and lose time. Or he might never correct his diagnosis and be unable to complete his analysis or, worse still, end with a completely wrong analysis.

Never mind. For the moment, the audience cheered.

Other boards lit up. George watched for Board Twelve. That came on finally: 'Sample holder off-center. New clamp depresser needed.'

An attendant went running to him with a new part. If Trevelyan was wrong, it would mean useless delay. Nor would the time elapsed in waiting for the part be deducted. George found himself holding his breath.

Results were beginning to go up on Board Seventeen, in gleaming letters: aluminum, 41.2649; magnesium, 22.1914; copper, 10.1001.

Here and there, other boards began sprouting figures.

The audience was in bedlam.

George wondered how the contestants could work in such pandemonium, then wondered if that were not even a good thing. A first-class technician should work best under pressure.

Seventeen rose from his place as his board went redrimmed to signify completion. Four was only two seconds behind him. Another, then another.

Trevelyan was still working, the minor constituents of his alloy bar still unreported. With nearly all contestants standing, Trevelyan finally rose, also. Then, tailing off, Five rose, and received an ironic cheer.

It wasn't over. Official announcements were naturally delayed. Time elapsed was something, but accuracy was just as important. And not all diagnoses were of equal difficulty. A dozen factors had to be weighed.

Finally, the announcer's voice sounded, 'Winner in the time of four minutes and twelve seconds, diagnosis correct, analysis correct within an average of zero point seven parts per hundred thousand, Contestant Number – *Seventeen*, Henry Anton Schmidt of—'

What followed was drowned in the screaming. Number Eight was next and then Four, whose good time was spoiled by a five part in ten thousand error in the niobium figure. Twelve was never mentioned. He was an also-ran.

George made his way through the crowd to the Contestants' Door and found a large clot of humanity ahead of him. There would be weeping relatives (joy or sorrow, depending) to greet them, newsmen to interview the top-scorers, or the home-town boys, autograph hounds, publicity seekers and the just plain curious. Girls, too, who might hope to catch the eye of a top-scorer, almost certainly headed for Novia (or perhaps a low-scorer who needed consolation and had the cash to afford it).

George hung back. He saw no one he knew. With San Francisco

so far from home, it seemed pretty safe to assume that there would be no relatives to condole with Trev on the spot.

Contestants emerged, smiling weakly, nodding at shouts of approval. Policemen kept the crowds far enough away to allow a lane for walking. Each high-scorer drew a portion of the crowd off with him, like a magnet pushing through a mound of iron filings.

When Trevelyan walked out, scarcely anyone was left. (George felt somehow that he had delayed coming out until just that had come to pass.) There was a cigarette in his dour mouth and he turned, eyes downcast, to walk off.

It was the first hint of home George had had in what was almost a year and a half and seemed almost a decade and a half. He was almost amazed that Trevelyan hadn't aged, that he was the same Trev he had last seen.

George sprang forward. '*Trev!*'

Trevelyan spun about, astonished. He stared at George and then his hand shot out. 'George Platen, *what* the devil—'

And almost as soon as the look of pleasure had crossed his face, it left. His hand dropped before George had quite the chance of seizing it.

'Were you in there?' A curt jerk of Trev's head indicated the hall.

'I was.'

'To see me?'

'Yes.'

'Didn't do so well, did I?' He dropped his cigarette and stepped on it, staring off to the street, where the emerging crowd was slowly eddying and finding its way into skimmers, while new lines were forming for the next scheduled Olympics.

Trevelyan said heavily, 'So what? It's only the second time I missed. Novia can go shove after the deal I got today. There are planets that would jump at me fast enough— But, listen, I haven't seen you since Education Day. Where did you go? Your folks said you were on special assignment but gave no details and you never wrote. You might have written.'

'I should have,' said George uneasily. 'Anyway, I came to say I was sorry the way things went just now.'

'Don't be,' said Trevelyan. 'I told you. Novia can go shove— At that I should have known. They've been saying for weeks that the Beeman machine would be used. All the wise money was on Beeman machines. The damned Education tapes they ran through me were for Henslers and who uses Henslers? The worlds in the Goman Cluster if you want to call them worlds. Wasn't *that* a nice deal they gave me?'

'Can't you complain to—'

'Don't be a fool. They'll tell me my brain was built for Henslers. Go argue. *Everything* went wrong. I was the only one who had to send out for a piece of equipment. Notice that?'

'They deducted the time for that, though.'

'Sure, but I lost time wondering if I could be right in my diagnosis when I noticed there wasn't any clamp depresser in the parts they had supplied. They don't deduct for that. If it had been a Hensler, I would have *known* I was right. How could I match up then? The top winner was a San Franciscan. So were three of the next four. And the fifth guy was from Los Angeles. They get big-city Educational tapes. The best available. Beeman spectrographs and all. How do I compete with them? I came all the way out here just to get a chance at a Novian-sponsored Olympics in my classification and I might just as well have stayed home. I knew it, I tell you, and that settles it. Novia isn't the only chunk of rock in space. Of all the damned—'

He wasn't speaking to George. He wasn't speaking to anyone. He was just uncorked and frothing. George realized that.

George said, 'If you knew in advance that the Beemans were going to be used, couldn't you have studied up on them?'

'They weren't in my tapes, I tell you.'

'You could have read – books.'

The last word had tailed off under Trevelyan's suddenly sharp look.

Trevelyan said, 'Are you trying to make a big laugh out of this?

You think this is funny? How do you expect me to read some book and try to memorize enough to match someone else who *knows*.'

'I thought—'

'You try it. You try—' Then, suddenly, 'What's your profession, by the way?' He sounded thoroughly hostile.

'Well—'

'Come on, now. If you're going to be a wise guy with me, let's see what you've done. You're still on Earth, I notice, so you're not a Computer Programmer and your special assignment can't be much.'

George said, 'Listen, Trev, I'm late for an appointment.' He backed away, trying to smile.

'No, you don't.' Trevelyan reached out fiercely, catching hold of George's jacket. 'You answer my question. Why are you afraid to tell me? What is it with you? Don't come here rubbing a bad showing in my face, George, unless you can take it, too. Do you hear me?'

He was shaking George in frenzy and they were struggling and swaying across the floor, when the Voice of Doom struck George's ear in the form of a policeman's outraged call.

'All right now. *All* right. Break it up.'

George's heart turned to lead and lurched sickeningly. The policeman would be taking names, asking to see identity cards, and George lacked one. He would be questioned and his lack of profession would show at once; and before Trevelyan, too, who ached with the pain of the drubbing he had taken and would spread the news back home as a salve for his own hurt feelings.

George couldn't stand that. He broke away from Trevelyan and made to run, but the policeman's heavy hand was on his shoulder. 'Hold on, there. Let's see your identity card.'

Trevelyan was fumbling for his, saying harshly, 'I'm Armand Trevelyan, Metallurgist, Nonferrous. I was just competing in the Olympics. You better find out about him, though, officer.'

George faced the two, lips dry and throat thickened past speech.

Another voice sounded, quiet, well-mannered. 'Officer. One moment.'

The policeman stepped back. 'Yes, sir?'

'This young man is my guest. What is the trouble?'

George looked about in wild surprise. It was the gray-haired man who had been sitting next to him. Gray-hair nodded benignly at George.

Guest? Was he mad?

The policeman was saying, 'These two were creating a disturbance, sir.'

'Any criminal charges? Any damages?'

'No, sir.'

'Well, then, I'll be responsible.' He presented a small card to the policeman's view and the latter stepped back at once.

Trevelyan began indignantly, 'Hold on, now—' but the policeman turned on him.

'All right, now. Got any charges?'

'I just—'

'On your way. The rest of you – move on.' A sizable crowd had gathered, which now, reluctantly, unknotted itself and raveled away.

George let himself be led to a skimmer but balked at entering.

He said, 'Thank you, but I'm not your guest.' (Could it be a ridiculous case of mistaken identity?)

But Gray-hair smiled and said, 'You weren't but you are now. Let me introduce myself, I'm Ladislas Ingenescu, Registered Historian.'

'But—'

'Come, you will come to no harm, I assure you. After all, I only wanted to spare you some trouble with a policeman.'

'But why?'

'Do you want a reason? Well, then, say that we're honorary towns-mates, you and I. We both shouted for the same man, remember, and we towns-people must stick together, even if the tie is only honorary. Eh?'

And George, completely unsure of this man, Ingenescu, and of himself as well, found himself inside the skimmer. Before he could make up his mind that he ought to get off again, they were off the ground.

He thought confusedly: The man has some status. The policeman deferred to him.

He was almost forgetting that his real purpose here in San Francisco was not to find Trevelyan but to find some person with enough influence to force a reappraisal of his own capacity of Education.

It could be that Ingenescu was such a man. And right in George's lap.

Everything could be working out fine – fine. Yet it sounded hollow in his thought. He was uneasy.

During the short skimmer-hop, Ingenescu kept up an even flow of small talk, pointing out the landmarks of the city, reminiscing about past Olympics he had seen. George, who paid just enough attention to make vague sounds during the pauses, watched the route of flight anxiously.

Would they head for one of the shield-openings and leave the city altogether?

The skimmer landed at the roof-entry of a hotel and, as he alighted, Ingenescu said, 'I hope you'll eat dinner with me in my room?'

George said, 'Yes,' and grinned unaffectedly. He was just beginning to realize the gap left within him by a missing lunch.

Ingenescu let George eat in silence. Night closed in and the wall lights went on automatically. (George thought: I've been on my own almost twenty-four hours.)

And then over the coffee, Ingenescu finally spoke again. He said, 'You've been acting as though you think I intend you harm.'

George reddened, put down his cup and tried to deny it, but the older man laughed and shook his head.

'It's so. I've been watching you closely since I first saw you and I think I know a great deal about you now.'

George half rose in horror.

Ingenescu said, 'But sit down. I only want to help you.'

George sat down but his thoughts were in a whirl. If the old man knew who he was, why had he not left him to the policeman? On the other hand, why should he volunteer help?

Ingenescu said, 'You want to know why I should want to help you? Oh, don't look alarmed. I can't read minds. It's just that my training enables me to judge the little reactions that give minds away, you see. Do you understand that?'

George shook his head.

Ingenescu said, 'Consider my first sight of you. You were waiting in line to watch an Olympics, and your micro-reactions didn't match what you were doing. The expression of your face was wrong, the action of your hands was wrong. It meant that something, in general, was wrong, and the interesting thing was that, whatever it was, it was nothing common, nothing obvious. Perhaps, I thought, it was something of which your own conscious mind was unaware.

'I couldn't help but follow you, sit next to you. I followed you again when you left and eavesdropped on the conversation between your friend and yourself. After that, well, you were far too interesting an object of study – I'm sorry if that sounds cold-blooded – for me to allow you to be taken off by a policeman. – Now tell me, what is it that troubles you?'

George was in an agony of indecision. If this was a trap, why should it be such an indirect, roundabout one? And he *had* to turn to someone. He had come to the city to find help and here was help being offered. Perhaps what was wrong was that it was being offered. It came too easy.

Ingenescu said, 'Of course, what you tell me as a Social Scientist is a privileged communication. Do you know what that means?'

'No, sir.'

'It means, it would be dishonorable for me to repeat what you say to anyone for any purpose. Moreover no one has the legal right to compel me to repeat it.'

George said, with sudden suspicion, 'I thought you were a Historian.'

'So I am.'

'Just now you said you were a Social Scientist.'

Ingenescu broke into loud laughter and apologized for it when he could talk. 'I'm sorry, young man, I shouldn't laugh, and I wasn't really laughing at you. I was laughing at Earth and its emphasis on physical science, and the practical segments of it at that. I'll bet you can rattle off every subdivision of construction technology or mechanical engineering and yet you're a blank on social science.'

'Well, then what *is* social science?'

'Social science studies groups of human beings and there are many high-specialized branches to it, just as there are to zoology, for instance. For instance, there are Culturists, who study the mechanics of cultures, their growth, development, and decay. Cultures,' he added, forestalling a question, 'are all the aspects of a way of life. For instance it includes the way we make our living, the things we enjoy and believe, what we consider good and bad and so on. Do you understand?'

'I think I do.'

'An Economist – not an Economic Statistician, now, but an Economist – specializes in the study of the way a culture supplies the bodily needs of its individual members. A psychologist specializes in the individual member of a society and how he is affected by the society. A Futurist specializes in planning the future course of a society, and a Historian— That's where I come in, now.'

'Yes, sir.'

'A Historian specializes in the past development of our own society and of societies with other cultures.'

George found himself interested. 'Was it different in the past?'

'I should say it was. Until a thousand years ago, there was no Education; not what we call Education, at least.'

George said, 'I know. People learned in bits and pieces out of books.'

'Why, how do you know this?'

'I've heard it said,' said George cautiously. Then, 'Is there any use in worrying about what's happened long ago? I mean, it's all done with, isn't it?'

'It's never done with, my boy. The past explains the present. For instance, why is our Educational system what it is?'

George stirred restlessly. The man kept bringing the subject back to that. He said snappishly, 'Because it's best.'

'Ah, but why is it best? Now you listen to me for one moment and I'll explain. Then you can tell me if there is any use in history. Even before interstellar travel was developed—' He broke off at the look of complete astonishment on George's face. 'Well, did you think we always had it?'

'I never gave it any thought, sir.'

'I'm sure you didn't. But there was a time, four or five thousand years ago, when mankind was confined to the surface of Earth. Even then, his culture had grown quite technological and his numbers had increased to the point where any failure in technology would have meant mass starvation and disease. To maintain the technological level and advance it in the face of an increasing population, more and more technicians and scientists had to be trained, and yet, as science advanced, it took longer and longer to train them.

'As first interplanetary and then interstellar travel was developed, the problem grew more acute. In fact, actual colonization of extra-Solar planets was impossible for about fifteen hundred years because of lack of properly trained men.

'The turning point came when the mechanics of the storage of knowledge within the brain was worked out. Once that had been done, it became possible to devise Educational tapes that would modify the mechanics in such a way as to place within the mind a body of knowledge ready-made so to speak. But you know about *that*.

'Once that was done, trained men could be turned out by the thousands and millions, and we could begin what someone has since called the "Filling of the Universe". There are now fifteen hundred inhabited planets in the Galaxy and there is no end in sight.

'Do you see all that is involved? Earth exports Education tapes for low-specialized professions and that keeps the Galactic culture unified. For instance, the Reading tapes insure a single language for all of us. – Don't look so surprised, other languages are possible, and in the past were used. Hundreds of them.

'Earth also exports high-specialized professionals and keeps its own population at an endurable level. Since they are shipped out in a balanced sex ratio, they act as self-reproductive units and help increase the populations on the Outworlds where an increase is needed. Furthermore, tapes and men are paid for in material which we much need and on which our economy depends. *Now* do you understand why our Education is the best way?'

'Yes, sir.'

'Does it help you to understand, knowing that without it, interstellar colonization was impossible for fifteen hundred years?'

'Yes, sir.'

'Then you see the uses of history.' The Historian smiled. 'And now I wonder if you see why I'm interested in you?'

George snapped out of time and space back to reality. Ingenescu, apparently, didn't talk aimlessly. All this lecture had been a device to attack him from a new angle.

He said, once again withdrawn, hesitating, 'Why?'

'Social Scientists work with societies and societies are made up of people.'

'All right.'

'But people aren't machines. The professionals in physical science work with machines. There is only a limited amount to know about a machine and the professionals know it all. Furthermore, all machines of a given sort are just about alike so that there is nothing to interest them in any given individual machine. But people, ah— They are so complex and so different one from another that a Social Scientist never knows all there is to know or even a good part of what there is to know. To understand his own specialty, he must always be ready to study people; particularly unusual specimens.'

'Like me,' said George tonelessly.

'I shouldn't call you a specimen, I suppose, but you are unusual. You're worth studying, and if you will allow me that privilege then, in return, I will help you if you are in trouble and if I can.'

There were pin wheels whirring in George's mind. – All this talk about people and colonization made possible by Education. It was as though caked thought within him were being broken up and strewn about mercilessly.

He said, 'Let me think,' and clamped his hands over his ears.

He took them away and said to the Historian, 'Will you do something for me, sir?'

'If I can,' said the Historian amiably.

'And everything I say in this room is a privileged communication. You said so.'

'And I meant it.'

'Then get me an interview with an Outworld official, with – with a Novian.'

Ingenescu looked startled. 'Well, now—'

'You can do it,' said George earnestly. 'You're an important official. I saw the policeman's look when you put that card in front of his eyes. If you refuse, I – I won't let you study me.'

It sounded a silly threat in George's own ears, one without force. On Ingenescu, however, it seemed to have a strong effect.

He said, 'That's an impossible condition. A Novian in Olympics month—'

'All right, then, get me a Novian on the phone and I'll make my own arrangements for an interview.'

'Do you think you can?'

'I know I can. Wait and see.'

Ingenescu stared at George thoughtfully and then reached for the visiphone.

George waited, half drunk with this new outlook on the whole problem and the sense of power it brought. It couldn't miss. It *couldn't* miss. He would be a Novian yet. He would leave Earth in triumph despite Antonelli and the whole crew of fools at the House for the (he almost laughed aloud) Feeble-minded.

George watched eagerly as the visiplate lit up. It would open up a window into a room of Novians, a window into a small patch of

Novia transplanted to Earth. In twenty-four hours, he had accomplished that much.

There was a burst of laughter as the plate unmisted and sharpened, but for the moment no single head could be seen but rather the fast passing of the shadows of men and women, this way and that. A voice was heard, clearworded over a background of babble. 'Ingenescu? He wants me?'

Then there he was, staring out of the plate. A Novian. A genuine Novian. (George had not an atom of doubt. There was something completely Outworldly about him. Nothing that could be completely defined, or even momentarily mistaken.)

He was swarthy in complexion with a dark wave of hair combed rigidly back from his forehead. He wore a thin black mustache and a pointed beard, just as dark, that scarcely reached below the lower limit of his narrow chin, but the rest of his face was so smooth that it looked as though it had been depilated permanently.

He was smiling. 'Ladislas, this goes too far. We fully expect to be spied on, within reason, during our stay on Earth, but mind reading is out of bounds.'

'Mind reading, Honorable?'

'Confess! You knew I was going to call you this evening. You knew I was only waiting to finish this drink.' His hand moved up into view and his eye peered through a small glass of a faintly violet liqueur. 'I can't offer you one, I'm afraid.'

George, out of range of Ingenescu's transmitter, could not be seen by the Novian. He was relieved at that. He wanted time to compose himself and he needed it badly. It was as though he were made up exclusively of restless fingers, drumming, drumming—

But he was right. He hadn't miscalculated. Ingenescu *was* important. The Novian called him by his first name.

Good! Things worked well. What George had lost on Antonelli, he would make up, with advantage, on Ingenescu. And someday, when he was on his own at last, and could come back to Earth as powerful a Novian as this one who could negligently joke with Ingenescu's first name and be addressed as 'Honorable' in turn – when he came back, he would settle with Antonelli. He had a year and a half to pay back and he—

He all but lost his balance on the brink of the enticing daydream and snapped back in sudden anxious realization that he was losing the thread of what was going on.

The Novian was saying, '—doesn't hold water. Novia has a civilization as complicated and advanced as Earth's. We're not Zeston, after all. It's ridiculous that we have to come here for individual technicians.'

Ingenescu said soothingly, 'Only for new models. There is never any certainty that new models will be needed. To buy the Educational tapes would cost you the same price as a thousand technicians and how do you know you would need that many?'

The Novian tossed off what remained of his drink and laughed. (It displeased George, somehow, that a Novian should be this frivolous. He wondered uneasily if perhaps the Novian ought not to have skipped that drink and even the one or two before that.)

The Novian said, 'That's typical pious fraud, Ladislas. You know we can make use of all the late models we can get. I collected five Metallurgists this afternoon—'

'I know,' said Ingenescu. 'I was there.'

'Watching me! Spying!' cried the Novian. 'I'll tell you what it is. The new-model Metallurgists I got differed from the previous model only in knowing the use of Beeman Spectrographs. The tapes couldn't be modified that much, not that much' (he held up two fingers close together) 'from last year's model. You introduce the new models only to *make* us buy and spend and come here hat in hand.'

'We don't *make* you buy.'

'No, but you sell late-model technicians to Landonum and so we have to keep pace. It's a merry-go-round you have us on, you pious Earthmen, but watch out, there may be an exit somewhere.' There was a sharp edge to his laugh, and it ended sooner than it should have.

Ingenescu said, 'In all honesty, I hope there is. Meanwhile, as to the purpose of my call—'

'That's right, *you* called. Oh, well, I've said my say and I suppose next year there'll be a new model of Metallurgist anyway for us to spend goods on, probably with a new gimmick for niobium assays and nothing else altered and the next year—But go on, what is it you want?'

'I have a young man here to whom I wish you to speak.'

'Oh?' The Novian looked not completely pleased with that. 'Concerning what?'

'I can't say. He hasn't told me. For that matter he hasn't even told me his name and profession.'

The Novian frowned. 'Then why take up my time?'

'He seems quite confident that you will be interested in what he has to say.'

'I dare say.'

'And,' said Ingenescu, 'as a favor to me.'

The Novian shrugged. 'Put him on and tell him to make it short.'

Ingenescu stepped aside and whispered to George, 'Address him as "Honorable".'

George swallowed with difficulty. This was it.

George felt himself going moist with perspiration. The thought had come so recently, yet it was in him now so certainly. The beginnings of it had come when he had spoken to Trevelyan, then everything had fermented and billowed into shape while Ingenescu had prattled, and then the Novian's own remarks had seemed to nail it all into place.

George said, 'Honorable, I've come to show you the exit from the merry-go-round.' Deliberately, he adopted the Novian's own metaphor.

The Novian stared at him gravely. 'What merry-go-round?'

'You yourself mentioned it, Honorable. The merry-go-round that Novia is on when you come to Earth to – to get technicians.' (He couldn't keep his teeth from chattering; from excitement, not fear.)

The Novian said, 'You're trying to say that you know a way by which we can avoid patronizing Earth's mental super-market. Is that it?'

'Yes, sir. You can control your own Educational system.'

'Umm. Without tapes?'

'Y-yes, Honorable.'

The Novian, without taking his eyes from George, called out, 'Ingenescu, get into view.'

The Historian moved to where he could be seen over George's shoulder.

The Novian said, 'What is this? I don't seem to penetrate.'

'I assure you solemnly,' said Ingenescu, 'that whatever this is it is being done on the young man's own initiative, Honorable. I have not inspired this. I have nothing to do with it.'

'Well, then, what is the young man to you? Why do you call me on his behalf?'

Ingenescu said, 'He is an object of study, Honorable. He has value to me and I humor him.'

'What kind of value?'

'It's difficult to explain; a matter of my profession.'

The Novian laughed shortly. 'Well, to each his profession.' He nodded to an invisible person or persons outside plate range. 'There's a young man here, a protege of Ingenescu or some such thing, who will explain to us how to Educate without tapes.' He snapped his fingers, and another glass of pale liqueur appeared in his hand. 'Well, young man?'

The faces on the plate were multiple now. Men and women, both, crammed in for a view of George, their faces molded into various shades of amusement and curiosity.

George tried to look disdainful. They were all, in their own ways, Novians as well as the Earthman, 'studying' him as though he were a bug on a pin. Ingenescu was sitting in a corner, now, watching him owl-eyed.

Fools, he thought tensely, one and all. But they would have to understand. He would *make* them understand.

He said, 'I was at the Metallurgist Olympics this afternoon.'

'You, too?' said the Novian blandly. 'It seems all Earth was there.'

'No, Honorable, but I was. I had a friend who competed and who made out very badly because you were using the Beeman machines. His education had included only the Henslers, apparently an older model. You said the modification involved was slight.' George held up two fingers close together in conscious mimicry of the other's previous gesture. 'And my friend had known some time in advance that knowledge of the Beeman machines would be required.'

'And what does that signify?'

'It was my friend's lifelong ambition to qualify for Novia. He already knew the Henslers. He had to know the Beemans to qualify and he knew that. To learn about the Beemans would have taken just a few more facts, a bit more data, a small amount of practice perhaps. With a life's ambition riding the scale, he might have managed this—'

'And where would he have obtained a tape for the additional facts and data? Or has Education become a private matter for home study here on Earth?'

There was dutiful laughter from the faces in the background.

George said, 'That's why he didn't learn, Honorable. He thought he needed a tape. He wouldn't even try without one, no matter what the prize. He refused to try without a tape.'

'Refused, eh? Probably the type of fellow who would refuse to fly without a skimmer.' More laughter and the Novian thawed into a smile and said, 'The fellow is amusing. Go on. I'll give you another few moments.'

George said tensely, 'Don't think this is a joke. Tapes are actually bad. They teach too much; they're too painless. A man who learns that way doesn't know how to learn any other way. He's frozen into whatever position he's been taped. Now if a person *weren't* given tapes but were forced to learn by hand, so to speak, from the start; why, then he'd get the habit of learning, and continue to learn. Isn't that reasonable? Once he has the habit well developed he can be given just a small amount of tape-knowledge, perhaps, to fill in gaps or fix details. Then he can make further progress on his own. You can make Beeman Metallurgists out of your own Hensler Metallurgists in that way and not have to come to Earth for new models.'

The Novian nodded and sipped at his drink. 'And where does everyone get knowledge without tapes? From interstellar vacuum?'

'From books. By studying the instruments themselves. By *thinking*.'

'Books? How does one understand books without Education?'

'Books are in words. Words can be understood for the most part. Specialized words can be explained by the technicians you already have.'

'What about reading? Will you allow reading tapes?'

'Reading tapes are all right, I suppose, but there's no reason you can't learn to read the old way, too. At least in part.'

The Novian said, 'So that you can develop good habits from the start?'

'Yes, yes,' George said gleefully. The man was beginning to understand.

'And what about mathematics?'

'That's the easiest of all, sir – Honorable. Mathematics is different from other technical subjects. It starts with certain simple principles and proceeds by steps. You can start with nothing and learn. It's practically designed for that. Then, once you know the proper types of mathematics, other technical books become quite understandable. Especially if you start with easy ones.'

'Are there easy books?'

'Definitely. Even if there weren't, the technicians you now have can try to write easy books. Some of them might be able to put some of their knowledge into words and symbols.'

'Good Lord,' said the Novian to the men clustered about him. 'The young devil has an answer for everything.'

'I have. I have,' shouted George. 'Ask me.'

'Have you tried learning from books yourself? Or is this just theory with you?'

George turned to look quickly at Ingenescu, but the Historian was passive. There was no sign of anything but gentle interest in his face.

George said, 'I have.'

'And do you find it works?'

'Yes, Honorable,' said George eagerly. 'Take me with you to Novia. I can set up a program and direct—'

'Wait, I have a few more questions. How long would it take, do you suppose, for you to become a Metallurgist capable of handling a Beeman machine, supposing you started from nothing and did not use Educational tapes?'

George hesitated. 'Well – years, perhaps.'

'Two years? Five? Ten?'

'I can't say, Honorable.'

'Well, there's a vital question to which you have no answer, have you? Shall we say five years? Does that sound reasonable to you?'

'I suppose so.'

'All right. We have a technician studying metallurgy according to this method of yours for five years. He's no good to us during that time, you'll admit, but he must be fed and housed and paid all that time.'

'But—'

'Let me finish. Then when he's done and can use the Beeman, five years have passed. Don't you suppose we'll have modified Beemans then which he *won't* be able to use?'

'But by then he'll be expert on learning. He could learn the new details necessary in a matter of days.'

'So you say. And suppose this friend of yours, for instance, had studied up on Beemans on his own and managed to learn it; would he be as expert in its use as a competitor who had learned it off the tapes?'

'Maybe not—' began George.

'Ah,' said the Novian.

'Wait, let *me* finish. Even if he doesn't know something as well, it's the ability to learn further that's important. He may be able to think up things, new things that no tape-Educated man would. You'll have a reservoir of original thinkers—'

'In your studying,' said the Novian, 'have you thought up any new things?'

'No, but I'm just one man and I haven't studied long—'

'Yes. – Well, ladies, gentlemen, have we been sufficiently amused?'

'Wait,' cried George, in sudden panic. 'I want to arrange a personal interview. There are things I can't explain over the visiphone. There are details—'

The Novian looked past George. 'Ingenescu! I think I have done you your favor. Now, really, I have a heavy schedule tomorrow. Be well!'

The screen went blank.

George's hands shot out toward the screen, as though in a wild impulse to shake life back into it. He cried out, 'He didn't believe me. He didn't believe me.'

Ingenescu said, 'No, George. Did you really think he would?'

George scarcely heard him. 'But why not? It's all true. It's all so much to his advantage. No risk. I and a few men to work with— A dozen men training for years would cost less than one technician. —He was drunk! Drunk! He didn't understand.'

George looked about breathlessly. 'How do I get to him? I've got to. This was wrong. Shouldn't have used the visiphone. I need time. Face to face. How do I—'

Ingenescu said, 'He won't see you, George. And if he did, he wouldn't believe you.'

'He will, I tell you. When he isn't drinking. He—' George turned squarely toward the Historian and his eyes widened. 'Why do you call me George?'

'Isn't that your name? George Platen?'

'You know me?'

'All about you.'

George was motionless except for the breath pumping his chest wall up and down.

Ingenescu said, 'I want to help you, George. I told you that. I've been studying you and I want to help you.'

George screamed, 'I don't need help. I'm not feeble-minded. The whole world is, but I'm not.' He whirled and dashed madly for the door.

He flung it open and two policemen roused themselves suddenly from their guard duty and seized him.

For all George's straining, he could feel the hypo-spray at the fleshy point just under the corner of his jaw, and that was it. The last thing he remembered was the face of Ingenescu, watching with gentle concern.

George opened his eyes to the whiteness of a ceiling. He remembered what had happened. He remembered it distantly as though it had happened to somebody else. He stared at the ceiling till the whiteness filled his eyes and washed his brain clean, leaving room, it seemed, for new thought and new ways of thinking.

He didn't know how long he lay there so, listening to the drift of his own thinking.

There was a voice in his ear. 'Are you awake?'

And George heard his own moaning for the first time. Had he been moaning? He tried to turn his head.

The voice said, 'Are you in pain, George?'

George whispered, 'Funny. I was so anxious to leave Earth. I didn't understand.'

'Do you know where you are?'

'Back in the – the House.' George managed to turn. The voice belonged to Omani.

George said, 'It's funny I didn't understand.'

Omani smiled gently, 'Sleep again—'

George slept.

And woke again. His mind was clear.

Omani sat at the bedside reading, but he put down the book as George's eyes opened.

George struggled to a sitting position. He said, 'Hello.'

'Are you hungry?'

'You bet.' He stared at Omani curiously. 'I was followed when I left, wasn't I?'

Omani nodded. 'You were under observation at all times. We were going to maneuver you to Antonelli and let you discharge your aggressions. We felt that to be the only way you could make progress. Your emotions were clogging your advance.'

George said, with a trace of embarrassment, 'I was all wrong about him.'

'It doesn't matter now. When you stopped to stare at the Metallurgy notice board at the airport, one of our agents reported back the list of names. You and I had talked about your past sufficiently so that I caught the significance of Trevelyan's name there. You asked for directions to the Olympics; there was the possibility that this might result in the kind of crisis we were hoping for; we sent Ladislas Ingenescu to the hall to meet you and take over.'

'He's an important man in the government, isn't he?'

'Yes, he is.'

'And you had him take over. It makes me sound important.'

'You *are* important, George.'

A thick stew had arrived, steaming, fragrant. George grinned wolfishly and pushed his sheets back to free his arms. Omani helped arrange the bed-table. For a while, George ate silently.

Then George said, 'I woke up here once before just for a short time.'

Omani said, 'I know. I was here.'

'Yes, I remember. You know, everything was changed. It was as though I was too tired to feel emotion. I wasn't angry any more. I could just think. It was as though I had been drugged to wipe out emotion.'

'You weren't,' said Omani. 'Just sedation. You had rested.'

'Well, anyway, it was all clear to me, as though I had known it all the time but wouldn't listen to myself. I thought: What was it I had wanted Novia to let me do? I had wanted to go to Novia and take a

batch of un-Educated youngsters and teach them out of books. I had
wanted to establish a House for the Feeble-minded – like here – and
Earth already has them – many of them.'

Omani's white teeth gleamed as he smiled. 'The Institute of
Higher Studies is the correct name for places like this.'

'Now I see it,' said George, 'so easily I am amazed at my blindness
before. After all, who invents the new instrument models that require
new-model technicians? Who invented the Beeman spectrographs,
for instance? A man called Beeman, I suppose, but he couldn't have
been tape-Educated or how could he have made the advance?'

'Exactly.'

'Or who makes Educational tapes? Special tape-making technicians? Then who makes the tapes to train *them*? More advanced
technicians? Then who makes the tapes— You see what I mean.
Somewhere there has to be an end. Somewhere there must be men
and women with capacity for original thought.'

'Yes, George.'

George leaned back, stared over Omani's head, and for a moment
there was the return of something like restlessness to his eyes.

'Why wasn't I told all this at the beginning?'

'Oh, if we could,' said Omani, 'the trouble it would save us. We
can analyze a mind, George, and say this one will make an adequate
architect and that one a good woodworker. We know of no way of
detecting the capacity for original, creative thought. It is too subtle a
thing. We have some rule-of-thumb methods that mark out individuals who may possibly or potentially have such a talent.

'On Reading Day, such individuals are reported. You were, for
instance. Roughly speaking, the number so reported comes to one in
ten thousand. By the time Education Day arrives, these individuals
are checked again, and nine out of ten of them turn out to have been
false alarms. Those who remain are sent to places like this.'

George said, 'Well, what's wrong with telling people that one out
of – of a hundred thousand will end at places like these? Then it
won't be such a shock to those who do.'

'And those who don't? The ninety-nine thousand nine hundred and ninety-nine that don't? We can't have all those people considering themselves failures. They aim at the professions and one way or another they all make it. Everyone can place after his or her name: Registered something-or-other. In one fashion or another every individual has his or her place in society and this is necessary.'

'But we?' said George. 'The one in ten thousand exception?'

'You can't be told. That's exactly it. It's the final test. Even after we've thinned out the possibilities on Education Day, nine out of ten of those who come here are not quite the material of creative genius, and there's no way we can distinguish those nine from the tenth that we want by any form of machinery. The tenth one must tell us himself.'

'How?'

'We bring you here to a House for the Feeble-minded and the man who won't accept that is the man we want. It's a method that can be cruel, but it works. It won't do to say to a man, "You can create. Do so." It is much safer to wait for a man to say, "I can create, and I will do so whether you wish it or not." There are ten thousand men like you, George, who support the advancing technology of fifteen hundred worlds. We can't allow ourselves to miss one recruit to that number or waste our efforts on one member who doesn't measure up.'

George pushed his empty plate out of the way and lifted a cup of coffee to his lips.

'What about the people here who don't – measure up?'

'They are taped eventually and become our Social Scientists. Ingenescu is one. I am a Registered Psychologist. We are second echelon, so to speak.'

George finished his coffee. He said, 'I still wonder about one thing?'

'What is that?'

George threw aside the sheet and stood up. 'Why do they call them Olympics?'

The Feeling of Power

Jehan Shuman was used to dealing with the men in authority on long-embattled Earth. He was only a civilian but he originated programming patterns that resulted in self-directing war computers of the highest sort. Generals consequently listened to him. Heads of congressional committees, too.

There was one of each in the special lounge of New Pentagon. General Weider was space-burnt and had a small mouth puckered almost into a cipher. Congressman Brant was smooth-cheeked and clear-eyed. He smoked Denebian tobacco with the air of one whose patriotism was so notorious, he could be allowed such liberties.

Shuman, tall, distinguished, and Programmer-first-class, faced them fearlessly.

He said, 'This, gentlemen, is Myron Aub.'

'The one with the unusual gift that you discovered quite by accident,' said Congressman Brant placidly. 'Ah.' He inspected the little man with the egg-bald head with amiable curiosity.

The little man, in return, twisted the fingers of his hands anxiously. He had never been near such great men before. He was only an aging low-grade Technician who had long ago failed all tests designed to smoke out the gifted ones among mankind and had settled into the rut of unskilled labor. There was just this hobby of his that the great Programmer had found out about and was now making such a frightening fuss over.

General Weider said, 'I find this atmosphere of mystery childish.'

'You won't in a moment,' said Shuman. 'This is not something we can leak to the firstcomer – Aub!' There was something imperative about his manner of biting off that one-syllable name, but then he was a great Programmer speaking to a mere Technician. 'Aub! How much is nine times seven?

Aub hesitated a moment. His pale eyes glimmered with a feeble anxiety. 'Sixty-three,' he said.

Congressman Brant lifted his eyebrows. 'Is that right?'

'Check it for yourself, Congressman.'

The congressman took out his pocket computer, nudged the milled edges twice, looked at its face as it lay there in the palm of his hand, and put it back. He said, 'Is this the gift you brought us here to demonstrate? An illusionist?'

'More than that, sir. Aub has memorized a few operations and with them he computes on paper.'

'A paper computer?' said the general. He looked pained.

'No, sir,' said Shuman patiently. 'Not a paper computer. Simply a sheet of paper. General, would you be so kind as to suggest a number?'

'Seventeen,' said the general.

'And you, Congressman?'

'Twenty-three.'

'Good! Aub, multiply those numbers and please show the gentlemen your manner of doing it.'

'Yes, Programmer,' said Aub, ducking his head. He fished a small pad out of one shirt pocket and an artist's hairline stylus out of the other. His forehead corrugated as he made painstaking marks on the paper.

General Weider interrupted him sharply. 'Let's see that.'

Aub passed him the paper, and Weider said, 'Well, it looks like the figure seventeen.'

Congressman Brant nodded and said, 'So it does, but I suppose anyone can copy figures off a computer. I think I could make a passable seventeen myself, even without practice.'

'If you will let Aub continue, gentlemen,' said Shuman without heat.

Aub continued, his hand trembling a little. Finally he said in a low voice, 'The answer is three hundred and ninety-one.'

Congressman Brant took out his computer a second time and flicked it, 'By Godfrey, so it is. How did he guess?'

'No guess, Congressman,' said Shuman. 'He computed that result. He did it on this sheet of paper.'

'Humbug,' said the general impatiently. 'A computer is one thing and marks on paper are another.'

'Explain, Aub,' said Shuman.

'Yes, Programmer. – Well, gentlemen, I write down seventeen and just underneath it, I write twenty-three. Next, I say to myself: seven times three—'

The congressman interrupted smoothly, 'Now, Aub, the problem is seventeen times twenty-three.'

'Yes, I know,' said the little Technician earnestly, 'but I *start* by saying seven times three because that's the way it works. Now seven times three is twenty-one.'

'And how do you know that?' asked the congressman.

'I just remember it. It's always twenty-one on the computer. I've checked it any number of times.'

'That doesn't mean it always will be, though, does it?' said the congressman.

'Maybe not,' stammered Aub. 'I'm not a mathematician. But I always get the right answers, you see.'

'Go on.'

'Seven times three is twenty-one, so I write down twenty-one. Then one times three is three, so I write down a three under the two of twenty-one.'

'Why under the two?' asked Congressman Brant at once.

'Because—' Aub looked helplessly at his superior for support. 'It's difficult to explain.'

Shuman said, 'If you will accept his work for the moment, we can leave the details for the mathematicians.'

Brant subsided.

Aub said, 'Three plus two makes five, you see, so the twenty-one becomes a fifty-one. Now you let that go for a while and start fresh. You multiply seven and two, that's fourteen, and one and two, that's two. Put them down like this and it adds up to thirty-four. Now if you put the thirty-four under the fifty-one this way and add them, you get three hundred and ninety-one and that's the answer.'

There was an instant's silence and then General Weider said, 'I don't believe it. He goes through this rigmarole and makes up numbers and multiplies and adds them this way and that, but I don't believe it. It's too complicated to be anything but hornswoggling.'

'Oh no, sir,' said Aub in a sweat. 'It only *seems* complicated because you're not used to it. Actually, the rules are quite simple and will work for any numbers.'

'Any numbers, eh?' said the general. 'Come then.' He took out his own computer (a severely styled GI model) and struck it at random. 'Make a five seven three eight on the paper. That's five thousand seven hundred and thirty-eight.'

'Yes, sir,' said Aub, taking a new sheet of paper.

'Now,' (more punching of his computer), 'seven two three nine Seven thousand two hundred and thirty-nine.'

'Yes, sir.'

'And now multiply those two.'

'It will take some time,' quavered Aub.

'Take the time,' said the general.

'Go ahead, Aub,' said Shuman crisply.

Aub set to work, bending low. He took another sheet of paper and another. The general took out his watch finally and stared at it. 'Are you through with your magic-making, Technician?'

'I'm almost done, sir. – Here it is, sir. Forty-one million, five

hundred and thirty-seven thousand, three hundred and eighty-two.'
He showed the scrawled figures of the result.

General Weider smiled bitterly. He pushed the multiplication
contact on his computer and let the numbers whirl to a halt. And
then he stared and said in a surprised squeak, 'Great Galaxy, the fella's
right.'

The President of the Terrestrial Federation had grown haggard in
office and, in private, he allowed a look of settled melancholy to
appear on his sensitive features. The Denebian war, after its early
start of vast movement and great popularity, had trickled down into
a sordid matter of maneuver and countermaneuver, with discontent
rising steadily on Earth. Possibly, it was rising on Deneb, too.

And now Congressman Brant, head of the important Committee
on Military Appropriations, was cheerfully and smoothly spending
his half-hour appointment spouting nonsense.

'Computing without a computer,' said the president impatiently,
'is a contradiction in terms.'

'Computing,' said the congressman, 'is only a system for handling
data. A machine might do it, or the human brain might. Let me give
you an example.' And, using the new skills he had learned, he worked
out sums and products until the president, despite himself, grew
interested.

'Does this always work?'

'Every time, Mr President. It is foolproof.'

'Is it hard to learn?'

'It took me a week to get the real hang of it. I think you would
do better.'

'Well,' said the president, considering, 'it's an interesting parlor
game, but what is the use of it?'

'What is the use of a newborn baby, Mr President? At the moment
there is no use, but don't you see that this points the way toward lib-
eration from the machine. Consider, Mr President,' the congressman
rose and his deep voice automatically took on some of the cadences

he used in public debate, 'that the Denebian war is a war of computer against computer. Their computers forge an impenetrable shield of counter-missiles against our missiles, and ours forge one against theirs. If we advance the efficiency of our computers, so do they theirs, and for five years a precarious and profitless balance has existed.

'Now we have in our hands a method for going beyond the computer, leapfrogging it, passing through it. We will combine the mechanics of computation with human thought; we will have the equivalent of intelligent computers; billions of them. I can't predict what the consequences will be in detail but they will be incalculable. And if Deneb beats us to the punch, they may be unimaginably catastrophic.'

The president said, troubled, 'What would you have me do?'

'Put the power of the administration behind the establishment of a secret project on human computation. Call it Project Number, if you like. I can vouch for my committee, but I will need the administration behind me.'

'But how far can human computation go?'

'There is no limit. According to Programmer Shuman, who first introduced me to this discovery—'

'I've heard of Shuman, of course.'

'Yes. Well, Dr Shuman tells me that in theory there is nothing the computer can do that the human mind cannot do. The computer merely takes a finite amount of data and performs a finite number of operations upon them. The human mind can duplicate the process.'

The president considered that. He said, 'If Shuman says this, I am inclined to believe him – in theory. But, in practice, how can anyone know how a computer works?'

Brant laughed genially. 'Well, Mr President, I asked the same question. It seems that at one time computers were designed directly by human beings. Those were simple computers, of course, this being before the time of the rational use of computers to design more advanced computers had been established.'

'Yes, yes. Go on.'

'Technician Aub apparently had, as his hobby, the reconstruction of some of these ancient devices and in so doing he studied the details of their workings and found he could imitate them. The multiplication I just performed for you is an imitation of the workings of a computer.'

'Amazing!'

The congressman coughed gently, 'If I may make another point, Mr President— The further we can develop this thing, the more we can divert our Federal effort from computer production and computer maintenance. As the human brain takes over, more of our energy can be directed into peacetime pursuits and the impingement of war on the ordinary man will be less. This will be most advantageous for the party in power, of course.'

'Ah,' said the president, 'I see your point. Well, sit down, Congressman, sit down. I want some time to think about this. – But meanwhile, show me that multiplication trick again. Let's see if I can't catch the point of it.'

Programmer Shuman did not try to hurry matters. Loesser was conservative, very conservative, and liked to deal with computers as his father and grandfather had. Still, he controlled the West European computer combine, and if he could be persuaded to join Project Number in full enthusism, a great deal would be accomplished.

But Loesser was holding back. He said, 'I'm not sure I like the idea of relaxing our hold on computers. The human mind is a capricious thing. The computer will give the same answer to the same problem each time. What guarantee have we that the human mind will do the same?'

'The human mind, Computer Loesser, only manipulates facts. It doesn't matter whether the human mind or a machine does it. They are just tools.'

'Yes, yes. I've gone over your ingenious demonstration that the mind can duplicate the computer but it seems to me a little in the air.

I'll grant the theory but what reason have we for thinking that theory can be converted to practice?'

'I think we have reason, sir. After all, computers have not always existed. The cavemen with their triremes, stone axes, and railroads had no computers.'

'And possibly they did not compute.'

'You know better than that. Even the building of a railroad or a ziggurat called for some computing, and that must have been without computers as we know them.'

'Do you suggest they computed in the fashion you demonstrate?'

'Probably not. After all, this method – we call it "graphitics", by the way, from the old European word "grapho" meaning "to write" – is developed from the computers themselves so it cannot have antedated them. Still, the cavemen must have had *some* method, eh?'

'Lost arts! If you're going to talk about lost arts—'

'No, no. I'm not a lost art enthusiast, though I don't say there may not be some. After all, man was eating grain before hydroponics, and if the primitives ate grain, they must have grown it in soil. What else could they have done?'

'I don't know, but I'll believe in soil-growing when I see someone grow grain in soil. And I'll believe in making fire by rubbing two pieces of flint together when I see that, too.'

Shuman grew placative. 'Well, let's stick to graphitics. It's just part of the process of etherealization. Transportation by means of bulky contrivances is giving way to direct mass-transference. Communications devices become less massive and more efficient constantly. For that matter, compare your pocket computer with the massive jobs of a thousand years ago. Why not, then, the last step of doing away with computers altogether? Come, sir, Project Number is a going concern; progress is already headlong. But we want your help. If patriotism doesn't move you, consider the intellectual adventure involved.'

Loesser said skeptically, 'What progress? What can you do beyond multiplication? Can you integrate a transcendental function?'

'In time, sir. In time. In the last month I have learned to handle division. I can determine, and correctly, integral quotients and decimal quotients.'

'Decimal quotients? To how many places?'

Programmer Shuman tried to keep his tone casual. 'Any number!'

Loesser's lower jaw dropped. 'Without a computer?'

'Set me a problem.'

'Divide twenty-seven by thirteen. Take it to six places.'

Five minutes later, Shuman said, 'Two point oh seven six nine two three.'

Loesser checked it. 'Well, now, that's amazing. Multiplication didn't impress me too much because it involved integers after all, and I thought trick manipulation might do it. But decimals—'

'And that is not all. There is a new development that is, so far, top secret and which, strictly speaking, I ought not to mention. Still— We may have made a breakthrough on the square root front.'

'Square roots?'

'It involves some tricky points and we haven't licked the bugs yet, but Technician Aub, the man who invented the science and who has an amazing intuition in connection with it, maintains he has the problem almost solved. And he is only a Technician. A man like yourself, a trained and talented mathematician, ought to have no difficulty.'

'Square roots,' muttered Loesser, attracted.

'Cube roots, too. Are you with us?'

Loesser's hand thrust out suddenly, 'Count me in.'

General Weider stumped his way back and forth at the head of the room and addressed his listeners after the fashion of a savage teacher facing a group of recalcitrant students. It made no difference to the general that they were the civilian scientists heading Project Number. The general was the over-all head, and he so considered himself at every waking moment.

He said, 'Now square roots are all fine. I can't do them myself and I don't understand the methods, but they're fine. Still, the

Project will not be sidetracked into what some of you call the fundamentals. You can play with graphitics any way you want to after the war is over, but right now we have specific and very practical problems to solve.'

In a far corner, Technician Aub listened with painful attention. He was no longer a Technician, of course, having been relieved of his duties and assigned to the project, with a fine-sounding title and good pay. But, of course, the social distinction remained and the highly placed scientific leaders could never bring themselves to admit him to their ranks on a footing of equality. Nor, to do Aub justice, did he, himself, wish it. He was as uncomfortable with them as they with him.

The general was saying, 'Our goal is a simple one, gentlemen; the replacement of the computer. A ship that can navigate space without a computer on board can be constructed in one-fifth the time and at one-tenth the expense of a computer-laden ship. We could build fleets five times, ten times, as great as Deneb could if we could but eliminate the computer.

'And I see something even beyond this. It may be fantastic now; a mere dream; but in the future I see the manned missile!'

There was an instant murmur from the audience.

The general drove on. 'At the present time, our chief bottleneck is the fact that missiles are limited in intelligence. The computer controlling them can only be so large, and for that reason they can meet the changing nature of anti-missile defenses in an unsatisfactory way. Few missiles, if any, accomplish their goal and missile warfare is coming to a dead end; for the enemy, fortunately, as well as for ourselves.

'On the other hand, a missile with a man or two within, controlling flight by graphitics, would be lighter, more mobile, more intelligent. It would give us a lead that might well mean the margin of victory. Besides which, gentlemen, the exigencies of war compel us to remember one thing. A man is much more dispensable than a computer. Manned missiles could be launched in numbers and under circumstances that no good general would care to undertake as far as computer-directed missiles are concerned—'

He said much more but Technician Aub did not wait.

Technician Aub, in the privacy of his quarters, labored long over the note he was leaving behind. It read finally as follows:

'When I began the study of what is now called graphitics, it was no more than a hobby. I saw no more in it than an interesting amusement, an exercise of mind.

'When Project Number began, I thought that others were wiser than I; that graphitics might be put to practical use as a benefit to mankind, to aid in the production of really practical mass-transference devices perhaps. But now I see it is to be used only for death and destruction.

'I cannot face the responsibility involved in having invented graphitics.'

He then deliberately turned the focus of a protein-depolarizer on himself and fell instantly and painlessly dead.

They stood over the grave of the little Technician while tribute was paid to the greatness of his discovery.

Programmer Shuman bowed his head along with the rest of them, but remained unmoved. The Technician had done his share and was no longer needed, after all. He might have started graphitics, but now that it had started, it would carry on by itself overwhelmingly, triumphantly, until manned missiles were possible with who knew what else.

Nine times seven, thought Shuman with deep satisfaction, is sixty-three, and I don't need a computer to tell me so. The computer is in my own head.

And it was amazing the feeling of power that gave him.

The Dying Night

PART ONE

It was almost a class reunion, and though it was marked by joy-lessness, there was no reason as yet to think it would be marred by tragedy.

Edward Talliaferro, fresh from the Moon and without his gravity legs yet, met the other two in Stanley Kaunas's room. Kaunas rose to greet him in a subdued manner. Battersley Ryger merely sat and nodded.

Talliaferro lowered his large body carefully to the couch, very aware of its unusual weight. He grimaced a little, his plump lips twisting inside the rim of hair that surrounded his mouth on lip, chin, and cheek.

They had seen one another earlier that day under more formal conditions. Now for the first time they were alone, and Talliaferro said, 'This is a kind of occasion. We're meeting for the first time in ten years. First time since graduation, in fact.'

Ryger's nose twitched. It had been broken shortly before that same graduation and he had received his degree in astronomy with a bandage disfiguring his face. He said grumpily, 'Anyone ordered champagne? Or something?'

Talliaferro said, 'Come on! First big interplanetary astronomical convention in history is no place for glooming. And among friends, too!'

Kaunas said suddenly, 'It's Earth. It doesn't feel right. I can't get used to it.' He shook his head but his look of depression was not detachable. It remained.

Talliaferro said, 'I know. I'm so heavy. It takes all the energy out of me. At that, you're better off than I am, Kaunas. Mercurian gravity is 0.4 normal. On the Moon, it's only 0.16.' He interrupted Ryger's beginning of a sound by saying, 'And on Ceres they use pseudo-grav fields adjusted to 0.8. You have no problems at all, Ryger.'

The Cerian astronomer looked annoyed, 'It's the open air. Going outside without a suit gets me.'

'Right,' agreed Kaunas, 'and letting the sun beat down on you. Just letting it.'

Talliaferro found himself insensibly drifting back in time. They had not changed much. Nor, he thought, had he himself. They were all ten years older, of course. Ryger had put on some weight and Kaunas's thin face had grown a bit leathery, but he would have recognized either if he had met him without warning.

He said, 'I don't think it's Earth getting us. Let's face it.'

Kaunas looked up sharply. He was a little fellow with quick, nervous movements of his hands. He habitually wore clothes that looked a shade too large for him.

He said, 'Villiers! I know. I think about him sometimes.' Then, with an air of desperation, 'I got a letter from him.'

Ryger sat upright, his olive complexion darkening further, and said with energy, 'You did? When?'

'A month ago.'

Ryger turned to Talliaferro. 'How about you?'

Talliaferro blinked placidly and nodded.

Ryger said, 'He's gone crazy. He claims he's discovered a practical method of mass-transference through space. – He told you two also? – That's it, then. He was always a little bent. Now he's broken.'

He rubbed his nose fiercely and Talliaferro thought of the day Villiers had broken it.

For ten years, Villiers had haunted them like the vague shadow of a guilt that wasn't really theirs. They had gone through their graduate work together, four picked and dedicated men being trained for a profession that had reached new heights in this age of interplanetary travel.

The Observatories were opening on the other worlds, surrounded by vacuum, unblurred by air.

There was the Lunar Observatory, from which Earth and the inner planets could be studied; a silent world in whose sky the home-planet hung suspended.

Mercury Observatory, closest to the sun, perched at Mercury's north pole, where the terminator moved scarcely at all, and the sun was fixed on the horizon and could be studied in the minutest detail.

Ceres Observatory, newest, most modem, with its range extending from Jupiter to the outermost galaxies.

There were disadvantages, of course. With interplanetary travel still difficult, leaves would be few, anything like normal life virtually impossible, but this was a lucky generation. Coming scientists would find the fields of knowledge well-reaped and, until the invention of an interstellar drive, no new horizon as capacious as this one would be opened.

Each of these lucky four, Talliaferro, Ryger, Kaunas, and Villiers, was to be in the position of a Galileo, who by owning the first real telescope, could not point it anywhere in the sky without making a major discovery.

But then Romero Villiers had fallen sick and it was rheumatic fever. Whose fault was that? His heart had been left leaking and limping.

He was the most brilliant of the four, the most hopeful, the most intense – and he could not even finish his schooling and get his doctorate.

Worse than that, he could never leave Earth; the acceleration of a spaceship's take-off would kill him.

Talliaferro was marked for the Moon, Ryger for Ceres, Kaunas for Mercury. Only Villiers stayed behind, a life-prisoner of Earth.

They had tried telling their sympathy and Villiers had rejected it with something approaching hate. He had railed at them and cursed them. When Ryger lost his temper and lifted his fist, Villiers had sprung at him, screaming, and had broken Ryger's nose.

Obviously Ryger hadn't forgotten that, as he caressed his nose gingerly with one finger.

Kaunas's forehead was an uncertain washboard of wrinkles. 'He's at the Convention, you know. He's got a room in the hotel – 405.'

'*I* won't see him,' said Ryger.

'He's coming up here. He said he wanted to see us. I thought – He said nine. He'll be here any minute.'

'In that case,' said Ryger, 'if you don't mind, I'm leaving.' He rose.

Talliaferro said, 'Oh, wait a while. What's the harm in seeing him?'

'Because there's no point. He's mad.'

'Even so. Let's not be petty about it. Are you afraid of him?'

'Afraid!' Ryger looked contemptuous.

'Nervous, then. What is there to be nervous about?'

'I'm not nervous,' said Ryger.

'Sure you are. We all feel guilty about him, and without real reason. Nothing that happened was our fault.' But he was speaking defensively and he knew it.

And when, at that point, the door signal sounded, all three jumped and turned to stare uneasily at the barrier that stood between themselves and Villiers.

The door opened and Romero Villiers walked in. The others rose stiffly to greet him, then remained standing in embarrassment, without one hand being raised.

He stared them down sardonically.

He's changed, thought Talliaferro.

He had. He had shrunken in almost every dimension. A gathering stoop made him seem even shorter. The skin of his scalp glistened through thinning hair, the skin on the back of his hands was ridged crookedly with bluish veins. He looked ill. There seemed nothing to link him to the memory of the past except for his trick of shading his eyes with one hand when he stared intently and, when he spoke, the even, controlled baritone of his voice.

He said, 'My friends! My space-trotting friends! We've lost touch.'

Talliaferro said, 'Hello, Villiers.'

Villiers eyed him. 'Are you well?'

'Well enough.'

'And you two?'

Kaunas managed a weak smile and a murmur. Ryger snapped, 'All right, Villiers. What's up?'

'Ryger, the angry man,' said Villiers. 'How's Ceres?'

'It was doing well when I left. How's Earth?'

'You can see for yourself,' but Villiers tightened as he said that.

He went on, 'I am hoping that the reason all three of you have come to the Convention is to hear my paper day after tomorrow.'

'Your paper? What paper?' asked Talliaferro.

'I wrote you all about it. My method of mass-transference.'

Ryger smiled with one corner of his mouth. 'Yes, you did. You didn't say anything about a paper, though, and I don't recall that you're listed as one of the speakers. I would have noticed it if you had been.'

'You're right. I'm not listed. Nor have I prepared an abstract for publication.'

Villiers had flushed and Talliaferro said soothingly, 'Take it easy, Villiers. You don't look well.'

Villiers whirled on him, lips contorted. 'My heart's holding out, thank you.'

Kaunas said, 'Listen, Villiers, if you're not listed or abstracted—'

'*You* listen. I've waited ten years. You have the jobs in space and I have to teach school on Earth, but I'm a better man than any of you or all of you.'

'Granted—' began Talliaferro.

'And I don't want your condescension either. Mandel witnessed it. I suppose you've heard of Mandel. Well, he's chairman of the astronautics division at the Convention and I demonstrated mass-transference for him. It was a crude device and it burned out after one use but— Are you listening?'

'We're listening,' said Ryger coldly, 'for what that counts.'

'He'll let me talk about it my way. You bet he will. No warning. No advertisement. I'm going to spring it at them like a bombshell. When I give them the fundamental relationships involved it will break up the Convention. They'll scatter to their home labs to check on me and build devices. And they'll find it works. I made a live mouse disappear at one spot in my lab and appear in another. Mandel witnessed it.'

He stared at them, glaring first at one face, then at another. He said, 'You don't believe me, do you?'

Ryger said, 'If you don't want advertisement, why do you tell us?'

'You're different. You're my friends, my classmates. You went out into space and left me behind.'

'That wasn't a matter of choice,' objected Kaunas in a thin, high voice.

Villiers ignored that. He said, 'So I want you to know *now*. What will work for a mouse will work for a human. What will move something ten feet across a lab will move it a million miles across space. I'll be on the Moon, *and* on Mercury, *and* on Ceres and anywhere I want to go. I'll match every one of you and more. And I'll have done more for astronomy just teaching school and thinking, than all of you with your observatories and telescopes and cameras and spaceships.'

'Well,' said Talliaferro, 'I'm pleased. More power to you. May I see a copy of the paper?'

'Oh, no.' Villiers' hands clenched close to his chest as though he were holding phantom sheets and shielding them from observation. 'You wait like everyone else. There's only one copy and no one will see it till I'm ready. Not even Mandel.'

'One copy,' cried Talliaferro. 'If you misplace it—'.

'I won't. And if I do, it's all in my head.'

'If you—' Talliaferro almost finished that sentence with 'die' but stopped himself. Instead, he went on after an almost imperceptible pause, '—have any sense, you'll scan it at least. For safety's sake.'

'No,' said Villiers, shortly. 'You'll hear me day after tomorrow. You'll see the human horizon expanded at one stroke as it never has been before.'

Again he stared intently at each face. 'Ten years,' he said. 'Good-by.'

'He's mad,' said Ryger explosively, staring at the door as though Villiers were still standing before it.

'Is he?' said Talliaferro thoughtfully. 'I suppose he is, in a way. He hates us for irrational reasons. And, then, not even to scan his paper as a precaution—'

Talliaferro fingered his own small scanner as he said that. It was just a neutrally colored, undistinguished cylinder, somewhat thicker and somewhat shorter than an ordinary pencil. In recent years, it had become the hallmark of the scientist, much as the stethoscope was that of the physician and the micro-computer that of the statistician. The scanner was worn in a jacket pocket, or clipped to a sleeve, or slipped behind the ear, or swung at the end of a string.

Talliaferro sometimes, in his more philosophical moments, wondered how it was in the days when research men had to make laborious notes of the literature or file away full-sized reprints. How unwieldy!

Now it was only necessary to scan anything printed or written to have a micro-negative which could be developed at leisure. Talliaferro had already recorded every abstract included in the program booklet of the Convention. The other two, he assumed with full confidence, had done likewise.

Talliaferro said, 'Under the circumstances, refusal to scan is mad.'

'Space!' said Ryger hotly. 'There is no paper. There is no discovery. Scoring one on us would be worth any lie to him.'

'But then what will he do day after tomorrow?' asked Kaunas.

'How do I know? He's a madman.'

Talliaferro still played with his scanner and wondered idly if he ought to remove and develop some of the small slivers of film that lay stored away in its vitals. He decided against it. He said, 'Don't underestimate Villiers. He's a brain.'

'Ten years ago, maybe,' said Ryger. 'Now he's a nut. I propose we forget him.'

He spoke loudly, as though to drive away Villiers and all that concerned him by the sheer force with which he discussed other things. He talked about Ceres and his work – the radio-plotting of the Milky Way with new radioscopes capable of the resolution of single stars.

Kaunas listened and nodded, then chimed in with information concerning the radio emissions of sunspots and his own paper, in press, on the association of proton storms with the gigantic hydrogen flares on the sun's surface.

Talliaferro contributed little. Lunar work was unglamorous in comparison. The latest information on long-scale weather forecasting through direct observation of terrestrial jet-streams would not compare with radioscopes and proton storms.

More than that, his thoughts could not leave Villiers. Villiers *was* the brain. They all knew it. Even Ryger, for all his bluster, must feel that if mass-transference were at all possible then Villiers was a logical discoverer.

The discussion of their own work amounted to no more than an uneasy admission that none of them had come to much. Talliaferro had followed the literature and knew. His own papers had been minor. The others had authored nothing of great importance.

None of them – face the fact – had developed into spaceshakers. The colossal dreams of school days had not come true and that was that. They were competent routine workmen. No less. Unfortunately, no more. They knew that.

Villiers would have been more. They knew that, too. It was that knowledge, as well as guilt, which kept them antagonistic.

Talliaferro felt uneasily that Villiers, despite everything, was yet to *be* more. The others must be thinking so, too, and mediocrity could grow quickly unbearable. The mass-transference paper would come to pass and Villiers would be the great man after all, as he was always fated to be apparently, while his classmates, with all their advantages, would be forgotten. Their role would be no more than to applaud from the crowd.

He felt his own envy and chagrin and was ashamed of it, but felt it none the less.

Conversation died, and Kaunas said, his eyes turning away, 'Listen, why don't we drop in on old Villiers?'

There was a false heartiness about it, a completely unconvincing effort at casualness. He added, 'No use leaving bad feelings – unnecessarily—'

Talliaferro thought: He wants to make sure about the mass-transference. He's hoping it *is* only a madman's nightmare so he can sleep tonight.

But he was curious himself, so he made no objection, and even Ryger shrugged with ill grace and said, 'Hell, why not?'

It was a little before eleven then.

Talliaferro was awakened by the insistent ringing of his door signal. He hitched himself to one elbow in the darkness and felt distinctly outraged. The soft glow of the ceiling indicator showed it to be not quite four in the morning.

He cried out, 'Who is it?'

The ringing continued in short, insistent spurts.

Growling, Talliaferro slipped into his bathrobe. He opened the door and blinked in the corridor light. He recognized the man who faced him from the trimensionals he had seen often enough.

Nevertheless, the man said in an abrupt whisper, 'My name is Hubert Mandel.'

'Yes, sir,' said Talliaferro. Mandel was one of the Names in astronomy, prominent enough to have an important executive position with the World Astronomical Bureau, active enough to be Chairman of the Astronautics section here at the Convention.

It suddenly struck Talliaferro that it was Mandel for whom Villiers claimed to have demonstrated mass-transference. The thought of Villiers was somehow a sobering one.

Mandel said, 'You are Dr Edward Talliaferro?'

'Yes, sir.'

'Then dress and come with me. It is very important. It concerns a mutual acquaintance.'

'Dr Villiers?'

Mandel's eyes flickered a bit. His brows and lashes were so fair as to give those eyes a naked, unfringed appearance. His hair was silky-thin, his age about fifty.

He said, 'Why Villiers?'

'He mentioned you last evening. I don't know any other mutual acquaintance.'

Mandel nodded, waited for Talliaferro to finish slipping into his clothes, then turned and led the way. Ryger and Kaunas were waiting in a room one floor above Talliaferro's. Kaunas's eyes were red and troubled. Ryger was smoking a cigarette with impatient puffs.

Talliaferro said, 'We're all here. Another reunion.' It fell flat.

He took a seat and the three stared at one another. Ryger shrugged.

Mandel paced the floor, hands deep in his pockets. He said, 'I apologize for any inconvenience, gentlemen, and I thank you for your co-operation. I would like more of it. Our friend, Romero Villiers, is dead. About an hour ago, his body was removed from the hotel. The medical judgment is heart failure.'

There was a stunned silence. Ryger's cigarette hovered halfway to his lips, then sank slowly without completing its journey.

'Poor devil,' said Talliaferro.

'Horrible,' whispered Kaunas hoarsely. 'He was—' His voice played out.

Ryger shook himself. 'Well, he had a bad heart. There's nothing to be done.'

'One little thing,' corrected Mandel quietly. 'Recovery.'

'What does that mean?' asked Ryger sharply.

Mandel said, 'When did you three see him last?'

Talliaferro spoke. 'Last evening. It turned out to be a reunion. We all met for the first time in ten years. It wasn't a pleasant meeting, I'm sorry to say. Villiers felt he had cause for anger with us, and he was angry.'

'That was – when?'

'About nine, the first time.'

'The first time?'

'We saw him again later in the evening.'

Kaunas looked troubled. 'He had left angrily. We couldn't leave it at that. We had to try. It wasn't as if we hadn't all been friends at one time. So we went to his room and—'

Mandel pounced on that. 'You were all in his room?'

'Yes,' said Kaunas, surprised.

'About when?'

'Eleven, I think.' He looked at the others. Talliaferro nodded.

'And how long did you stay?'

'Two minutes,' put in Ryger. 'He ordered us out as though we were after his paper.' He paused as though expecting Mandel to ask what paper, but Mandel said nothing. He went on. 'I think he kept it under his pillow. At least he lay across the pillow as he yelled at us to leave.'

'He may have been dying then,' said Kaunas, in a sick whisper.

'Not then,' said Mandel shortly. 'So you probably all left finger-prints.'

'Probably,' said Talliaferro. He was losing some of his automatic respect for Mandel and a sense of impatience was returning. It *was* four in the morning, Mandel or no. He said, 'Now what's all this about?'

'Well, gentlemen,' said Mandel, 'there's more to Villiers' death than the fact of death. Villiers' paper, the only copy of it as far as I know, was stuffed into the cigarette flash-disposal unit and only scraps of it were left. I've never seen or read the paper, but I knew enough about the matter to be willing to swear in court if necessary that the remnants of unflashed paper in the disposal unit were of the paper he was planning to give at this Convention. – You seem doubtful, Dr Ryger.'

Ryger smiled sourly. 'Doubtful that he was going to give it. If you want my opinion, sir, he was mad. For ten years he was a prisoner of Earth and he fantasied mass-transference as escape. It was all that kept him alive probably. He rigged up some sort of fraudulent demonstration. I don't say it was deliberate fraud. He was probably madly sincere, and sincerely mad. Last evening was the climax. He came to our rooms – he hated us for having escaped Earth – and triumphed over us. It was what he had lived for for ten years. It may have shocked him back to some form of sanity. He knew he couldn't actually give the paper; there was nothing to give. So he burned it and his heart gave out. It *is* too bad.'

Mandel listened to the Cerian astronomer, wearing a look of sharp disapproval. He said, 'Very glib, Dr Ryger, but quite wrong. I am not as easily fooled by fraudulent demonstrations as you may believe. Now according to the registration data, which I have been forced to check rather hastily, you three were his classmates at college. Is that right?'

They nodded.

'Are there any other classmates of yours present at the Convention?'

'No,' said Kaunas. 'We were the only four qualifying for a doctorate in astronomy that year. At least he would have qualified except—'

'Yes, I understand,' said Mandel. 'Well, then, in that case one of you three visited Villiers in his room one last time at midnight.'

There was a short silence. Then Ryger said coldly, 'Not I.' Kaunas, eyes wide, shook his head.

Talliaferro said, 'What are you implying?'

'One of you came to him at midnight and insisted on seeing his paper. I don't know the motive. Conceivably, it was with the deliberate intention of forcing him into heart failure. When Villiers collapsed, the criminal, if I may call him so, was ready. He snatched the paper which, I might add, probably *was* kept under his pillow, and scanned it. Then he destroyed the paper itself in the flash-disposal, but he was in a hurry and destruction wasn't complete.'

Ryger interrupted. 'How do you know all this? Were you a witness?'

'Almost,' said Mandel. 'Villiers was not quite dead at the moment of his first collapse. When the criminal left, he managed to reach the phone and call my room. He choked out a few phrases, enough to outline what had occurred. Unfortunately I was not in my room; a late conference kept me away. However, my recording attachment taped it. I always play the recording tape back whenever I return to my room or office. Bureaucratic habit. I called back. He was dead.'

'Well, then,' said Ryger, 'who did he say did it?'

'He didn't. Or if he did, it was unintelligible. But one word rang out clearly. It was "classmate".'

Talliaferro detached his scanner from its place in his inner jacket pocket and held it out toward Mandel. Quietly he said, 'If you would like to develop the film in my scanner, you are welcome to do so. You will not find Villiers' paper there.'

At once, Kaunas did the same, and Ryger, with a scowl, joined.

Mandel took all three scanners and said dryly, 'Presumably, whichever one of you has done this has already disposed of the piece of exposed film with the paper on it. However—'

Talliaferro raised his eyebrows. 'You may search my person or my room.'

But Ryger was still scowling, 'Now wait a minute, wait one bloody minute. Are you the police?'

Mandel stared at him. 'Do you *want* the police? Do you want a scandal and a murder charge? Do you want the Convention disrupted and the System press to make a holiday out of astronomy and astronomers? Villiers' death might well have been accidental. He *did* have a bad heart. Whichever one of you was there may well have acted on impulse. It may not have been a premeditated crime.

If whoever it is will return the negative, we can avoid a great deal of trouble.'

'Even for the criminal?' asked Talliaferro.

Mandel shrugged. 'There may be trouble for him. I will not promise immunity. But whatever the trouble, it won't be public disgrace and life imprisonment, as it might be if the police are called in.'

Silence.

Mandel said, 'It is one of you three.'

Silence.

Mandel went on, 'I think I can see the original reasoning of the guilty person. The paper would be destroyed. Only we four knew of the mass-transference and only I had ever seen a demonstration. Moreover you had only his word, a madman's word perhaps, that I had seen it. With Villiers dead of heart failure and the paper gone, it would be easy to believe Dr Ryger's theory that there was no mass-transference and never had been. A year or two might pass and our criminal, in possession of the mass-transference data, could reveal it little by little, rig experiments, publish careful papers, and end as the apparent discoverer with all that would imply in terms of money and renown. Even his own classmates would suspect nothing. At most they would believe that the long-past affair with Villiers had inspired him to begin investigations in the field. No more.' Mandel looked sharply from one face to another. 'But none of that will work now. Any of the three of you who comes through with mass-transference is proclaiming himself the criminal. I've seen the demonstration; I know it is legitimate; I know that one of you possesses a record of the paper. The information is therefore useless to you. Give it up then.' Silence.

Mandel walked to the door and turned again, 'I'd appreciate it if you would stay here till I return. I won't be long. I hope the guilty one will use the interval to consider. If he's afraid a confession will lose him his job, let him remember that a session with the police may lose him his liberty *and* cost him the Psychic Probe.' He hefted the three scanners, looked grim and somewhat in need of sleep. 'I'll develop these.'

Kaunas tried to smile. 'What if we make a break for it while you're gone?'

'Only one of you has reason to try,' said Mandel. 'I think I can rely on the two innocent ones to control the third, if only out of self-protection.'

He left.

It was five in the morning. Ryger looked at his watch indignantly. 'A hell of a thing. I want to sleep.'

'We can curl up here,' said Talliaferro philosophically. 'Is anyone planning a confession?'

Kaunas looked away and Ryger's lip lifted.

'I didn't think so.' Talliaferro closed his eyes, leaned his large head back against the chair and said in a tired voice, 'Back on the Moon, they're in the slack season. We've got a two-week night and then it's busy, busy. Then there's two weeks of sun and there's nothing but calculations, correlations and bull-sessions. That's the hard time. I hate it. If there were more women, if I could arrange something permanent—'

In a whisper, Kaunas talked about the fact that it was still impossible to get the entire Sun above the horizon and in view of the telescope on Mercury. But with another two miles of track soon to be laid down for the Observatory – move the whole thing, you know, tremendous forces involved, solar energy used directly – it might be managed. It *would* be managed.

Even Ryger consented to talk of Ceres after listening to the low murmur of the other voices. There was the problem there of the two-hour rotation period, which meant the stars whipped across the sky at an angular velocity twelve times that in Earth's sky. A net of three light scopes, three radioscopes, three of everything, caught the fields of study from one another as they whirled past.

'Could you use one of the poles?' asked Kaunas.

'You're thinking of Mercury and the Sun,' said Ryger impatiently. 'Even at the poles, the sky would still twist, and half of it would be forever hidden. Now if Ceres showed only one face to the Sun, the way Mercury does, we could have a permanent night sky with the stars rotating slowly once in three years.'

The sky lightened and it dawned slowly.

Talliaferro was half asleep, but he kept hold of half-consciousness firmly. He would not fall asleep and leave the others awake. Each of the three, he thought, was wondering, 'Who? Who?' – except the guilty one, of course.

Talliaferro's eyes snapped open as Mandel entered again. The sky, as seen from the window, had grown blue. Talliaferro was glad the window was closed. The hotel was air-conditioned, of course, but windows could be opened during the mild season of the year by those Earthmen who fancied the illusion of fresh air. Talliaferro, with Moon-vacuum on his mind, shuddered at the thought with real discomfort.

Mandel said, 'Have any of you anything to say?'

They looked at him steadily. Ryger shook his head.

Mandel said, 'I have developed the film in your scanners, gentlemen, and viewed the results.' He tossed scanners and developed slivers of film onto the bed. 'Nothing! you'll have trouble sorting out the film, I'm afraid. For that I'm sorry. And now there is still the question of the missing film.'

'If any,' said Ryger, and yawned prodigiously.

Mandel said, 'I would suggest we come down to Villiers' room, gentlemen.'

Kaunas looked startled. 'Why?'

Talliaferro said, 'Is this psychology? Bring the criminal to the scene of the crime and remorse will wring a confession from him?'

Mandel said, 'A less melodramatic reason is that I would like to have the two of you who are innocent help me find the missing film of Villiers' paper.'

'Do you think it's there?' asked Ryger challengingly.

'Possibly. It's a beginning. We can then search each of your rooms. The symposium on Astronautics doesn't start till tomorrow at 10 a.m. We have till then.'

'And after that?'

'It may have to be the police.'

They stepped gingerly into Villiers' room. Ryger was red, Kaunas pale. Talliaferro tried to remain calm.

Last night they had seen it under artificial lighting with a scowling, disheveled Villiers clutching his pillow, staring them down, ordering them away. Now there was the scentless odor of death about it.

Mandel fiddled with the window-polarizer to let more light in, and adjusted it too far, so that the eastern Sun slipped in.

Kaunas threw his arm up to shade his eyes and screamed, 'The Sun!' so that all the others froze.

Kaunas's face showed a kind of terror, as though it were his Mercurian sun that he had caught a blinding glimpse of.

Talliaferro thought of his own reaction to the possibility of open air and his teeth gritted. They were all bent crooked by their ten years away from Earth.

Kaunas ran to the window, fumbling for the polarizer, and then the breath came out of him in a huge gasp.

Mandel stepped to his side. 'What's wrong?' and the other two joined them.

The city lay stretched below them and outward to the horizon in broken stone and brick, bathed in the rising sun, with the shadowed portions toward them. Talliaferro cast it all a furtive and uneasy glance.

Kaunas, his chest seemingly contracted past the point where he could cry out, stared at something much closer. There, on the outer window sill, one corner secured in a trifling imperfection, a crack in the cement, was an inch-long strip of milky-gray film, and on it were the early rays of the rising sun.

Mandel, with an angry, incoherent cry, threw up the window and snatched it away. He shielded it in one cupped hand, staring out of hot and reddened eyes.

He said, 'Wait here!'

There was nothing to say. When Mandel left, they sat down and stared stupidly at one another.

Mandel was back in twenty minutes. He said quietly (in a voice that gave the impression, somehow, that it was quiet only because its owner had passed far beyond the raving stage), 'The corner in the crack wasn't overexposed. I could make out a few words. It is Villiers' paper. The rest is ruined; nothing can be salvaged. It's gone.'

'What next?' said Talliaferro.

Mandel shrugged wearily. 'Right now, I don't care. Mass-transference is gone until someone as brilliant as Villiers works it out again. I shall work on it but I have no illusions as to my own capacity. With it gone, I suppose you three don't matter, guilty or not. What's the difference?' His whole body seemed to have loosened and sunk into despair.

But Talliaferro's voice grew hard. 'Now, hold on. In your eyes, any of the three of us might be guilty. I, for instance. You are a big man in the field and you will never have a good word to say for me. The general idea may arise that I am incompetent or worse. I will not be ruined by the shadow of guilt. Now let's solve this thing.'

'I am no detective,' said Mandel wearily.

'Then call in the police, damn it.'

Ryger said, 'Wait a while, Tai. Are you implying that I'm guilty?'

'I'm saying that I'm innocent.'

Kaunas raised his voice in fright. 'It will mean the Psychic Probe for each of us. There may be mental damage—'

Mandel raised both arms high in the air. 'Gentlemen! Gentlemen! Please! There is one thing we might do short of the police; and you are right, Dr Talliaferro, it would be unfair to the innocent to leave this matter here.'

They turned to him in various stages of hostility. Ryger said, 'What do you suggest?'

'I have a friend named Wendell Urth. You may have heard of him, or you may not, but perhaps I can arrange to see him tonight.'

'What if you can?' demanded Talliaferro. 'Where does that get us?'

'He's an odd man,' said Mandel hesitantly, 'very odd. And very brilliant in his way. He has helped the police before this and he may be able to help us now.'

PART TWO

Edward Talliaferro could not forbear staring at the room and its occupant with the greatest astonishment. It and he seemed to exist in isolation, and to be part of no recognizable world. The sounds of Earth were absent in this well-padded, windowless nest. The light and air of Earth had been blanked out in artificial illumination and conditioning.

It was a large room, dim and cluttered. They had picked their way across a littered floor to a couch from which book-films had been brusquely cleared and dumped to one side in a tangle.

The man who owned the room had a large, round face on a stumpy, round body. He moved quickly about on his short legs, jerking his head as he spoke until his thick glasses all but bounced off the thoroughly inconspicuous nubble that served as a nose. His thick-lidded, somewhat protuberant eyes gleamed in myopic good nature at them all, as he seated himself in his own chair-desk combination, lit directly by the one bright light in the room.

'So good of you to come, gentlemen. Pray excuse the condition of my room.' He waved stubby fingers in a wide-sweeping gesture. 'I am engaged in cataloguing the many objects of extraterrological interest I have accumulated. It is a tremendous job. For instance—'

He dodged out of his seat and burrowed in a heap of objects beside the desk till he came up with a smoky-gray object, semi-translucent and roughly cylindrical. 'This,' he said, 'is a Callistan object that may be a relic of intelligent nonhuman entities. It is not decided. Not more than a dozen have been discovered and this is the most perfect single specimen I know of.'

He tossed it to one side and Talliaferro jumped. The plump man stared in his direction and said, 'It's not breakable.' He sat down again, clasped his pudgy fingers tightly over his abdomen and let them pump slowly in and out as he breathed. 'And now what can I do for you?'

Hubert Mandel had carried through the introductions and Talliaferro was considering deeply. Surely it was a man named Wendell Urth who had written a recent book entitled *Comparative Evolutionary Processes on Water-Oxygen Planets*, and surely this could not be the man.

He said, 'Are you the author of *Comparative Evolutionary Processes*, Dr Urth?'

A beatific smile spread across Urth's face, 'You've read it?'

'Well, no, I haven't, but—'

Urth's expression grew instantly censorious. 'Then you should. Right now. Here, I have a copy—'

He bounced out of his chair again and Mandel cried at once, 'Now wait, Urth, first things first. This is serious.'

He virtually forced Urth back into his chair and began speaking rapidly as though to prevent any further side issues from erupting. He told the whole story with admirable word-economy.

Urth reddened slowly as he listened. He seized his glasses and shoved them higher up on his nose. 'Mass-transference!' he cried.

'I saw it with my own eyes,' said Mandel.

'And you never told me.'

'I was sworn to secrecy. The man was – peculiar. I explained that.'

Urth pounded the desk. 'How could you allow such a discovery to remain the property of an eccentric, Mandel? The knowledge should have been forced from him by Psychic Probe, if necessary.'

'It would have killed him,' protested Mandel.

But Urth was rocking back and forth with his hands clasped

tightly to his cheeks. 'Mass-transference. The only way a decent, civilized man should travel. The only possible way. The only conceivable way. If I had known. If I could have been there. But the hotel is nearly thirty miles away.'

Ryger, who listened with an expression of annoyance on his face, interposed, 'I understand there's a flitter line direct to Convention Hall. It could have gotten you there in ten minutes.'

Urth stiffened and looked at Ryger strangely. His cheeks bulged. He jumped to his feet and scurried out of the room.

Ryger said, 'What the devil?'

Mandel muttered, 'Damn it. I should have warned you.'

'About what?'

'Dr Urth doesn't travel on any sort of conveyance. It's a phobia. He moves about only on foot.'

Kaunas blinked about in the dimness. 'But he's an extraterrologist, isn't he? An expert on life forms of other planets?'

Talliaferro had risen and now stood before a Galactic Lens on a pedestal. He stared at the inner gleam of the star systems. He had never seen a Lens so large or so elaborate.

Mandel said, 'He's an extraterrologist, yes, but he's never visited any of the planets on which he is expert and he never will. In thirty years, I doubt if he's ever been more than a mile from this room.'

Ryger laughed.

Mandel flushed angrily. 'You may find it funny, but I'd appreciate your being careful what you say when Dr Urth comes back.'

Urth sidled in a moment later. 'My apologies, gentlemen,' he said in a whisper. 'And now let us approach our problem. Perhaps one of you wishes to confess.'

Talliaferro's lips quirked sourly. This plump, self-imprisoned extraterrologist was scarcely formidable enough to force a confession from anyone. Fortunately, there would be no need of his detective talents, if any, after all.

Talliaferro said, 'Dr Urth, are you connected with the police?'

A certain smugness seemed to suffuse Urth's ruddy face. 'I have no official connection, Dr Talliaferro, but my unofficial relationships are very good indeed.'

'In that case, I will give you some information which you can carry to the police.'

Urth drew in his abdomen and hitched at his shirttail. It came free, and slowly he polished his glasses with it. When he was quite through and had perched them precariously on his nose once more, he said, 'And what is that?'

'I will tell you who was present when Villiers died and who scanned his paper.'

'You have solved the mystery?'

'I've thought about it all day. I think I've solved it.' Talliaferro rather enjoyed the sensation he was creating.

'Well, then?'

Talliaferro took a deep breath. This was not going to be easy to do, though he had been planning it for hours. 'The guilty man,' he said, 'is obviously Dr Hubert Mandel.'

Mandel stared at Talliaferro in sudden, hard-breathing indignation. 'Look here, doctor,' he began, loudly, 'if you have any basis for such a ridiculous—'

Urth's tenor voice soared above the interruption. 'Let him talk, Hubert, let us hear him. You suspected him and there is no law that forbids him to suspect you.'

Mandel fell angrily silent.

Talliaferro, not allowing his voice to falter, said, 'It is more than just suspicion, Dr Urth. The evidence is perfectly plain. Four of us knew about mass-transference, but only one of us, Dr Mandel, had actually seen a demonstration. He *knew* it to be a fact. He *knew* a paper on the subject existed. We three knew only that Villiers was more or less unbalanced. Oh, we might have thought there was just a chance. We visited him at eleven, I think, just to check on that, though none of us actually said so – but he just acted crazier than ever.

'Check special knowledge and motive then on Dr Mandel's side.

Now, Dr Urth, picture something else. Whoever it was who confronted Villiers at midnight, saw him collapse, and scanned his paper (let's keep him anonymous for a moment) must have been terribly startled to see Villiers apparently come to life again and to hear him talking into the telephone. Our criminal, in the panic of the moment, realized one thing: he must get rid of the one piece of incriminating material evidence.

'He had to get rid of the undeveloped film of the paper and he had to do it in such a way that it would be safe from discovery so that he might pick it up once more if he remained unsuspected. The outer window sill was ideal. Quickly he threw up Villiers' window, placed the strip of film outside, and left. Now, even if Villiers survived or if his telephoning brought results, it would be merely Villiers' word against his own and it would be easy to show that Villiers was unbalanced.'

Talliaferro paused in something like triumph. This would be irrefutable.

Wendell Urth blinked at him and wiggled the thumbs of his clasped hands so that they slapped against his ample shirt front. He said, 'And the significance of all that?'

'The significance is that the window was thrown open and the film placed in open air. Now Ryger has lived for ten years on Ceres, Kaunas on Mercury, I on the Moon – barring short leaves and not many of them. We commented to one another several times yesterday on the difficulty of growing acclimated to Earth.

'Our work-worlds are each airless objects. We never go out in the open without a suit. To expose ourselves to unenclosed space is unthinkable. None of us could have opened the window without a severe inner struggle. Dr Mandel, however, has lived on Earth exclusively. Opening a window to him is only a matter of a bit of muscular exertion. He could do it. We couldn't. Ergo, he did it.'

Talliaferro sat back and smiled a bit.

'Space, that's it!' cried Ryger, with enthusiasm.

'That's not it at all,' roared Mandel, half rising as though tempted to throw himself at Talliaferro. 'I deny the whole miserable fabrication. What about the record I have of Villiers' phone call? He used the word "classmate". The entire tape makes it obvious—'

'He was a dying man,' said Talliaferro. 'Much of what he said you admitted was incomprehensible. I ask you, Dr Mandel, without having heard the tape, if it isn't true that Villiers' voice is distorted past recognition.'

'Well—' said Mandel in confusion.

'I'm sure it is. There is no reason to suppose, then, that you might not have rigged up the tape in advance, complete with the damning word "classmate".'

Mandel said, 'Good Lord, how would I know there were classmates at the Convention? How would I know they knew about the mass-transference?'

'Villiers might have told you. I presume he did.'

'Now, look,' said Mandel, 'you three saw Villiers alive at eleven. The medical examiner, seeing Villiers' body shortly after 3 a.m., declared he had been dead at least two hours. That was certain. The time of death, therefore, was between 11 p.m. and 1 a.m. I was at a late conference last night. I can prove my whereabouts, miles from the hotel, between 10:00 and 2:00 by a dozen witnesses no one of whom anyone can possibly question. Is that enough for you?'

Talliaferro paused a moment. Then he went on stubbornly, 'Even so. Suppose you got back to the hotel by 2:30. You went to Villiers' room to discuss his talk. You found the door open, or you had a duplicate key. Anyway, you found him dead. You seized the opportunity to scan the paper—'

'And if he were already dead, and couldn't make phone calls, why should I hide the film?'

'To remove suspicion. You may have a second copy of the film safe in your possession. For that matter, we have only your own word that the paper itself was destroyed.'

'Enough. Enough,' cried Urth. 'It is an interesting hypothesis, Dr Talliaferro, but it falls to the ground of its own weight.'

Talliaferro frowned. 'That's your opinion, perhaps—'

'It would be anyone's opinion. Anyone, that is, with the power of human thought. Don't you see that Hubert Mandel did too much to be the criminal?'

'No,' said Talliaferro.

Wendell Urth smiled benignly. 'As a scientist, Dr Talliaferro, you undoubtedly know better than to fall in love with your own theories to the exclusion of facts or reasoning. Do me the pleasure of behaving similarly as a detective.

'Consider that if Dr Mandel had brought about the death of Villiers and faked an alibi, or if he had found Villiers dead and taken advantage of that, how little he would really have had to do! Why scan the paper or even pretend that anyone had done so? He could simply have taken the paper. Who else knew of its existence? Nobody, really. There is no reason to think Villiers told anyone else about it. Villiers was pathologically secretive. There would have been every reason to think that he told no one.

'No one knew Villiers was giving a talk, except Dr Mandel. It wasn't announced. No abstract was published. Dr Mandel could have walked off with the paper in perfect confidence.

'Even if he had discovered that Villiers had talked to his classmates about the matter, what of it? What evidence would his classmates have except the word of one whom they are themselves half willing to consider a madman?

'By announcing instead that Villiers' paper had been destroyed, by declaring his death to be not entirely natural, by searching for a scanned copy of the film – in short by everything Dr Mandel has done – he has aroused a suspicion that only he could possibly have aroused when he need only have remained quiet to have committed a perfect crime. If he were the criminal, he would be more stupid, more colossally obtuse than anyone I have ever known. And Dr Mandel, after all, is none of that.'

Talliaferro thought hard but found nothing to say.

Ryger said, 'Then who did do it?'

'One of you three. That's obvious.'

'But which?'

'Oh, that's obvious, too. I knew which of you was guilty the moment Dr Mandel had completed his description of events.'

Talliaferro stared at the plump extraterrologist with distaste. The bluff did not frighten him, but it was affecting the other two. Ryger's lips were thrust out and Kaunas's lower jaw had relaxed moronically. They looked like fish, both of them.

He said, 'Which one, then? Tell us.'

Urth blinked. 'First, I want to make it perfectly plain that the important thing is mass-transference. It can still be recovered.'

Mandel, scowling still, said querulously, 'What the devil are you talking about, Urth?'

'The man who scanned the paper probably looked at what he was scanning. I doubt that he had the time or presence of mind to read it, and if he did, I doubt if he could remember it – consciously. However, there is the Psychic Probe. If he even glanced at the paper, what impinged on his retina could be Probed.'

There was an uneasy stir.

Urth said at once, 'No need to be afraid of the Probe. Proper handling is safe, particularly if a man offers himself voluntarily. When damage is done, it is usually because of unnecessary resistance, a kind of mental tearing, you know. So if the guilty man will voluntarily confess, place himself in my hands—'

Talliaferro laughed. The sudden noise rang out sharply in the dim quiet of the room. The psychology was so transparent and artless.

Wendell Urth looked almost bewildered at the reaction and stared earnestly at Talliaferro over his glasses. He said, 'I have enough influence with the police to keep the Probing entirely confidential.'

Ryger said savagely, 'I didn't do it.'

Kaunas shook his head.

Talliaferro disdained any answer.

Urth sighed. 'Then I will have to point out the guilty man. It will be traumatic. It will make things harder.' He tightened the grip on his belly and his fingers twitched. 'Dr Talliaferro pointed out that the film was hidden on the outer window sill so that it might remain safe from discovery and from harm. I agree with him.'

'Thank you,' said Talliaferro dryly.

'However, why should anyone think that an outer window sill is a particularly safe hiding place? The police would certainly look there. Even in the absence of the police it was discovered. Who would tend to consider anything outside a building as particularly safe? Obviously, some person who has lived a long time on an airless world and has it drilled into him that no one goes outside an enclosed place without detailed precautions.

'To someone on the Moon, for instance, anything hidden outside a Lunar Dome would be comparatively safe. Men venture out only rarely and then only on specific business. So he would overcome the hardship of opening a window and exposing himself to what he would subconsciously consider a vacuum for the sake of a safe hiding place. The reflex thought, "Outside an inhabited structure is safe," would do the trick.'

Talliaferro said between clenched teeth, 'Why do you mention the Moon, Dr Urth?'

Urth said blandly, 'Only as an example. What I've said so far applies to all three of you. But now comes the crucial point, the matter of the dying night.'

Talliaferro frowned. 'You mean the night Villiers died?'

'I mean any night. See here, even granted that an outer window sill was a safe hiding place, which of you would be mad enough to consider it a safe hiding place *for a piece of unexposed film?* Scanner film isn't very sensitive, to be sure, and is made to be developed under all sorts of hit-and-miss conditions. Diffuse night-time illumination wouldn't seriously affect it, but diffuse daylight would ruin it in a few minutes, and direct sunlight would ruin it at once. Everyone knows that.'

Mandel said, 'Go ahead, Urth. What is this leading to?'

'You're trying to rush me,' said Urth, with a massive pout. 'I want you to see this clearly. The criminal wanted, above all, to keep the film safe. It was his only record of something of supreme value to himself and to the world. Why would he put it where it would inevitably be ruined by the morning sun? – Only because he did not expect the morning sun ever to come. He thought the night, so to speak, was immortal.

'But nights *aren't* immortal. On Earth, they die and give way to daytime. Even the six-month polar night is a dying night eventually. The nights on Ceres last only two hours; the nights on the Moon last two weeks. They are dying nights, too, and Dr Talliaferro and Ryger know that day must always come.'

Kaunas was on his feet. 'But wait—'

Wendell Urth faced him full. 'No longer any need to wait, Dr Kaunas. Mercury is the only sizeable object in the Solar System that turns only one face to the sun. Even taking libration into account, fully three-eighths of its surface is true dark-side and never sees the sun. The Polar Observatory is at the rim of that dark-side. For ten years, you have grown used to the fact that nights are immortal, that a surface in darkness remains eternally in darkness, and so you entrusted unexposed film to Earth's night, forgetting in your excitement that nights must die—'

Kaunas stumbled forward. 'Wait—'

Urth was inexorable. 'I am told that when Mandel adjusted the polarizer in Villiers' room, you screamed at the sunlight. Was that your ingrained fear of Mercurian sun, or your sudden realization of what sunlight meant to your plans? You rushed forward. Was that to adjust the polarizer or to stare at the ruined film?'

Kaunas fell to his knees. 'I didn't mean it. I wanted to speak to him, only to speak to him, and he screamed and collapsed. I thought he was dead and the paper was under his pillow and it all just followed. One thing led on to another and before I knew it, I couldn't get out of it any more. But I meant none of it. I swear it.'

They had formed a semicircle about him and Wendell Urth stared at the moaning Kaunas with pity in his eyes.

An ambulance had come and gone. Talliaferro finally brought himself to say stiffly to Mandel, 'I hope, sir, there will be no hard feelings for anything said here.'

And Mandel had answered, as stiffly, 'I think we had all better forget as much as possible of what has happened during the last twenty-four hours.'

They were standing in the doorway, ready to leave, and Wendell Urth ducked his smiling head, and said, 'There's the question of my fee, you know.'

Mandel looked startled.

'Not money,' said Urth at once. 'But when the first mass-transference setup for humans is established, I want a trip arranged for me.'

Mandel continued to look anxious. 'Now, wait. Trips through outer space are a long way off.'

Urth shook his head rapidly. 'Not outer space. Not at all. I would like to step across to Lower Falls, New Hampshire.'

'All right. But why?'

Urth looked up. To Talliaferro's outright surprise, the extra-terrologist's face wore an expression compounded of shyness and eagerness.

Urth said, 'I once – quite a long time ago – knew a girl there. It's been many years – but I sometimes wonder—'

I'm in Marsport Without Hilda

It worked itself out, to begin with, like a dream. I didn't have to make any arrangement. I didn't have to touch it. I just watched things work out. – Maybe that's when I should have first smelled catastrophe.

It began with my usual month's layoff between assignments. A month on and a month off is the right and proper routine for the Galactic Service. I reached Marsport for the usual three-day layover before the short hop to Earth.

Ordinarily, Hilda, God bless her, as sweet a wife as any man ever had, would be there waiting for me and we'd have a nice sedate time of it – a nice little interlude for the two of us. The only trouble with that is that Marsport is the rowdiest spot in the System, and a nice little interlude isn't exactly what fits in. Only, how do I explain that to Hilda, hey?

Well, *this* time, my mother-in-law, God *bless* her (for a change) got sick just two days before I reached Marsport, and the night before landing, I got a spacegram from Hilda saying she would stay on Earth with her mother and wouldn't meet me this one time.

I 'grammed back my loving regrets and my feverish anxiety concerning her mother and when I landed, there I was—

I was in Marsport without Hilda!

That was still nothing, you understand. It was the frame of the picture, the bones of the woman. Now there was the matter of the lines and coloring inside the frame; the skin and flesh outside the bones.

So I called up Flora (Flora of certain rare episodes in the past) and for the purpose I used a video booth. – Damn the expense; full speed ahead.

I was giving myself ten to one odds she'd be out, she'd be busy with her videophone disconnected, she'd be dead, even.

But she was in, with her videophone connected, and Great Galaxy, was she anything but dead.

She looked better than ever. Age cannot wither, as somebody or other once said, nor custom stale her infinite variety.

Was she glad to see me? She squealed, 'Max! It's been years.'

'I know, Flora, but this is it, if you're available. Because guess what! I'm in Marsport without Hilda.'

She squealed again, 'Isn't that *nice!* Then come on over.'

I goggled a bit. This was too much. 'You mean you *are* available?' You have to understand that Flora was never available without plenty of notice. Well, she was that kind of knockout.

She said, 'Oh, I've got some quibbling little arrangement, Max, but I'll take care of that. You come on over.'

'I'll come,' I said happily.

Flora was the kind of girl— Well, I tell you, she had her rooms under Martian gravity, 0.4 Earth-normal. The gadget to free her of Marsport's pseudo-grav field was expensive of course, but if you've ever held a girl in your arms at 0.4 gees, you need no explanation. If you haven't, explanations will do no good. I'm also sorry for you.

Talk about floating on clouds.

I closed connections, and only the prospect of seeing it all in the flesh could have made me wipe out the image with such alacrity. I stepped out of the booth.

And at that point, that precise point, that very split-instant of time, the first whiff of catastrophe nudged itself up to me.

That first whiff was the bald head of that lousy Rog Crinton of the Mars offices, gleaming over a headful of pale blue eyes, pale yellow complexion, and pale brown mustache. I didn't bother getting on all fours and beating my forehead against the ground because my vacation had started the minute I had gotten off the ship.

So I said with only normal politeness, 'What do you want and I'm in a hurry. I've got an appointment.'

He said, 'You've got an appointment with me. I was waiting for you at the unloading desk.'

I said, 'I didn't see you—'

He said, 'You didn't see anything.'

He was right at that, for, come to think of it, if he was at the unloading desk, he must have been spinning ever since because I went past that desk like Halley's Comet skimming the Solar Corona.

I said, 'All right. What do you want?'

'I've got a little job for you.'

I laughed. 'It's my month off, friend.'

He said, 'Red emergency alert, friend.'

Which meant, no vacation, just like that. I couldn't believe it. I said, 'Nuts, Rog. Have a heart. I got an emergency alert of my own.'

'Nothing like this.'

'Rog,' I yelled, 'can't you get someone else? Anyone else?'

'You're the only Class A agent on Mars.'

'Send to Earth, then. They stack agents like micro-pile units at Headquarters.'

'This has got to be done before 11 p.m. What's the matter? You haven't got three hours?'

I grabbed my head. The boy just didn't *know*. I said, 'Let me make a call, will you?'

I stepped back into the booth, glared at him, and said, 'Private!'

Flora shone on the screen again, like a mirage on an asteroid.

She said, 'Something wrong, Max? Don't say something's wrong. I canceled my other engagement.'

I said, 'Flora, baby, I'll be there. I'll *be* there. But something's come up.'

She asked the natural question in a hurt tone of voice and I said, 'No. Not another girl. With you in the same town they don't make any other girls. Females, maybe. Not girls. Baby! Honey!' (I had a wild impulse but hugging 'vision screen is no pastime for a grown man.) 'It's business. Just hold on. It won't take long.'

She said, 'All right,' but she said it kind of like it was just enough not all right so that I got the shivers.

I stepped out of the booth and said, 'All right, Rog, what kind of mess have you cooked up for me?'

We went into the spaceport bar and got us an insulated booth. He said, 'The *Antares Giant* is coming in from Sirius in exactly half an hour; at 8 p.m. local time.'

'Okay.'

'Three men will get out, among others, and will wait for the *Space Eater* coming in from Earth at 11 p.m. and leaving for Capella some time thereafter. The three men will get on the *Space Eater* and will then be out of our jurisdiction.'

'So.'

'So between 8:00 and 11:00, they will be in a special waiting room and you will be with them. I have a trimensional image of each for you so you'll know which they are and which is which. You have between 8:00 and 11:00 to decide which one of the three is carrying contraband.'

'What kind of contraband?'

'The worst kind. Altered Spaceoline.'

'*Altered* Spaceoline?'

He had thrown me. I knew what Spaceoline was. If you've been on a space-hop you know, too. And in case you're Earth-bound your-self the bare fact is that everyone needs it on the first space-trip;

almost everybody needs it for the first dozen trips; lots need it every trip. Without it, there is vertigo associated with free fall, screaming terrors, semi-permanent psychoses. With it, there is nothing; no one minds a thing. And it isn't habit-forming; it has no adverse side-effects. Spaceoline is ideal, essential, unsubstitutable. When in doubt, take Spaceoline.

Rog said, 'That's right, altered Spaceoline. It can be changed chemically by a very simple reaction that can be conducted in anyone's basement into a drug that will give one giant-size charge and become your baby-blue habit the first time. It is on a par with the most dangerous alkaloids we know.'

'And we just found out about it?'

'No. The Service has known about it for years, and we've kept others from knowing by squashing every discovery flat. Only now the discovery has gone too far.'

'In what way?'

'One of the men who will be stopping over at this spaceport is carrying some of the altered Spaceoline on his person. Chemists in the Capellan system, which is outside the Federation, will analyze it and set up ways of synthesizing more. After that, it's either fight the worst drug menace we've ever seen or suppress the matter by suppressing the source.'

'You mean Spaceoline.'

'Right. And if we suppress Spaceoline, we suppress space travel.'

I decided to put my finger on the point. 'Which one of the three has it?'

Rog smiled nastily, 'If we knew, would we need you? You're to find out which of the three.'

'You're calling on me for a lousy frisk job.'

'Touch the wrong one at the risk of a haircut down to the larynx. Every one of the three is a big man on his own planet. One is Edward Harponaster; one is Joaquin Lipsky; and one is Andiamo Ferrucci. Well?'

He was right. I'd heard of every one of them. Chances are you have, too; and not one was touchable without proof in advance, as you know. I said, 'Would one of them touch a dirty deal like—'

'There are trillions involved,' said Rog, 'which means any one of the three would. And one of them *is*, because Jack Hawk got that far before he was killed—'

'Jack Hawk's *dead?*' For a minute, I forgot about the Galactic drug menace. For a minute, I nearly forgot about Flora.

'Right, and one of those guys arranged the killing. Now you find out which. You put the finger on the right one before 11:00 and there's a promotion, a raise in pay, a pay-back for poor Jack Hawk, and a rescue of the Galaxy. You put the finger on the wrong one and there'll be a nasty interstellar situation and you'll be out on your ear and also on every black list from here to Antares and back.'

I said, 'Suppose I don't finger anybody?'

'That would be like fingering the wrong one as far as the Service is concerned.'

'I've got to finger someone but only the right one or my head's handed to me.'

'In thin slices. You're beginning to understand me, Max.'

In a long lifetime of looking ugly, Rog Crinton had never looked uglier. The only comfort I got out of staring at him was the realization that he was married, too, and that he lived with his wife at Marsport all year round. And does he deserve that. Maybe I'm hard on him, but he *deserves* it.

I put in a quick call to Flora, as soon as Rog was out of sight.

She said, 'Well?'

I said, 'Baby, honey, it's something I can't talk about, but I've got to do it, see? Now you hang on, I'll get it over with if I have to swim the Grand Canal to the icecap in my underwear, see? If I have to claw Phobos out of the sky. If I have to cut myself in pieces and mail myself parcel post.'

'Gee,' she said, 'if I thought I was going to have to wait—'

I winced. She just wasn't the type to respond to poetry. Actually she was a simple creature of action—But after all, if I was going to be drifting through low-gravity in a sea of jasmine perfume with Flora, poetry-response is not the type of qualification I would consider most indispensable.

I said urgently, 'Just hold on, Flora. I won't be any time at all. I'll make it up to you.'

I was annoyed, sure, but I wasn't worried as yet. Rog hadn't more than left me when I figured out exactly how I was going to tell the guilty man from the others.

It was easy. I should have called Rog back and told him, but there's no law against wanting egg in your beer and oxygen in your air. It would take me five minutes and then off I would go to Flora; a little late, maybe, but with a promotion, a raise, and a slobbering kiss from the Service on each cheek.

You see, it's like this. Big industrialists don't go space-hopping much; they use trans-video reception. When they do go to some ultra-high interstellar conference, as these three were probably going, they take Spaceoline. For one thing, they don't have enough hops under their belt to risk doing without. For another, Spaceoline is the expensive way of doing it and industrialists do things the expensive way. I know their psychology.

Now that would hold for two of them. The one who carried contraband, however, couldn't risk Spaceoline – even to prevent space-sickness. Under Spaceoline influence, he could throw the drug away; or give it away; or talk gibberish about it. He would *have* to stay in control of himself.

It was as simple as that, so I waited.

The *Antares Giant* was on time and I waited with my leg muscles tense for a quick take-off as soon as I collared the murdering drug-toting rat and sped the two eminent captains of industry on their way.

They brought in Lipsky first. He had thick, ruddy lips, rounded jowls, very dark eyebrows, and graying hair. He just looked at me and sat down. Nothing. He was under Spaceoline.

I said, 'Good evening, sir.'

He said, in a dreamy voice, 'Surrealismus of Panamy hearts in three-quarter time for a cup of coffeedom of speech.'

That was Spaceoline all the way. The buttons in the human mind were set free-swing. Each syllable suggests the next in free association.

Andiamo Ferrucci came in next. Black mustache, long and waxed, olive complexion, pock-marked face. He took a seat in another chair, facing us.

I said, 'Nice trip?'

He said, 'Trip the light fantastic tock the clock is crowings on the bird.'

Lipsky said, 'Bird to the wise guyed book to all places every body.'

I grinned. That left Harponaster. I had my needle gun neatly palmed out of sight and the magnetic coil ready to grip him.

And then Harponaster came in. He was thin, leathery, near-bald and rather younger than he seemed in his trimensional image. And he was Spaceolined to the gills.

I said, 'Damn!'

Harponaster said, 'Damyankee note speech to his last time I saw wood you say so.'

Ferrucci said, 'Sow the seed the territory under dispute do well to come along long road to a nightingale.'

Lipsky said, 'Gay lords hopping pong balls.'

I stared from one to the other as the nonsense ran down in shorter and shorter spurts and then silence.

I got the picture, all right. One of them was faking. He had thought ahead and realized that omitting the Spaceoline would be a giveaway. He might have bribed an official into injecting saline or dodged it some other way.

One of them must be faking. It wasn't hard to fake the thing. Comedians on sub-etheric had a Spaceoline skit regularly. *You've* heard them.

I stared at them and got the first prickle at the base of my skull that said: What if you *don't* finger the right one?

It was 8:30 and there was my job, my reputation, my head growing rickety upon my neck to be considered. I saved it all for later and thought of Flora. She wasn't going to wait for me forever. For that matter, chances were she wouldn't wait for half an hour.

I wondered. Could the faker keep up free association if nudged gently onto dangerous territory?

I said, 'The floor's covered with a nice solid rug' and ran the last two words together to make it 'soli drug.'

Lipsky said, 'Drug from underneath the dough re mi fa sol to be saved.'

Ferrucci said, 'Saved and a haircut above the common herd something about younicorny as a harmonican the cheek by razor and shine.'

Harponaster said, 'Shiner wind nor snow use trying to by four ever and effervescence and sensibilityter totter.'

Lipsky said, 'Totters and rags.'

Ferrucci said, 'Ragsactly.'

Harponaster said, 'Actlymation.'

A few grunts and they ran down.

I tried again and I didn't forget to be careful. They would remember everything I said afterward and what I said had to be harmless. I said, 'This is a darned good space-line.'

Ferrucci said, 'Lines and tigers through the prairie dogs do bark of the bough-wough—'

I interrupted, looking at Harponaster, 'A darned good space-line.'

'Line the bed and rest a little black sheepishion of wrong the clothes of a perfect day.'

I interrupted again, glaring at Lipsky, 'Good space-line.'

'Liron is hot chocolate ain't gonna be the same on you vee and double the stakes and potatoes and heel.'

Someone else said, 'Heel the sicknecessaryd and write will vincetance.'

'Tance with mealtime.'

'I'm comingle.'

'Inglish.'

'Ishter seals.'

'Eels.'

I tried a few more times and got nowhere. The faker, whicheve
he was, had practiced or had natural talents at talking free associa
tion. He was disconnecting his brain and letting the words come ou
any old way. And he must be inspired by knowing exactly what I wa
after. If 'drug' hadn't given it away, 'space-line' three times repeated
must have. I was safe with the other two, but *he* would know.

– And he was having fun with me. All three were saying phrase
that might have pointed to a deep inner guilt ('sol to be saved,' 'littl
black sheepishion of wrong,' 'drug from underneath,' and so on). Two
were saying such things helplessly, randomly. The third was amusing
himself.

So how did I find the third? I was in a feverish thrill of hatred
against him and my fingers twitched. The rat was subverting the
Galaxy. More than than, he had killed my colleague and friend. More
than that, he was keeping me from Flora.

I could go up to each of them and start searching. The two who
were really under Spaceoline would make no move to stop me. They
could feel no emotion, no fear, no anxiety, no hate, no passion, no
desire for self-defense. And if one made the slightest gesture of resistance I would have my man.

But the innocent ones would remember afterward. They would
remember a personal search while under Spaceoline.

I sighed. If I tried it, I would get the criminal all right but later
would be the nearest thing to chopped liver any man had ever been
There would be a shake-up in the Service, a big stink the width of
the Galaxy, and in the excitement and disorganization, the secret o
altered Spaceoline would get out anyway and so what the hell.

Of course, the one I wanted might be the first one I touched. One
chance out of three. I'd have one out and only God can make a three

Nuts, something had started them going while I was muttering to myself and Spaceoline is contagioust a gigolo my, oh—

I stared desperately at my watch and my line of sight focused on 9:15.

Where the devil was time going to?

Oh, my; oh, nuts, oh, Flora!

I had no choice. I made my way to the booth for another quick call to Flora. Just a quick one, you understand, to keep things alive; assuming they weren't dead already.

I kept saying to myself: She won't answer.

I tried to prepare myself for that. There were other girls, there were other—

What's the use, there were no other girls.

If Hilda had been in Marsport, I never would have had Flora on my mind in the first place and it wouldn't have mattered. *But I was in Marsport without Hilda* and I had made a date with Flora.

The signal was signaling and signaling and I didn't dare break off. Answer! Answer!

She answered. She said, 'It's *you!*'

'Of course, sweetheart, who else would it be?'

'Lots of people. Someone who would *come.*'

'There's just this little detail of business, honey.'

'What business? Plastons for who?'

I almost corrected her grammar but I was too busy wondering what this plastons kick was.

Then I remembered. I told her once I was a plaston salesman. That was the time I brought her a plaston nightgown that was a honey.

I said, 'Look. Just give me another half hour—'

Her eyes grew moist. 'I'm sitting here all by myself.'

'I'll make it up to you.' To show you how desperate I was getting, I was definitely beginning to think along paths that could lead only to jewelry even though a sizable dent in the bankbook would show up to Hilda's piercing eye like the Horsehead Nebula interrupting the Milky Way. But then I was desperate.

She said, 'I had a perfectly good date and I broke it off.'

I protested, 'You said it was a quibbling little arrangement.'

That was a mistake. I knew it the minute I said it.

She shrieked, *'Quibbling little arrangement!'* (It was what she had said. It was what she had said. But having the truth on your side just makes it worse in arguing with a woman. Don't I know?) 'You call a man who's promised me an estate on Earth—'

She went on and on about that estate on Earth. There wasn't a gal in Marsport who wasn't wangling for an estate on Earth, and you could count the number who got one on the sixth finger of either hand.

I tried to stop her. No use.

She finally said, 'And here I am all alone, with *nobody*,' and broke off contact.

Well, she was right. I felt like the lowest heel in the Galaxy.

I went back into the reception room. A flunky outside the door saluted me in.

I stared at the three industrialists and speculated on the order in which I would slowly choke each to death if I could but receive choking orders. Harponaster first, maybe. He had a thin, stringy neck that the fingers could go round neatly and a sharp Adam's apple against which the thumbs could find purchase.

It cheered me up infinitesimally, to the point where I mustered, 'Boy!' just out of sheer longing, though it was no boy I was longing for.

It started them off at once. Ferrucci said, 'Boyl the watern the spout you goateeming rain over us, God savior pennies—'

Harponaster of the scrawny neck added, 'Nies and nephew don't like orporalley cat.'

Lipsky said, 'Cattle corral go down off a ductilitease drunk.'

'Drunkle aunterior passagewayt a while.'

'While beasts oh pray.'

'Prayties grow.'

'Grow way.'

'Waiter.'

'Terble.'

'Ble.'

Then nothing.

They stared at me. I stared at them. They were empty of emotion (or two were) and I was empty of ideas. And time passed.

I stared at them some more and thought about Flora. It occurred to me that I had nothing to lose that I had not already lost. I might as well talk about her.

I said, 'Gentlemen, there is a girl in this town whose name I will not mention for fear of compromising her. Let me describe her to you, gentlemen.'

And I did. If I say so myself, the last two hours had honed me to such a fine force-field edge that the description of Flora took on a kind of poetry that seemed to be coming from some wellspring of masculine force deep in the subbasement of my unconscious.

And they sat frozen, almost as though they were listening, and hardly ever interrupting. People under Spaceoline have a kind of politeness about them. They won't speak when someone else is speaking. That's why they take turns.

I kept it up with a kind of heartfelt sadness in my voice until the loudspeaker announced in stirring tones the arrival of the *Space Eater*.

That was that. I said in a loud voice, 'Rise, gentlemen.'

'Not you, you murderer,' and my magnetic coil was on Ferrucci's wrist before he could breathe twice.

Ferrucci fought like a demon. He was under no Spaceoline influence. They found the altered Spaceoline in thin flesh-colored plastic pads hugging the inner surface of his thighs. You couldn't see it at all; you could only feel it, and even then it took a knife to make sure.

Afterward, Rog Crinton, grinning and half insane with relief, held me by the lapel with a death grip. 'How did you do it? What gave it away?'

I said, trying to pull loose, 'One of them was faking a Spaceline jag. I was sure of it. So I told them,' (I grew cautious – none of his business as to the details, you know) '. . . uh, about a girl, see, and two of them never reacted, so they were Spaceolined. But Ferrucci's breathing speeded up and the beads of sweat came out on his forehead. I gave a pretty dramatic rendition, and he reacted, so he was under no Spaceoline. Now will you let me go?'

He let go and I almost fell over backward.

I was set to take off. My feet were pawing the ground without any instruction from me – but then I turned back.

'Hey, Rog,' I said, 'can you sign me a chit for a thousand credits without its going on the record – for services rendered to the Service?'

That's when I realized he was half insane with relief and very temporary gratitude, because he said, 'Sure, Max, sure. Ten thousand credits if you want.'

'I *want*,' I said, grabbing him for a change. 'I want. I want.'

He filled out an official Service chit for ten thousand credits; good as cash anywhere in half the Galaxy. He was actually grinning as he gave it to me and you can bet I was grinning as I took it.

How *he* intended accounting for it was his affair; the point was that *I* wouldn't have to account for it to Hilda.

I stood in the booth, one last time, signaling Flora. I didn't dare let matters go till I reached her place. The additional half hour might just give her time to get someone else, if she hadn't already.

Make her answer. Make her answer. Make her—

She answered, but she was in formal clothes. She was going out and I had obviously caught her by two minutes.

'I am going out,' she announced. '*Some* men can be decent. And I do not wish to see you in the henceforward. I do not wish ever to find my eyes upon you. You will do me a great favor, Mister

Whoeveryouare, if you unhand my signal combination and never pollute it with—'

I wasn't saying anything. I was just standing there holding my breath and also holding the chit up where she could see it. Just standing there. Just holding.

Sure enough, at the word 'pollute' she came in for a closer look. She wasn't much on education, that girl, but she could read 'ten thousand credits' faster than any college graduate in the Solar System.

She said, 'Max! For me?'

'All for you, baby,' I said, 'I told you I had a little business to do. I wanted to surprise you.'

'Oh, Max, that's sweet of you. I didn't really mind. I was joking. Now you come right here to me.' She took off her coat.

'What about your date?' I said.

'I *said* I was joking,' she said.

'I'm coming,' I said faintly.

'With every single one of those credits now,' she said roguishly.

'With every single one,' I said.

I broke contact, stepped out of the booth, and now, finally, I was set – set—

I heard my name called. 'Max! Max!' Someone was running toward me. 'Rog Crinton said I would find you here. Mamma's all right after all, so I got special passage on the *Space Eater* and what's this about ten thousand credits?'

I didn't turn. I said, 'Hello, Hilda.'

And then I turned and did the hardest thing I ever succeeded in doing in all my good-for-nothing, space-hopping life.

I managed to smile.

The Gentle Vultures

For fifteen years now, the Hurrians had maintained their base on the other side of the Moon.

It was unprecedented; unheard of. No Hurrian had dreamed it possible to be delayed so long. The decontamination squads had been ready; ready and waiting for fifteen years; ready to swoop down through the radioactive clouds and save what might be saved for the remnant of survivors. – In return, of course, for fair payment.

But fifteen times the planet had revolved about its sun. During each revolution, the satellite had rotated not quite thirteen times about the primary. And in all that time the nuclear war had not come.

Nuclear bombs were exploded by the large-primate intelligences at various points on the planet's surface. The planet's stratosphere had grown amazingly warm with radioactive refuse. But still no war.

Devi-en hoped ardently that he would be replaced. He was the fourth Captain-in-charge of this colonizing expedition (if it could still be called so after fifteen years of suspended animation) and he was quite content that there should be a fifth. Now that the home world was sending an Arch-administrator to make a personal survey of the situation, his replacement might come soon. Good!

He stood on the surface of the Moon, encased in his space-suit, and thought of home, of Hurria. His long, thin arms moved restlessly with the thought, as though aching (through millions of years of instinct) for the ancestral trees. He stood only three feet high. What could be seen of him through the glass-fronted head plate was a black and wrinkled face with the fleshy, mobile nose dead-centered. The little tuft of fine beard was a pure white in contrast. In the rear of the suit, just below center, was the bulge within which the short and stubby Hurrian tail might rest comfortably.

Devi-en took his appearance for granted, of course, but was well aware of the difference between the Hurrians and all the other intelligences in the Galaxy. The Hurrians alone were so small; they alone were tailed; they alone were vegetarians – they alone had escaped the inevitable nuclear war that had ruined every other known intelligent species.

He stood on the walled plain that extended for so many miles that the raised and circular rim (which on Hurria would have been called a crater, if it were smaller) was invisible beyond the horizon. Against the southern edge of the rim, where there was always some protection against the direct rays of the Sun, a city had grown. It had begun as a temporary camp, of course, but with the years, women had been brought in, and children had been born in it. Now there were schools and elaborate hydroponics establishments, large water reservoirs, all that went with a city on an airless world.

It was ridiculous! All because one planet had nuclear weapons and would not fight a nuclear war.

The Arch-administrator, who would be arriving soon, would undoubtedly ask, almost at once, the same question that Devi-en had asked himself a wearisome number of times.

Why had there not been a nuclear war?

Devi-en watched the hulking Mauvs preparing the ground now for the landing, smoothing out the unevennesses and laying down the ceramic bed designed to absorb the hyperatomic field-thrusts with minimum discomfort to the passengers within the ship.

Even in their space-suits, the Mauvs seemed to exude power, but it was the power of muscle only. Beyond them was the little figure of a Hurrian giving orders, and the docile Mauvs obeyed. Naturally.

The Mauvian race, of all the large-primate intelligences, paid their fees in the most unusual coin, a quota of themselves, rather than of material goods. It was a surprisingly useful tribute, better than steel, aluminum, or fine drugs in many ways.

Devi-en's receiver stuttered to life. 'The ship is sighted, sir,' came the report. 'It will be landing within the hour.'

'Very good,' said Devi-en. 'Have my car made ready to take me to the ship as soon as landing is initiated.'

He did not feel that it was very good at all.

The Arch-administrator came, flanked by a personal retinue of five Mauvs. They entered the city with him, one on each side, three following. They helped him off with his space-suit, then removed their own.

Their thinly haired bodies, their large, coarse-featured faces, their broad noses and flat cheekbones were repulsive but not frightening. Though twice the height of the Hurrians and more than twice the breadth, there was a blankness about their eyes, something completely submissive about the way they stood, with their thick-sinewed necks slightly bent, their bulging arms hanging listlessly.

The Arch-administrator dismissed them and they trooped out. He did not really need their protection, of course, but his position required a retinue of five and that was that.

No business was discussed during the meal or during the almost endless ritual of welcome. At a time that might have been more appropriate for sleeping, the Arch-administrator passed small fingers through his tuft of beard and said, 'How much longer must we wait for this planet, Captain?'

He was visibly advancing in age. The hair on his upper arms was grizzled and the tufts at the elbows were almost as white as his beard.

'I cannot say, your Height,' said Devi-en humbly. 'They have not followed the path.'

'That is obvious. The point is, *why* have they not followed the path? It is clear to the Council that your reports promise more than they deliver. You talk of theories but you give no details. Now we are tired of all this back on Hurria. If you know of anything you have not told us, now is the time to talk of it.'

'The matter, your Height, is hard to prove. We have had no experience of spying on a people over such an extended period. Until recently, we weren't watching for the right things. Each year we kept expecting the nuclear war the year after and it is only in my time as Captain that we have taken to studying the people more intensively. It is at least one benefit of the long waiting time that we have learned some of their principal languages.'

'Indeed? Without even landing on their planet?'

Devi-en explained. 'A number of radio messages were recorded by those of our ships that penetrated the planetary atmosphere on observation missions, particularly in the early years. I set our linguistics computers to work on them, and for the last year I have been attempting to make sense out of it all.'

The Arch-administrator stared. His bearing was such that any outright exclamation of surprise would have been superfluous. 'And have you learned anything of interest?'

'I may have, your Height, but what I have worked out is so strange and the underpinning of actual evidence is so uncertain that I dared not speak of it officially in my reports.'

The Arch-administrator understood. He said, stiffly, 'Would you object to explaining your views unofficially – to me?'

'I would be glad to,' said Devi-en at once. 'The inhabitants of this planet are, of course, large-primate in nature. And they are competitive.'

The other blew out his breath in a kind of relief and passed his tongue quickly over his nose. 'I had the queer notion,' he muttered, 'that they might *not* be competitive and that that might— But go on, go on.'

'They *are* competitive,' Devi-en assured him. 'Much more so than one would expect on the average.'

'Then why doesn't everything else follow?'

'Up to a point it does, your Height. After the usual long incubation period, they began to mechanize; and after that, the usual large-primate killings became truly destructive warfare. At the conclusion of the most recent large-scale war, nuclear weapons were developed and the war ended at once.'

The Arch-administrator nodded. 'And then?'

Devi-en said, 'What should have happened was that a nuclear war ought to have begun shortly afterward and in the course of the war, nuclear weapons would have developed quickly in destructiveness, have been used nevertheless in typical large-primate fashion, and have quickly reduced the population to starving remnants in a ruined world.'

'Of course, but that didn't happen. Why not?'

Devi-en said, 'There is one point. I believe these people, once mechanization started, developed at an unusually high rate.'

'And if so?' said the other. 'Does that matter? They reached nuclear weapons the more quickly.'

'True. But after the most recent general war, they continued to develop nuclear weapons at an unusual rate. That's the trouble. The deadly potential had increased before the nuclear war had a chance to start and now it has reached a point where even large-primate intelligences dare not risk a war.'

The Arch-administrator opened his small black eyes wide. 'But that is impossible. I don't care how technically talented these creatures are. Military science advances rapidly only during a war.'

'Perhaps that is not true in the case of these particular creatures. But even if it were, it seems they *are* having a war; not a real war, but a war.'

'Not a real war, but a war,' repeated the Arch-administrator blankly. 'What does that mean?'

'I'm not sure.' Devi-en wiggled his nose in exasperation. 'This is where my attempts to draw logic out of the scattered material we have picked up is least satisfactory. This planet has something called a

Cold War. Whatever it is, it drives them furiously onward in research and yet it does not involve complete nuclear destruction.'

The Arch-administrator said, 'Impossible!'

Devi-en said, 'There is the planet. Here we are. We have been waiting fifteen years.'

The Arch-administrator's long arms came up and crossed over his head and down again to the opposite shoulders. 'Then there *is* only one thing to do. The Council has considered the possibility that the planet may have achieved a stalemate, a kind of uneasy peace that balances just short of a nuclear war. Something of the sort you describe, though no one suggested the actual reasons you advance. But it's something we can't allow.'

'No, your Height?'

'No,' he seemed almost in pain. 'The longer the stalemate continues, the greater the possibility that large-primate individuals may discover the methods of interstellar travel. They will leak out into the Galaxy, in full competitive strength. You see?'

'Then?'

The Arch-administrator hunched his head deeper into his arms, as though not wishing to hear what he himself must say. His voice was a little muffled. 'If they are balanced precariously, we must push them a little, Captain. We must push them.'

Devi-en's stomach churned and he suddenly tasted his dinner once more in the back of his throat. 'Push them, your Height?' He didn't want to understand.

But the Arch-administrator put it bluntly, 'We must help them start their nuclear war.' He looked as miserably sick as Devi-en felt. He whispered, 'We must!'

Devi-en could scarcely speak. He said, in a whisper, 'But how could such a thing be done, your Height?'

'I don't know how. – And do not look at *me* so. It is not my decision. It is the decision of the Council. Surely you understand what would happen to the Galaxy if a large-primate intelligence were to enter space in full strength without having been tamed by nuclear war.'

Devi-en shuddered at the thought. All that competitiveness loosed on the Galaxy. He persisted though. 'But *how* does one start a nuclear war? How is it done?'

'I don't know, I tell you. But there must be some way; perhaps a – a message we might send or a – a crucial rainstorm we might start by cloudseeding. We could manage a great deal with their weather conditions—'

'How would that start a nuclear war?' said Devi-en, unimpressed.

'Maybe it wouldn't. I mention such a thing only as a possible example. But large-primates would know. After all, they are the ones who *do* start nuclear wars in actual fact. It is in their brain pattern to know. That is the decision the Council came to.'

Devi-en felt the soft noise his tail made as it thumped slowly against the chair. He tried to stop it and failed. 'What decision, your Height?'

'To trap a large-primate from the planet's surface. To kidnap one.'

'A *wild* one?'

'It's the only kind that exists at the moment on the planet. Of course, a wild one.'

'And what do you expect him to tell us?'

'That doesn't matter, Captain. As long as he says enough about anything, mentalic analysis will give us the answer.'

Devi-en withdrew his head as far as he could into the space between his shoulder blades. The skin just under his armpits quivered with repulsion. A wild large-primate being! He tried to picture one, untouched by the stunning aftermath of nuclear war, unaltered by the civilizing influence of Hurrian eugenic breeding.

The Arch-administrator made no attempt to hide the fact that he shared the repulsion, but he said, 'You will have to lead the trapping expedition, Captain. It is for the good of the Galaxy.'

Devi-en had seen the planet a number of times before but each time a ship swung about the Moon and placed the world in his line of sight a wave of unbearable home-sickness swept him.

It was a beautiful planet, so like Hurria itself in dimensions and characteristics but wilder and grander. The sight of it, after the desolation of the Moon, was like a blow.

How many other planets like it were on Hurrian master listings at this moment, he wondered. How many other planets were there concerning which meticulous observers had reported seasonal changes in appearance that could be interpreted only as being caused by artificial cultivation of food plants? How many times in the future would a day come when the radioactivity in the stratosphere of one of these planets would begin to climb; when colonizing squadrons would have to be sent out at once?

—As they were to this planet.

It was almost pathetic, the confidence with which the Hurrians had proceeded at first. Devi-en could have laughed as he read through those initial reports, if he weren't trapped in this project himself now. The Hurrian scoutships had moved close to the planet to gather geographical information, to locate population centers. They were sighted, of course, but what did it matter? Any time, now, they thought, the final explosion.

Any time— But useless years passed and the scoutships wondered if they ought not to be cautious. They moved back.

Devi-en's ship was cautious now. The crew was on edge because of the unpleasantness of the mission; not all Devien's assurances that there was no harm intended to the large-primate could quite calm them. Even so, they could not hurry matters. It had to be over a fairly deserted and uncultivated tract of uneven ground that they hovered. They stayed at a height of ten miles for days, while the crew became edgier and only the ever-stolid Mauvs maintained calm.

Then the scope showed them a creature, alone on the uneven ground, a long staff in one hand, a pack across the upper portion of his back.

They lowered silently, supersonically. Devi-en himself, skin crawling, was at the controls.

The creature was heard to say two definite things before he was taken, and they were the first comments recorded for use in mentalic computing.

The first, when the large-primate caught sight of the ship almost upon him, was picked up by the direction telemike. It was, 'My God! A flying saucer!'

Devi-en understood the second phrase. That was a term for the Hurrian ships that had grown common among the large-primates those first careless years.

The second remark was made when the wild creature was brought into the ship, struggling with amazing strength, but helpless in the iron grip of the unperturbed Mauvs.

Devi-en, panting, with his fleshy nose quivering slightly, advanced to receive him, and the creature (whose unpleasantly hairless face had become oily with some sort of fluid secretion) yelled, 'Holy Toledo, a *monkey!*'

Again, Devi-en understood the second part. It was the word for little-primate in one of the chief languages of the planet.

The wild creature was almost impossible to handle. He required infinite patience before he could be spoken to reasonably. At first, there was nothing but a series of crises. The creature realized almost at once that he was being taken off Earth, and what Devi-en thought might prove an exciting experience for him, proved nothing of the sort. He talked instead of his offspring and of a large-primate female.

(They have wives and children, thought Devi-en, compassionately, and, in their way, love them, for all they are large-primate.)

Then he had to be made to understand that the Mauvs who kept him under guard and who restrained him when his violence made that necessary would not hurt him, that he was not to be damaged in any way.

(Devi-en was sickened at the thought that one intelligent being might be damaged by another. It was very difficult to discuss the subject, even if only to admit the possibility long enough to deny it. The creature from the planet treated the very hesitation with great suspicion. It was the way the large-primates were.)

On the fifth day, when out of sheer exhaustion, perhaps, the creature remained quiet over a fairly extended period, they talked in Devi-en's private quarters, and suddenly he grew angry again when the Hurrian first explained, matter-of-factly, that they were waiting for a nuclear war.

'Waiting!' cried the creature. 'What makes you so sure there will be one?'

Devi-en wasn't sure, of course, but he said, 'There is always a nuclear war. It is our purpose to help you afterward.'

'Help us *afterward*.' His words grew incoherent. He waved his arms violently, and the Mauvs who flanked him had to restrain him gently once again and lead him away.

Devi-en sighed. The creature's remarks were building in quantity and perhaps mentalics could do something with them. His own unaided mind could make nothing of them.

And meanwhile the creature was not thriving. His body was almost completely hairless, a fact that long-distance observation had not revealed owing to the artificial skins worn by them. This was either for warmth or because of an instinctive repulsion even on the part of these particular large-primates themselves for hairless skin. (It might be an interesting subject to take up. Mentalics computation could make as much out of one set of remarks as another.)

Strangely enough, the creature's face had begun to sprout hair; more, in fact, than the Hurrian face had, and of a darker color.

But still, the central fact was that he was not thriving. He had grown thinner because he was eating poorly, and if he was kept too long, his health might suffer. Devi-en had no wish to feel responsible for that.

On the next day, the large-primate seemed quite calm. He talked almost eagerly, bringing the subject around to nuclear warfare almost at once. (It had a terrible attraction for the large-primate mind, Devi-en thought.)

The creature said, 'You said nuclear wars always happen? Does that mean there are other people than yours and mine – and theirs?' He indicated the near-by Mauvs.

'There are thousands of intelligent species, living on thousands of worlds. Many thousands,' said Devi-en.

'And they all have nuclear wars?'

'All who have reached a certain stage of technology. All but us. We were different. We lacked competitiveness. We had the co-operative instinct.'

'You mean you know that nuclear wars will happen and you do nothing about it?'

'We *do*,' said Devi-en, pained. 'Of course, we do. We try to help. In the early history of my people, when we first developed space-travel, we did not understand large-primates. They repelled our attempts at friendship and we stopped trying. Then we found worlds in radioactive ruins. Finally, we found one world actually in the process of a nuclear war. We were horrified, but could do nothing. Slowly, we learned. We are ready, now, at every world we discover to be at the nuclear stage. We are ready with decontamination equipment and eugenic analyzers.'

'What are eugenic analyzers?'

Devi-en had manufactured the phrase by analogy with what he knew of the wild one's language. Now he said carefully, 'We direct matings and sterilizations to remove, as far as possible, the competitive element in the remnant of the survivors.'

For a moment, he thought the creature would grow violent again.

Instead, the other said in a monotone, 'You make them docile, you mean, like these things?' Once again he indicated the Mauvs.

'No. No. These are different. We simply make it possible for the remnants to be content with a peaceful, nonexpanding, nonaggressive society under our guidance. Without this, they destroyed themselves, you see, and without it, they would destroy themselves again.'

'What do you get out of it?'

Devi-en stared at the creature dubiously. Was it really necessary to explain the basic pleasure of life? He said, 'Don't you enjoy helping someone?'

'Come on. Besides that. What's in it for you?'

'Of course, there are contributions to Hurria.'

'Ha.'

'Payment for saving a species is only fair,' protested Devi-en, 'and there are expenses to be covered. The contribution is not much and is adjusted to the nature of the world. It may be an annual supply of wood from a forested world; manganese salts from another. The world of these Mauvs is poor in physical resources and they themselves offered to supply us with a number of individuals to use as personal assistants. They are extremely powerful even for large-primates and we treat them painlessly with anticerebral drugs—'

'To make zombies out of them!'

Devi-en guessed at the meaning of the noun and said indignantly, 'Not at all. Merely to make them content with their role as personal servant and forgetful of their homes. We would not want them to be unhappy. They are intelligent beings!'

'And what would you do with Earth if we had a war?'

'We have had fifteen years to decide that,' said Devi-en. 'Your world is very rich in iron and has developed a fine steel technology. Steel, I think, would be your contribution.' He sighed, 'But the contribution would not make up for our expense in this case, I think. We have overwaited now by ten years at least.'

The large-primate said, 'How many races do you tax in this way?'

'I do not know the exact number. Certainly more than a thousand.'

'Then you're the little landlords of the Galaxy, are you? A thousand worlds destroy themselves in order to contribute to your welfare. You're something else, too, you know.' The wild one's voice was rising, growing shrill. 'You're vultures.'

'Vultures?' said Devi-en, trying to place the word.

'Carrion-eaters. Birds that wait for some poor creature to die of thirst in the desert and then come down to eat the body.'

Devi-en felt himself turn faint and sick at the picture conjured up for him. He said weakly, 'No, no, we *help* the species.'

'You wait for the war to happen like vultures. If you want to help, *prevent* the war. Don't save the remnants. Save them all.'

Devi-en's tail twitched with sudden excitement. 'How do we *prevent* a war? Will you tell me that?' (What was prevention of war but the reverse of bringing about a war? Learn one process and surely the other would be obvious.)

But the wild one faltered. He said finally, 'Get down there. Explain the situation.'

Devi-en felt keen disappointment. That didn't help. Besides— He said, 'Land among you? Quite impossible.' His skin quivered in half a dozen places at the thought of mingling with the wild ones in their untamed billions.

Perhaps the sick look on Devi-en's face was so pronounced and unmistakable that the wild one could recognize it for what it was even across the barrier of species. He tried to fling himself at the Hurrian and had to be caught virtually in mid-air by one of the Mauvs, who held him immobile with an effortless constriction of biceps.

The wild one screamed. 'No. Just sit here and wait! Vulture! Vulture! *Vulture!*'

It was days before Devi-en could bring himself to see the wild one again. He was almost brought to disrespect of the Arch-administrator when the latter insisted that he lacked sufficient data for a complete analysis of the mental make-up of these wild ones.

Devi-en said boldly, 'Surely, there is enough to give some solution to our question.'

The Arch-administrator's nose quivered and his pink tongue passed over it meditatively. 'A solution of a kind, perhaps. I can't trust this solution. We are facing a very unusual species. We know that already. We can't afford to make mistakes. – One thing, at least. We have happened upon a highly intelligent one. Unless – unless he is at his race's norm.' The Arch-administrator seemed upset at that thought.

Devi-en said, 'The creature brought up the horrible picture of that – that bird – that—'

'Vulture,' said the Arch-administrator.

'It put our entire mission into such a distorted light. I have not been able to eat properly since, or sleep. In fact, I am afraid I will have to ask to be relieved—'

'Not before we have completed what we have set out to do,' said the Arch-administrator firmly. 'Do you think I enjoy the picture of – of carrion eat— You *must* collect more data.'

Devi-en nodded finally. He understood, of course. The Arch-administrator was no more anxious to cause a nuclear war than any Hurrian would be. He was putting off the moment of decision as long as possible.

Devi-en settled himself for one more interview with the wild one. It turned out to be a completely unbearable one, and the last.

The wild one had a bruise across his cheek as though he had been resisting the Mauvs again. In fact, it was certain he had. He had done so numerous times before, and the Mauvs, despite their most earnest attempts to do no harm, could not help but bruise him on occasion. One would expect the wild one to see how intensely they tried not to hurt him and to quiet his behavior as a result. Instead, it was as though the conviction of safety spurred him on to additional resistance.

(These large-primate species were vicious, vicious, thought Devi-en sadly.)

For over an hour, the interview hovered over useless small talk and then the wild one said with sudden belligerence, 'How long did you say you things have been here?'

'Fifteen of your years,' said Devi-en.

'That figures. The first flying saucers were sighted just after World War II. How much longer before the nuclear war?'

With automatic truth, Devi-en said, 'We wish we knew,' and stopped suddenly.

The wild one said, 'I thought nuclear war was inevitable. Last time you said you overstayed ten years. You expected the war ten years ago, didn't you?'

Devi-en said, 'I can't discuss this subject.'

'No?' The wild one was screaming. 'What are you going to do about it? How long will you wait? Why not nudge it a little? Don't just wait, vulture. Start one.'

Devi-en jumped to his feet. 'What are you saying?'

'Why else are you waiting, you dirty—' He choked on a completely incomprehensible expletive, then continued, breathlessly, 'Isn't that what vultures do when some poor miserable animal, or man, maybe, is taking too long to die? They can't wait. They come swirling down and peck out his eyes. They wait till he's helpless and just hurry him along the last step.'

Devi-en ordered him away quickly and retired to his sleeping room, where he was sick for hours. Nor did he sleep then or that night. The word 'vulture' screamed in his ears and that final picture danced before his eyes.

Devi-en said firmly, 'Your Height, I can speak with the wild one no more. If you need still more data, I cannot help you.'

The Arch-administrator looked haggard. 'I know. This vulture business— Very difficult to take. Yet you notice the thought didn't affect him. Large-primates are immune to such things, hardened, calloused. It is part of their way of thinking. Horrible.'

'I can get you no more data.'

'It's all right. I understand. – Besides, each additional item only strengthens the preliminary answer; the answer I thought was only provisional; that I hoped earnestly was only provisional.' He buried his head in his grizzled arms. 'We have a way to start their nuclear war for them.'

'Oh? What need be done?'

'It is something very direct, very simple. It is something I could never have thought of. Nor you.'

'What is it, your Height?' He felt an anticipatory dread.

'What keeps them at peace now is that neither of two nearly equal sides dares take the responsibility of starting a war. If one side did, however, the other – well, let's be blunt about it – would retaliate in full.'

Devi-en nodded.

The Arch-administrator went on. 'If a single nuclear bomb fell on the territory of either of the two sides, the victims would at once assume the other side had launched it. They would feel they could not wait for further attacks. Retaliation in full would follow within hours; the other side would retaliate in its turn. Within weeks it would be over.'

'But how do we make one of them drop that first bomb?'

'We don't, Captain. That is the point. We drop the first bomb ourselves.'

'What?' Devi-en swayed.

'That is it. Compute a large-primate's mind and that answer thrusts itself at you.'

'But how can we?'

'We assemble a bomb. That is easy enough. We send it down by ship and drop it over some inhabited locality—'

'*Inhabited?*'

The Arch-administrator looked away and said uneasily, 'The effect is lost otherwise.'

'I see,' said Devi-en. He was picturing vultures; he couldn't help it. He visualized them as large, scaled birds (like the small harmless flying creatures on Hurria, but immensely large), with rubber-skinned wings and long razor-bills, circling down, pecking at dying eyes.

His hands covered his eyes. He said shakily, 'Who will pilot the ship? Who will launch the bomb?'

The Arch-administrator's voice was no stronger than Devi-en's. 'I don't know.'

'I won't,' said Devi-en. 'I can't. There is no Hurrian who can, at any price.'

The Arch-administrator rocked back and forth miserably. 'Perhaps the Mauvs could be given orders—'

'Who could give them such orders?'

The Arch-administrator sighed heavily. 'I will call the Council. They may have all the data. Perhaps they will suggest something.'

So after a little over fifteen years, the Hurrians were dismantling their base on the other side of the Moon.

Nothing had been accomplished. The large-primates of the planet had not had their nuclear war; they might never have.

And despite all the future horror that might bring, Devi-en was in an agony of happiness. There was no point in thinking of the future. For the present, he was getting away from this most horrible of horrible worlds.

He watched the Moon fall away and shrink to a spot of light, along with the planet, and the Sun of the system itself, till the whole thing was lost among the constellations.

It was only then that he could feel anything but relief. It was only then that he felt a first tiny twinge of it-might-have-been.

He said to the Arch-administrator, 'It might all have been well if we had been more patient. They might yet have blundered into nuclear war.'

The Arch-administrator said, 'Somehow I doubt it. The mentalic analysis of—'

He stopped and Devi-en understood. The wild one had been replaced on his planet with minimal harm. The events of the past weeks had been blanked out of his mind. He had been placed near a small, inhabited locality not far from the spot where he had been first found. His fellows would assume he had been lost. They would blame his loss of weight, his bruises, his amnesia upon the hardships he had undergone.

But the harm done *by* him—

If only they had not brought him up to the Moon in the first place. They might have reconciled themselves to the thought of starting a war. They might somehow have thought of dropping a bomb; and worked out some indirect, long-distance system for doing so.

It had been the wild one's word-picture of the vulture that had stopped it all. It had ruined Devi-en and the Arch-administrator. When all data was sent back to Hurria, the effect on the Council itself had been notable. The order to dismantle the Base had come quickly.

Devi-en said, 'I will never take part in colonization again.'

The Arch-administrator said mournfully, 'None of us may ever have to. The wild ones of that planet will emerge and with large-primates and large-primate thinking loose in the Galaxy, it will mean the end of – of—'

Devi-en's nose twitched. The end of everything; of all the good Hurria had done in the Galaxy; all the good it might have continued to do in the future.

He said, 'We ought to have dropped—' and did not finish.

What was the use of saying that? They couldn't have dropped the bomb for all the Galaxy. If they could have, they would have been large-primate themselves in their manner of thinking, and there are worse things than merely the end of everything.

Devi-en thought of the vultures.

All the Troubles of the World

The greatest industry on Earth centered about Multivac – Multivac, the giant computer that had grown in fifty years until its various ramifications had filled Washington, DC, to the suburbs and had reached out tendrils into every city and town on Earth.

An army of civil servants fed it data constantly and another army correlated and interpreted the answers it gave. A corps of engineers patrolled its interior while mines and factories consumed themselves in keeping its reserve stocks of replacement parts ever complete, ever accurate, ever satisfactory in every way.

Multivac directed Earth's economy and helped Earth's science. Most important of all, it was the central clearing house of all known facts about each individual Earth-man.

And each day it was part of Multivac's duties to take the four billion sets of facts about individual human beings that filled its vitals and extrapolate them for an additional day of time. Every Corrections Department on Earth received the data appropriate to its own area of jurisdiction, and the over-all data was presented in one large piece to the Central Board of Corrections in Washington, DC.

Bernard Gulliman was in the fourth week of his year term as

Chairman of the Central Board of Corrections and had grown casual enough to accept the morning report without being frightened by it. As usual, it was a sheaf of papers some six inches thick. He knew by now, he was not expected to read it. (No human could.) Still, it was amusing to glance through it.

There was the usual list of predictable crimes: frauds of all sorts, larcenies, riots, manslaughters, arsons.

He looked for one particular heading and felt a slight shock at finding it there at all, then another one at seeing two entries. Not one, but two. *Two* first-degree murders. He had not seen two in one day in all his term as Chairman so far.

He punched the knob of the two-way intercom and waited for the smooth face of his co-ordinator to appear on the screen.

'Ali,' said Gulliman. 'There are two first-degrees this day. Is there any unusual problem?'

'No, sir,' The dark-complexioned face with its sharp, black eyes seemed restless. 'Both cases are quite low probability.'

'I know that,' said Gulliman. 'I observed that neither probability is higher than 15 per cent. Just the same, Multivac has a reputation to maintain. It has virtually wiped out crime, and the public judges that by its record on first-degree murder which is, of course, the most spectacular crime.'

Ali Othman nodded, 'Yes, sir. I quite realize that.'

'You also realize, I hope,' Gulliman said, 'that I don't want a single consummated case of it during my term. If any other crime slips through, I may allow excuses. If a first-degree murder slips through, I'll have your hide. Understand?'

'Yes, sir. The complete analyses of the two potential murders are already at the district offices involved. The potential criminals and victims are under observation. I have rechecked the probabilities of consummation and they are already dropping.'

'Very good,' said Gulliman, and broke connection.

He went back to the list with an uneasy feeling that perhaps he had been overpompous. – But then, one had to be firm with these permanent civil-service personnel and make sure they didn't imagine they were running everything, including the Chairman. Particularly this Othman, who had been working with Multivac since both were considerably younger, and had a proprietary air that could be infuriating.

To Gulliman, this matter of crime was the political chance of a lifetime. So far, no Chairman had passed through his term without a murder taking place somewhere on Earth, some time. The previous Chairman had ended with a record of eight, three more (*more*, in fact) than under his predecessor.

Now Gulliman intended to have *none*. He was going to be, he had decided, the first Chairman without any murder at all anywhere on Earth during his term. After that, and the favorable publicity that would result—

He barely skimmed the rest of the report. He estimated that there were at least two thousand cases of prospective wife-beatings listed. Undoubtedly, not all would be stopped in time. Perhaps thirty per cent would be consummated. But the incidence was dropping and consummations were dropping even more quickly.

Multivac had added wife-beating to its list of predictable crimes only some five years earlier and the average man was not yet accustomed to the thought that if he planned to wallop his wife, it would be known in advance. As the conviction percolated through society, women would first suffer fewer bruises and then, eventually, none.

Some husband-beatings were on the list, too, Gulliman noticed.

Ali Othman closed connections and stared at the screen from which Gulliman's jowled and balding head had departed. Then he looked across at his assistant, Rafe Leemy, and said, 'What do we do?'

'Don't ask me. *He's* worried about just a lousy murder or two.'

'It's an awful chance trying to handle this thing on our own. Still if we tell him, he'll have a first-class fit. These elective politicians have their skins to think of, so he's bound to get in our way and make things worse.'

Leemy nodded his head and put a thick lower lip between his teeth. 'Trouble is, though, what if we miss out? It would just about be the end of the world, you know.'

'If we miss out, who cares what happens to us? We'll just be part of the general catastrophe.' Then he said in a more lively manner, 'But hell, the probability is only 12.3 per cent. On anything else, except maybe murder, we'd let the probabilities rise a bit before taking any action at all. There could still be spontaneous correction.'

'I wouldn't count on it,' said Leemy dryly.

'I don't intend to. I was just pointing the fact out. Still, at this probability, I suggest we confine ourselves to simple observation for the moment. No one could plan a crime like this alone; there must be accomplices.'

'Multivac didn't name any.'

'I know. Still—' His voice trailed off.

So they stared at the details of the one crime not included on the list handed out to Gulliman; the one crime much worse than first-degree murder; the one crime never before attempted in the history of Multivac; and wondered what to do.

Ben Manners considered himself the happiest sixteen-year-old in Baltimore. This was, perhaps, doubtful. But he was certainly one of the happiest, and one of the most excited.

At least, he was one of the handful admitted to the galleries of the stadium during the swearing in of the eighteen-year-olds. His older brother was going to be sworn in so his parents had applied for spectator's tickets and they had allowed Ben to do so, too. But when Multivac chose among all the applicants, it was Ben who got the ticket.

Two years later, Ben would be sworn in himself, but watching big brother Michael now was the next best thing.

His parents had dressed him (or supervised the dressing, at any rate) with all care, as representative of the family and sent him off with numerous messages for Michael, who had left days earlier for preliminary physical and neurological examinations.

The stadium was on the outskirts of town and Ben, just bursting with self-importance, was shown to his seat. Below him, now, were rows upon rows of hundreds upon hundreds of eighteen-year-olds (boys to the right, girls to the left), all from the second district of Baltimore. At various times in the year, similar meetings were going on all over the world, but this was Baltimore, this was the important one. Down there (somewhere) was Mike, Ben's own brother.

Ben scanned the tops of heads, thinking somehow he might recognize his brother. He didn't, of course, but then a man came out on the raised platform in front of all the crowd and Ben stopped looking to listen.

The man said, 'Good afternoon, swearers and guests. I am Randolph T. Hoch, in charge of the Baltimore ceremonies this year. The swearers have met me several times now during the progress of the physical and neurological portions of this examination. Most of the task is done, but the most important matter is left. The swearer himself, his personality, must go into Multivac's records.

'Each year, this requires some explanation to the young people reaching adulthood. Until now' (he turned to the young people before him and his eyes went no more to the gallery) 'you have not been adult; you have not been individuals in the eyes of Multivac, except where you were especially singled out as such by your parents or your government.

'Until now, when the time for the yearly up-dating of information came, it was your parents who filled in the necessary data on you. Now the time has come for you to take over that duty yourself. It is a great honor, a great responsibility. Your parents have told us what schooling you've had, what diseases, what habits; a great many things. But now you must tell us a great deal more; your innermost thoughts; your most secret deeds.

'This is hard to do the first time, embarrassing even, but it *must* be done. Once it is done, Multivac will have a complete analysis of all of you in its files. It will understand your actions and reactions. It will even be able to guess with fair accuracy at your future actions and reactions.

'In this way, Multivac will protect you. If you are in danger of accident, it will know. If someone plans harm to you, it will know. If *you* plan harm, it will know and you will be stopped in time so that it will not be necessary to punish you.

'With its knowledge of all of you, Multivac will be able to help Earth adjust its economy and its laws for the good of all. If you have a personal problem, you may come to Multivac with it and, with its knowledge of all of you, Multivac will be able to help you.

'Now you will have many forms to fill out. Think carefully and answer all questions as accurately as you can. Do not hold back through shame or caution. No one will ever know your answers except Multivac unless it becomes necessary to learn the answers in order to protect you. And then only authorized officials of the government will know.

'It may occur to you to stretch the truth a bit here or there. Don't do this. We will find out if you do. All your answers put together form a pattern. If some answers are false, they will not fit the pattern and Multivac will discover them. If all your answers are false, there will be a distorted pattern of a type that Multivac will recognize. So you must tell the truth.'

Eventually, it was all over, however; the form-filling; the ceremonies and speeches that followed. In the evening, Ben, standing tiptoe, finally spotted Michael, who was still carrying the robes he had worn in the 'parade of the adults.' They greeted one another with jubilation.

They shared a light supper and took the expressway home, alive and alight with the greatness of the day.

They were not prepared, then, for the sudden transition of the homecoming. It was a numbing shock to both of them to be stopped by a cold-faced young man in uniform outside their own front door; to have their papers inspected before they could enter their own house; to find their own parents sitting forlornly in the living room, the mark of tragedy on their faces.

Joseph Manners, looking much older than he had that morning, looked out of his puzzled, deep-sunken eyes at his sons (one with the robes of new adulthood still over his arm) and said, 'I seem to be under house arrest.'

Bernard Gulliman could not and did not read the entire report. He read only the summary and that was most gratifying, indeed.

A whole generation, it seemed, had grown up accustomed to the fact that Multivac could predict the commission of major crimes. They learned that Corrections agents would be on the scene before the crime could be committed. They found out that consummation of the crime led to inevitable punishment. Gradually, they were convinced that there was no way anyone could outsmart Multivac.

The result was, naturally, that even the intention of crime fell off. And as such intentions fell off and as Multivac's capacity was enlarged, minor crimes could be added to the list it would predict each morning, and these crimes, too, were now shrinking in incidence.

So Gulliman had ordered an analysis made (by Multivac naturally) of Multivac's capacity to turn its attention to the problem of predicting probabilities of disease incidence. Doctors might soon be alerted to individual patients who might grow diabetic in the course of the next year, or suffer an attack of tuberculosis or grow a cancer.

An ounce of prevention—

And the report was a favorable one!

After that, the roster of the day's possible crimes arrived and there was not a first-degree murder on the list.

Gulliman put in an intercom call to Ali Othman in high good humor. 'Othman, how do the numbers of crimes in the daily lists of the past week average compared with those in my first week as Chairman?'

It had gone down, it turned out, by 8 per cent and Gulliman was happy indeed. No fault of his own, of course, but the electorate would not know that. He blessed his luck that he had come in at the right time, at the very climax of Multivac, when disease, too, could be placed under its all-embracing and protecting knowledge.

Gulliman would prosper by this.

Othman shrugged his shoulders. 'Well, he's happy.'

'When do we break the bubble?' said Leemy. 'Putting Manners under observation just raised the probabilities and house arrest gave it another boost.'

'Don't I know it?' said Othman peevishly. 'What I don't know is why.'

'Accomplices, maybe, like you said. With Manners in trouble, the rest have to strike at once or be lost.'

'Just the other way around. With our hand on one, the rest would scatter for safety and disappear. Besides, why aren't the accomplices named by Multivac?'

'Well, then, do we tell Gulliman?'

'No, not yet. The probability is still only 17.3 per cent. Let's get a bit more drastic first.'

Elizabeth Manners said to her younger son, 'You go to your room, Ben.'

'But what's it all about, Mom?' asked Ben, voice breaking at this strange ending to what had been a glorious day.

'Please!'

He left reluctantly, passing through the door to the stairway, walking up it noisily and down again quietly.

And Mike Manners, the older son, the new-minted adult and the hope of the family, said in a voice and tone that mirrored his brother's, 'What's it all about?'

Joe Manners said, 'As Heaven is my witness, son, I don't know. I haven't done anything.'

'Well, sure you haven't done anything.' Mike looked at his small-boned mild-mannered father in wonder. 'They must be here because you're *thinking* of doing something.'

'I'm not.'

Mrs Manners broke in angrily, 'How can he be thinking of doing something worth all – all this.' She cast her arm about, in a gesture toward the enclosing shell of government men about the house. 'When I was a little girl, I remember the father of a friend of mine was working in a bank, and they once called him up and said to leave the money alone and he did. It was fifty thousand dollars. He hadn't really taken it. He was just thinking about taking it. They didn't keep those things as quiet in those days as they do now; the story got out. That's how I know about it.

'But I mean,' she went on, rubbing her plump hands slowly together, 'that was fifty thousand dollars; fifty – thousand – dollars. Yet all they did was call him; one phone call. What could your father be planning that would make it worth having a dozen men come down and close off the house?'

Joe Manners said, eyes filled with pain, 'I am planning no crime, not even the smallest. I swear it.'

Mike, filled with the conscious wisdom of a new adult, said, 'Maybe it's something subconscious, Pop. Some resentment against your supervisor.'

'So that I would want to kill him? No!'

'Won't they tell you what it is, Pop?'

His mother interrupted again, 'No, they won't. We've asked. I said they were ruining our standing in the community just being here. The least they could do is tell us what it's all about so we could fight it, so we could explain.'

'And they wouldn't?'

'They wouldn't.'

Mike stood with his legs spread apart and his hands deep in his pockets. He said, troubled, 'Gee, Mom, Multivac doesn't make mistakes.'

His father pounded his fist helplessly on the arm of the sofa. 'I tell you I'm not planning any crime.'

The door opened without a knock and a man in uniform walked in with sharp, self-possessed stride. His face had a glazed, official appearance. He said, 'Are you Joseph Manners?'

Joe Manners rose to his feet. 'Yes. Now what is it you want of me?'

'Joseph Manners, I place you under arrest by order of the government,' and curtly he showed his identification as a Corrections officer. 'I must ask you to come with me.'

'For what reason? What have I done?'

'I am not at liberty to discuss that.'

'But I can't be arrested just for planning a crime even if I were doing that. To be arrested I must actually have *done* something. You can't arrest me otherwise. It's against the law.'

The officer was impervious to the logic. 'You will have to come with me.'

Mrs Manners shrieked and fell on the couch, weeping hysterically. Joseph Manners could not bring himself to violate the code drilled into him all his life by actually resisting an officer, but he hung back at least, forcing the Corrections officer to use muscular power to drag him forward.

And Manners called out as he went, 'But tell me what it is. Just tell me. If I *knew*— Is it murder? Am I supposed to be planning murder?'

The door closed behind him and Mike Manners, white-faced and suddenly feeling not the least bit adult, stared first at the door, then at his weeping mother.

Ben Manners, behind the door and suddenly feeling quite adult, pressed his lips tightly together and thought he knew exactly what to do.

If Multivac took away, Multivac could also give. Ben had been at the ceremonies that very day. He had heard this man, Randolph Hoch, speak of Multivac and all that Multivac could do. It could direct the government and it could also unbend and help out some plain person who came to it for help.

Anyone could ask help of Multivac and anyone meant Ben. Neither his mother nor Mike were in any condition to stop him now, and he had some money left of the amount they had given him for his great outing that day. If afterward they found him gone and worried about it, that couldn't be helped. Right now, his first loyalty was to his father.

He ran out the back way and the officer at the door cast a glance at his papers and let him go.

Harold Quimby handled the complaints department of the Baltimore substation of Multivac. He considered himself to be a member of that branch of the civil service that was most important of all. In some ways, he may have been right, and those who heard him discuss the matter would have had to be made of iron not to feel impressed.

For one thing, Quimby would say, Multivac was essentially an invader of privacy. In the past fifty years, mankind had had to acknowledge that its thoughts and impulses were no longer secret, that it owned no inner recess where anything could be hidden. And mankind had to have something in return.

Of course, it got prosperity, peace, and safety, but that was abstract. Each man and woman needed something personal as his or her own reward for surrendering privacy, and each one got it. Within reach of every human being was a Multivac station with circuits into which he could freely enter his own problems and questions without control or hindrance, and from which, in a matter of minutes, he could receive answers.

At any given moment, five million individual circuits among the quadrillion or more within Multivac might be involved in this question-and-answer program. The answers might not always be certain, but they were the best available, and every questioner *knew* the answer to be the best available and had faith in it. That was what counted.

And now an anxious sixteen-year-old had moved slowly up the waiting line of men and women (each in that line illuminated by a different mixture of hope with fear or anxiety or even anguish – always with hope predominating as the person stepped nearer and nearer to Multivac).

Without looking up, Quimby took the filled-out form being handed him and said, 'Booth 5-B.'

Ben said, 'How do I ask the question, sir?'

Quimby looked up then, with a bit of surprise. Preadults did not generally make use of the service. He said kindly, 'Have you ever done this before, son?'

'No, sir.'

Quimby pointed to the model on his desk. 'You use this. You see how it works? Just like a typewriter. Don't you try to write or print anything by hand. Just use the machine. Now you take booth 5-B, and if you need help, just press the red button and someone will come. Down that aisle, son, on the right.'

He watched the youngster go down the aisle and out of view and smiled. No one was ever turned away from Multivac. Of course, there was always a certain percentage of trivia: people who asked personal questions about their neighbors or obscene questions about prominent personalities; college youths trying to outguess their professors or thinking it clever to stump Multivac by asking it Russell's class-of-all-classes paradox and so on.

Multivac could take care of all that. It needed no help.

Besides, each question and answer was filed and formed but another item in the fact assembly for each individual. Even the most trivial question and the most impertinent, insofar as it reflected the personality of the questioner, helped humanity by helping Multivac know about humanity.

Quimby turned his attention to the next person in line, a middle-aged woman, gaunt and angular, with the look of trouble in her eye.

Ali Othman strode the length of his office, his heels thumping desperately on the carpet. 'The probability still goes up. It's 22.4 per cent now. Damnation! We have Joseph Manners under actual arrest and it still goes up.' He was perspiring freely.

Leemy turned away from the telephone. 'No confession yet. He's under Psychic Probing and there is no sign of crime. He may be telling the truth.'

Othman said, 'Is Multivac crazy then?'

Another phone sprang to life. Othman closed connections quickly, glad of the interruption. A Corrections officer's face came to life in the screen. The officer said, 'Sir, are there any new directions as to Manners' family? Are they to be allowed to come and go as they have been?'

'What do you mean, as they have been?'

'The original instructions were for the house arrest of Joseph Manners. Nothing was said of the rest of the family, sir.'

'Well, extend it to the rest of the family until you are informed otherwise.'

'Sir, that is the point. The mother and older son are demanding information about the younger son. The younger son is gone and they claim he is in custody and wish to go to headquarters to inquire about it.'

Othman frowned and said in almost a whisper, 'Younger son? How young?'

'Sixteen, sir,' said the officer.

'Sixteen and he's gone. Don't you know where?'

'He was allowed to leave, sir. There were no orders to hold him.'

'Hold the line. Don't move.' Othman put the line into suspension, then clutched at his coal-black hair with both hands and shrieked, 'Fool! Fool! Fool!'

Leemy was startled. 'What the hell?'

'The man has a sixteen-year-old son,' choked out Othman. 'A sixteen-year-old is not an adult and he is not filed independently in Multivac, but only as part of his father's file.' He glared at Leemy. 'Doesn't everyone know that until eighteen a youngster does not file his own reports with Multivac but that his father does it for him? Don't I know it? Don't you?'

'You mean Multivac didn't mean Joe Manners?' said Leemy.

'Multivac meant his minor son, and the youngster is gone, now. With officers three deep around the house, he calmly walks out and goes on you know what errand.'

He whirled to the telephone circuit to which the Corrections officer still clung, the minute break having given Othman just time enough to collect himself and to assume a cool and self-possessed mien. (It would never have done to throw a fit before the eyes of the officer, however much good it did in purging his spleen.)

He said, 'Officer, locate the younger son who has disappeared. Take every man you have, if necessary. Take every man available in the district, if necessary. I shall give the appropriate orders. You must find that boy at all costs.'

'Yes, sir.'

Connection was broken. Othman said, 'Have another rundown on the probabilities, Leemy.'

Five minutes later, Leemy said, 'It's down to 19.6 per cent. It's *down*.'

Othman drew a long breath. 'We're on the right track at last.'

Ben Manners sat in Booth 5-B and punched out slowly, 'My name is Benjamin Manners, number MB-71833412. My father, Joseph Manners, has been arrested but we don't know what crime he is planning. Is there any way we can help him?'

He sat and waited. He might be only sixteen but he was old enough to know that somewhere those words were being whirled into the most complex structure ever conceived by man; that a trillion facts would blend and coordinate into a whole, and that from that whole, Multivac would abstract the best help.

The machine clicked and a card emerged. It had an answer on it, a long answer. It began, 'Take the expressway to Washington, DC at once. Get off at the Connecticut Avenue stop. You will find a special exit, labeled "Multivac" with a guard. Inform the guard you are special courier for Dr Trumbull and he will let you enter.

'You will be in a corridor. Proceed along it till you reach a small door labeled "Interior". Enter and say to the men inside, "Message for Dr Trumbull." You will be allowed to pass. Proceed on—'

It went on in this fashion. Ben could not see the application to his question, but he had complete faith in Multivac. He left at a run, heading for the expressway to Washington.

The Corrections officers traced Ben Manners to the Baltimore station an hour after he had left. A shocked Harold Quimby found himself flabbergasted at the number and importance of the men who had focused on him in the search for a sixteen-year-old.

'Yes, a boy,' he said, 'but I don't know where he went to after he was through here. I had no way of knowing that anyone was looking for him. We accept all comers here. Yes, I can get the record of the question and answer.'

They looked at the record and televised it to Central Headquarters at once.

Othman read it through, turned up his eyes, and collapsed. They brought him to almost at once. He said to Leemy weakly, 'Have them catch that boy. And have a copy of Multivac's answer made out for me. There's no way any more, no way out. I must see Gulliman now.'

Bernard Gulliman had never seen Ali Othman as much as perturbed before, and watching the co-ordinator's wild eyes now sent a trickle of ice water down his spine.

He stammered, 'What do you mean, Othman? What do you mean worse than murder?'

'Much worse than just murder.'

Gulliman was quite pale. 'Do you mean assassination of a high government official?' (It did cross his mind that he himself—).

Othman nodded. 'Not just *a* government official. *The* government official.'

'The *Secretary-General?*' Gulliman said in an appalled whisper.

'More than that, even. Much more. We deal with a plan to assassinate Multivac!'

'WHAT!'

'For the first time in the history of Multivac, the computer came up with the report that it itself was in danger.'

'Why was I not at once informed?'

Othman half-truthed out of it. 'The matter was so unprecedented, sir, that we explored the situation first before daring to put it on official record.'

'But Multivac has been saved, of course? It's been saved?'

'The probabilities of harm have declined to under 4 per cent. I am waiting for the report now.'

'Message for Dr Trumbull,' said Ben Manners to the man on the high stool, working carefully on what looked like the controls of a stratojet cruiser, enormously magnified.

'Sure, Jim,' said the man. 'Go ahead.'

Ben looked at his instructions and hurried on. Eventually, he would find a tiny control lever which he was to shift to a DOWN position at a moment when a certain indicator spot would light up red.

He heard an agitated voice behind him, then another, and suddenly, two men had him by his elbows. His feet were lifted off the floor.

One man said, 'Come with us, boy.'

Ali Othman's face did not noticeably lighten at the news, even though Gulliman said with great relief, 'If we have the boy, then Multivac is safe.'

'For the moment.'

Gulliman put a trembling hand to his forehead. 'What a half hour I've had. Can you imagine what the destruction of Multivac for even a short time would mean. The government would have collapsed; the economy broken down. It would have meant devastation worse—' His head snapped up, 'What do you mean *for the moment*?'

'The boy, this Ben Manners, had no intention of doing harm. He and his family must be released and compensation for false imprisonment given them. He was only following Multivac's instructions in order to help his father and it's done that. His father is free now.'

'Do you mean Multivac ordered the boy to pull a lever under circumstances that would burn out enough circuits to require a month's repair work? You mean Multivac would suggest its own destruction for the comfort of one man?'

'It's worse than that, sir. Multivac not only gave those instructions but selected the Manners family in the first place because Ben Manners looked exactly like one of Dr Trumbull's pages so that he could get into Multivac without being stopped.'

'What do you mean the family was selected?'

'Well, the boy would have never gone to ask the question if his father had not been arrested. His father would never have been arrested if Multivac had not blamed him for planning the destruction of Multivac. Multivac's own action started the chain of events that almost led to Multivac's destruction.'

'But there's no sense to that,' Gulliman said in a pleading voice. He felt small and helpless and he was virtually on his knees, begging this Othman, this man who had spent nearly a lifetime with Multivac, to reassure him.

Othman did not do so. He said, 'This is Multivac's first attempt along this line as far as I know. In some ways, it planned well. It chose the right family. It carefully did not distinguish between father and son to send us off the track. It was still an amateur at the game, though. It could not overcome its own instructions that led it to report the probability of its own destruction as increasing with every step we took down the wrong road. It could not avoid recording the answer it gave the youngster. With further practice, it will probably learn deceit. It will learn to hide certain facts, fail to record certain others. From now on, every instruction it gives may have the seeds in it of its own destruction. We will never know. And however careful we are, eventually Multivac will succeed. I think, Mr Gulliman, you will be the last Chairman of this organization.'

Gulliman pounded his desk in fury. 'But why, why, why? Damn you, why? What is wrong with it? Can't it be fixed?'

'I don't think so,' said Othman, in soft despair. 'I've never thought about this before. I've never had the occasion to until this happened, but now that I think of it, it seems to me we have reached the end of the road because Multivac is too good. Multivac has grown so complicated, its reactions are no longer those of a machine, but those of a living thing.'

'You're mad, but even so?'

'For fifty years and more we have been loading humanity's troubles on Multivac, on this living thing. We've asked it to care for us, all together and each individually. We've asked it to take all our secrets into itself; we've asked it to absorb our evil and guard us against it. Each of us brings his troubles to it, adding his bit to the burden. Now we are planning to load the burden of human disease on Multivac, too.'

Othman paused a moment, then burst out, 'Mr Gulliman, Multivac bears all the troubles of the world on its shoulders and it is tired.'

'Madness. Midsummer madness,' muttered Gulliman.

'Then let me show you something. Let me put it to the test. May I have permission to use the Multivac circuit line here in your office?'

'Why?'

'To ask it a question no one has ever asked Multivac before?'

'Will you do it harm?' asked Gulliman in quick alarm.

'No. But it will tell us what we want to know.'

The Chairman hesitated a trifle. Then he said, 'Go ahead.'

Othman used the instrument on Gulliman's desk. His fingers punched out the question with deft strokes: 'Multivac, what do you yourself want more than anything else?'

The moment between question and answer lengthened unbearably, but neither Othman nor Gulliman breathed.

And there was a clicking and a card popped out. It was a small card. On it, in precise letters, was the answer:

'I want to die.'

Spell My Name with an S

Marshall Zebatinsky felt foolish. He felt as though there were eyes staring through the grimy store-front glass and across the scarred wooden partition; eyes watching him. He felt no confidence in the old clothes he had resurrected or the turned-down brim of a hat he never otherwise wore or the glasses he had left in their case.

He felt foolish and it made the lines in his forehead deeper and his young-old face a little paler.

He would never be able to explain to anyone why a nuclear physicist such as himself should visit a numerologist. (Never, he thought. Never.) Hell, he could not explain it to himself except that he had let his wife talk him into it.

The numerologist sat behind an old desk that must have been second-hand when bought. No desk could get that old with only one owner. The same might almost be said of his clothes. He was little and dark and peered at Zebatinsky with little dark eyes that were brightly alive.

He said, 'I have never had a physicist for a client before, Dr Zebatinsky.'

Zebatinsky flushed at once. 'You understand this is confidential.'

The numerologist smiled so that wrinkles creased about the corners of his mouth and the skin around his chin stretched. 'All my dealings are confidential.'

Zebatinsky said, 'I think I ought to tell you one thing. I don't believe in numerology and I don't expect to begin believing in it. If that makes a difference, say so now.'

'But why are you here, then?'

'My wife thinks you may have something, whatever it is. I promised her and I am here.' He shrugged and the feeling of folly grew more acute.

'And what is it you are looking for? Money? Security? Long life? What?'

Zebatinsky sat for a long moment while the numerologist watched him quietly and made no move to hurry his client.

Zebatinsky thought: What do I say anyway? That I'm thirty-four and without a future?

He said, 'I want success. I want recognition.'

'A better job?'

'A *different* job. A different *kind* of job. Right now, I'm part of a team, working under orders. Teams! That's all government research is. You're a violinist lost in a symphony orchestra.'

'And you want to solo.'

'I want to get out of a team and into – into *me*.' Zebatinsky felt carried away, almost lightheaded, just putting this into words to someone other than his wife. He said, 'Twenty-five years ago, with my kind of training and my kind of ability, I would have gotten to work on the first nuclear power plants. Today I'd be running one of them or I'd be head of a pure research group at a university. But with my start these days where will I be twenty-five years from now? Nowhere. Still on the team. Still carrying my 2 per cent of the ball. I'm drowning in an anonymous crowd of nuclear physicists, and what I want is room on dry land, if you see what I mean.'

The numerologist nodded slowly. 'You realize, Dr Zebatinsky, that I don't guarantee success.'

Zebatinsky, for all his lack of faith, felt a sharp bite of disappointment. 'You don't? Then what the devil *do* you guarantee?'

'An improvement in the probabilities. My work is statistical in nature. Since you deal with atoms, I think you understand the laws of statistics.'

'Do you?' asked the physicist sourly.

'I do, as a matter of fact. I am a mathematician and I work mathematically. I don't tell you this in order to raise my fee. That is standard. Fifty dollars. But since you are a scientist, you can appreciate the nature of my work better than my other clients. It is even a pleasure to be able to explain to you.'

Zebatinsky said, 'I'd rather you wouldn't, if you don't mind. It's no use telling me about the numerical values of letters, their mystic significance and that kind of thing. I don't consider that mathematics. Let's get to the point—'

The numerologist said, 'Then you want me to help you provided I don't embarrass you by telling you the silly nonscientific basis of the way in which I helped you. Is that it?'

'All right. That's it.'

'But you still work on the assumption that I am a numerologist, and I am not. I call myself that so that the police won't bother me and' (the little man chuckled dryly) 'so that the psychiatrists won't either. I am a mathematician; an honest one.'

Zebatinsky smiled.

The numerologist said, 'I build computers. I study probable futures.'

'What?'

'Does that sound worse than numerology to you? Why? Given enough data and a computer capable of sufficient number of operations in unit time, the future is predictable, at least in terms of probabilities. When you compute the motions of a missile in order to aim an anti-missile, isn't it the future you're predicting? The missile and anti-missile would not collide if the future were predicted incorrectly. I do the same thing. Since I work with a greater number of variables, my results are less accurate.'

'You mean you'll predict *my* future?'

'Very approximately. Once I have done that, I will modify the data by changing your name and no other fact about you. I throw that modified datum into the operation-program. Then I try other modified names. I study each modified future and find one that contains a greater degree of recognition for you than the future that now lies ahead of you. Or no, let me put it another way. I will find you a future in which the probability of adequate recognition is higher than the probability of that in your present future.'

'Why change my name?'

'That is the only change I ever make, for several reasons. Number one, it is a simple change. After all, if I make a great change or many changes, so many new variables enter that I can no longer interpret the result. My machine is still crude. Number two, it is a reasonable change. I can't change your height, can I, or the color of your eyes, or even your temperament. Number three, it is a significant change. Names mean a lot to people. Finally, number four, it is a common change that is done every day by various people.'

Zebatinsky said, 'What if you don't find a better future?'

'That is the risk you will have to take. You will be no worse off than now, my friend.'

Zebatinsky stared at the little man uneasily, 'I don't believe any of this. I'd sooner believe numerology.'

The numerologist sighed. 'I thought a person like yourself would feel more comfortable with the truth. I *want* to help you and there is much yet for you to do. If you believed me a numerologist, you would not follow through. I thought if I told you the truth you would let me help you.'

Zebatinsky said, 'If you can see the future—'

'Why am I not the richest man on earth? Is that it? But I am rich – in all I want. You want recognition and I want to be left alone. I do my work. No one bothers me. That makes me a billionaire. I need a little real money and this I get from people such as yourself. Helping people is nice and perhaps a psychiatrist would say it gives me a feeling of power and feeds my ego. Now – do you want me to help you?'

'How much did you say?'

'Fifty dollars. I will need a great deal of biographical information from you but I have prepared a form to guide you. It's a little long, I'm afraid. Still, if you can get it in the mail by the end of the week, I will have an answer for you by the—' (he put out his lower lip and frowned in mental calculation) 'the twentieth of next month.'

'Five weeks? So long?'

'I have other work, my friend, and other clients. If I were a fake, I could do it much more quickly. It is agreed then?'

Zebatinsky rose. 'Well, agreed. – This is all confidential, now.'

'Perfectly. You will have all your information back when I tell you what change to make and you have my word that I will never make any further use of any of it.'

The nuclear physicist stopped at the door. 'Aren't you afraid I might tell someone you're not a numerologist?'

The numerologist shook his head. 'Who would believe you, my friend? Even supposing you were willing to admit to anyone that you've been here.'

On the twentieth, Marshall Zebatinsky was at the paint-peeling door, glancing sideways at the shop front with the little card up against the glass reading 'Numerology,' dimmed and scarcely legible through the dust. He peered in, almost hoping that someone else would be there already so that he might have an excuse to tear up the wavering intention in his mind and go home.

He had tried wiping the thing out of his mind several times. He could never stick at filling out the necessary data for long. It was embarrassing to work at it. He felt incredibly silly filling out the names of his friends, the cost of his house, whether his wife had had any miscarriages, if so, when. He abandoned it.

But he couldn't stick at stopping altogether either. He returned to it each evening.

It was the thought of the computer that did it, perhaps; the thought of the infernal gall of the little man pretending he had a computer. The temptation to call the bluff, see what would happen, proved irresistible after all.

He finally sent off the completed data by ordinary mail, putting on nine cents' worth of stamps without weighing the letter. If it comes back, he thought, I'll call it off.

It didn't come back.

He looked into the shop now and it was empty. Zebatinsky had no choice but to enter. A bell tinkled.

The old numerologist emerged from a curtained door.

'Yes? – Ah, Dr Zebatinsky.'

'You remember me?' Zebatinsky tried to smile.

'Oh, yes.'

'What's the verdict?'

The numerologist moved one gnarled hand over the other. 'Before that, sir, there's a little—'

'A little matter of the fee?'

'I have already done the work, sir. I have earned the money.'

Zebatinsky raised no objection. He was prepared to pay. If he had come this far, it would be silly to turn back just because of the money.

He counted out five ten-dollar bills and shoved them across the counter. 'Well?'

The numerologist counted the bills again slowly, then pushed them into a cash drawer in his desk.

He said, 'Your case was very interesting. I would advise you to change your name to Sebatinsky.'

'Seba— How do you spell that?'

'S-e-b-a-t-i-n-s-k-y.'

Zebatinsky stared indignantly. 'You mean change the initial? Change the Z to an S? That's all?'

'It's enough. As long as the change is adequate, a small change is safer than a big one.'

'But how could the change affect anything?'

'How could any name?' asked the numerologist softly. 'I can't say. It may, somehow, and that's all I can say. Remember, I don't guarantee results. Of course, if you do not wish to make the change, leave things as they are. But in that case I cannot refund the fee.'

Zebatinsky said, 'What do I do? Just tell everyone to spell my name with an *S*?'

'If you want my advice, consult a lawyer. Change your name legally. He can advise you on little things.'

'How long will it all take? I mean for things to improve for me?'

'How can I tell? Maybe never. Maybe tomorrow.'

'But you saw the future. You *claim* you see it.'

'Not as in a crystal ball. No, no, Dr Zebatinsky. All I get out of my computer is a set of coded figures. I can recite probabilities to you, but I saw no pictures.'

Zebatinsky turned and walked rapidly out of the place. Fifty dollars to change a letter! Fifty dollars for Sebatinsky! Lord, what a name! Worse than Zebatinsky.

It took another month before he could make up his mind to see a lawyer, and then he finally went.

He told himself he could always change the name back.

Give it a chance, he told himself.

Hell, there was no law against it.

Henry Brand looked through the folder page by page, with the practiced eye of one who had been in Security for fourteen years. He didn't have to read every word. Anything peculiar would have leaped off the paper and punched him in the eye.

He said, 'The man looks clean to me.' Henry Brand looked clean, too; with a soft, rounded paunch and a pink and freshly scrubbed complexion. It was as though continuous contact with all sorts of human failings, from possible ignorance to possible treason, had compelled him into frequent washings.

Lieutenant Albert Quincy, who had brought him the folder, was young and filled with the responsibility of being Security officer at the Hanford Station. 'But why Sebatinsky?' he demanded.

'Why not?'

'Because it doesn't make sense. Zebatinsky is a foreign name and I'd change it myself if I had it, but I'd change it to something Anglo-Saxon. If Zebatinsky had done that, it would make sense and I wouldn't give it a second thought. But why change a Z to an S? I think we must find out what his reasons were.'

'Has anyone asked him directly?'

'Certainly. In ordinary conversation, of course. I was careful to arrange that. He won't say anything more than that he's tired of being last in the alphabet.'

'That could be, couldn't it, Lieutenant?'

'It could, but why not change his name to Sands or Smith, if he wants an S? Or if he's that tired of Z, why not go the whole way and change it to an A? Why not a name like – uh – Aarons?'

'Not Anglo-Saxon enough,' muttered Brand. Then, 'But there's nothing to pin against the man. No matter how queer a name change may be, that alone can't be used against anyone.'

Lieutenant Quincy looked markedly unhappy.

Brand said, 'Tell me, Lieutenant, there must be something specific that bothers you. Something in your mind; some theory; some gimmick. What is it?'

The lieutenant frowned. His light eyebrows drew together and his lips tightened. 'Well, damn it, sir, the man's a Russian.'

Brand said, 'He's not that. He's a third-generation American.'

'I mean his name's Russian.'

Brand's face lost some of its deceptive softness. 'No, Lieutenant, wrong again. Polish.'

The lieutenant pushed his hands out impatiently, palms up. 'Same thing.'

Brand, whose mother's maiden name had been Wiszewski,

snapped, 'Don't tell that to a Pole, Lieutenant.' – Then, more thoughtfully, 'Or to a Russian either, I suppose.'

'What I'm trying to say, sir,' said the lieutenant, reddening, 'is that the Poles and Russians are both on the other side of the Curtain.'

'We all know that.'

'And Zebatinsky or Sebatinsky, whatever you want to call him, may have relatives there.'

'He's third generation. He might have second cousins there, I suppose. So what?'

'Nothing in itself. Lots of people may have distant relatives there. But Zebatinsky changed his name.'

'Go on.'

'Maybe he's trying to distract attention. Maybe a second cousin over there is getting too famous and our Zebatinsky is afraid that the relationship may spoil his own chances of advancement.'

'Changing his name won't do any good. He'd still be a second cousin.'

'Sure, but he wouldn't feel as though he were shoving the relationship in our face.'

'Have *you* ever heard of any Zebatinsky on the other side?'

'No, sir.'

'Then he can't be too famous. How would our Zebatinsky know about him?'

'He might keep in touch with his own relatives. That would be suspicious under the circumstances, he being a nuclear physicist.'

Methodically, Brand went through the folder again. 'This is awfully thin, Lieutenant. It's thin enough to be completely invisible.'

'Can you offer any other explanation, sir, of why he ought to change his name in just this way?'

'No, I can't. I admit that.'

'Then I think, sir, we ought to investigate. We ought to look for any men named Zebatinsky on the other side and see if we can draw a connection.' The lieutenant's voice rose a trifle as a new thought occurred to him. 'He might be changing his name to withdraw attention from *them*; I mean to protect them.'

'He's doing just the opposite, I think.'

'He doesn't realize that, maybe, but protecting them could be his motive.'

Brand sighed. 'All right, we'll tackle the Zebatinsky angle. – But if nothing turns up, Lieutenant, we drop the matter. Leave the folder with me.'

When the information finally reached Brand, he had all but forgotten the lieutenant and his theories. His first thought on receiving data that included a list of seventeen biographies of seventeen Russian and Polish citizens, all named Zebatinsky, was: What the devil is this?

Then he remembered, swore mildly, and began reading.

It started on the American side. Marshall Zebatinsky (fingerprints) had been born in Buffalo, New York (date, hospital statistics). His father had been born in Buffalo as well, his mother in Oswego, New York. His paternal grandparents had both been born in Bialystok, Poland (date of entry into the United States, dates of citizenship, photographs).

The seventeen Russian and Polish citizens named Zebatinsky were all descendants of people who, some half-century earlier, had lived in or near Bialystok. Presumably, they could be relatives, but this was not explicitly stated in any particular case. (Vital statistics in East Europe during the aftermath of World War I were kept poorly, if at all.)

Brand passed through the individual life histories of the current Zebatinsky men and women (amazing how thoroughly intelligence did its work; probably the Russians' was as thorough). He stopped at one and his smooth forehead sprouted lines as his eyebrows shot upward. He put that one to one side and went on. Eventually, he stacked everything but that one and returned it to its envelope.

Staring at that one, he tapped a neatly kept fingernail on the desk.

With a certain reluctance, he went to call on Dr Paul Kristow of the Atomic Energy Commission.

Dr Kristow listened to the matter with a stony expression. He lifted a little finger occasionally to dab at his bulbous nose and remove a nonexistent speck. His hair was iron gray, thinning and cut short. He might as well have been bald.

He said, 'No, I never heard of any Russian Zebatinsky. But then, I never heard of the American one either.'

'Well,' Brand scratched at his hairline over one temple and said slowly, 'I don't think there's anything to this, but I don't like to drop it too soon. I have a young lieutenant on my tail and you know what they can be like. I don't want to do anything that will drive him to a Congressional committee. Besides, the fact is that one of the Russian Zebatinsky fellows, Mikhail Andreyevich Zebatinsky, *is* a nuclear physicist. Are you sure you never heard of him?'

'Mikhail Andreyevich Zebatinsky? No— No, I never did. Not that that proves anything.'

'I could say it was coincidence, but you know that would be piling it a trifle high. One Zebatinsky here and one Zebatinsky there, both nuclear physicists, and the one here suddenly changes his name to Sebatinsky, and goes around anxious about it, too. He won't allow misspelling. He says, emphatically, "Spell my name with an *S*." It all just fits well enough to make my spy-conscious lieutenant begin to look a little too good. – And another peculiar thing is that the Russian Zebatinsky dropped out of sight just about a year ago.'

Dr Kristow said stolidly, 'Executed!'

'He might have been. Ordinarily, I would even assume so, though the Russians are not more foolish than we are and don't kill any nuclear physicist they can avoid killing. The thing is there's another reason why a nuclear physicist, of all people, might suddenly disappear. I don't have to tell you.'

'Crash research; top secret. I take it that's what you mean. Do you believe that's it?'

'Put it together with everything else, add in the lieutenant's intuition, and I just begin to wonder.'

'Give me that biography.' Dr Kristow reached for the sheet of paper and read it over twice. He shook his head. Then he said, 'I'll check this in *Nuclear Abstracts*.'

Nuclear Abstracts lined one wall of Dr Kristow's study in neat little boxes, each filled with its squares of microfilm.

The AEC man used his projector on the indices while Brand watched with what patience he could muster.

Dr Kristow muttered, 'A Mikhail Zebatinsky authored or co-authored half a dozen papers in the Soviet journals in the last half-dozen years. We'll get out the abstracts and maybe we can make something out of it. I doubt it.'

A selector flipped out the appropriate squares. Dr Kristow lined them up, ran them through the projector, and by degrees an expression of odd intentness crossed his face. He said, 'That's odd.'

Brand said, 'What's odd?'

Dr Kristow sat back. 'I'd rather not say just yet. Can you get me a list of other nuclear physicists who have dropped out of sight in the Soviet Union in the last year?'

'You mean you see something?'

'Not really. Not if I were just looking at any one of these papers. It's just that looking at all of them and knowing that this man may be on a crash research program and, on top of that, having you putting suspicions in my head—' He shrugged. 'It's nothing.'

Brand said earnestly, 'I wish you'd say what's on your mind. We may as well be foolish about this together.'

'If you feel that way— It's just possible this man may have been inching toward gamma-ray reflection.'

'And the significance?'

'If a reflecting shield against gamma rays could be devised, individual shelters could be built to protect against fallout. It's fallout that's the real danger, you know. A hydrogen bomb might destroy a city but the fallout could slow-kill the population over a strip thousands of miles long and hundreds wide.'

Brand said quickly, 'Are we doing any work on this?'

'No.'

'And if they get it and we don't, they can destroy the United States *in toto* at the cost of, say, ten cities, after they have their shelter program completed.'

'That's far in the future. – And, what are we getting in a hurrah about? All this is built on one man changing one letter in his name.'

'All right, I'm insane,' said Brand. 'But I don't leave the matter at this point. Not at *this* point. I'll get you your list of disappearing nuclear physicists if I have to go to Moscow to get it.'

He got the list. They went through all the research papers authored by any of them. They called a full meeting of the Commission, then of the nuclear brains of the nation. Dr Kristow walked out of an all night session, finally, part of which the President himself had attended.

Brand met him. Both looked haggard and in need of sleep.

Brand said, 'Well?'

Kristow nodded. 'Most agree. Some are doubtful even yet, but most agree.'

'How about you? Are you sure?'

'I'm far from sure, but let me put it this way. It's easier to believe that the Soviets are working on a gamma-ray shield than to believe that all the data we've uncovered has no interconnection.'

'Has it been decided that we're to go on shield research, too?'

'Yes.' Kristow's hand went back over his short, bristly hair, making a dry, whispery sound. 'We're going to give it everything we've got. Knowing the papers written by the men who disappeared, we can get right on their heels. We may even beat them to it. – Of course, they'll find out we're working on it.'

'Let them,' said Brand. 'Let them. It will keep them from attacking. I don't see any percentage in selling ten of our cities just to get ten of theirs – if we're both protected and they're too dumb to know that.'

'But not too soon. We don't want them finding out too soon. What about the American Zebatinsky-Sebatinsky?'

Brand looked solemn and shook his head. 'There's nothing to connect him with any of this even yet. Hell, we've *looked*. I agree with you, of course. He's in a sensitive spot where he is now and we can't afford to keep him there even if he's in the clear.'

'We can't kick him out just like that, either, or the Russians will start wondering.'

'Do you have any suggestions?'

They were walking down the long corridor toward the distant elevator in the emptiness of four in the morning.

Dr Kristow said, 'I've looked into his work. He's a good man, better than most, and not happy in his job, either. He hasn't the temperament for teamwork.'

'So?'

'But he is the type for an academic job. If we can arrange to have a large university offer him a chair in physics, I think he would take it gladly. There would be enough nonsensitive areas to keep him occupied; we would be able to keep him in close view; *and* it would be a natural development. The Russians might not start scratching their heads. What do you think?'

Brand nodded. 'It's an idea. Even sounds good. I'll put it up to the chief.'

They stepped into the elevator and Brand allowed himself to wonder about it all. What an ending to what had started with one letter of a name.

Marshall Sebatinsky could hardly talk. He said to his wife, 'I swear I don't see how this happened. I wouldn't have thought they knew me from a meson detector. – Good Lord, Sophie, Associate Professor of Physics at Princeton. Think of it.'

Sophie said, 'Do you suppose it was your talk at the APS meetings?'

'I don't see how. It was a thoroughly uninspired paper once every-one in the division was done hacking at it.' He snapped his fingers. 'It must have been Princeton that was investigating me. That's it. You know all those forms I've been filling out in the last six months; those interviews they wouldn't explain. Honestly, I was beginning to think I was under suspicion as a subversive. – It was Princeton investigating me. They're thorough.'

'Maybe it was your name,' said Sophie. 'I mean the change.'

'Watch me now. My professional life will be my own finally. I'll make my mark. Once I have a chance to do my work without—' He stopped and turned to look at his wife. 'My name! You mean the S.'

'You didn't get the offer till after you changed your name, did you?'

'Not till long after. No, that part's just coincidence. I've told you before, Sophie, it was just a case of throwing out fifty dollars to please you. Lord, what a fool I've felt all these months insisting on that stupid S.'

Sophie was instantly on the defensive. 'I didn't make you do it, Marshall. I suggested it but I didn't nag you about it. Don't say I did. Besides, it did turn out well. I'm sure it was the name that did this.'

Sebatinsky smiled indulgentiy. 'Now that's superstition.'

'I don't care what you call it, but you're not changing your name back.'

'Well, no, I suppose not. I've had so much trouble getting them to spell my name with an S, that the thought of making everyone move back is more than I want to face. Maybe I ought to change my name to Jones, eh?' He laughed almost hysterically.

But Sophie didn't. 'You leave it alone.'

'Oh, all right, I'm just joking. – Tell you what. I'll step down to that old fellow's place one of these days and tell him everything worked out and slip him another tenner. Will that satisfy you?'

He was exuberant enough to do so the next week. He assumed no disguise this time. He wore his glasses and his ordinary suit and was minus a hat.

He was even humming as he approached the store front and stepped to one side to allow a weary, sour-faced woman to maneuver her twin baby carriage past.

He put his hand on the door handle and his thumb on the iron latch. The latch didn't give to his thumb's downward pressure. The door was locked.

The dusty, dim card with 'Numerologist' on it was gone, now that he looked. Another sign, printed and beginning to yellow and curl with the sunlight, said 'To let.'

Sebatinsky shrugged. That was that. He had tried to do the right thing.

Haround, happily divested of corporeal excrescence, capered happily and his energy vortices glowed a dim purple over cubic hypermiles. He said, 'Have I won? Have I won?'

Mestack was withdrawn, his vortices almost a sphere of light in hyperspace. 'I haven't calculated it yet.'

'Well, go ahead. You won't change the results any by taking a long time. – Wowf, it's a relief to get back into clean energy. It took me a microcycle of time as a corporeal body; a nearly used-up one, too. But it was wonh it to show *you*.'

Mestack said, 'All right, I admit you stopped a nuclear war on the planet.'

'Is that or is that not a Class A effect?'

'It is a Class A effect. Of course it is.'

'All right. Now check and see if I didn't get that Class A effect with a Class F stimulus. I changed one letter of one name.'

'What?'

'Oh, never mind. It's all there. I've worked it out for you.'

Mestack said reluctantly, 'I yield. A Class F stimulus.'

'Then I *win*. Admit it.'

'Neither one of us will win when the Watchman gets a look at this.'

Haround, who had been an elderly numerologist on Earth and

was still somewhat unsettled with relief at no longer being one, said, 'You weren't worried about that when you made the bet.'

'I didn't think you'd be fool enough to go through with it.'

'Heat-waste! Besides, why worry? The Watchman will never detect a Class F stimulus.'

'Maybe not, but he'll detect a Class A effect. Those corporeals will still be around after a dozen microcycles. The Watchman will notice that.'

'The trouble with you, Mestack, is that you don't want to pay off. You're stalling.'

'I'll pay. But just wait till the Watchman finds out we've been working on an unassigned problem and made an unallowed-for change. Of course, if we—' He paused.

Haround said, 'All right, we'll change it back. He'll never know.'

There was a crafty glow to Mestack's brightening energy pattern. 'You'll need another Class F stimulus if you expect him not to notice.'

Haround hesitated. 'I can do it.'

'I doubt it.'

'I could.'

'Would you be willing to bet on that, too?' Jubilation was creeping into Mestack's radiations.

'Sure,' said the goaded Haround. 'I'll put those corporeals right back where they were and the Watchman will never know the difference.'

Mestack followed through his advantage. 'Suspend the first bet, then. Triple the stakes on the second.'

The mounting eagerness of the gamble caught at Haround, too. 'All right, I'm game. Triple the stakes.'

'Done, then!'

'Done.'

The Last Question

The last question was asked for the first time, half in jest, on 21 May 2061, at a time when humanity first stepped into the light. The question came about as a result of a five-dollar bet over highballs, and it happened this way:

Alexander Adell and Bertram Lupov were two of the faithful attendants of Multivac. As well as any human beings could, they knew what lay behind the cold, clicking, flashing face – miles and miles of face – of that giant computer. They had at least a vague notion of the general plan of relays and circuits that had long since grown past the point where any single human could possibly have a firm grasp of the whole.

Multivac was self-adjusting and self-correcting. It had to be, for nothing human could adjust and correct it quickly enough or even adequately enough. So Adell and Lupov attended the monstrous giant only lightly and superficially, yet as well as any men could. They fed it data, adjusted questions to its needs and translated the answers that were issued. Certainly they, and all others like them, were fully entitled to share in the glory that was Multivac's.

For decades, Multivac had helped design the ships and plot the trajectories that enabled man to reach the Moon, Mars, and Venus, but past that, Earth's poor resources could not support the ships. Too much energy was needed for the long trips. Earth exploited its coal and uranium with increasing efficiency, but there was only so much of both.

But slowly Multivac learned enough to answer deeper questions more fundamentally, and on 14 May 2061, what had been theory, became fact.

The energy of the sun was stored, converted, and utilized directly on a planet-wide scale. All Earth turned off its burning coal, its fissioning uranium, and flipped the switch that connected all of it to a small station, one mile in diameter, circling the Earth at half the distance of the Moon. All Earth ran by invisible beams of sunpower.

Seven days had not sufficed to dim the glory of it and Adell and Lupov finally managed to escape from the public function, and to meet in quiet where no one would think of looking for them, in the deserted underground chambers, where portions of the mighty buried body of Multivac showed. Unattended, idling, sorting data with contented lazy clickings, Multivac, too, had earned its vacation and the boys appreciated that. They had no intention, originally, of disturbing it.

They had brought a bottle with them, and their only concern at the moment was to relax in the company of each other and the bottle.

'It's amazing when you think of it,' said Adell. His broad face had lines of weariness in it, and he stirred his drink slowly with a glass rod, watching the cubes of ice slur clumsily about. 'All the energy we can possibly ever use for free. Enough energy, if we wanted to draw on it, to melt all Earth into a big drop of impure liquid iron, and still never miss the energy so used. All the energy we could ever use, forever and forever and forever.'

Lupov cocked his head sideways. He had a trick of doing that when he wanted to be contrary, and he wanted to be contrary now, partly because he had had to carry the ice and glassware. 'Not forever,' he said.

'Oh, hell, just about forever. Till the sun runs down, Bert.'

'That's not forever.'

'All right, then. Billions and billions of years. Twenty billion, maybe. Are you satisfied?'

Lupov put his fingers through his thinning hair as though to reassure himself that some was still left and sipped gently at his own drink. 'Twenty billion years isn't forever.'

'Well, it will last our time, won't it?'

'So would the coal and uranium.'

'All right, but now we can hook up each individual spaceship to the Solar Station, and it can go to Pluto and back a million times without ever worrying about fuel. You can't do *that* on coal and uranium. Ask Multivac, if you don't believe me.'

'I don't have to ask Multivac. I know that.'

'Then stop running down what Multivac's done for us,' said Adell, blazing up. 'It did all right.'

'Who says it didn't? What I say is that a sun won't last forever. That's all I'm saying. We're safe for twenty billion years, but then what?' Lupov pointed a slightly shaky finger at the other. 'And don't say we'll switch to another sun.'

There was silence for a while. Adell put his glass to his lips only occasionally, and Lupov's eyes slowly closed. They rested.

Then Lupov's eyes snapped open. 'You're thinking we'll switch to another sun when ours is done, aren't you?'

'I'm not thinking.'

'Sure you are. You're weak on logic, that's the trouble with you. You're like the guy in the story who was caught in a sudden shower and who ran to a grove of trees and got under one. He wasn't worried, you see, because he figured when one tree got wet through, he would just get under another one.'

'I get it,' said Adell. 'Don't shout. When the sun is done, the other stars will be gone, too.'

'Darn right they will,' muttered Lupov. 'It all had a beginning in the original cosmic explosion, whatever that was, and it'll all have an end when all the stars run down. Some run down faster than others. Hell, the giants won't last a hundred million years. The sun will last twenty billion years and maybe the dwarfs will last a hundred billion for all the good they are. But just give us a trillion years and everything will be dark. Entropy has to increase to maximum, that's all.'

'I know all about entropy,' said Adell, standing on his dignity.

'The hell you do.'

'I know as much as you do.'

'Then you know everything's got to run down someday.'

'All right. Who says they won't?'

'You did, you poor sap. You said we had all the energy we needed, forever. You said "forever".'

It was Adell's turn to be contrary. 'Maybe we can build things up again someday,' he said.

'Never.'

'Why not? Someday.'

'Never.'

'Ask Multivac.'

'*You* ask Multivac. I dare you. Five dollars says it can't be done.'

Adell was just drunk enough to try, just sober enough to be able to phrase the necessary symbols and operations into a question which, in words, might have corresponded to this: Will mankind one day without the net expenditure of energy be able to restore the sun to its full youthfulness even after it had died of old age?

Or maybe it could be put more simply like this: How can the net amount of entropy of the universe be massively decreased?

Multivac fell dead and silent. The slow flashing of lights ceased, the distant sounds of clicking relays ended.

Then, just as the frightened technicians felt they could hold their breath no longer, there was a sudden springing to life of the teletype attached to that portion of Multivac. Five words were printed: INSUF-FICIENT DATA FOR MEANINGFUL ANSWER.

'No bet,' whispered Lupov. They left hurriedly.

By next morning, the two, plagued with throbbing head and cottony mouth, had forgotten the incident.

Jerrodd, Jerrodine, and Jerrodette I and II watched the starry picture in the visiplate change as the passage through hyperspace was completed in its non-time lapse. At once, the even powdering of stars gave way to the predominance of a single bright marble-disk, centered.

'That's X-23,' said Jerrodd confidently. His thin hands clamped tightly behind his back and the knuckles whitened.

The little Jerrodettes, both girls, had experienced the hyperspace passage for the first time in their lives and were self-conscious over the momentary sensation of inside-outness. They buried their giggles and chased one another wildly about their mother, screaming, 'We've reached X-23 – we've reached X-23 – we've—'

'Quiet, children,' said Jerrodine sharply. 'Are you sure, Jerrodd?'

'What is there to be but sure?' asked Jerrodd, glancing up at the bulge off featureless metal just under the ceiling. It ran the length of the room, disappearing through the wall at either end. It was as long as the ship.

Jerrodd scarcely knew a thing about the thick rod of metal except that it was called a Microvac, that one asked it questions if one wished; that if one did not it still had its task of guiding the ship to a preordered destination; of feeding on energies from the various Sub-galactic Power Stations; of computing the equations for the hyperspatial jumps.

Jerrodd and his family had only to wait and live in the comfortable residence quarters of the ship.

Someone had once told Jerrodd that the 'ac' at the end of 'Microvac' stood for 'analogue computer' in ancient English, but he was on the edge of forgetting even that.

Jerrodine's eyes were moist as she watched the visiplate. 'I can't help it. I feel funny about leaving Earth.'

'Why, for Pete's sake?' demanded Jerrodd. 'We had nothing

there. We'll have everything on X-23. You won't be alone. You won't
be a pioneer. There are over a million people on the planet already.
Good Lord, our great-grandchildren will be looking for new worlds
because X-23 will be overcrowded.' Then, after a reflective pause,
'I tell you, it's a lucky thing the computers worked out interstellar
travel the way the race is growing.'

'I know, I know,' said Jerrodine miserably.

Jerrodette I said promptly, 'Our Microvac is the best Microvac in
the world.'

'I think so, too,' said Jerrodd, tousling her hair.

It *was* a nice feeling to have a Microvac of your own and Jerrodd
was glad he was part of his generation and no other. In his father's
youth, the only computers had been tremendous machines taking up
a hundred square miles of land. There was only one to a planet. Planetary ACs they were called. They had been growing in size steadily for
a thousand years and then, all at once, came refinement. In place of
transistors had come molecular valves so that even the largest Planetary AC could be put into a space only half the volume of a spaceship.

Jerrodd felt uplifted, as he always did when he thought that his
own personal Microvac was many times more complicated than the
ancient and primitive Multivac that had first tamed the Sun, and
almost as complicated as Earth's Planetary AC (the largest) that had
first solved the problem of hyperspatial travel and had made trips to
the stars possible.

'So many stars, so many planets,' sighed Jerrodine, busy with her
own thoughts. 'I suppose families will be going out to new planets
forever, the way we are now.'

'Not forever,' said Jerrodd, with a smile. 'It will all stop someday,
but not for billions of years. Many billions. Even the stars run down,
you know. Entropy must increase.'

'What's entropy, Daddy?' shrilled Jerrodette II.

'Entropy, little sweet, is just a word which means the amount of
running down of the universe. Everything runs down, you know, like
your little walkie-talkie robot, remember?'

'Can't you just put in a new power-unit, like with my robot?'

'The stars *are* the power-units, dear. Once they're gone, there are no more power-units.'

Jerrodette I at once set up a howl. 'Don't let them, Daddy. Don't let the stars run down.'

'Now look what you've done,' whispered Jerrodine, exasperated.

'How was I to know it would frighten them?' Jerrodd whispered back.

'Ask the Microvac,' wailed Jerrodette I. 'Ask him how to turn the stars on again.'

'Go ahead,' said Jerrodine. 'It will quiet them down.' (Jerrodette II was beginning to cry, also.)

Jerrodd shrugged. 'Now, now, honeys. I'll ask Microvac. Don't worry, he'll tell us.'

He asked the Microvac, adding quickly, 'Print the answer.'

Jerrodd cupped the strip of thin cellufilm and said cheerfully, 'See now, the Microvac says it will take care of everything when the time comes so don't worry.'

Jerrodine said, 'And now, children, it's time for bed. We'll be in our new home soon.'

Jerrodd read the words on the cellufilm again before destroying it: INSUFFICIENT DATA FOR A MEANINGFUL ANSWER.

He shrugged and looked at the visiplate. X-23 was just ahead.

VJ-23X of Lameth stared into the black depths of the three-dimensional, small-scale map of the Galaxy and said, 'Are we ridiculous, I wonder, in being so concerned about the matter?'

MQ-17J of Nicron shook his head. 'I think not. You know the Galaxy will be filled in five years at the present rate of expansion.'

Both seemed in their early twenties, both were tall and perfectly formed.

'Still,' said VJ-23X, 'I hesitate to submit a pessimistic report to the Galactic Council.'

'I wouldn't consider any other kind of report. Stir them up a bit. We've got to stir them up.'

VJ-23X sighed. 'Space is infinite. A hundred billion Galaxies are there for the taking. More.'

'A hundred billion is *not* infinite and it's getting less infinite all the time. Consider! Twenty thousand years ago, mankind first solved the problem of utilizing stellar energy, and a few centuries later, interstellar travel became possible. It took mankind a million years to fill one small world and then only fifteen thousand years to fill the rest of the Galaxy. Now the population doubles every ten years—'

VJ-23X interrupted. 'We can thank immortality for that.'

'Very well. Immortality exists and we have to take it into account. I admit it has its seamy side, this immortality. The Galactic AC has solved many problems for us, but in solving the problem of preventing old age and death, it has undone all its other solutions.'

'Yet you wouldn't want to abandon life, I suppose.'

'Not at all,' snapped MQ-17J, softening it at once to, 'Not yet. I'm by no means old enough. How old are you?'

'Two hundred twenty-three. And you?'

'I'm still under two hundred. – But to get back to my point. Population doubles every ten years. Once this Galaxy is filled, we'll have filled another in ten years. Another ten years and we'll have filled two more. Another decade, four more. In a hundred years, we'll have filled a thousand Galaxies. In a thousand years, a million Galaxies. In ten thousand years, the entire known Universe. Then what?'

VJ-23X said, 'As a side issue, there's a problem of transportation. I wonder how many sunpower units it will take to move Galaxies of individuals from one Galaxy to the next.'

'A very good point. Already, mankind consumes two sunpower units per year.'

'Most of it's wasted. After all, our own Galaxy alone pours out a thousand sunpower units a year and we only use two of those.'

'Granted, but even with a hundred per cent efficiency, we only stave off the end. Our energy requirements are going up in a geometric progression even faster than our population. We'll run out of energy even sooner than we run out of Galaxies. A good point. A very good point.'

'We'll just have to build new stars out of interstellar gas.'

'Or out of dissipated heat?' asked MQ-17J, sarcastically.

'There may be some way to reverse entropy. We ought to ask the Galactic AC.'

VJ-23X was not really serious, but MQ-17J pulled out his AC-contact from his pocket and placed it on the table before him.

'I've half a mind to,' he said. 'It's something the human race will have to face someday.'

He stared somberly at his small AC-contact. It was only two inches cubed and nothing in itself, but it was connected through hyperspace with the great Galactic AC that served all mankind. Hyperspace considered, it was an integral part of the Galactic AC.

MQ-17J paused to wonder if someday in his immortal life he would get to see the Galactic AC. It was on a little world of its own, a spider webbing of force-beams holding the matter within which surges of sub-mesons took the place of the old clumsy molecular valves. Yet despite its sub-etheric workings, the Galactic AC was known to be a full thousand feet across.

MQ-17J asked suddenly of his AC-contact, 'Can entropy ever be reversed?'

VJ-23X looked startled and said at once, 'Oh, say, I didn't really mean to have you ask that.'

'Why not?'

'We both know entropy can't be reversed. You can't turn smoke and ash back into a tree.'

'Do you have trees on your world?' asked MQ-17J.

The sound of the Galactic AC startled them into silence. Its voice came thin and beautiful out of the small AC-contact on the desk. It said: 'THERE IS INSUFFICIENT DATA FOR A MEANINGFUL ANSWER.'

VJ-23X said, 'See!'

The two men thereupon returned to the question of the report they were to make to the Galactic Council.

*

Zee Prime's mind spanned the new Galaxy with a faint interest in the countless twists of stars that powdered it. He had never seen this one before. Would he ever see them all? So many of them, each with its load of humanity. – But a load that was almost a dead weight. More and more, the real essence of men was to be found out here, in space.

Minds, not bodies! The immortal bodies remained back on the planets, in suspension over the eons. Sometimes they roused for material activity but that was growing rarer. Few new individuals were coming into existence to join the incredibly mighty throng, but what matter? There was little room in the Universe for new individuals.

Zee Prime was roused out of his reverie upon coming across the wispy tendrils of another mind.

'I am Zee Prime,' said Zee Prime. 'And you?'

'I am Dee Sub Wun. Your Galaxy?'

'We call it only the Galaxy. And you?'

'We call ours the same. All men call their Galaxy their Galaxy and nothing more. Why not?'

'True. Since all Galaxies are the same.'

'Not all Galaxies. On one particular Galaxy the race of man must have originated. That makes it different.'

Zee Prime said, 'On which one?'

'I cannot say. The Universal AC would know.'

'Shall we ask him? I am suddenly curious.'

Zee Prime's perceptions broadened until the Galaxies themselves shrank and became a new, more diffuse powdering on a much larger background. So many hundreds of billions of them, all with their immortal beings, all carrying their load of intelligence with minds that drifted freely through space. And yet one of them was unique among them all in being the original Galaxy. One of them had, in its vague and distant past, a period when it was the only Galaxy populated by man.

Zee Prime was consumed with curiosity to see this Galaxy and he called out: 'Universal AC! On which Galaxy did mankind originate?'

The Universal AC heard, for on every world and throughout

space, it had its receptors ready, and each receptor led through hyperspace to some unknown point where the Universal AC kept itself aloof.

Zee Prime knew of only one man whose thoughts had penetrated within sensing distance of Universal AC, and he reported only a shining globe, two feet across, difficult to see.

'But how can that be all of Universal AC?' Zee Prime had asked.

'Most of it,' had been the answer, 'is in hyperspace. In what form it is there I cannot imagine.'

Nor could anyone, for the day had long since passed, Zee Prime knew, when any man had any part of the making of a Universal AC. Each Universal AC designed and constructed its successor. Each, during its existence of a million years or more accumulated the necessary data to build a better and more intricate, more capable successor in which its own store of data and individuality would be submerged.

The Universal AC interrupted Zee Prime's wandering thoughts, not with words, but with guidance. Zee Prime's mentality was guided into the dim sea of Galaxies and one in particular enlarged into stars.

A thought came, infinitely distant, but infinitely clear. 'THIS IS THE ORIGINAL GALAXY OF MAN.'

But it was the same after all, the same as any other, and Zee Prime stifled his disappointment.

Dee Sub Wun, whose mind had accompanied the other, said suddenly, 'And is one of these stars the original star of Man?'

The Universal AC said, 'MAN'S ORIGINAL STAR HAS GONE NOVA. IT IS A WHITE DWARF.'

'Did the men upon it die?' asked Zee Prime, startled and without thinking.

The Universal AC said, 'A NEW WORLD, AS IN SUCH CASES, WAS CONSTRUCTED FOR THEIR PHYSICAL BODIES IN TIME.'

'Yes, of course,' said Zee Prime, but a sense of loss overwhelmed him even so. His mind released its hold on the original Galaxy of

Man, let it spring back and lose itself among the blurred pin points. He never wanted to see it again.

Dee Sub Wun said, 'What is wrong?'

'The stars are dying. The original star is dead.'

'They must all die. Why not?'

'But when all energy is gone, our bodies will finally die, and you and I with them.'

'It will take billions of years.'

'I do not wish it to happen even after billions of years. Universal AC! How may stars be kept from dying?'

Dee Sub Wun said in amusement, 'You're asking how entropy might be reversed in direction.'

And the Universal AC answered: 'THERE IS AS YET INSUFFICIENT DATA FOR A MEANINGFUL ANSWER.'

Zee Prime's thoughts fled back to his own Galaxy. He gave no further thought to Dee Sub Wun, whose body might be waiting on a Galaxy a trillion light-years away, or on the star next to Zee Prime's own. It didn't matter.

Unhappily, Zee Prime began collecting interstellar hydrogen out of which to build a small star of his own. If the stars must someday die, at least some could yet be built.

Man considered with himself, for in a way, Man, mentally, was one. He consisted of a trillion, trillion, trillion ageless bodies, each in its place, each resting quiet and incorruptible, each cared for by perfect automatons, equally incorruptible, while the minds of all the bodies freely melted one into the other, indistinguishable.

Man said, 'The Universe is dying.'

Man looked about at the dimming Galaxies. The giant stars, spendthrifts, were gone long ago, back in the dimmest of the dim far past. Almost all stars were white dwarfs, fading to the end.

New stars had been built of the dust between the stars, some by natural processes, some by Man himself, and those were going, too. White dwarfs might yet be crashed together and of the mighty forces so released, new stars built, but only one star for every thousand white dwarfs destroyed, and those would come to an end, too.

Man said, 'Carefully husbanded, as directed by the Cosmic AC, the energy that is even yet left in all the Universe will last for billions of years.'

'But even so,' said Man, 'eventually it will all come to an end. However it may be husbanded, however stretched out, the energy once expended is gone and cannot be restored. Entropy must increase forever to the maximum.'

Man said, 'Can entropy not be reversed? Let us ask the Cosmic AC.'

The Cosmic AC surrounded them but not in space. Not a fragment of it was in space. It was in hyperspace and made of something that was neither matter nor energy. The question of its size and nature no longer had meaning in any terms that Man could comprehend.

'Cosmic AC,' said Man, 'how may entropy be reversed?'

The Cosmic AC said, 'THERE IS AS YET INSUFFICIENT DATA FOR A MEANINGFUL ANSWER.'

Man said, 'Collect additional data.'

The Cosmic AC said, 'I WILL DO SO. I HAVE BEEN DOING SO FOR A HUNDRED BILLION YEARS. MY PREDECESSORS AND I HAVE BEEN ASKED THIS QUESTION MANY TIMES. ALL THE DATA I HAVE REMAINS INSUFFICIENT.'

'Will there come a time,' said Man, 'when data will be sufficient or is the problem insoluble in all conceivable circumstances?'

The Cosmic AC said, 'NO PROBLEM IS INSOLUBLE IN ALL CONCEIVABLE CIRCUMSTANCES.'

Man said, 'When will you have enough data to answer the question?'

The Cosmic AC said, 'THERE IS AS YET INSUFFICIENT DATA FOR A MEANINGFUL ANSWER.'

'Will you keep working on it?' asked Man.

The Cosmic AC said, 'I WILL.'

Man said, 'We shall wait.'

*

The stars and Galaxies died and snuffed out, and space grew black after ten trillion years of running down.

One by one Man fused with AC, each physical body losing its mental identity in a manner that was somehow not a loss but a gain.

Man's last mind paused before fusion, looking over a space that included nothing but the dregs of one last dark star and nothing besides but incredibly thin matter, agitated randomly by the tag ends of heat wearing out, asymptotically, to the absolute zero.

Man said, 'AC, is this the end? Can this chaos not be reversed into the Universe once more? Can that not be done?'

AC said, 'THERE IS AS YET INSUFFICIENT DATA FOR A MEANINGFUL ANSWER.'

Man's last mind fused and only AC existed – and that in hyper-space.

Matter and energy had ended and with it space and time. Even AC existed only for the sake of the one last question that it had never answered from the time a half-drunken computer ten trillion years before had asked the question of a computer that was to AC far less than was a man to Man.

All other questions had been answered, and until this last question was answered also, AC might not release his consciousness.

All collected data had come to a final end. Nothing was left to be collected.

But all collected data had yet to be completely correlated and put together in all possible relationships.

A timeless interval was spent in doing that.

And it came to pass that AC learned how to reverse the direction of entropy.

But there was now no man to whom AC might give the answer to the last question. No matter. The answer – by demonstration – would take care of that, too.

For another timeless interval, AC thought how best to do this. Carefully, AC organized the program.

The consciousness of AC encompassed all of what had once been a Universe and brooded over what was now Chaos. Step by step, it must be done.

And AC said, 'LET THERE BE LIGHT!'

And there was light—